One called Soothsayer shall arise, with heart of blackness and powers great. His strong arm reaches far in unknown ways. The Soothsayer shall try to conquer the mind of the Dream Warrior. . . .

Other Books by D. J. Conway

The Ancient & Shining Ones
Animal Magick
Astral Love
By Oak, Ash, & Thorn
Celtic Magic
The Dream Warrior (fiction)
Dancing With Dragons
Falcon Feather & Valkyrie Sword
Flying Without a Broom
Lord of Light & Shadow
Magickal, Mythical, Mystical Beasts
Maiden, Mother, Crone
Moon Magick
Norse Magic

Forthcoming

Warrior of Shadows (fiction)

Sooth Slayer

A MAGICKAL FANTASY BY

D. J. Conway

1997
Llewellyn Publications
St. Paul, Minnesota 55164-0383 U.S.A.

FIRST EDITION
First Printing, 1997

Cover art by Kris Waldherr
Cover design by Anne Marie Garrison
Book design and editing by Jessica Thoreson and Rebecca Zins

Cataloging-in-Publication Data

Conway, D. J. (Deanna J.)
   Soothslayer: a magickal fantasy / by D. J. Conway.
     p. cm.
   ISBN 1-56718-162-7
   I. Title.
   PS3553.05455S65 1997
   813'.54—dc21   97-3558
                                              CIP

Llewellyn Publications
A Division of Llewellyn Worldwide, Ltd.
P.O. Box 64383
St. Paul, MN 55164-0383

In memory of Sharon Elizabeth
1959-1975.

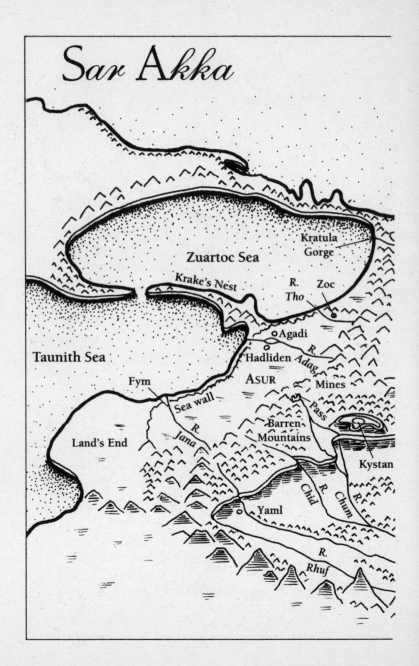

Sar Akka

Zuartoc Sea

Kratula
Gorge

Krake's Nest

R.
Tho

Zoc

Taunith Sea

Agadi

Hadliden

R.
Adag

ASUR

Mines

Fym

Sea wall

Pass

R.
Jana

Barren
Mountains

Land's End

Kystan

Chid

R.
Chum

R.

Yaml

R.
Rhuf

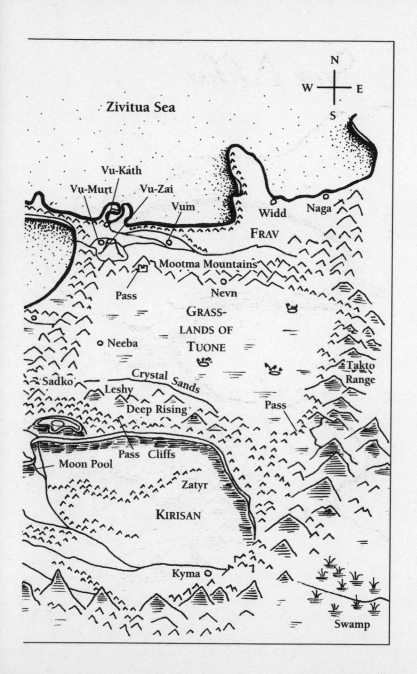

Pronunciation Guide

Adag: Aye´ (long "a")-dag
Agadi: Ah-gah´-dee
Asperel: Ass´-per-el
Asur: Aye´ (long "a")-sir
Athdar: Ath´ (as in "am")-dar
Ayron: Aye´ (long "a")-ron

Baba: Bah´-bah
Babbel: Bay´-bull
Balqama: Ball-kah´-mah
Barsark: Bar´-sark
Breela: Bree´-lah
Burrak: Burr´-ack

Cabiria: Cah-beer´-ee-ah
Cassyr: Cass´-seer
Charissa: Chur-iz´-zah
Chid: Chid (as in "kid")
Chum: Chum
Cleeman: Clee´-mon
Clua: Clue´-ah
Corri: Core´-ee
Croyna: Croy´ (as in "troy")
   -nah

Daduku: Dah-doo´-koo
Dakhma: Dahk´-mah
Druk: Druk (as in "truck")

Fenlix: Fen´-licks
Feya: Fay´ (long "a")-yah

Fravashi: Frah-vah´-shee
Frayma: Fray´ (long "a")
   -mah
Friama: Free-ah´-mah
Fym: Fim

Gadavar: Gad´-a-var
Gertha: Grr´-thah
Geyti: Guy´-tee
Gran: Gran (as in "bran")
Grimmel: Grim´-ell

Hachino: Hah-chee´-no
Hadliden: Had´-li-dan
Halka: Hall´-kah
Halman: Hall´-mon
Hari-Hari: Har´-ee
Hindjall: Hind´ (as in
   "hinge")-yall

Imandoff: im´ (as in "imp")
   -an-doff
Iodan: Ee´-o-dan

Jabed: Jah´-bed
Jana: Jah´-nah
Jehennette: Gee´-en-et
Jevotan: Jay´ (long "a")
   -vo-tan
Jinniyah: Gin-ee´-yah

ix

Kaaba: Kay-ah´-bah
Kaballoi: Cab´-ah-loy
  (as in "toy")
Kanlath: Can´-lath
Kayth: Kay´-th
Keffin: Keff´-in
Kirisan: Kier´ (as in "tier")
  -i (as in "it")-sahn
Korud: Core´-ud (as in
  "thud")
Krake: Krake (as in "brake")
Kratula: Kraw-too´-lah
Krynap: Cry´-nap
Kulkar: Kool´-kar
Kyma: Ky´ (as in "eye")-mah
Kystan: Ky´ (as in "eye")
  -stan

Leshy: Lesh´ (as in
  "mesh")-ee
Limna: Lim´ (as "limb")-nah

Magni: Mahg´-nee
Malya: Mahl´-yah
Medha: May´-dah
Melaina: Mee-lane´-ah
Menec: Men´-ek
Merra: Meer´-ah
Minepa: Min-e´ (as the "e"
  in "egg")-paw
Minna: Mee´-nah
Mootma: Moot´-mah
Morvrana: Morv (as
  "more")-rah´-nah

Naga: Nah´-gah
Natira: Nah-tier´-rah
Neeba: Nee´-bah
Nevn: Nev´-n
Norya: Nor´-yah
Nu-Sheek: New-sheek´
Nu-Sheeka: New-shee´-kah

Odran: O´ (as in "oh")
  -dran (as in "bran")

Qishua: Kish´-oo-ah

Rhuf: Rough
Rissa: Ris´-sah
Roggkin: Rog´ (as in
  "dog")-kin
Rushina: Roo-shee´-nah
Rympa: Rim´-pah

Sadko: Sod´-koh
Sallin: Say´-linn
Sejda: Say´-dah
Shakka: Shah´-kah
Sharrock: Shar´-rock
Shilluk: Shill´-uck
Simi: Sim´-ee
Sussa: Soo´-sah

Taillefer: Tal´ (as in "alley")
  -ee-fur
Takra: Tahk´-rah
Takto: Tahk´-toe
Tamia: Tay´-mee-ah

Taunith: Tow´ (as in "ow")
  -nith
Taymin: Tay´-men
Thalassa: Thal (as in
  "alley")-ass´-ah
Thidrick: Thid´ (as in
  "kid")-rick
Tho: Tho (as in "throw")
Tirkul: Tur´-kull
Tujyk: Too´-yek
Tuone: Too´-own
Tuonela: Too-oh-nell´-ah
Tuulikki: Too-oo-lee´-kee

Utha Unop: Oo´-thah
  Oh´-nap
Uunlak: Oo´-un-lack
Uzza: Oo´-zah

Vairya: Vair´-yah
Varanna: Var-ah´-nah
Vayhall: Vay´ (as in "way")
  -hall
Vu-Murt: Voo´-murt
Vu-Zai: Voo-zai´ (as in
  "eye")
Vum: Vum (as in "come")

Wella: Well´-ah
Wermod: Were´-mode
Widd: Widd (as in "lid")
Willa: Will´-ah

Xephena: Zeh-fee´-nah

Yaml: Yam´-el
Yngona: In-go´-nah

Zaitan: Zai´ (as in "eye")-tan
Zalmoxis: Zal (as in
  "alley")-mox´-iz
Zatyr: Zah-tier´
Zingas: Zing´-gahs
Zivitua: Zi (as the "e" in
  "egg")-vi´ (as in "it")
  -too-ah
Zoc: Zock
Zuartoc: Zoo-are´-tock

The Prophecy of the Dream Warrior
From the Bahrhatta, the Ancient Book

A great prophecy came to Tirkul and the two Maidens chosen by the flames. Each dreamed a dream, and when they met together, they learned that each dream was the same.

The prophecy is thus: A way will be shown to the Four Peoples, across many lands and seas, to a new land. There, the Peoples will prosper. Future-times become past-times. Out of Light and Darkness the One has become Three, but the Three are not complete. Future-times and future-times, one silver sky ship sails from the heavens, once more bringing star travelers to Sar Sakka. For many seasons they shall live among the Peoples, their origin unknown. A black force shall arise from the star wanderers to resurrect again the old evil from the Abyss of Jevotan, setting free the dark forces to threaten the land. Only the ancient armor of Varanna in the hands of the Dream Warrior can breach the walls and strike the heart of evil.

One called Soothsayer shall arise, with heart of blackness and powers great. His strong arm reaches far in unknown ways. With him shall ride the reborn Jinniyah. The Soothsayer shall try to conquer the mind of the Dream Warrior and will be burned at the crown.

Out of the darkness opened by the star travelers shall come two seeds. One walks in Darkness, unfriend to Frayma. The other cries after, sword in hand. A star woman takes up the challenge, killing the Footed Serpent at the gate and cutting the web that snares the minds of the Peoples. All Sar Akka lives under shadow of the sword. Past-times become future-times.

Imandoff's Tale of the Prophecy

Varanna was born to star parents who chose to live with the Fravashi. But as a young girl, before the war, she rebelled and fled across the harsh mountains into the lands of the Goddess, the owl stone with her. By sword and cunning, she brought with her a band of children, each a holder of mystic power, each self-dedicated to the Goddess. A priestess of Frayma found and sheltered the children, dispersing them among the Peoples for safety, but keeping Varanna with her. Eventually Varanna was chosen as High Priestess because of her ability to far-see with the stone.

Varanna had a vision through her star stone of the coming battle with Frav. The High Priest Tirkul dreamed it also. She went to the Asur Clan and had them fashion armor and shield from the scales of great sea beasts. This she wore with charmed sword in the last great battle.

Jinniyah, who led Frav as their High Priest, knew much Dark Magic. He called forth from the Abyss great other-world forces of Jevotan, and these rode the blackened skies above the battlefield, aiding his magic. The Clans of Light were encircled, and all seemed lost until Varanna leaped forward to face Jinniyah alone. Tirkul lay wounded, unable to lend his strength, and no light of the Lady or Her Lord could pierce the blackened skies to aid her.

Jinniyah called upon his magic powers and, with his black rod, sent forth such a wave of death that it pierced the eye-piece of Varanna's war helm, killing her and twenty warriors who had leaped to her aid. But in her dying breath, one silver moonbeam broke through the black sky horde of Jevotan and touched her heart. She died with her sword's point out toward Jinniyah, and his magic flowed back out through the sword to kill him. Even his bones were burned to ashes. Varanna's body was cremated and her ashes brought on the long journey.

The magical battle caused great quakes and eruptions. The land was upturned, shaken out and made desolate. In the end, even the Fravashi begged to go with them, saying they had destroyed the great Books of Darkness written by Jinniyah in a secret tongue. There followed a long journey, full of hardships for the Four Peoples, a journey that took nearly two years by ship and land.

But people do not change easily, if at all. Very soon it was discovered that the books of Jinniyah had been brought with the Fravashi. Another great war followed, and the Fravashi were driven to the north, beyond the mountains, where they now live. The border between Frav and Tuone was sealed with powerful ancient spells, so that no Fravashi may cross. And the Books still await one who can break the code and learn again to use the terrible Dark Magic.

The Prophecy says that in some future time another star vessel will come. One traveler will aid the Fravashi, once again unlocking the power of Jinniyah's books. But a star-woman, the Dream Warrior, will take up the challenge, killing the Footed Serpent at the gate and cutting the net that snares the minds of the Peoples. Into her hand will come the stone of Varanna, the stone that was lost in this new land. Only through her powers will the Peoples walk free.

Chapter 1

"How can Imandoff have vanished?" Corri Farblood turned to look at the Tuonela warrior woman reclining on a sleeping mat behind her. "And where is this city of Nevn?"

Corri stood at the door of the tent-wagon and stared off across miles of rolling Tuonela grasslands to the south while she waited for Takra's answer. On the northern horizon lay the hazy forms of the Mootma Mountains, the rocky tree-studded barrier that separated Frav from Tuone. She pushed up the leather headband to rub at the scar burned by the owl stone on the center of her forehead.

The spring season was almost gone. Promise of the building heat of summer could be felt in the ever-present winds that swept over the Tuonela grasslands out of the eastern mountains. The sound of the sweeping wind reminded Corri of the distant roll of surf, a sound she knew well during her life in the Asuran city of Hadliden as the best thief Grimmel had in his employ.

In a way I miss that sound, Corri thought as she continued to watch the grass bending in waves before the winds. *I could hear the soft, whispering call of the sea in the deepest part of night when I wandered the city or lay in bed. I cannot remember a time growing up when I could not hear it. Yes, I miss that sound, but not enough to return to that way of existence or under some man's control. Still, loss of the sea's voice makes me sad inside.*

"Imandoff Silverhair comes and goes as he wishes. You know that, Dream Warrior," Takra Wind-Rider finally answered. "Just because we have had no word of him does not mean he has vanished." Takra rose from her sleeping mat and stretched. "As to Nevn, that is to the north in Tuone, up along the mountains."

The Tuonela warrior woman hugged her bare breasts in the morning chill, her silver amulet catching the light from the door as she moved. The thin scar crossing the delicate blue swirl of her Clan tattoo pulled across her cheek as she yawned.

"Is it like Neeba?" Corri's sun-streaked dark red hair glowed in the morning sun as she turned back to stare out at the grasslands, new-green and rippling under the wind's touch.

The shy little hachino, the drab-looking prairie quail, whistled their calls to each other as they scratched for seeds in the tall grass beyond the camp, and bleats from the herds of silky longhaired goats punctuated the grassland's sounds. Corri tugged at one red curl along her cheek, glad that the bleaching done on her hair in Neeba was gone.

"Nevn is a trading city for the Clans when they journey north," Takra answered. "Sometimes certain traders come with exotic goods they say are from Frav, although I do not see how that can be."

Corri looked at Takra with dark blue-green eyes, the tiny wrinkles at their corners deepening. "Perhaps Imandoff left Nevn for somewhere else."

"No, there was no trace of him after he entered Nevn. It was as if he suddenly stepped Between Worlds. But if that had happened, I would know." Takra's mellow voice was soft as she grinned shyly. She quickly pulled on her leather tunic and trousers. "I asked every Rider who had been up that way, but no one of the Clans knows exactly where Imandoff has gone or why." She combed out her long white-blonde hair and twisted the front portions into two braids. "You know how he is, Corri. When the sorcerer finds some old clue to the Forgotten Ones, or some bit of strange knowledge, he completely forgets everything else."

Corri turned away from the view of waving grass and came to sit on a chest facing Takra. She stretched her long, muscled legs and stared at her worn half-boots. "I think you love him, Takra. Have the two of you exchanged heart oath without telling anyone?"

Takra pulled on her worn boots, then shook her head, her pale braids swaying with the movement. "Neither of us has spoken of feelings. Perhaps he does not feel as I do."

"Spoken words often mean nothing," Corri said with sudden bitterness.

Takra looked up at her friend, amber eyes intent. "Corri, bide your time. I know Tirkul spoke in the heat of anger. Hot words are later regretted. He loves you. He will forget about breaking heart oath by the time he returns."

"I will not forget. He took back his heart oath because I would not yield to his wishes." Corri raised her thin face to stare at Takra with angry eyes. "He wants me to give up my dream-flying, the powers I am just learning to control. As if I have a choice or wanted to change. I worked hard to learn to control my powers. Why should I give them up at his whim?" She clenched her slender hands together. "He has changed, Takra. Where once he respected my life and what I have to do, now he orders that I follow his wishes."

"He is afraid for you to ride into danger. So am I, but I know that you follow the Goddess, that through Her you are our only possible defense between the Peoples and the evil that breeds in Frav." Takra adjusted her sword belt and gathered up her saddlebags. "But Tirkul has always been strong-willed, determined that he knows best. I am with you, sister-friend. I too will not bend to any man's orders."

"I wish you were staying here." Corri rose and walked with Takra out of the tent-wagon into the rapidly warming new day. "I do not yet feel comfortable here with the Clan of the Feathered Spear."

"Norya is a good shakka. She is wise in the ways of talking with animals, of reading weather-signs. You can learn much from her. Imandoff thinks so, too. That is why he and Halka of the Clan of the Asperel insisted you come here for a time."

"It is not Norya who makes me uncomfortable." Corri matched Takra's long stride as they wove their way through the camp to the horse herd beyond. "I have heard whispers calling me an Out-Clanner. And Melaina. . . ."

"That one is a troublemaker. I do not understand why Norya keeps her as apprentice." Takra stopped at the edge of the herd of horses and whistled for Lightfoot. "Beware of Melaina, Corri. She had her heart set on Tirkul. I think she does not take lightly to his love for you."

"Then she should be pleased, as soon as she finds out Tirkul has broken heart oath."

"Does anyone know besides me?" Takra asked, and Corri shook her head. "Leave it that way, Dream Warrior. Melaina has used rumor and information to hurt others before."

The warrior woman picked up her saddle from where she had placed it the night before. Lightfoot trotted out of the herd, her ears pricked forward, braided gray forelock swinging, and nuzzled Takra's shoulder. She threw the saddle on the horse's back and tightened the cinch.

"Do you not worry that someone will steal your things?" Corri gestured at the saddle and the bags now tied in place. "All Tuonela seem to drop their possessions wherever they please, without a care."

"The penalty for theft is high. Remember that, Corri. I know you do not steal as you once did, but others might blame you if something goes missing." Takra slid her spear into its holder near her left stirrup. "The punishment is public whipping, adult or child, if the child is old enough to know better. And no one will speak to the offender for a time set by the shakka. The Clan of the Feathered Spear is not as open to Out-Clanners as are the Clan of the Asperel and others."

"I wish you were staying," Corri said again.

"It is only five days' ride to the post of Frayma's Mare from here." Takra tied her barsark-fur jacket behind the saddle, then pulled on her leather helmet. The thin scar running through the delicate blue tattoo on her cheek shone nearly white against her sun-browned skin as she turned back to the tall, thin girl beside her. "I will not be far away should you need me."

"I know. Watch your back, Takra Wind-Rider. And I will try to mind-seek for Imandoff. If I discover where he is and what he does, I will send word."

"And you, sister-friend, watch your own back. Melaina would be unwise to cause trouble around Norya, but she might try. Jealousy can be a sharp sword. Do you have words for me to take to Tirkul?"

"No. Let him think on what he already said," Corri answered bitterly. "Take care, sister-friend."

The two embraced. Takra swung up onto Lightfoot, gave a raised fist in salute, then rode off through the wind-swept grasslands toward the guard posts in the distant northern mountains.

Corri watched the gray-speckled black horse for some time before picking her way back through the cluster of tent-wagons to her temporary home with the shakka. As she walked, her instincts prickled at the silent glances from the Tuonela whom she passed. One hand fell automatically onto the worn wire-hilt of her belt dagger.

There is danger here for me, she thought. *I feel it as strongly as I did when I went out on thefts for Grimmel. The feeling grows stronger each day I stay here. Perhaps I should return to Halka.*

The image of the stooped-shouldered old shakka of the Clan of the Asperel rose in her mind. The bird-bright eyes that saw to the very soul of a person stared back at Corri. With a sigh, the girl accepted the fact that she could not return to Halka until she had learned new things from this shakka Norya. This was part of the training set for her by Halka and Imandoff.

Corri's reverie was broken by the taunting calls of children gathered in a mass before the next wagon. At first she thought the words were for her, but then she saw a small child in the center of the shoving group.

"Out-Clanner!" The insult came from several children. "You lie! Dakhma is an Out-Clanner! Dakhma is a liar!" The taunts rose in the crisp morning air like the screams of attacking birds.

Corri watched several Tuonela adults pass the children without a word of protest or an attempt to stop the children from shoving and pinching the little girl. Her anger flared, and before she thought, Corri was wading through the children, pushing them aside as she went.

"Enough." Her quiet voice, heavy with controlled rage, silenced the voices. "Who are you to behave worse than the lowest of animals? How dare you do this! Begone, or I will cast a fire spell and set your pants alight." The children scattered without a word.

"And who are you, Farblood, to threaten Tuonela children?" A woman's cold voice came from the shadows beside the wagon where Corri and the child stood. "Out-Clanners stand together, and always they bring trouble. Beware that you do not strain Tuonela guest rights."

A tall young woman stepped out of the shadows into the sunlight. Her light brown eyes glared hatred as she approached. The child slipped behind Corri and peeked fearfully out at the woman.

"Do you threaten me, Melaina?" Corri glared back. "This ill treatment of a child is not allowed by any Clan, and I have been among many. Those of the Feathered Spear are more closed of mind than any Tuonela I have met, but until now I have never seen them mistreat children. If they had their way, no one not of full Clan blood would ever darken the horizons of Tuone. You feed their suspicions, I know for I have heard you. But this is inexcusable. As apprentice to Norya, I have a duty to stop this kind of behavior, as do you. Why did you not protect this child?"

"She is an Out-Clanner and carries the seed of evil magic within her." Melaina threw her long golden hair back over her shoulders as she looked down her nose at Corri. "She is not wanted here."

"Horse dung! Her parents are Tuonela. There is no evil in this girl, Melaina." Corri's hand dropped once more onto her dagger hilt.

"Her mother may be Tuonela, but her father was a trader from outside Tuone, perhaps even a Fravashi. This girl has the look of one. Even her mother rejects her, Farblood. And she has evil powers growing within her. I say so." Melaina's hand slipped to her own belt knife.

"Who are you to say anything, nathling!" Corri spat out the deadliest insult she could think of. "Draw your dagger, Melaina. I think you will not score blood with me. I have faced poisonous snakes before, and crushed them with my boot heel."

Melaina's face flushed a deep red. She turned on her heel and swiftly disappeared among the tent-wagons.

"Do not be afraid." Corri reached back to draw the little girl from behind her. "Melaina has a poisonous tongue but little courage to face danger from one who can fight back." She smiled down at the child.

"She spoke true." The gray eyes, rimmed around the iris with dark blue, looked up at Corri out of a thin, tear-streaked face. "My mother does not want me. And I am an Out-Clan-ner."

Corri smoothed back the light brown hair, noting the scratches and bruises on the child's face and arms. *I had that frightened, wild look in my eyes when I was her age,* Corri thought as she cupped the child's thin cheek with her hand. *I remember seeing it in a mirror. Whatever the cost to me, I will not leave her to this daily torture. By the Goddess, somehow I will see her to a safe place before the great battle begins.*

"I am Corri Farblood, a friend of Takra Wind-Rider and Imandoff the sorcerer," she said.

"I know. I am Dakhma." The girl's thin body cringed as two Tuonela walked by and frowned at her. "My mother Sussa has a boy baby now that she likes better. She told me so."

"Dakhma! Come at once and watch the baby." A tall woman at the entrance to one of the wagons stood with her hands on her hips, staring at Corri.

"I must go." The little girl quickly ran across the pounded ground of the encampment, ducking a slap as she entered the wagon.

What is happening here? Corri frowned as she walked back to the shakka's wagon, deep in thought. *I have never known a Tuonela to treat a child like this. Children are loved and cherished by all in a Clan. Imandoff said those of the Feathered Spear are fanatical about blood-purity, but I never thought it would be this bad.*

The shakka's wagon was empty when Corri arrived. Norya was still across the camp checking on a pregnant woman who showed signs of giving birth at any time. Melaina spent little time in the shakka's wagon unless Norya was there, living instead in her family's wagon. Corri set a kettle of water spiced with herbs over the burning fire-pot to heat for the morning drink.

Corri was glad of the solitude as she sat cross-legged on a mat before the shakka's altar. She gazed up at the statue of the Mother of Mares; the goddess called Friama by the Asurans and Frayma by those of Kirisan. *Lady, what am I to do now? This child is much like I was, unloved, unwanted. I cannot stand by while she is tormented and mistreated.*

Her mind slipped back through her childhood memories, her fears that Grimmel would find out what powers she had and force her to use them for him, the isolation in which she lived by Grimmel's command. The toad-like face of the master thief rose unbidden in her mind's eye, his round, almost lidless eyes and wide slit of a mouth as clear as if he were still alive and standing before her.

I was so lonely. No matter what I did to please Grimmel and those within his house, I never could. Even though he is dead, the memories still hurt, the fear of not doing things right still plagues me. She shivered with old dreads and pushed the vision away.

Gradually, Corri sank deeper into her daily meditation, the camp sounds receding beyond her senses. With each deep breath she took, she felt herself drawing closer to the quiet center of her innermost being. At last, she drifted in a place of peace and calmness, a space where she knew she would eventually find the Lady. She waited, aware of the blood pumping through her veins, the wind currents in the sky above, the life forms of prairie birds and animals in the tall grass outside the camp. Slowly, the golden glow surrounding the Goddess broke through the inner darkness; the healing rays soothing Corri's mind.

Peace, Dream Warrior. All things have a pattern and a purpose. The Lady smiled. *You are My messenger and the one whom I send to turn back the tides of evil on Sar Akka. Trust in yourself, daughter.* Her face grew serious. *Beware of the Soothsayer. You will know him by the evil he does. Beware, for he hunts down and binds souls to evil.*

A series of faces flashed rapidly through Corri's inner sight. She recognized some of them, Takra, Imandoff, Tirkul, Gadavar, but others were strangers to her. *All these will play a part in the battle for freedom,* the Lady said. *Some will help; others will hinder if they can. Remember them.* The woman's image started to fade at the edges.

Wait, Lady. Corri reached out. *Who is the Soothsayer? No one has told me of him.*

She struggled up out of her meditative state, more confused than ever. The light tread of boots on the wagon steps brought her fully awake. Her hand dropped instinctively to her dagger hilt as she turned to face the entrance.

"Corri?" The rod-straight form of Norya darkened the doorway. "What troubles you? I felt your distress across the camp."

Corri bit her lip and kept silent. *She has daily tested me in some small way since I came. Why does she not believe I am the true Dream Warrior? In spite of how she thinks of me, I must learn all I can, so I can be gone all the sooner.*

"Come, girl. Tell me what troubles your heart and mind." The shakka sat on a chest near Corri, her gray-streaked braids falling over her square shoulders. She bent closer and peered at the girl with sharp hazel eyes.

Corri hesitated before she spoke. "I am having trouble with animal-talk," she said at last. "I did all you said, but I receive nothing."

"Perhaps you are listening for the wrong things. Animals speak to us in different ways. But this is not the source of your unease. Tell me."

"There is a child here, one called Dakhma." Corri chose her words carefully. "I had to rescue her from other children who were beating on her."

"Again?" The shakka settled back with a sigh. "I have warned them. I told Sussa to put a stop to this."

"Melaina stood by and did nothing." Corri's anger grew with every word, bringing back the painful scene. "She called her an evil Out-Clanner."

"So." The shakka's wrinkled hands tightened on her knees. "Melaina does not bridle her sharp tongue and hateful mind. This must not be allowed to continue." She sighed as she leaned forward to pat Corri's shoulder. "Your sympathy for Dakhma reveals the goodness you hide under a prickly exterior. I know you think me a harsh teacher, but I wanted to be certain you were not another false prophet. I have seen many who claimed to be the Dream Warrior over the years. The one telling sign of the Dream Warrior for which I waited, a sign given only in Tuonela prophecy, was the purity of heart that ached for the crying children."

"At first being the Dream Warrior was an honor thrust upon me, not one I claimed. Now I accept it, for I cannot stand aside and do nothing to help the Peoples. I have found too many truly good people to ever think of not trying to help." Corri's chin went up in defiance. "As for Dakhma, she knows only the goodness of a child, and I cannot turn away from her either, for she reminds me how I was treated as a child."

"Dakhma suffers from her mother's unhappiness. Sussa once took heart oath with a trader. He left her with child and never returned." The shakka shook her head sadly. "When Dakhma was born, she was a footling, a baby born feet first. This is a sign of great powers to come, usually healing. But Sussa rejected the baby. Only because I threatened her with outcasting did she care for the child at all. When she exchanged heart oath with a Tuonela of this Clan, and the boy was born, little by little Sussa again pushed Dakhma away."

"Melaina does not help the matter." Corri set her jaw in anger. "She called her Out-Clanner and evil to her face. That is a terrible thing to tell a child."

"Dakhma is no Out-Clanner. A child takes the mother's blood. She is as Tuonela as I am." The shakka slapped her hands against her knees in frustration. "And evil? Never! Dakhma must be trained to control her powers, and I have yet to determine what those powers are. But evil? No!" The shakka rose and paced back and forth across the wagon. "This must stop. Melaina has gone too far this time. I can no longer overlook her petty spitefulness and malicious tongue. These are not qualities of a true shakka."

Corri rose from her position before the altar and stretched the kinks from her legs. "The child has bruises and cuts on her face and arms. I saw them. If she is not protected, the other children will eventually harm her by more than shoving."

"I know, but Clan law will not allow me to take her from her mother without consent of the parents or a Clan assembly." The shakka shook her head and continued her pacing. "And I cannot force Sussa to love her. True love must come from the heart and soul."

"What can we do then?"

"We can only wait," Norya answered. "Imandoff said a strange thing before he left, something I have given much thought to since. He believes that in some way Dakhma will play a part in the final battle with Frav."

I saw her face in my vision! Corri thought, but said nothing. *Takra, Gadavar, Imandoff, and Tirkul I know will aid me, just as Malya and Roggkin will not. But how can I judge the faces belonging to people I have not met?*

"Norya, may I enter?" Melaina's syrupy voice came from outside.

"Enter." The shakka's brows pulled down in a frown.

Melaina slipped gracefully through the doorway. Then her mouth pinched tight in dislike at the sight of Corri standing beside the altar.

"I wished to speak to you in private," the tall girl said, fixing Corri with a hateful stare. "I will return at another time."

"No, you will speak now." The shakka's tones were rigid and cold.

Melaina bristled with indignation. "What tales has this one been telling you?" She pointed at Corri. "Did she tell you she called me a nathling?" The girl quivered with rage.

"Yes, I called you a nathling, and you are." Corri's soft voice carried across the wagon, striking Melaina with its coldness. "What you said and did was not only against Clan law, it was cruel and wrong."

"If you take offense at the insult, you have the right to draw knife with Farblood." The shakka folded her arms and stared at Melaina. "First blood drawn settles the insult."

"She has poisoned you against me." Melaina clenched her fists in anger.

"Silence!" The shakka's voice was barely above a whisper, but Corri felt its power run through her. Melaina blanched and bit her lip. "I warned you before about your sharp tongue, Melaina. Now I have learned of the evil you spread with it. To attack a child with words, no shakka does that."

"She is a tale-bearer!" Melaina stamped her foot in frustration.

"And what are you? Do you think me so powerless that I must rely on the words of others to know what you say?" Norya spoke with deadly softness. "You have overstepped your position as my apprentice." The shakka pointed her finger at the Tuonela girl. "I cast you out. I cast you out. I cast you out."

At each sharp sentence, Melaina involuntarily backed farther out of the wagon, as if she were physically pushed, until she stood on the steps outside. "You will pay, Farblood," she hissed. "You will pay." She jumped down the steps and ran across the encampment.

The shakka stood quietly for a time, then beckoned to someone standing in the shadows near the bottom of the steps. "Come, little one. There is nothing to fear."

The slight form of Dakhma was silhouetted in the doorway. She looked nervously around her as she entered.

"I came to see Farblood," she said, looking around the wagon. "I brought her a friend-gift."

"And your mother?" Norya gently stroked the child's hair.

"Please, shakka, do not tell her I was here." Fright filled the girl's eyes.

"You are safe here." Norya took the thin hand and led the little girl to the chests near the altar. "Sit, and we will share the morning drink."

Dakhma fidgeted as the shakka poured out the hot tea-water that bubbled over the fire-pot. She accepted the cup, watching Corri from beneath half-lowered eyelids.

"How many summers are you now, Dakhma?" Norya set aside her cup and stared across the tent-wagon, eyes half-closed.

"Seven summers, shakka." Dakhma turned her head quickly to look at the shakka. Her mouth tightened.

"So you can shield yourself. Good." Norya looked back at the child with a smile. The fear and resentment dropped from the child's face at the words.

"It is right for me to shield?" she asked in wonder, and Norya nodded.

Norya reads the life-force. Corri wondered how much she had given away inadvertently to Norya's gentle probings.

As if she had spoken aloud, Norya answered her. "No, Farblood, I cannot read your life-force. Unlike Dakhma, who can shield her life-force at will, you are a blank to me at all times. I have never experienced such a thing before. That is why I tested you."

"I must go. My mother will be looking for me." Dakhma hurriedly set down her cup. "This is for you, Farblood. A friend-gift." The girl untied a tiny woven grass-bag hanging from her belt and thrust it into Corri's hands, then bolted out the door.

"Poor child." Norya shook her head. "What little thing has she given you?"

Corri carefully opened the bag and tipped out a stone into the palm of her hand. "Something she found on the grasslands, no doubt. It is just a stone."

"She has little enough for herself, let alone to share." Norya carefully sorted through bags of herbs kept in one of the chests. She took her healing bag from its peg on the wall and packed it with the herbs. "I must return to Lyna. The baby could come at any time. I may not return here for some time as I fear it will be a long, difficult labor." She slung the bag-strap over her shoulder. "Practice your animal-talk, Farblood. The sorcerer and Halka will be interested in your progress."

Corri nodded as the old shakka left. She turned the strange stone over and over in her hands, staring at it intently. The smooth stone was a pale, translucent red, like watery blood. *I have never seen a stone like this. Deep within are hair-thin black lines like twisted spider webs. And it feels as if it is coated with invisible slime.* She rubbed the stone against her pants, then slipped it into the pouch at her belt.

Back to the animal-talk, she reminded herself. *Although I cannot understand what animals have to say to me.*

With a sigh, she left the wagon and wandered through the camp in the direction of the horse herd. As she passed the flocks of silky-haired goats, one of the djow raced to greet her. With a laugh, she steadied herself against the dog's weight as he jumped to stand with his front feet on her shoulders.

Good boy, pretty boy. Corri thought-talked with the djow as she scratched behind its long floppy ears. *Do you understand me?* The dog looked straight into her eyes, its large head completely blocking her view. Its strong jaws were open in a grin as it panted its approval of the girl. She relaxed, putting aside her efforts to read the dog's mind.

Suddenly, pictures jumped into Corri's mind, scenes that made her feel she was racing very fast across the grasslands, closer to the ground, as if on four feet instead of two. Before her low-ground view, several longhaired goats darted back into the herd.

So you can talk with me! Corri laughed and hugged the big djow. *All this time I was listening for words instead of looking for pictures. Good boy!*

The djow dropped down and rubbed against Corri's hip, nearly knocking her over. It lifted its head to stare at her with yellow eyes, then whirled to race back toward the goats.

So animals talk in pictures. Why did Norya not tell me this is how they communicate? In answer to the question, the thought came to Corri's mind: *She was testing my powers.*

She continued to wander around the edges of the camp, reaching out her thoughts to the horses, then to the invisible prairie birds and the hachino she heard calling from the tall grass. Her horse Mouse immediately answered her mind-talk by trotting out of the herd to her side, nuzzling against her shoulder and neck. The other horses, however, ignored her mental call. When reaching out to the grassland birds, Corri felt only wariness and distrust.

As she stood watching the horses graze near the camp, her thoughts slid back to the faces she had seen in her vision. The face of Gadavar, a Green Man of Deep Rising, rose unbidden and filled her mind with memories of their meeting high in the forest-covered mountains near the Valley of Whispers. *He had such a quiet confidence about him. I wish I could know him better, perhaps count him as a close friend.* She found herself comparing him to Tirkul. *I never felt as if Gadavar would be one to order his friends or lover about. But what do I know of lovers?* She felt guilt rise with her next thought. *How would it feel to stand in Gadavar's arms? If I had truly loved Tirkul, I would not have kept him at arm's length; I would have shared his bed.* She shook her head and moved on.

As the sun climbed high overhead, the camp became quiet. Except for a few guards, the Tuonela went to their tent-wagons to rest or to work on their crafts. Corri returned to Norya's wagon, but the shakka was still gone.

After she caught herself nodding off to sleep several times, she gave up and lay down on her sleeping mat. Instantly, she drifted off to sleep.

Corri hung in a gray place without a sense of up or down to it. Gradually, she became aware of voices and flashes of movement, but try as she would, she could not force anything into focus. She relaxed, floating without thought or purpose for some time. Little by little, a room took form; its walls were a slick black, the furnishings rich in gilt and rare woods and gems. Rolled scrolls, their edges tattered with age, filled a shelf by the door. On a dark table lay a rare bound book, open to the light of two thick yellowish candles.

Where is this place? Corri gazed about the room, searching for something familiar. *Is this where Imandoff is?*

Nothing belonging to the sorcerer was in sight. Corri shivered, as if with cold.

The door opened, and a very tall, emaciated man wearing a long dull black robe entered the room. Ebony hair hung matted over his bony shoulders. He stopped, looking around the room with a puzzled expression. Then with a shrug, he sat down at the table and began to turn the pages of the opened book.

I have seen you before! But where? she thought. Corri stared at the sharp jutting beak of a nose, the pointed chin. The skin of the man's face was pulled tightly over the heavy bones, giving him a look of death. *I remember! I saw your shadow-self when I dream-flew and later your face in the Lady's vision.*

The man looked up in suspicion, his wide slash of a mouth rimmed with thin lips. He pushed against the table with his talon-nailed fingers and stood up to stare at each part of the room in turn. When he reached the area where Corri's dream-form floated, his thick black brows drew together in a deep frown. The almost colorless yellow eyes stared straight through her.

"Minepa." A quiet rap on the door brought the man's head around with a jerk. "The sacrifice is prepared."

Let me out! Corri thought frantically as a whiff of evil stench reached her. *This is Frav! That is the High Priest Minepa! I must leave!*

She awoke in a cold sweat, her heart pounding, gasping for breath as if she had run for her life. She sat with her head on her knees for a long time, trying to understand what had happened.

It was too real to be a nightmare, she told herself. *And somehow it was different from the way I usually dream-fly. I had no wish to be anywhere near Minepa!* She ran her slender hands through her hair. *It was more like a calling. But a calling needs a touch-point, something to connect.*

Corri's thoughts darted back to the earring she had unknowingly worn for years, a device Grimmel used to keep track of her. The assassin Druk had worn such a device also. Both touchpoints were now destroyed. *Perhaps Kayth has made others.* She fumbled at her belt pouch, pulling out the friend-gift from Dakhma. She stared at the crazy black lines within the blood-watery stone.

Dakhma is not a servant of Frav. Norya and I would have felt it. Corri rose and hunted for the rare moly herb that Norya kept. Wrapping some of the moly around the stone, she then slipped it back into her pouch. *That should break any contact if this is the cause. I must find out where the child got this stone. Something is not right about it. I will keep it for Imandoff.*

Corri set off across the quiet encampment in search of the little Tuonela girl.

Chapter 2

$\mathcal{B}$efore Corri could find the child Dakhma, the camp came alive as three strange Tuonela riders came into camp. Their tattoos marked them as members of other Tuonela Clans: the Gray Wolf, the Sun Seekers, and the Sword Talkers. The warrior-messengers, two women and a man, left their mounts with the other horses, then went straight to the tent-wagon of the Feathered Spear chieftain Burrak.

Corri followed the growing crowd, listening to the mur-mured comments from the people around her, at the same time watching for Dakhma's small form.

"The Baba has found more of the old Prophecies," one man said to his neighbor. "He has sent riders to all of the Clans with this news."

"What can it mean?" the other replied. "It must be impor-tant for the Baba to do this."

Corri's thoughts flew back to the city of Neeba when she had been presented to the Baba and made a member of the

Clans. His calm young face rose briefly, but clearly, in her thoughts.

The Baba seemed such an intelligent man, yet gentle and strong at the same time. I cannot believe him to be one who would panic at doubtful prophecies.

The crowd quietly arranged itself in a semicircle before the chieftain's wagon with the messengers grouped at the bottom of the steps. Burrak came down to meet them, his long silver-threaded braids glistening in the brilliant sunlight. He talked with them for several minutes, the voices low and indistinguishable to Corri, who stood at the far side of the circle.

Then Burrak raised his hands and spoke, his deep voice reaching easily to the farthest of the Clan members. "The Baba has sent a message for the ears of the Dream Warrior and the Clans. Listen well to the messengers."

"If she is the Dream Warrior," mumbled the man standing next to Corri, his dark eyes flicking across her, then glancing quickly away.

One of the women, the tattoo of the Clan of the Sun Seekers plain on her cheek, stepped forward and looked around with narrowed brown eyes. "The Baba has discovered a new portion of the Prophecies. A part that has been lost to the Tuonela for many long years, so long that it has been forgotten. The Baba does not understand its message but feels it may be important." She straightened her armored shoulders, the long yellow braids rasping across the chain mail shirt.

She must have had to memorize the words, Corri thought as she watched the woman close her eyes and begin to chant.

"One called Soothsayer shall arise, with heart of blackness and powers great. His strong arm reaches far in unknown ways. With him shall ride the reborn Jinniyah. The Soothsayer shall try to conquer the mind of the Dream Warrior and will be burned at the crown. Out of the darkness opened by the star travelers shall come two seeds. One walks the shadowland, unfriend to Frayma. The other cries after, sword in hand.

A star woman takes up the challenge, killing the Footed Serpent at the gate and cutting the web that snares the minds of the Peoples. All Sar Akka lives under shadow of the sword. Past-times become future-times."

The warrior woman opened her eyes and stepped back with her companions. The crowd looked at one another, uneasy.

"We all know of one who calls himself the Soothsayer," one warrior said, stepping forward into the open space between the gathered people and the messengers. "He is a young man from Kirisan who journeys sometimes through the Clans. But if he were of Frav, the shakkas would have sensed it."

There were murmurs of agreement. The Clan messengers nodded.

"We, too, know of this Soothsayer." The man with the Sword Talkers tattoo on his arm spoke. "The Baba does not condemn this man as a servant of Frav, for the signs do not point to him. However, the Baba sends word to ride with care until the truth becomes known about this portion of the Prophecy. Walk in wariness, alert to all things."

"You will stay this night with us?" The chieftain gestured to his tent-wagon. "The Dream Warrior dwells among us."

"We can only rest our horses until this sunset, no longer," one of the women answered. "Then we must ride on to the northern border to carry the message and take our places with the guards there. If the Dream Warrior is here, as you say, she has heard our words. There is nothing more to add."

The crowd began to break apart, low voices murmuring questions and opinions. Corri felt a tug at her leather tunic and turned to find Dakhma standing beside her. There was a new bruise along the child's cheekbone.

"Farblood, I would speak with you." Dakhma caught her hand and pulled her toward the shakka's wagon. "Hurry! They must not see us."

The child nearly ran as she urged Corri back to the shakka's tent-wagon. Corri pulled loose the ties of the leather door-curtain, letting the painted cover drop into place, a signal for privacy.

"Stand still, Dakhma," she said as she felt her way through the darkened wagon. "I will light a lamp." Corri reached out with her mind, as Imandoff had taught her. A tiny bright spark flared over the altar lamp; the wick caught and the lamp burst into flame.

"I can do that," the child said softly. She shut her eyes and concentrated, her small forehead wrinkled in the attempt. The second altar lamp took fire. When Corri moved toward her, Dakhma cringed.

"What troubles you?" Corri reached out slowly to touch the girl's arm. "I will not harm you. Making fire with the mind is a talent honored by shakkas and sorcerers."

Dakhma's head was down as she answered. "I am not to do that, my mother says. I am not to use any of my powers. If I do, she punishes me."

Corri sat on one of the chests and pulled the child onto her lap. "What are your powers?" There was no answer.

"When I was as old as you, I did many things of power, and I too kept them secret." Corri began to tell Dakhma the story of her youth, about the dream-flying and her special memory, of Grimmel, and of Imandoff and Takra.

"Imandoff spoke with my mother," Dakhma finally said. "He promised that he would take me away to the Temple of the Great Mountain when he returned from his journey. He said my powers are not evil, and that some day I will help you when the Darkness comes. My mother is afraid of the sorcerer and promised I could go."

"What are your powers?" Corri asked again.

"Just little things." Dakhma clasped and unclasped her thin hands as she spoke. "I can light lamps. I can animal-talk. And I can call things to me. I have always known how to do these things."

"I just learned how to animal-talk. It was very difficult for me." Corri smiled down at her.

"Truly?" Dakhma's gray eyes were wide in wonder. Corri nodded. "But I cannot dream-fly."

"Each person has their own talents, Dakhma. Not everyone can do the same things; some have no talents at all. I cannot call things to me. I do not even know what that is."

"I can make things come to me. I feel the life-force of something and call it." The child struggled with putting a concept into words. "Not calling animals, but calling things."

"I do not understand."

"I will show you, but you must not tell. My mother says it is stealing."

Dakhma closed her eyes, held out one of her hands, and concentrated. Corri felt a small twitching inside her belt pouch. The watery red stone suddenly materialized on Dakhma's palm.

"Where did you find this stone?" Corri asked as the child returned it to her.

"A strange woman came here with a Tuonela warrior. It fell from inside her dress, and I felt its call. So I spoke to it, and it came to me. I would have returned it, but I was afraid of the warrior. Norya told them to leave the camp and not return."

"This warrior, what did he look like?" Corri felt a cold creeping along her neck.

"He was from the Clan of the Black Moon, with a scar across his cheek and part of his ear gone." The child touched her own ear in explanation. "I think the shakka called him Roggkin."

"Roggkin and Malya!" Corri spoke in a whisper. "You did right, Dakhma. You must stay away from those two." She hugged the child to her and kissed her cheek.

The child twisted in her arms and stared at the altar. "The shakka has something here which calls to me each time I come near this wagon. I can always feel its power." She pointed to a small dark blue-purple, tear-shaped stone near the statue of Frayma. "She told me it was a Qishua Tear from the far southern mountains. When the shakka was young, she went on a journey there and found the Tear. Can you not hear its voice, Farblood?"

"No, that is not my talent. Be careful not to let others know you can call things to you, Dakhma. They would not understand. Imandoff is right. You should go to the Temple for training. When the Darkness tries to cover this land, those for the Light will need all the help we can find." She smoothed back the child's light brown hair.

Dakhma's eyes suddenly went wide with fright. "My mother is seeking me. I must go!" She broke from Corri's arms and fled from the wagon.

Once more Corri sat cross-legged before the altar and sank deep into meditation. Although she reached the quiet center, she found no answers to her questions. As she began her ascent to consciousness, her senses registered stealthy movement of the hide curtain over the door. Corri came fully awake with her belt knife in one hand, but no one was there.

A faint rasping sound of something sliding across the wagon floor prickled the hair on her neck. Corri leaped up into a crouch, knife poised to strike. Halfway across the floor slithered a bright green snake, its diamond-shaped head raised.

A *tujyk!* Corri knew well the effects of the bite of this poisonous snake. Lightning-fast, striking without provocation, the tujyk was feared by the Tuonela. They hunted and killed it at each new campsite to prevent the death of children, djow, and herd animals. *If I knock it outside, it may strike one of the children. And I cannot leave it in here to hide somewhere.*

Walking slowly, as she had on many a thieving excursion in years past, Corri moved across the wagon, constantly watching the tujyk. With one hand she reached out and took hold of the long forked stick Norya kept for catching and killing the reptiles.

I cannot hold it down on the floor, she thought. *I will have to get it outside, then kill it.*

With one swift movement she knocked the snake back against the leather door-curtain. Its dry scales rasped against the curtain, as it slithered through, falling down the steps to the dirt. As she leaped down, the snake struck at her booted foot, but Corri trapped the tujyk with the forked pole. She ground the forks deep into the pounded earth of the encampment.

"You must die, snake," she said as she leaned down and severed the reptile's body where it joined the head. The jaws still opened and closed in death convulsions. Using the end of the pole, she dug a pit in the soft earth under the wagon and buried both the body and head.

That thing did not crawl into the wagon by itself, she thought as she went back inside. She eased back a slit at the edge of the curtain and looked around the camp. Near one of the wagons she saw Melaina, back stiff and eyes narrowed in hatred.

Norya did not return to the tent-wagon that night. Corri ate the evening meal alone, then took Mouse on a brief ride out into the grasslands before dark. It was nearly owl-light when she returned. As she walked through the camp after wiping down Mouse, Dakhma met her near the edge of the clustered wagons.

"It will not return." Tears ran down the child's face as she threw her arms around the tall girl. "I know I should not have called it, but I did. Now it will not go back!"

"What will not return, Dakhma?" Corri tipped up the child's chin and looked into her eyes.

"This." Dakhma opened her clenched hand. On the palm lay the shakka's Qishua Tear. "The others said I was lying, that I could not call such a powerful thing. When I tried, they ran away, saying I would be whipped if the Tear came to me, for it was stealing. Truly, I did not mean to keep it, Farblood!"

"I will take it back and no one will know." Corri took the Tear and slid it into her belt pouch. "Dry your tears, little one. No one will whip you."

"There she is!" Melaina's shrieking voice made Corri jump. "She has stolen the shakka's sacred Qishua Tear!"

Dakhma screamed and ran, while Corri whirled in anger to face the accusing apprentice. The warriors with the tall, golden-haired woman ignored the fleeing child, instead surrounding Corri and quickly pinning her arms to her sides.

"She carries it," said Melaina, dipping her hand into the girl's belt pouch and withdrawing the Tear. "See! It is as I said. Take her to Burrak. You all know the punishment for stealing."

The gathering Clan murmured angrily as the warriors dragged Corri through the camp to the chieftain's wagon. There her hands were bound with a rawhide thong, and she was shoved into a sitting position at the bottom of the steps.

"Where is the shakka?" Burrak stood over her, hands on hips. "Clan law says the shakka must be here."

"I stand in her place," answered Melaina. "Norya cannot leave Lyna. As the shakka's apprentice, the law says I can fulfill her duties at a Clan gathering."

"She cast you out, Melaina. You are no longer her apprentice." Corri glared up at the haughty woman.

"Liar!" Melaina's open hand struck her full in the mouth, and Corri tasted blood as her lip split. "Have any here heard the shakka cast me out? Will you take the word of this Out-Clanner against me?"

Corri looked around at the angry faces of the Clan as the blood ran down her chin. *Melaina must have known that Dakhma called the Tear,* she thought. *Now she uses this against me. Well, better me than a helpless child.* She set her jaw and remained silent.

"Is there anyone to speak for Farblood?" Burrak looked around the gathering. No one spoke. "Who speaks against her?"

Two warriors stepped forward. "We saw Melaina take the Qishua Tear from Farblood's belt pouch," said one, and the other nodded agreement. "All know that she was a thief in Hadliden before she came to the Clans."

"The law is clear." Melaina's eyes gleamed in triumph. "She is guilty. I myself found the Tear in her belt pouch. And these saw it." She pointed to the warriors. "As the shakka's apprentice, I demand six cuts of the whip and outcasting."

"Outcasting?" Burrak looked uneasily from Corri to Melaina. "The law says no speaking for a chosen time, but not outcasting. Besides, the Baba himself has called her the prophesied Dream Warrior."

"This Clan did not swallow the Baba's decision whole without giving a single thought to what he decreed. This Clan, and you, Burrak, said they wanted proof." There was a murmur of agreement from the crowd. "I have seen no proof she is the Dream Warrior. Have you, Burrak? Farblood is an Out-Clanner, not one of us. We must teach Out-Clanners to respect the laws of the Clans. How better than outcasting?" Melaina stared back at the chieftain. "Outcasting with nothing, not even a horse. That is my decision."

Shouts of agreement rose all around. The crowd pressed forward, some shaking their fists at Corri.

A young warrior stepped forward. "Many of us of the Feathered Spear think the Baba was mislead by Darkness when he proclaimed this one as Dream Warrior." He lifted his lip in scorn as he stared at Corri. "The Prophecy could not possibly mean an Asuran thief. She is no warrior, just a thief and liar, one having the traits that bring outcasting in this Clan."

Burrak sighed. "So be it. By our laws the apprentice can give judgment if the shakka cannot. The shakka's apprentice has determined the punishment."

She knows I will not accuse Dakhma, Corri thought. *So be it, Melaina. But I promise I will have my revenge.*

Rough hands jerked Corri to her feet and whirled her to face the high wheel of the tent-wagon. Her tunic was yanked up over her head to fall around her bound hands, exposing her bared torso. Strong hands stretched her arms up over her head and tied them to top of the wheel.

"If she faints, douse her with water until she comes to."
Melaina's voice hissed near her ear. "I want her to feel every
kiss of the whip."

"No! She did not steal the Tear!" Dakhma screamed as
Sussa knocked the child to the ground.

Corri flinched as the chosen warrior cracked the tough
leather whip to its full length on the ground. Before she could
draw another breath, the whip tore into her back. She bit into
her lip, stifling the scream that rose in her throat. Her slender
hands clenched over the rough wood of the wheel as she felt
her knees give way. Daggers of hot pain ripped through her
back and shoulders; blood trickled down her chin. The whip
struck again, and Corri hung half-conscious against the wheel,
determined not to cry aloud. The blood-lust in the shouts of
the gathered people roared like distant ocean breakers in her
ears.

"Stop!" Norya's sharp voice stilled the crowd. "What goes
here?"

"We follow Clan law in exacting justice for stealing." Burrak
sounded uncertain under the angry stare of the shakka. "You
were not here, so your apprentice. . . ."

"Melaina is not my apprentice." Corri turned her head and
saw Norya jerk her thumb downward before Melaina. "I cast
her out. If she demanded this judgment, then let her take the
blows left as punishment for lying. No one will speak to this
one for four moons. But all here are guilty for willingly believing the lies. I charge the entire Clan of the Feathered Spear to
walk softly, lest I withdraw my aid and declare you all outcast.
I, the shakka of the Clan of the Feathered Spear, have spoken."

Corri felt a rough robe slide against her side and the cool-
ness of a knife blade on her wrists. She sagged down with a
muffled cry as the leather thongs binding her snapped apart
under the sharp edge.

"Easy," a deep voice said softly in her ear as strong arms caught her. "Quickly, while Norya argues with these nathlings." The man half-dragged her behind the wagon, then helped her pull the leather tunic back over her bleeding body. "You will be safe in the shakka's wagon until I can get you out of camp."

"She was an accomplished thief and liar for the Master thief of Hadliden, even married to him by Asuran law." Corri heard Melaina's voice rise to a scream of rage. "Who knows what controlling magic she learned from that sorcerer with whom she companies? I am a Tuonela, free of her evil spellworkings. Farblood is an Out-Clanner! I, myself, found your Qishua Tear in her belt pouch."

"Imandoff Silverhair is no evil man, nor would Farblood steal my Tear. Must I call for a foretelling trance to bear out my words?" Norya's words were clipped with anger. "Carry out the punishment."

The strange man hurried Corri out of sight among the wagons as Melaina tried to fight off the warriors who bound her to the place where the girl had hung on the wheel.

"Who are you?" Corri whispered as they used the covering shadows to pass unseen. She leaned against the tall man, barely able to walk.

"The Soothsayer." He turned toward her briefly, and she caught a glimpse of dark golden hair and pale hazel eyes framed by dark lashes and brows. "Quickly, inside." He pushed her ahead of him into Norya's wagon and dropped the leather curtain into place. The sharp crack of whip and an answering scream of pain filled the camp outside.

Corri collapsed on one of the chests near the altar. She began to shake, her teeth chattering uncontrollably. The bright lamps showed the Soothsayer hunting among the packs on the floor, finally coming up with a flask. He pulled the stopper and tipped the liquid into Corri's mouth.

"Drink it," he said when she choked and tried to turn her head. "You need it. You have not felt the full pain yet." He made her swallow another mouthful of the fiery mountain water.

The whip-cracks and the screams continued, slicing across Corri's already raw nerves.

"Why did you help me?" Corri gasped when she moved, the tunic pulling against the wounds on her back. *Are you the Soothsayer the Lady warned me about? I did not see your face in my vision.*

"Because you covered for the child." The Soothsayer sat down on the floor in front of her. The light gilded his flat cheekbones, beaked nose, and strong chin, casting pools of shadow around his strange, light-colored, almost lidless eyes. "I understand how it feels to be called a freak, to be ridiculed and harassed." As he leaned toward her, the neck of his tunic slipped to one side, revealing extraordinarily white skin.

Corri stared at the man's face, uneasy memories pricking at her mind through the sharp pain of her body. "Do I know you?" she asked. "You seem familiar."

"We have never met, Dream Warrior, although I have heard many things about you." The Soothsayer smiled, his thick lips rimming the wide slash of a mouth. His hand fell suddenly to his belt knife, then relaxed as Norya pushed aside the curtain and entered.

"Fair greetings, Ayron the Soothsayer," Norya said as she nodded to the man at Corri's side. "You chose a dangerous time to visit me, but I thank you for quick action while I distracted the others."

"The rebellious nature of those of the Feathered Spear have at last found a target in this woman." He tilted his head, listening to the rumble of voices in the camp outside. "And now they also have Melaina to fuel their inner angers against all not of Tuonela blood. I saw it coming in my dreams."

"Yes, Melaina." Norya shook her head as she opened a chest to take out carefully wrapped boxes and jars. "Her family has much influence, blood-tied as they are to Burrak. By dawn I will no longer be able to protect you from her and the hot-bloods who hang on her words. You must leave tonight." A wry smile lifted one corner of the old woman's mouth at the surprise and concern on Corri's face. "If you travel with Ayron, you will be safe enough crossing Tuone. He has come to our camp for three summers now and knows all trails from Tuone into Kirisan."

"This is a dangerous time for you, Farblood," the shakka continued as she poured out a basin of water and prepared bandages and her herbal salves. "I hold control for a time, but in my heart I know that Melaina will divide the Clan of the Feathered Spear against you. She is a coward and liar, but with great pride and influence among the people. She will never forgive you for being my apprentice and exposing her to me for what she truly is. And many of this Clan have only waited for the right time to explode in their fear against strangers. I must ask you to accept another burden also. When you leave, take Dakhma with you to Kystan. Her mother wants rid of her."

"Melaina's hot-bloods fear to challenge me. The Dream Warrior will be safe at my side." The Soothsayer rose from his place at Corri's feet. "Should not the child come here at once, where she will be safe from her mother's heavy hand?"

"One of the messengers has gone to bring her." Norya motioned to the door. "Best if you stand guard until they come."

The Soothsayer nodded and slipped through the curtain.

"Now I shall do what I can, Farblood. For your own safety, and Dakhma's, surely you must ride before dawn."

The shakka pulled up the tunic and began to wash the blood from Corri's lacerated back. Clenching her teeth against the pain, silent tears running down her cheeks, Corri sat rigid under the gentle hands. The herbal salves stung at first, then slowly deadened the sharpness of the pain.

"You were brave to take the blows for the child." Norya gathered up her healing supplies. "Not many would have taken such punishment brought about by the actions of another."

"You knew about Dakhma calling the Tear?"

"I knew she called things. Since you would not have taken the Tear, I guessed the rest."

"Your Qishua Tear, did Melaina return it to you?" Corri's breath hissed as she pulled the tunic back into place. She wiped her wet cheeks with the back of her hand.

"Not freely." The shakka's jaw set as she reached into her pouch and placed the Tear back on the altar. "Burrak forced it from her hand as she hung on the wheel." She turned without a word and began to stuff containers of herbs and salves into Corri's saddlebags that hung on the wagon wall. To these the shakka added pouches of dried meat and ground grain. "You must leave very soon. By dawn, Melaina will have stirred high the fires of superstitious fear in those who think and feel as she does about Out-Clanners."

Why does trouble always ride wherever I go? Corri watched Norya's busy hands. *Even though I was not happy here, it was home for a time, a place to rest and learn. But if I must take to the road again to save Dakhma, I will, rather than have her endure more ill treatment. I remember too well how it felt.*

There was a quiet murmur of voices outside. The shakka listened, then went back to her packing. The messengers from the Baba entered with the child and the Soothsayer behind them.

"War-fever rises," one of the women said to the shakka. "We leave tonight for the border. As messengers of the Baba, and believers in the Prophecies, we can take no part in what will happen here."

"Take care, Norya." The Soothsayer gathered Dakhma into his lap, sheltering her frightened form with his arms. "The camp is dividing against you. Perhaps you should ride on to the border with these Tuonela."

Besides, Melaina tried to kill me earlier with a tujyk she put in here, Corri thought. *It would be easy for her to kill you with one when you are tired to the bone. She would have no difficulty getting her warrior friends to capture another poisonous snake.*

"That is the way of it?" Norya asked.

"That is the way of it," answered one of the women. "Come with us."

The shakka nodded her agreement. "I foresaw this possibility. Lyna's child is here safely. But I feel Farblood and the child should leave first. I will use what power and influence I still have to stand shield at their backs against Melaina and any who agree with her."

"The horses of the Dream Warrior and the Soothsayer are even now waiting outside." The man from the Sword Talkers gestured toward the curtained doorway.

"Then we shall leave at once, while the camp is still debating what to do." The Soothsayer gathered Dakhma's meager bundle in one thick-fingered hand. "Can you ride now, Dream Warrior?"

Corri rose and nodded. The pain in her back had dulled, but she was still aware of the fire-hot injuries. She turned to the women and asked, "Takra Wind-Rider, do you know her?"

"She rides with Frayma's Mare," they answered.

"Tell her . . . I have gone to Kystan."

The shakka followed them out into the darkening night. The Soothsayer lifted Dakhma up onto her mount, then tied all the saddlebags and bundles behind his and Corri's saddles. Corri gritted her teeth as she swung up onto Mouse.

"Ride fair, Dream Warrior," Norya said quietly, one hand on Corri's leg. "Yes, I call you Dream Warrior, for only such a one would do what you have done this day. May the wind be at your backs, travelers."

"Ride fair, Norya." Corri looked down at the shakka through a haze of half-felt pain, the chill grasslands night sliding across her face. "And watch your back."

She wheeled Mouse, and the three fugitives rode off into the grasslands.

That night was a blur of memories for Corri. The bouncing of the trotting Mouse renewed the tearing pain in her back. By the time the Soothsayer called a halt in the early dawn hours, Corri swayed in the saddle, only half-conscious. He helped her dismount, then rubbed down the horses while Dakhma opened the bags and laid out food.

The first thing Corri did was check her saddlebags for her owl stone set in the silver circlet. *It is here,* she thought with relief when her fingers closed around it. *Norya knew how important you are to me and did what I could not do in my pain, make certain you were among my things.* Her thoughts jumped back over the owl stone's first strange calling to her in Hadliden and its importance in the battle over the sky-ship.

Corri tied the flaps of the bag and hunkered against the bank of the arroyo, miserable with the gnawing pain and angry at Melaina. Dakhma coaxed her to eat and began to cry when she refused.

"Please, Farblood. It is all my fault." Silent tears ran down the child's face.

"No," Corri answered, her jaw set with pain. "It was Melaina's doing, not yours."

"Drink this." The Soothsayer pressed a cup into Corri's hand. The bitter smell of sharp herbs rose from it. "It will help deaden the pain. We cannot rest too long, Dream Warrior, for some of the Clan may decide to ride after us. We are still too close to the encampment."

"How long till we reach Deep Rising?" Corri choked down the bitter brew.

"At least another fourteen days." The Soothsayer stared at her, a puzzled frown on his brow, but he said nothing else. Instead he reached out and drew Dakhma into the circle of his arms.

"Dakhma, play a game with me as we ride," Corri said as she handed back the cup and pulled herself stiffly to her feet. "I will picture something in my mind. You must see if you can learn what it is."

"Not a guessing game." The Soothsayer smiled as he helped the child put the saddlebags back on the horses. "You must try to see within her mind. I will play the game, too."

They rode on, not pushing the horses as they had, but letting them go at a steady pace toward the distant blur of blue mountains.

Dakhma proved to have a small ability to read whatever the Soothsayer held in his mind, but could not see within Corri's. The Soothsayer could read Dakhma if she did not shield. Whenever he tried with Corri, he would smile, a puzzled frown on his brow, and shake his head.

"You have unscalable walls, Dream Warrior."

Why does this fret at him? Corri thought. *Not being able to read my mind makes him uneasy, as if I threaten him in some way.*

By the time they reached the foothills of Deep Rising, blanketed with oak and fir, the Soothsayer and Dakhma were friends. But Corri found herself watching and waiting for something she could not put a name to. The Soothsayer did nothing to cause suspicion; he talked freely of his journeys and adventures, but never once did he mention anything that would give the girl clues to his real self.

He reminds me of someone, Corri thought as they went single-file up the trail into the mountains. *Something is not right about him. But what?* To that the Soothsayer gave her no answers.

After two weeks of riding, and the second night in the lower slopes of Deep Rising, they came to a small cup of a meadow with a spring. Corri and Dakhma bathed while the Soothsayer went off to gather tubers. Dakhma cried when she saw the pink scars beneath the scabbed wounds on the girl's back.

"It is over," Corri comforted her. "Bad things happen sometimes. We endure them and go on. That is the way of life."

"But it is my fault," Dakhma sobbed into her shoulder.

"No, I chose. You must think only of the wonderful things you will learn in Kystan at the Temple. There is a young girl there called the Oracle. You will like her."

The child was still fretful when they rolled out their blankets, so the Soothsayer brewed her a drink from herbs in his saddlebags.

"It will help her to sleep," he told Corri. "Poor little thing, life has not been kind to her."

He appears to care about Dakhma and what happens to her, yet something within me warns that this caring is a mask. What are you really like, Soothsayer?

Corri lay for a time, staring into the gathering darkness at the thick darkening forms of fir and pine, the lacy outlines of newly budded oaks. Alders whispered together at the edge of the forest, their new leaves filtering her view of the night sky. She listened a long time to Dakhma's even breathing before she drifted off herself.

When awareness entered Corri's mind, she found herself floating high over their mountain campsite. The full moon shone round and bright high above, bathing the trees and rocky slopes with its light, casting pools of black shadows under the tree branches and in the rock crevices.

Takra! I will seek Takra. She turned in the air to face the north where she knew the Wind-Rider stood guard with Frayma's Mare on the borderland with Frav. Instantly, she streaked high over the Tuone grasslands to the Mootma Mountains.

Corri kept her thoughts centered on her friend as she hovered over the Tuonela camp she saw below her. Forms rolled in blankets lay around a small fire in the midst of a clearing surrounded by thick groves of fir and pine, huge boulders and a scattering of smaller debris marking the upper slopes. Moonlight winked on spearhead and armor of the guards who patrolled within arrow flight of the invisible spellbound border. The snort and blow of horses came clearly to her.

Takra? Corri mentally called to her sister-friend. She saw one of the solitary guards look upward. Flying lower, she saw Takra's scar-marked face bathed in moonlight. She hovered in the air, inches above the ground, facing the Tuonela warrior woman.

Takra, I go to Kystan. I am with the Soothsayer and the Tuonela child Dakhma.

Takra's eyes were wide in the darkness, looking straight through Corri. She quietly paced three steps away, then returned to her post, a puzzled expression on her face.

She cannot hear me, Corri told herself. She cautiously reached out and touched the center of Takra's forehead. *Remember my message when you dream this night,* she told her friend.

Takra stood still, listening intently to the night sounds as Corri lifted herself once more into the night sky high over the border. She thought of Imandoff and drifted slowly toward the west. Below she saw a great cleft in the earth, dark rushing water roaring through its shadowed channel.

The Kratula Gorge! Corri recalled the Tuonela speaking of this great abyss which marked a long portion of the border between Tuone and Frav, an impassable barrier broken only by the legendary land bridge that stretched across the Gorge from Vu-Murt.

Her curiosity led her to dream-fly along the Gorge until she hung over the bridge itself. On the distant side, inside Frav, she saw the tall cone of the Fire Mountain, inky-black and startling white in the moonlight, and at its feet the walled city-temple of the Volikvis.

Imandoff, where are you? Corri's thoughts once more reached out, seeking the sorcerer.

At last, daughter, you have come to me. Come. I can teach you such magic as you have only dreamed of.

The confident voice froze her movements. Before her, the face of Kayth, her father, wavered in the wind above the Gorge. Corri drew back and stared at the rapidly coalescing form. The sun-browned face, bright red hair, and blue eyes were as clear to her inner sight as if she faced him in reality. One part of her mind prickled with a sense of danger, while another part calmly noted a taint of blackness in Kayth's life-force.

You are not here. She threw the mental words like a spear at the face. *You cannot dream-fly.*

You think this dream-flying is so great a force? Corri bristled at the derisive laughter. *You have no idea of my powers, daughter. I have grown in strength since last we met. Come to me, and together we shall rule Sar Akka.*

Never! There are no blood-ties between us, Kayth. I will kill you before I let you destroy my world!

A dark tendril of power, sparking with a fiery red deep within, struck out at her. Her dream form fled, a snarl of anger echoing in her ears. She halted her sky-skimming flight only when she was well over the safety of the Tuonela lands once more. *Imandoff, where are you?* She mind-shouted her words into the night. There was no answer. As she turned and streaked back to her campsite in Deep Rising, Corri felt only a tiny flicker of awareness behind her, quickly gone and untraceable.

The camp in Deep Rising was quiet as Corri slid back into her sleeping body. Once returned to the physical, however, she felt a prickle of uneasiness. She opened her eyes to a slit and stared at Dakhma's silent form, wrapped in its blanket.

Beside the girl sat the Soothsayer, bending over the child and whispering. When Corri moved slightly, the Soothsayer drew back to his own bedroll.

Corri willed herself to lie quietly, deepening her breathing as if she still slept. The Soothsayer sat as still as stone in the inky shadows, his light-colored eyes watching. Corri felt a slight push against her mind.

What is it you seek to do, Soothsayer, she thought. *Who are you really?* She held the mind-probe at bay, felt it push again, then snap back. *I am warned now, Soothsayer. The shakkas may be right, that you are not the evil Soothsayer of the Prophecies, but something is wrong about you. And I will not let you harm Dakhma.*

Corri stretched and sat up. The far eastern tips of the mountains were just lightening with the coming dawn, still several hours away. The Soothsayer sat unmoving in his shadowed place.

"Awake so early?" Corri asked, trying to keep the suspicion out of her voice.

"The child was restless." The Soothsayer lay down and pulled the blanket over him. "Wake me when you are ready to move on."

You are lying, Corri thought as she stared at Dakhma. *But why? What is there in Dakhma that interests you?*

Corri's mind touched upon her own past, Grimmel's perverse interest in her, the master thief's desires and plans that had caused her to flee with Imandoff.

If you plan such a thing for Dakhma, you are dead, Soothsayer. Corri put a tight rein on her anger, instead reaching out to the Soothsayer's life-force. She found only a blank space, more frightening than if she had encountered a mind-shield. *What are you?* Corri sat, arms around her knees, watching the Soothsayer until dawn broke over the mountaintops.

Chapter 3

 $\mathcal{T}$ akra Wind-Rider stood, hands on hips, as she watched the shakka's tent-wagon make its way cautiously up the narrow mountain trail. The long, needled branches of evergreens brushed against the wagon sides as the tired team of horses strained up the slope. Before the wagon rode a Tuonela warrior woman, one hand resting on her sword hilt. The other women of Frayma's Mare clustered around Takra, their low voices like the hum of bees above the rising morning wind sweeping down from the east.

"A shakka here? What is happening among the Clans?" Charissa asked. The raw-boned woman twisted the end of one long blonde braid as she turned to Takra.

"Something not good," Takra answered. "When have you ever known a shakka to leave a Clan? See, those are the symbol-markings of Norya of the Clan of the Feathered Spear." Takra pointed at the decorated side of the wagon.

"Did your friend not stop with them?" Charissa asked, her dark eyes narrowed against the sunlight.

"Yes." Takra felt a coldness in her gut and remembered her strange dreams of the night before. "If anything happened to Corri, I will take my revenge." She strode to the wagon as the sweating horses pulled it into the Tuonela camp.

"Takra Wind-Rider, I bring a message for you." The warrior woman riding beside the wagon raised a fist in greeting. "But first, help the shakka. The trek has been a hard one."

The women clustered around the steaming horses, unhitching them, rubbing them down, and then leading them off to graze on the rich spring grass with the other horses. Others blocked the wagon wheels with rocks. Takra held out her strong hand to the shakka as the old woman limped down from the high seat.

"Call a Gathering," Norya ordered. "I would speak with all here."

"Call in the guards?" One of the tall armored women raised her pale brows in question.

"Even the guards." Norya limped to the low fire where the ever-present Clan stew simmered in a kettle. She sank down on a blanket there, rubbing at her red-rimmed eyes with one hand. "All must be warned of the evil growing among the Clans."

Without further questions, two runners dashed from the camp to bring in the border guards, while the other warriors gathered about the shakka. One ladled up a bowl of stew, pressing it into the wrinkled hands along with a horn spoon; another set a flask of mountain water by Norya's side.

"What of Corri Farblood?" Takra's words broke the tense silence. "If harm has come to her. . . ."

Norya raised tired dark eyes to meet Takra's pale amber ones. "Harm came and has fled. The Dream Warrior even now rides for Kystan. Last night I felt her spirit fly across the grass-lands toward these mountains." The shakka indicated the rugged peaks around them with one hand. "Perhaps to you, Wind-Rider?"

Takra nodded. "I dreamed of her. She spoke of a Soothsayer and a child. But I also felt pain coming from her."

"The bite of the whip must still pain her." Norya sighed and shook her head. "The deed was done before I could stop it."

Takra hissed through her clenched teeth, her hand falling to her sword hilt.

"Tell me," she growled. "Tell me all, shakka."

Norya raised her hand for silence as the warriors and the incoming guards gathered around to hear. "First, the Baba's messenger will tell you her tale of the new-found Prophecies. Then I will add my story."

The woman-messenger stood and chanted out the Prophecy found by the Baba and sent out to the Clans. When she finished and dropped down to sit beside Norya, the shakka told of the treachery of Melaina and the backing of the apprentice's decision by Clan members.

"As we rode out," Norya continued, "we saw a division of Clan wagons. Melaina has caused a split among the Clan of the Feathered Spear. Most stayed with her, acknowledging her as shakka."

"But she has no complete training and has not been accepted by the other shakkas!" said one of the warriors.

"Do you think that matters to Melaina?" Norya's hard eyes glanced around the circle of women. " I withheld the inner-most secrets of the shakkas, for my mind was not easy about her. But Melaina thinks she knows all there is to be shakka. She craves the power, not the responsibility. It is against all Clan laws to create such a splitting in a Clan, but that did not stop her. I am now outcast from my Clan, a wanderer, by my own choice." Norya took a long drink of the mountain water.

"Join with us as our shakka," said Charissa. "Frayma's Mare has long been without such help."

"Join us!" shouted a chorus of voices around the circle.

"Long ago, before I gave myself to being a shakka, I once rode with Frayma's Mare." The wrinkles fanning out from Norya's eyes deepened as the corners of her firm mouth turned up in a half-smile. "It seems the Goddess calls me once more to take up sword, this time as both a shakka and a warrior. Yes, I will be shakka for Frayma's Mare."

The women's shouts rang among the huge boulders and leaning trees around the camp.

"This Soothsayer with whom Farblood rides, is he the one of the Prophecies?" Takra asked.

"The Baba is not certain," the shakka answered, "and I found no evil of Frav in him."

"Give me leave to go after Farblood." Takra rose to stand with her hand on sword. "This is a blood oath, shakka."

"And Melaina?" The shakka's hard eyes lifted to Takra's even harder ones.

"Her time will come," Takra answered, her jaw set in determination. "My soul will not forget the insult to my sister-friend and to you."

"Ride with the Goddess, Wind-Rider. And watch your back."

"The message, it has gone out to the border guards of the Clan of the Asperel?" Takra turned to the messenger.

"Halman carried it, along with the shakka's news," the woman answered. "Rushina went to the third guard post. By this time, all at the border know of the Prophecy and the treachery on the grasslands."

"Then I ride for Deep Rising." Takra strode off to gather her belongings and Lightfoot.

This news comes at a bad time." The Tuonela war leader stood, spear in hand, as he narrowed his eyes at the shimmering in the air ahead of their position. "The Fravashi are preparing to attack. We can spare no one, Tirkul, for there are only thirty of us." His watchful eyes never left the milling mass of warriors pressed close to the other side of the border.

"I know." Tirkul eyed the break beginning in the spell-bound border. "What is that thing near the gray-streaked rock?" He pointed across the open, gravel-strewn space toward a black box near the rear of the Fravashi position. Squatted beside it was a Volikvi priest, his long tangled hair swaying in the morning breeze. A second priest stood behind him.

"I have seen its like before," Kulkar said. "Each time the Fravashi managed to break through the spells, one of the Volikvis carried such a box."

"Can an arrow reach the Volikvi from here?" Tirkul narrowed his eyes against the wavering spells.

"Not until the spells break. To get within range to use the bow will be dangerous, for the cowardly Volikvi stay well back."

Tirkul motioned to another warrior for his bow and quiver of bolts. As he strung the horn bow, he said, "When the spell breaks, Kulkar, I will try to get that box. Perhaps Imandoff or one of the shakkas can learn how it works."

War cries rose from the Tuonela warriors as the shimmering spells broke apart, leaving a clear-edged hole in the shimmering energy field. The dark-armored Fravashi war-band, outnumbering the Tuonela two to one, poured through the opening to meet with flashing swords.

If I am to capture that box, it must be now! Tirkul thought as he readied himself.

Tirkul dashed through the melee, dodging warriors, until he stood an arrow's flight away from the Volikvi. He drew the bow string to his cheek and let the bolt fly, straight and true. It took the Volikvi in the throat. As the priest fell, the second priest reached out a hand and slapped hard against the top of the box. The hole in the spells closed, leaving Tirkul to smash against an invisible wall.

"Beware, Tirkul!" The cry brought the Tuonela around in a crouch. A curved sword sang over his head. Drawing his long dagger, he thrust upward into the Fravashi soldier standing over him. The man dropped with a surprised grunt, the sound lost in the screaming war-cries of both armies.

Tirkul dodged back through the fighting, slashing with his long dagger as he went. When he reached a cleared space, he turned and drew his sword. *They are trapped here,* he thought as he slashed and ducked, dodged and parried blows. The Fravashi warriors retreated in a body until they huddled against the invisible spell-wall, unable to return across the border.

Snarling defiance, the Fravashi formed a wall of swords, as they fought without hope. The Tuonela laughed and withdrew to bow range. They notched their bows and slowly, carefully picked off the enemy.

Tirkul was aware of warm blood trickling from a shallow cut on his thigh. He stared across the border as the remaining Volikvi took the black box and slunk off among the far trees.

By the hell-fires of Frav! They will be back and soon, I know it. His thoughts returned to the message about Corri. *I was right to worry about danger, Corri. If you had given up this quest of the Dream Warrior, as I wanted, perhaps this would not have happened. Now I cannot help you. Like a willful horse, you have gone your own way, and I must be here.*

Perhaps she is right, and you are wrong, his conscience whispered. *You smother her with what you call love.*

It is love, Tirkul demanded. *I want her in my life. I need her!*

But does she need or want you? You think controlling her life will make her docile, yet your demands drove her away. Would you really want a docile woman at your side?

"They will try again, but not here I think." Kulkar's voice broke into Tirkul's thoughts as he wiped the blood from his sword. "Where next is the question."

"Two miles from here is another narrow place, easily crossed, where the Gorge has not yet begun." A second warrior spoke as he cleaned his splattered leather armor. "But what of the bridge at Vu-Murt?"

"We dare not split our force," Kulkar answered. "That bridge is a constant danger, I know. However, it leads straight out of the Fire Temple. I think they will not allow common warriors to enter that place."

"A band of Volikvis could cross." Tirkul slid his sword back into its sheath. "One Tuonela could go there, then ride back if any tried to get across the border at that point. The Volikvis would be inside Tuone, true, but we would know."

Kulkar looked at him, eye to eye, and nodded.

"I will take Hellstorm. If any cross the bridge, Hellstorm is swift as the wind, even among these rocks and trees. I can get word to you before the Volikvis get far into Tuone."

"Ride fair, Tirkul." Kulkar clapped him on the shoulder with one callused hand.

As Tirkul gathered his supplies, his thoughts reached out to Imandoff. *Sorcerer, I wish you were with the Dream Warrior. The Baba thinks the Soothsayer with whom she rides is no threat, but I am uneasy in my heart.*

Imandoff sat at the scrubbed table with a tankard of ale between his long sword-callused fingers, his prominent cheekbones and straight nose highlighted by the faint sunlight coming in the open door. He sighed with weariness and took a deep drink.

Such things I have discovered! he thought. *If I tell this news to the Clans, they will surely kill innocent people. These Fravashi traders harm no one. They hate the Volikvis. Yet the secret of their passing the spellbound border will cause the Peoples to fear them. And fear most often brings with it swift death.*

The sorcerer stared around the dim Nevn inn, his dark smoke-colored eyes noting each person there and dismissing them as any threat. He stirred uneasily on the rough bench, stretching his long, muscled legs under the scrubbed table and absently tracing the blue stone buckle on his belt.

Corri, where have you gone that I cannot reach you? Imandoff sent out a shaft of mind-seeking thought to the place where he had left Corri Farblood with the shakka Norya. He met once more with only confusion, hatred, and no life-spark of the girl. *I must return,* he thought as he picked up his staff and left the inn. *Something has happened. I should have listened more closely when I felt her dream-form pass in the night.*

The sorcerer strode through the mid-day empty streets of Nevn, the hard line of his sword visible under his swinging robe. His probing eyes passed over the shadowed alleyways and half-open doors of the shops until he found a merchant he knew.

"Any news from the Clans?" he asked as the little man weighed out journey bread and hard-dried travel meat, adding a full leather bottle of mountain water to the supplies.

"Rumblings about a new Prophecy discovered by the Baba." The little man peered up at Imandoff, eyes bright with gossip. "And a rumor of troubles within the Clan of the Feathered Spear."

"What troubles?" Imandoff leaned both sun-browned hands on the counter, his silver-flecked black hair sliding over his shoulders.

The merchant shrugged. "They are said to be running out all Out-Clanners. You know how that Clan is, always quick to jump at shadows cast by people who are different. All I have heard are bits and pieces, something about troubles between an Out-Clanner and the shakka's apprentice."

As he tied the supplies behind Sun Dancer's saddle, Imandoff cursed himself for being too involved in the pursuit of knowledge. When he rode out of the Tuonela city on Sun

Dancer, the sorcerer turned toward the east where he had last seen Corri in the camp of the Feathered Spear.

They will tell me what has happened and where she has gone, or they will wish for an easy death, something they will not get from me if there has been treachery.

Imandoff scowled against the bright afternoon sun as he rode across the grasslands.

Malya sat wrapped in her cloak before the tiny fire. The mole at the left corner of her mouth was plainly visible as she turned to face the Tuonela warrior who sat at her side.

"Now, tell me, Roggkin. Why are you here instead of with the Clan of the Black Moon? You were to stay there for two more moons before joining me at Leshy." Her pale blue eyes narrowed with displeasure. "When I left you at the Clan of the Feathered Spear, you were to ride back to your Clan. You were to find out all you could about Corri Farblood, where she went and what she did."

The Tuonela fidgeted under the pinning stare of those ice-cold eyes. He nervously pulled at his lobeless ear. "I could not stay," he grumbled, his words barely audible. "News spread from that girl and the sorcerer about my doings with you and Kayth."

"But your father is an important warrior in the Clan," Malya purred, stroking his bronzed arm with a slender white hand. "Surely he could protect you."

"At first he did." Roggkin stared into the fire. "He had an agreement with the chieftain that there would be no punishment. But the Clan members complained to the shakka, and she reprimanded them both before all the people. The shakka placed my father and the chieftain on threat of outcasting until the Baba can hear the complaints at the next Gathering." Roggkin exploded in anger as he sprang to his feet. "Do you know what outcasting is, you pampered Kirisani woman? No one will speak to you, give you any aid, even allow you in their company!" His fists were clenched, his jaw set, as he rounded on the slender form still seated at his feet.

"All because the girl said you were with me, or because you did the compelling magic I taught you?" She laughed up at Roggkin's flushed face. "I told you the dangers of trying to force that one to bed with you, Tuonela. Now you are left with only me."

Malya opened her cloak, the curves of her delicate slender form revealed by a clinging robe. Her long dark hair showed the glints of deep red from the firelight as she tipped her oval face upward to laugh at him again. She brushed his hands away roughly when he pulled her to her feet.

"You know the bargain, Roggkin. Not until this task is finished will I lie with you." She stepped back, watching his dark eyes. *And you will be dead by then,* she thought.

Roggkin's large hand shot out and grabbed her arm, pulling her close to him. "I have no desire to wait any longer." A sheen of perspiration beaded above his lip.

"Think again, Tuonela." Malya's free arm slid against his belly, and he saw the glint of steel in her hand. "This blade is tipped with tujyk poison," she said, her lips twisted in anger. "And it is not the only poison I carry with me at all times. If you wish to die an agonizing death alone, leave your hand where it is."

Roggkin dropped his hold and shoved her away. His eyes flicked across the dark coating on the slender needle knife, then rose once more to stare at the oval face. "You would scratch me with that, and then ride out?" he asked.

"I could not stay to watch you die," Malya answered calmly. "I do not like to see things die." She tucked the knife back into its secret sheath and sat down on her blanket. "Why quarrel with me, Tuonela? You cannot win. Besides, you long for the power that only my father Kayth and I can give you."

"Where do we go now?" Roggkin poked up the small fire, then moved to sit opposite the woman. "We are at the foothills of Deep Rising now. We know that the Soothsayer and Far-blood went up into the mountains, but we do not know why."

"Oh, but I do know." Malya held up the pendant strung on its silver chain. The watery red stone glistened in the firelight as she twirled it on the chain. "I was sent another stone to aid me in contacting Kayth. My father tells me that they take the Tuonela child to the Temple at Kystan."

"And how does he know all this?" Roggkin lifted his lip in a sneer. "The other spies he has here among the Peoples do not dare go into Tuone now. The Clans are turning unfriend to all Out-Clanners."

"He has his ways." Malya let the pendant fall back on her breast. "He cannot leave Frav now, or he would be here with us. If he left, Minepa would usurp the position of power my father has made. Kayth alone holds the secret of the strange boxes that can break the spells at the border. Besides, Kayth is finishing the translations of the Books of Jinniyah, the great Books of Darkness." Her tongue licked across her lips as she thought of her dreams of joining Kayth. "And when he is finished, all Sar Akka will grovel at his feet."

"Imandoff the sorcerer will stop him if he can." Roggkin kicked a stick farther into the fire. "Why does Kayth not mind-send the old man lies to lead him astray?"

"The sorcerer's mind-shield is too strong now," answered Malya. "But my father will have his revenge, never think he will not."

"And what do we do when we catch this Soothsayer we trail?" The flickering fire revealed clearly the scar that zigzagged across Roggkin's cheek, the nose bent from an old break. "He is not without power of his own. Will he join with Kayth, or do we kill him?"

"My father says the Soothsayer will join with us when the Temple refuses him again." Malya smiled to herself and idly pulled at a curl that hung about her face. "We will meet him at Kystan and take the child to Kayth. He recognizes the girl's powers, even if Minepa does not. And the Soothsayer will join our cause. Like me, that one knows the value of power. Besides, we know where his son is."

"I know what you dream of with your father, and it is not power alone, although you prattle of your importance in the Great War." Roggkin made the sign against evil across the fire. "To bear a child to close blood is forbidden!"

"It will give me even greater power!" Malya's soft words sliced across the night silence. "That is your problem, Roggkin, you are afraid to take risks. You hide behind others, striking in the back from the shadows or trying to work dark magicks to control a woman. You run from a fair fight, Tuonela, just as you did when Grimmel and the others met their death in the Taktos."

"Some day I will kill you, Malya." Roggkin clenched his fists and glared at her.

"I think not, Tuonela." Her laughter made his face flush; he ground his teeth in frustration. "You have no stomach for blood, especially if it might be yours. And I have my poisons." She passed her hand slowly before her face, palm toward him. He saw the bright glint of a disk held there. "Sleep, Roggkin. Sleep, for it is a long ride to Kystan."

The warrior felt his eyelids growing heavy. "I will still have Farblood," he said as he pulled his blanket around him. "Then I will kill her."

Malya's mocking laughter followed him down into sleep.

She journeys to Kystan." The Oracle turned from her seeing-stone, her narrow face pale from the effort. "She brings the child with her." The faint candlelight winked on the rare crystal in the center of the silver circlet across her brow. "The child is important, Vairya, important in some hidden manner to the outcome of this battle against Darkness. If I could only find a way to see what the child will do."

"Oracle, you must not keep foreseeing." The High Priestess Vairya touched the young girl's slender hands. "You have not been well since the attack upon you by the intruder when last the Dream Warrior was here." Her deep brown eyes were shadowed with concern.

"That is not the problem," the Oracle answered. She ran her thin hands lightly over her temples, rubbing at the ache she felt there. "The Dream Warrior is difficult to foresee, Vairya. I can find her presence in the future, but I cannot discover why she is in certain places or what she will do. All possibilities of the Dream Warrior's future come to me, scrambled together, as if she writes it minute by minute, day by day."

The High Priestess stared at the young face before her, the pale skin stretched tight over the wide cheekbones, the sooty lashes drooping over dark tired eyes. The delicate bones seemed to glow through the girl's skin with her weariness.

She stretches herself too thin, Vairya thought. *She never really believed that war with Frav was inevitable. Now that possibility stares her in the eye, and she must accept it as real and true.* The High Priestess pressed a goblet of cold water into the Oracle's shaking hands. *Words and good thoughts will not bring peace, as she supposed. She must reconcile herself to the fact that the land will be drenched in blood and battles.*

"Call the Jabed." The Oracle smoothed back a drooping black curl from her forehead. "We must prepare the warriors as never before. Two warriors of the Kaballoi must be chosen to ride to the Dream Warrior. She will need their aid soon, that much I know." The girl pulled the violet veil over her head once more.

"It shall be done, Oracle." Vairya stood, her regal form shining in her white robe. "But where is the Dream Warrior?"

"Somewhere in Deep Rising, with the Soothsayer and the child."

"The Soothsayer?" Vairya raised her eyebrows in question. "Is he safe? You know he was rejected once by the Temple. He has never forgiven us."

"Who knows?" The Oracle slumped back in her chair. "He can mask his feelings and shield his true being whenever he wishes. But this I do know: his powers have grown in strength since he was last in Kystan."

"How is that possible? Power is power. It can lie dormant until training brings it forth in its full strength, but to grow stronger than when first assessed, that I have never heard."

"Nevertheless, it is true with the Soothsayer. Call the Jabed and the Kaballoi, Vairya. We have little time. The future I have seen races to meet us."

Imandoff saw the wagons of the Clan of the Feathered Spear at the same time he spotted Takra Wind-Rider coming from the north across the grasslands. He sat on Sun Dancer, waiting for the Tuonela warrior woman to reach his side. The roan snorted and fidgeted, pricking its ears at the milling camp beyond.

Takra reined Lightfoot close, her booted foot touching Imandoff's. "You heard?" she asked, a scowl wrinkling her sun-browned brow.

"I spoke with the shakkas of the Clans of the Black Moon and Sword Talkers." Imandoff narrowed his dark gray eyes against the ceaseless wind. "Roggkin stirred deep trouble within his Clan before the shakka outcast him. She says he rode to the south. Rumor also runs of the trouble Farblood found in this Clan."

"And the Prophecy discovered by the Baba?" Takra fingered the silver amulet around her neck. "Is the Soothsayer of the Prophecy the same as the one who now rides with Corri?"

"I do not know." Imandoff stared at three riders coming from the camp beyond. "It is not a thing I would risk. We must follow Corri as soon as we can."

"First I have business here, with Melaina." Takra's amber eyes were hard. "A whip laid to my sister-friend is lifted against me."

Imandoff laid a restraining hand on Takra's arm. "I heard of this injustice, but we are in danger here, Wind-Rider," he said softly. "Many of the Clans have lifted dagger against Out-Clanners. They are now afraid of everyone and everything that is different."

Takra smiled grimly, the scar across her cheek drawing tight against the bone. "I am Tuonela. If they deny my right to enter the camp, I shall take sword and slash my way in. This is blood oath, Imandoff."

The sorcerer grinned and dropped his callused hand to the worn hilt of his sword at his belt. "That is to my liking. Corri is my friend also."

The Clan riders swept up on their horses, rearing the mounts before the two wanderers. Neither Takra nor Imandoff flinched. Sun Dancer laid back his ears and bared his teeth, while Lightfoot danced in her eagerness for battle.

"Travel on, Out-Clanner." Burrak met the sorcerer's gaze. "You are not welcome here."

"Take care, Burrak. Hasty words often bring swift pain." Takra stared at the riders haughtily. "I have blood business within this Clan."

"And by Tuonela law one who gives heart oath can enter with the chosen one." Imandoff smiled. "Do you challenge me, Burrak? If you do, let us dismount and fight here. I will leave your body for the rats and birds, your bones to dry in the grassland heat."

Takra gave a quick startled glance at Imandoff, then turned her watchful eyes back on the riders. *Heart oath? Well, a lie will get us into camp where I can find Melaina.*

"Out-Clanner is Out-Clanner in these times," Burrak answered stubbornly. "But I will not cross swords with you, sorcerer. Ride in only for the space of daylight hours. You both must be gone before nightfall."

"Do not think to send us to Vayhall by a dagger in the back." Takra spat the words. "That is a coward's way, and I will kill anyone who tries. As I will kill any man or woman who stands between me and Melaina."

"Our shakka can care for herself," Burrak answered stiffly, his quick glance silencing the other riders. "She has the power."

"Shakka?" Imandoff's voice purred above the wind. "To be a true shakka requires one to go before an assembly of all shakkas. You and I both know this has not been done, Burrak."

Without a word, the three Clan riders whirled their mounts and started back to the encampment, Takra and Imandoff behind them. The gathered people spoke in whispers as the group passed among the wagons.

"Burrak, why do you let Out-Clanners come here?" Melaina's sharp voice demanded from the door of a wagon.

Takra was instantly down from Lightfoot, dropping the horse's reins to trail on the ground. With one swift movement, her long dagger was in her hand. She leaped up the wagon steps toward the tall woman.

Melaina gave a startled cry and tried to retreat into the wagon, but Takra caught her arm and threw her off the steps to the ground. In a flash, Takra leaped down beside her, yanking the screaming woman to her feet, the dagger blade held up before her face.

"Silence, or by the hell-fires of Frav I will slit your throat." Takra's words were sharp-edged and filled with promise. She heard the hiss of a drawn sword behind her, but trusted Imandoff to keep the crowd at bay.

"I hear, Melaina, that you passed false judgment on Far-blood and by your word she was whipped." Takra brought the sharp point of the dagger closer to Melaina's frightened face. "And that your actions and lies drove the true shakka from this Clan. You should have known that a whip laid to my sis-ter-friend is a whip laid to me."

There was the loud burst of a fireball over the heads of the crowd, along with Imandoff's quiet words, "Stay back."

"Burrak, help me!" Melaina's wide eyes turned to look at the Clan chieftain, who stood with folded arms. Beside him was the sorcerer, sword in hand, eyes narrowed against the crowd.

"Hell-spawn! If I find that Farblood came to any more grief because of you, I shall return and slit your nostrils up to your eyes." Takra pressed the edge of the blade against Melaina's nose, bringing a trickle of blood. She lightly twisted the blade, opening a small cut along one cheek. "You disgust me! The Clan of the Feathered Spear deserves no better than you, you liar and trouble-brewer. I will not dirty my blade further on such as you."

She sheathed her dagger, then shoved the woman away and turned toward Imandoff.

"Beware!" Imandoff's shout brought Takra around in a crouch; Melaina's dagger whistled over her head.

Takra's clenched fist drove into the woman's stomach. Melaina gave a gasping sound and folded up, only to have her head jerked up by the Wind-Rider's hand in her hair. Takra then hit Melaina across the cheek with the flat of her hand, leaving a bright red mark that would later leave a dark bruise. The woman collapsed at her feet.

"Take care, Burrak," Takra said, watching Melaina moaning on the ground. "You may find a tujyk in your wagon some night or poison in your food."

Imandoff kept his bared sword in hand until they were both mounted and outside the camp. Takra's last look at the Clan of the Feathered Spear showed Melaina dragging herself into her wagon while the people stood apart, watching her.

"Well, we dare not return there," the sorcerer said with a grin as he slid the long blade back into its sheath.

Takra wiped the blood from her skinned knuckles against her leather trousers. "My business with Melaina is finished."

They rode on in silence for several miles before Imandoff called a halt and spoke again.

"Something worries at you, Takra. Will you tell me, or shall we ride without speaking all the way to Kystan?"

Takra chewed her lip before answering. "What did you mean by telling Burrak we had heart oath?"

"I meant to ask you first, Takra." Imandoff reached out to grasp her arm. "Look at me, Takra."

Amber eyes met dark gray. Imandoff gently pulled her toward him until their lips met. Lightfoot shied at a prairie quail, pulling the two apart again.

"The time that is left to us, let us spend it together." Imandoff's eyes pleaded with her.

"You would take heart oath with me? I am a Tuonela warrior woman, scarred and tough as saddle leather." She ducked her head shyly.

"I love every inch of you, Takra Wind-Rider, from your Clan tattoo to your little toe. As I have shown you already in the nights we spent in love under the stars."

"Love-making does not always mean loving, sorcerer." Takra turned her face away, afraid of what he might say.

"With me it does." Imandoff reached out to grasp her arm again. "I will walk beside you in fairness, keep your life as my own, ride with you wherever the wind blows." His deep voice faltered as she turned to look into his eyes.

"True?" she asked.

"True."

"Then I will give heart oath also." Takra smiled, then lifted her head to look to the east. "A storm is coming. We must push on while we can, Imandoff. Deep Rising is a long journey from here."

"And Corri may have need of us."

They urged the horses faster, riding as far and as fast as the light and coming rain would allow. But Takra's thoughts about Imandoff swirled like a whirlwind in her mind.

Now I understand Corri's confusion and anger over Tirkul.
Takra looked sideways at the sorcerer. *Part of me loves Imand-off, but the other part fears he will try to control my life, my actions, my desires. If he treats me as Tirkul has Corri, I will walk away, leaving the love behind. No love, no man, is worth the loss of my power as a woman. Corri was forced to live under such dominance for years in Hadliden! Best you find another, Tirkul, and let Corri grow in her own way.*

After the worst of the storm passed, they stopped for the night. On the driest side of a grasslands hill Imandoff fashioned a crude tent of their blankets to shelter them from the wind.

"We should rest the horses and then ride on," Takra protested. "Corri may be in danger."

"We cannot hope to catch up with her tonight." Imandoff reached out gently to cup Takra's cheek, then moved closer to kiss her. "The Goddess will care for Corri."

"Imandoff, why did you choose me?" Takra's words were breathy as they crawled into the tent. "There are many more beautiful women." She pulled off her boots and threw them next to Imandoff's near the tent opening.

"I thought you the most alive, fascinating woman I ever met. I never thought you would love me in return, my beautiful warrior," he whispered as he unlaced her tunic and drew it over her head. "I have seen twice as many summers as you, yet when you first smiled at me, I felt as I did when I was younger, riding the grasslands and rejoicing in the life of every day. Each day I have waited for you to turn aside, but your heart was true to me, as mine is to you."

"I would turn away only if you tried to cage me." Takra's lips moved softly over his bared chest. "Then my heart would weep the rest of my life because we could never be together."

"I would never do that, I promise," Imandoff answered as he stripped off his robe and trousers. "That would destroy what I love best about you: your wildness, your free spirit, the very essence of what is you, Takra."

Takra pushed aside the tangle of their clothes and wrapped one bare leg around Imandoff as she snuggled her whole body against him. "Perhaps our lovemaking will burn you out," she giggled.

"Then I plan to die the happiest man who ever lived." Imandoff tightened his arms around her and kissed her into silence as the grasslands wind thrummed against the blanket-tent.

Chapter 4

"My mother was a feya woman, Cassyr of the village of Springwell," the Soothsayer said as he pushed tubers into the coals to roast. "She died five years ago."

"Did you have no father?" Dakhma played with the rag and stick doll the Soothsayer had made for her.

"Like you, I had no father to live with us." The man frowned. "It was difficult for my mother. The man who fathered me went away, leaving her to raise me alone."

"Did your mother train you in your powers?" Corri asked, watching the man's face through her lashes. *Something about him is familiar, but what?* She raised her head, her eyes wide, as a memory slipped into her mind. *His eyes, his mouth, remind me of Grimmel's!*

"Cassyr taught me all she knew," the Soothsayer answered. "She taught me to cast charms and to foresee. Since then I have strengthened my powers with fenlix spores and wermod." His lidless eyes watched Corri closely.

"I know nothing of those herbs," she said, uncomfortable in his stare.

The Soothsayer relaxed and smiled. "They are known among the feya women of the mountains. My mother had a rare seeing crystal, something which should have been mine." His wide mouth was set in a firm line, his eyes seeing back into the past. "The villagers buried it with her." His voice was bitter.

"Why would they do that?" Corri took out her belt knife and began sharpening it on the whetstone she carried in her pouch.

"The mountain people follow many barbaric customs," the Soothsayer sneered. "They say doing such a thing keeps the spirit of the dead from walking at night."

Corri felt a push against her mind and looked up to see the Soothsayer staring at her intently. *You cannot read my thoughts, no use to keep trying.* She smiled to herself and went on with her sharpening.

"Has anyone ever foretold for you, Dream Warrior?" he asked. "I can do it for you."

Corri slid the knife back into her belt. "And why would you foresee for me?" *If you think I will drop my mind-shield, think again.*

"I know you have a heavy journey before you." The Soothsayer answered. "I know well the Prophecies of the Dream Warrior. Being aware of any possible dangers can help you avoid them. I will need to touch something you wear."

I know I did not see your face in my vision, but I saw a small boy, one whose eyes were much like yours. Corri pursed her mouth as she thought. *Was it you as a child, or only another? If I let you touch my amulet, perhaps I can then read you, Soothsayer. I will gamble it.*

Corri slipped off the amulet she wore about her neck, a parting gift from the shakka Halka. She dropped the gleaming disk into the Soothsayer's outstretched hand.

He closed his eyes, bowing his head over the amulet he cupped in both hands. A frown puckered his brow as he concentrated.

"Strange, but your future is a jumble of many things, none of them clear." He opened his pale hazel eyes, staring first at the amulet, then at Corri. "I can see you in certain places, but I get no answer as to why you are there or what you do. I know you quarreled with a Tuonela warrior, parting from him in anger. I see your flight from Hadliden with the sorcerer. I can follow your first journey to the Temple in Kystan, then on to a great battle with one from Frav." He slapped his knee in frustration. "But I get no clear picture of your future. This has never happened before."

Corri fingered the amulet carefully as she took it back. *What is this? There is nothing of you on the amulet, as if it never left my possession.* She dropped the amulet back around her neck, tucking it inside her tunic. "Perhaps there is no future for me."

"No. When there is no future, it is different. Not jumbled. Sometimes the end is seen clearly, other times just blank." The Soothsayer began brewing the nightly herbal drink he gave Dakhma. "Perhaps I see this confusion because I am tired."

He stared at Corri. His memories clicked into place, and he remembered her. As a child he had looked into his mother's crystal to see his father Grimmel. There in Hadliden, in Grimmel's great house, he had seen this red-haired girl. His mother explained that the girl too was the child of a star-wanderer.

He continued to watch Corri as she went to check on the horses before bedding down for the night. *What are you, Dream Warrior, that you fight against your own father? And what am I, except one robbed of his birthright?*

Corri looked back at the Soothsayer as he mixed the herbal brew for Dakhma. *You remembered me in some way, I saw it in the way your eyes changed. Now I sense a bitterness toward me, though we have never met before this.*

The Soothsayer smiled as he watched Dakhma drink down the nightly brew. "Soon, little one," he said as he gently touched the child's cheek, "you will use your great powers of calling to bring my mother's crystal back to me."

"Farblood will not like that." The child's eyes began to take on a glazed look.

"We will not tell her. It will be our secret." The Soothsayer helped her to the sleeping blankets and tucked them around her. "You will not be punished for calling something this time, Dakhma. Those at the Temple in Kystan will be surprised and pleased at what you can do." The child smiled in her drugged sleep.

You will buy my way into the Temple this time, child, he thought to himself. *If they want you, and they shall, they must take me also.*

Corri cautiously watched the Soothsayer and Dakhma from the corner of her eye as she stood beside the horses.

So Grimmel got you on some feya woman. I know that as surely as if you told me. Are you like him, Soothsayer? Do you have an unhealthy desire for little girls as that old toad did? If you do, best you ride out now, for if I find you plan such a thing, I will cut your throat! Surprised at her strong emotions for Dakhma, Corri thought hard as she caressed Mouse. *It is as if I see myself in Dakhma. If I keep her from the same events that made my life so terrible, perhaps in my heart I truly believe I can cast out the last bitter memories of my childhood. In a way, I am reliving that part of my life through her.*

She walked back to the fire and dropped down on her own blankets. Digging through her saddlebags, she closed her hand on the owl stone, set in its circlet, reassuring herself it was still safe. Then she closed the bags and pillowed them under her head.

During the dark hours of the night, Corri rose from a sound sleep, trying to place what woke her. The camp was quiet; the horses shifted their feet but gave no sound of alarm. She turned over and drifted back to sleep.

The Soothsayer gently took the owl stone circlet from Dakhma's limp hand. "You did a wonderful thing," he whispered into the child's ear. "Soon we will go to find the crystal."

Corri felt groggy and thick-minded the next morning as they rode on up into Deep Rising in the pale light of early dawn. The Soothsayer hurried them on their way, giving her little time to do anything other than eat quickly and saddle the horses. The oaks had given way to thick masses of fir and pine with the wide purple leaves of the meppe starring the slopes about them. What dreams Corri could remember had been unsettling; she felt as if she had spent all night running and searching for someone, someone she never saw or found.

"Soothsayer, wait," she called to the tall figure ahead as he turned his horse into a narrow fork of the trail. "That leads to the west, not to Kystan."

The Soothsayer reined in his mount, turning in the saddle to watch her ride to his side. "We must go around," he answered. "Winter snows brought down a slide on the other trail."

Corri nodded as he rode on. *What he says is logical,* she told herself. *Yet I feel uneasy with his explanation.* She glanced at the brief glimpse of pale skin exposed when the sleeve of his tunic pulled back. *He marked you with more than his eyes, Soothsayer. Strange. You may be of Grimmel's blood, but I do not think you have his perverse desires for little girls. Why then do you press your friendship with Dakhma?* She shrugged as they rode on. *Perhaps I am too suspicious.*

The sun had reached its high point when the Soothsayer and Dakhma stopped in a grassy place along the trail. The heat bounced off the layered rocky outcroppings, creating black shadows in the deep cracks and under the thick trees.

Corri, uneasiness growing, gave her attention to the surrounding forest as she urged Mouse toward them.

The horse began to quiver beneath her, then threw its head wildly as it fought the reins. Before Corri realized what was happening, Mouse gave a stiff-legged buck and bounced her onto the hard-packed trail before galloping back the way they had come. She stared up at the Soothsayer and Dakhma in surprise. The little girl sat quietly, her eyes closed, as if in deep thought. The Soothsayer watched her with his strange pale eyes, a secret smile turning up the corners of his thin mouth.

"Do you wish my help?" the tall man asked.

"Mouse will not come to anyone but me." Corri stared at him with calculating eyes. "It will only take me a few minutes to get her back." *You expected that,* she thought. *How did you know?*

"We will wait here, then." He laid his hand on Dakhma's arm and spoke quietly.

What is happening? Corri asked herself as she ran back down the twisting trail in search of her horse. *Mouse has never done such a thing before. It is as if something spooked her, yet I saw nothing!*

She paused and sent out a mental call. Mouse nickered from farther down the trail, a thread of fear plain to Corri's questing thought. Coaxing by verbal word and animal-talk, Corri walked down the pebble-strewn trail until she found Mouse. The horse stood with head down, flanks quivering; her eyes rolled with fear.

"Why are you afraid?" she asked as she ran her hands slowly over the horse's heaving sides. "I saw nothing."

Speaking softly, Corri mounted and turned the mousy-brown horse back up the path toward her companions. Mouse went with no hesitation until they were in sight of the grassy space. Then she balked and refused to go farther. Corri looked around in surprise. The Soothsayer and Dakhma were gone.

"What is it?" Corri felt around the area with her inner senses. The heat-reflecting rocks and thick stands of trees were barren of any life except for the flick of a lizard and the call of birds. "I see nothing." With a jerk of apprehension, the girl stared at the middle of the trail ahead.

"I feel it now," she said quietly to the horse, "but I cannot see it. It cannot be real. Tujyk do not live in the mountains, that I know. Yet I feel the presence of one here."

Talking softly to Mouse, she dismounted. With knife in hand the girl slowly walked up the trail, her eyes alert for any sign of the snake. She found nothing; even the lizards were quiet. Reaching out with her inner senses, she could sense traces of Dakhma's thoughts.

"The tujyk must have been created by Dakhma's thoughts, but why?" Corri was baffled about the little girl's actions. "Dakhma would never do anything to hurt Mouse or me." *Not unless she were controlled in some way.* Corri's fists clenched at the sudden thought that sprang into her mind. *It has to be the herbs he gives her!*

"There is no tujyk. It is just an illusion," Corri said. But try as she would, she could not dispel the mental image of the waiting snake.

Although she talked quietly to Mouse, urging the horse to move ahead as she held the reins and walked, it was nearly an hour before the animal would pass the spelled place in the trail. Even then, Mouse quivered and snorted, her eyes rolling in fear, as Corri led her past.

Corri fumed at the Soothsayer for leaving her behind, and was anxious to catch up with him. However, she wiped down Mouse's sweating hide with dry grass before moving on.

"Perhaps if I used the owl stone, I can see where he has taken her." Corri dug into her saddlebag for the circlet. The cloth that had wrapped it was empty.

"Gone!" She gripped the flap of the bag in her fist, conscious of the hard beddle beads that decorated it. "Soothsayer, you have proved yourself to be unfriend. I think you are not only a liar, but a coward, one who uses a child to do your evil. I cannot guess why you have taken Dakhma, but I know it is for nothing good. You are now my enemy, son of Grimmel. I will get Dakhma back, and then, when the child is in a place of safety, I will see that you get the punishment you deserve."

She swung up on Mouse and turned the horse up the trail to the west, away from Kystan and toward the Barren Mountains that separated Asur and Kirisan.

*W*hy must we leave Farblood behind?" Dakhma's thin voice reached the Soothsayer riding in front of her.

"She will meet us later. First we must hurry to my mother's grave so you can call the crystal buried there." The Soothsayer turned and smiled.

"Why do you have Farblood's stone?" The child was persistent in her search for answers. She was beginning to fear this tall, pale-eyed man who had once seemed so friendly.

"I did not take the stone, you did," the Soothsayer said over his shoulder. "We will return it to the Dream Warrior when next we see her."

A tear trickled down the little girl's cheek. "I will be whipped for stealing." Her lip quivered.

The Soothsayer reined in his horse, waiting for her to ride alongside. "She did not allow you to be whipped before, did she?" He wiped away the silent tears with his thick-fingered hand. "We will tell her it was a mistake. Everything will be fine, Dakhma. Trust me."

The child followed him silently on into the mountains, but she tossed away the stick and rag doll. On the evening of the third day, they left the main trail, descending into a narrow valley that ran like a bare finger back into the higher ranges along the border with Asur. Mounds taller than a horseman, and covered with a velvet carpet of green grass, covered the valley floor.

"What is this place?" Dakhma asked, her eyes wide as she turned her head back and forth to look at the strange mounds. The edge of the sun peered from behind the far mountains, its last rays deepening the shadows about the mounds. "There are many things buried here, many things calling to my mind."

The Soothsayer reined in his horse. "Are they powerful things?" he asked as the little girl rode up beside him.

"Some feel like they are. They were once sacred things." Dakhma shook her head in bewilderment. "But they are tainted with a bad sickness. I do not understand, Soothsayer."

"These are the burial mounds of the Peoples who died in long-ago wars with Frav. Our history says that many of those buried here died of a strange plague sent by the Volikvis." The Soothsayer pointed beyond the high mounds among which they rode. "At the end of the valley lie the barrows of some of the Forgotten Ones. Perhaps you will find something there of even greater importance."

"This is a place of the ancient dead?" Dakhma's eyes went wide with fear. She stared around her, at the fading sunlight falling over the mountains to the west, at the burial mounds casting long, black shadows.

"Come, Dakhma, you knew you were to bring the crystal from my mother's grave." The Soothsayer frowned down at the child. "I thought the Tuonela were brave. Are you a coward, then?" His thick lips lifted in a sneer.

"I am no coward!" The child's face flushed across the cheekbones.

"My mother is buried just beyond the next mound." The Soothsayer smiled in triumph, then urged his horse forward. Dakhma followed him, a look of deep thought on her young face.

Cassyr's burial mound was only a low hump, covered with grass and wild flowers, a tiny hill among giants. At the foot of the mound lay a cup of water and a chunk of hard bread, pieces pecked out of it by the birds.

"I see Uzza still comes here." The Soothsayer dismounted, pulled loose their supply bag, and dropped the reins so the horse could graze among the mounds. He lifted Dakhma down, then turned her mount loose to graze with his.

"The full moon will be up soon," he said as he spread blankets near the mound. "We will wait. Moonlight, such as will be tonight, is very powerful."

"I do not like this place. Let me call the crystal now," Dakhma pleaded.

"No!" The Soothsayer swung to face the child, anger drawing down his brows. "Uzza sealed the grave with her magic. You will need the extra power of the moon and my herbs to retrieve the crystal."

"I do not want your drink." Dakhma crouched on her blanket, fear plain on her little face. "It makes me feel strange."

The Soothsayer squatted at her side, his pale eyes almost shining in the dusk. "You will drink what I give you, Dakhma, or I will tie you and leave you here until you do. Do you understand?" He shook the child by her thin arm until she nodded in agreement.

Dakhma lay down on the blanket and curled up into a ball, while the Soothsayer built a tiny fire to brew the herbal drink. Her little body shook, but she made no sound as she sobbed with terror. Ignoring her, the tall man took his flask and walked off into the darkness to dip water from a hidden spring.

When she could no longer hear his footsteps, Dakhma sat up and wiped her face with a grimy hand. The jingle of the horses' bridles reached her ears, along with the hunting cry of the little meemee owls ghosting through the night. She stared around at the mounds, black with shadows and dusted with the first silver light of the rising moon. The Soothsayer was nowhere in sight.

Dakhma cautiously got to her feet, then crept in the direction of the horses. The Soothsayer's mount snorted and backed away from her, but the horse she had ridden nuzzled her outstretched hand as she caught at the reins. She tried several times to pull herself into the saddle but failed. Finally, she looked about for something to stand on, but saw only the shadowed forms of the graves; she pulled the horse close to one of the mounds. Wiping her perspiring hands on her trousers, the little girl climbed up the sloping side of the burial mound. Just as she leaned out to mount the horse, it shied and she sprawled to the ground.

"So you would run away." The Soothsayer's deep voice filled her ears as he yanked her to her feet. "I meant what I said. You will not leave this place until you call my mother's crystal out of her grave."

The Soothsayer took a piece of rope from his saddlebags, dragged the reluctant child back to the campsite, and threw her on the blanket. He trapped her hands in his thick-fingered grip and bound them before her with the rope.

Dakhma bent her head onto her knees as he went back to the fire. The Soothsayer sprinkled bright green leaves marked at the edges with purple into the water, stirring it until the thick odor of wermod filled the stagnant air between the mounds. He dipped out the leaves and poured the liquid into a cup.

"Drink this," he ordered as he pressed the cup against Dakhma's mouth. "The sooner you do everything I say, the sooner we can be gone from this place."

She gulped down the hot liquid. The Soothsayer watched her closely for some time, until the child's eyes took on a dreamy, vacant stare. He smiled as he sat beside her, one arm around her thin shoulders. When the child's eyes began to glaze, he untied her hands, tucking the rope into his belt. The moon broke free of the clutching trees on the forested mountains, bathing the valley in sharp contrasts.

"Now, my little Tuonela girl," he said softly, "this is what you must seek." He droned on in a whispered voice no louder than the wind in her ears as he described what he wanted.

Dakhma stared at the low grave, holding out her hands. She whimpered, drawing back in fear at what she found there, but the Soothsayer shook her roughly.

"Do it!" he ordered.

She held out her hands again. There was a shimmer in the air between her and the grave. A moon-bright piece of crystal materialized on her palms, filling her hands.

"At last." The Soothsayer snatched the crystal from the child and held it up to the moon. "This should have been mine five years ago." He turned the perfectly clear crystal round and round, the moonlight flashing from its globular surface. Looking deep into its fist-sized form was like looking into a deep, clear pool.

"Eat now before we travel on to Kystan," he said as he pressed a portion of journey bread and dried meat into the child's hands. Obediently, the child chewed and swallowed. The Soothsayer turned again to the crystal. "Mine at last. So much for your powers, Uzza." He laughed as he carefully wrapped the crystal and placed it in the supply bag.

A dry twig snapped somewhere among the mounds. The Soothsayer instantly stamped out the tiny fire and stood listening, his head turning slowly from side to side. There was a faint rustle of grass, then silence.

"Come, we must leave." He pulled the child to her feet, gathering the blanket in his other arm.

"I am tired," she whimpered. "I want to sleep."

"We will sleep in another place," he answered as he led her to the horses. "Soon you can sleep, Dakhma, but for now you must be strong and ride." He lifted her onto the horse, mounted his own, and led the way out of the burial valley.

$\mathcal{C}$orri trailed the Soothsayer and Dakhma for three days, never coming any closer to them. Several times she felt an itch between her shoulder blades, that old warning of being watched. But she caught sight of no one in the thick forest or rocky mountain bones of outcroppings along the trail.

She began to dread the night and sleep. Each time she drifted into deep rest, faint and disjointed scenes of Minepa, the head of the Fravashi priesthood, rose to meet her. Her only consolation was that Minepa seemed to be unaware of her dream-form presence as he went about his shadowed room. Her nerves stretched tight and screaming with dread, Corri would watch him reading in ancient scrolls and books, performing magic that stunk of evil, and once opening the door of his room to Kayth. Always she fled back into her physical body before she was discovered, to awaken shaking, perspiration dripping down her face, and gasping for breath. She would spend the rest of the night huddled close to her low fire.

Late on the third day, Corri came upon a village set high in the mountains, the log huts built in a clearing near a sun-gilded creek. After her recent experience with the Tuonela, and her long solitary journey with only Mouse for company, she was reluctant to speak with these strange villagers. As she turned Mouse away, a young woman came down the trail, bags of herbs slung over her back.

"Greetings, stranger. Do you have need of me?" The woman leaned on her walking staff and looked up at Corri with bright green eyes that missed nothing. Her glance flicked over the worn wire-hilt of the girl's belt knife, the dust on her leather Tuonela trousers. "You are no Tuonela, although you wear their garb." The woman's long skirt was tucked up under her belt, revealing a thinly worn petticoat underneath. Her waist-length brown hair hung in a single braid down her back.

"Is this Springwell? I seek a man called the Soothsayer. He came this way with a girl-child."

"This is the village of Tree-Home. And why would you seek the Soothsayer?" The woman spat on the ground. "I am the feya woman of this village, and I tell you to beware of that one." She leaned against her walking staff, her eyes narrowed against the sunset.

"I must find him. He kidnapped the child from me when we journeyed toward Kystan." Corri hesitated, then plunged on. "I am Corri Farblood. The Soothsayer told me he came from Springwell, here in these mountains. I fear for the child's safety."

"The Dream Warrior!" The woman's eyes widened in surprise. "The feya women know of you, girl, but we did not think it would be one so young." She motioned with her hand. "I am called Thalassa. Come to my hut. You look tired and hungry. There, we can talk without being disturbed. It is too dangerous to travel at night in these mountains."

What choice have I? This woman will know the places the Sooth- sayer would go to hide. I must find Dakhma quickly and get her out of his hands.

Corri turned Mouse and followed the woman down the slope. The feya woman turned aside before she reached the village to a hut half-hidden in the shadows of overhanging tree branches. The creek ran close by, singing over the smooth rocks and around moss-covered trees that had fallen into it.

Thalassa waited silently while Corri rubbed down Mouse and tethered the horse near the creek where the grass was tall. She held the hut door open in welcome as Corri, laden with her saddlebags, wearily stumbled inside.

The wooden shutters at the windows were thrown back, letting in filtered patches of fading sunlight and air rich with the scent of firs and pines. Whispering in the breeze coasting along the creek, a purple-leafed meppe tree rustled against the log wall. A low fire smoked in the fireplace, with an iron pot hung over it by a hook.

Corri looked up at the open rafters, where bunches of dried herbs hung. Two narrow sleeping shelves, covered with blankets, hung on the wall. Plank tables, covered with pots and mortars and small jars, filled most of the room.

The feya woman carefully laid out her herb bags, then turned to dip out a bowl of stew from the cauldron. Corri sank down on a stool beside the fireplace, the wooden bowl and horn spoon in her hands.

"So the Soothsayer is up to new tricks." Thalassa sat across from Corri, her strong weather-browned hands on her knees. "That one strives always to be more than he is. It rankled him to be rejected by the Temple of the Great Mountain."

"He was rejected? Why?" Corri watched her as she ate.

"He has no self-discipline," the feya woman answered. "It takes no High Priestess to see that Ayron, son of the feya woman Cassyr, wants power for his own purposes, not to use to help the Peoples." She sniffed in disdain. "When he found his powers were not as strong as he wanted, he began to take fenlix spores and wermod—a dangerous thing to do."

Corri paused, the horn spoon poised above the bowl. "How are they dangerous?"

"Fenlix spores are addictive if taken too often. And wermod has dual properties. It can make one's powers sharpen, true, but too strong doses of it can make one pliable to the will of another. These herbs are used carefully by the feya women for trance, contacting those dead, and foreseeing."

"Oh, Goddess." Corri dropped the spoon into the bowl as she stared at the woman. "The child with whom the Soothsayer travels has powers not yet tested. And each night he gave her an herb drink, saying it would help her sleep."

Thalassa shook her head sadly. "Ayron will come to a bad end, Dream Warrior. In the morning I myself will take you to Springwell to get the child. She must not stay with him."

"You called him Ayron. That is his given name then?" Corri set the bowl on the hearth. "Among the Clan of the Feathered Spear, he was known only as the Soothsayer. The shakka

Norya called him Ayron, but I thought it a Kirisani word I did
not know."

"He tries to wrap an air of mystery about him. Ayron, it
means one born from sorrow. I met his mother Cassyr once,
when I trained to be a feya under Uzza, the other feya woman
of the village of Springwell." The woman stared into the tiny
crackling flames of the fire. "Uzza says that she and the villagers warned Cassyr to abort the baby, but she refused. Later,
she regretted her decision many times. Ayron was a willful
child, always wanting more, never patient to wait for anything.

"His father was a strange-looking and evil man, not of the
Peoples." Grimmel's image rose in Corri's mind.

"The villagers say that two men, not of the Peoples, came
into these mountains long ago. Ayron's father drugged Cassyr
and raped her, leaving her with child. The other man, one
with bright red hair," the feya woman's eyes flicked to Corri's
sun-streaked curls, "lived for a time with a Priestess from the
Temple. He, too, left before the child was born." She gripped
her knees, her knuckles white, the tendons standing clear.
"Are you the child of that Priestess, Dream Warrior?"

"Yes," Corri sighed. "Now I stand with the Peoples against
the man who fathered me and who would turn the land red
with blood."

"So the Dream Warrior who fights for us comes from the
blood of our enemy. It is said the Lady can draw good from
evil. Now I truly believe it." She paused. "But why would
Ayron return to Springwell?" Thalassa frowned in thought.
"He is not welcome there. Uzza has declared him outcast."

"His mother's crystal!" both said at the same time.

"He would desecrate her grave." The woman twisted the
end of her braid.

"Not in the way you think," Corri answered. "The child
with him can call things to her. Dakhma can bring things to
her through walls and across distance. A grave would be no

obstacle to the child. The Soothsayer will use her to get the crystal."

"This power you say the child has. I have heard of it, but never have I seen one who could do it. Ayron will stop at nothing, will use anything and anyone to give himself more power and control over others."

"Dakhma has this calling power, for I have seen her use it." Corri thought of her owl stone. *So you think to use the power of the owl stone, Soothsayer. Beware, lest it turn on you.* She pushed up her leather headband and rubbed at the scar in the center of her forehead.

"I will take you to Springwell at first light," the feya woman said. "The trail is too dangerous to travel in the dark. There have been many strange and dangerous animals abroad in the night lately."

Corri and Thalassa learned they were too late when dawn brought news by messenger that the Soothsayer and Dakhma had been to Springwell and gone. The villagers were angry and frightened at the story the messenger told. A late hunter had seen the child call forth the crystal from the grave of Ayron's mother. Then the Soothsayer and Dakhma had vanished into the black forest.

"Where will he go now?" the feya woman asked. "He dare not stay in our mountains, for the men will hunt him down as a grave-robber. He has given them reason enough to fear him in the past. Now his actions make him truly outcast and such an enemy as to be killed on sight."

"He will go to Kystan, to bargain for a place in the Temple," Corri said with certainty as she saddled Mouse. "He spoke of it, but at the time I did not understand what he meant. The Soothsayer had best watch his back, for I will follow him. And if I catch him, in the Temple or out, I will kill him for what he has done to the child."

"Go with the Goddess, Dream Warrior. But I warn you, take care, for the Prophecies say you are our only hope in the coming war with Frav." Thalassa smiled at Corri's raised brows. "Yes, we in the mountains, isolated though we are, know a little of what happens beyond our forests. The feya women have had foreseeing of the approaching war, dire dreams and haunting visions. When the time comes, we will fight, as will all the free Peoples. Our freedom is precious to us. We would die rather than submit to the god of the Fravashi."

"Can you get word to the Green Men about the Soothsayer?"

"We shall do this," the woman answered. "But be assured, Ayron has not passed the Green Men unobserved. However, they will have no reason to detain him until they learn of his unlawful taking of the child and the desecrating of the grave."

"Then I must ride to Kystan." Corri fastened the saddlebags in place and pulled herself up on Mouse. "If others come seeking me, a Tuonela warrior woman and a sorcerer, tell them where I have gone and why."

"This I shall do. Ride with the Goddess."

Corri took the mountain trails back to the east, the damp morning chill against her face. *Soothsayer, you should have been more like your mother's blood-line,* she thought bitterly. *When you chose to be like your father Grimmel, you opened the door to your own death.*

Cold gripped Corri's heart as she thought of her own childhood under the control of the Master Thief and what she knew Dakhma must now be enduring under the control of the Soothsayer.

The shakkas were wrong. You have to be the Soothsayer of the Prophecy. And I shall fulfill the ancient words and send you down into darkness. Corri pursed her mouth in deep thought. *Yet, there is a puzzle. I felt no evil within you toward the Peoples or toward me as a fellow traveler. The only evil seems to be in the way you use Dakhma for your own thirst after power. How can this be, if you are the Soothsayer of the Prophecy?*

Chapter 5

The influence of the wermod was gone by the time the Soothsayer and Dakhma found a secure resting place just off the trail. They had traveled throughout the night, stopping after dawn-light broke over the tall sharp peaks of Deep Rising. The exhausted child curled up on her sleeping blanket and immediately fell into a deep sleep. The Soothsayer tended to the horses, then spread his blanket close to the girl.

Now the Temple cannot refuse me, he thought as he unwrapped the grave-crystal. *My powers have grown to such an extent that I am now more powerful than the Jabed himself. Goddess knows, that old man never had any talents to begin with. Once admitted to the Temple, it should not take long for them to recognize my powers and replace the Jabed with me.*

The Soothsayer cradled the icy-cold globe of clear crystal in both his hands and stared deep within its flawless depths. For a time he silently watched the scenes he saw there. A frown pulled down his brows as he again wrapped the crystal and stowed it in his bags.

Farblood is still shielded, even from the crystal. But why? I see Dakhma clearly enough. She will be in the Temple by late summer. And I see myself both in the Temple and in my mountain cabin. He shook his head in frustration. *Farblood follows us, according to the crystal. But I cannot clearly see if she will upset my plans.* He lay back on the blanket, arms behind his head, staring up at the swaying green fir branches. *My mother always said that the crystal can lie. It can show only what the seer wants to see, truth or not, or it can show the true future. But my mind is strong and I see only the truth.* A mental image of the owl stone rose in his mind. *There is a strange and powerful energy in that stone. I will get Dakhma to try it first. The child's mind is open and pure, therefore she should come to no harm. After I have explored the stone's energy through her, I will use it on my own.* He closed his eyes and slept.

Dakhma found herself conscious of an unfamiliar place. Her surroundings flickered in and out of view, briefly revealing a vast cavern. Hundreds of gigantic stone pillars dropped from ceiling to floor; oil lamps on pedestals illuminated a pathway to a backdrop of glowing smoke. A thin young woman dressed in a violet robe and veil sat there on a bronze stool, her white hands outstretched. Near her feet coiled a great white grassland python, the hari-hari.

Where am I? the child asked.

This is the Temple of the Great Mountain, and I am the Oracle. The young woman smiled, weaving her hands as if to draw Dakhma closer. *Do not be afraid.*

The Dream Warrior was bringing me to you. Dakhma tried to bring the surroundings into better focus, but failed. Everything around the Oracle was a dreamlike mist. *Are you friend or unfriend?*

I am friend, child. Where are you now?

I do not know. The Soothsayer left Farblood behind and took me into the mountains. He made me call a crystal out of his mother's grave. The little girl shivered. *I am afraid of him, Oracle.*

He is evil, the Oracle replied. *Not evil as the Fravashi are, but evil in that he seeks to use you to gain what is not rightfully his.* The vision of the Oracle began to break apart. *We have been together in other lives, little sister. I can mind-talk with you a little, but your training is insufficient. Fight against his control, Dakhma.*

How? The child panicked as the Oracle faded from view.

Use your mind-powers to delay him. And drink nothing he brews for you.

The Oracle's words echoed in Dakhma's mind as she came out of sleep. She lay on the blanket, her heart thumping wildly as she listened to the swish of the wind through the trees, the jingle of horse brass from the grazing mounts. Carefully, she turned her head until she could see the Soothsayer asleep nearby. In her mind she felt the call of the dead Cassyr's crystal but resisted the urge to make it appear in her hands.

I know you take me to the Temple, the girl thought. *I will do what you want, but you shall no longer control my mind.*

Dakhma reached out with her thoughts and felt the life-force of the owl stone stolen from Corri. Instead of calling it to her as she once would have done, the little girl used her mind to explore the layers of power and emotions connected with the ancient stone.

You are so old! I can feel the sadness and blood spilled over you. The power you hold is great, greater than Farblood knows, but you are not for me, little owl stone.

Dakhma withdrew her probing senses and slipped back into dreamless sleep.

The child woke to find the Soothsayer's hand over her mouth. She lay quietly at his whispered instructions. On the trail below them she heard the jingle of horse bridles and the low voice of a man. When a woman's derisive laughter rose in the mountain air, Dakhma stiffened, eyes wide.

"They are gone now." The Soothsayer removed his hand and quietly opened the supply bag. "Those two who passed are enemies." His pale eyes stared at Dakhma and saw that the child recognized the voices. "You know them?"

"The woman, she was once with the Clan," Dakhma whispered. "The shakka made her and the Tuonela with her leave."

The Soothsayer nodded as he handed Dakhma her noon-day portion of journey bread and dried meat. "She is an evil one, working for Frav. Even when we were children, Malya yearned after power and importance."

"Like you." Dakhma stared at the tall man.

"My yearnings are different," he answered sharply. "I would use my powers for the good of the Temple in Kystan." He gazed dreamily into the surrounding trees.

Dakhma ate her meal and kept her thoughts to herself. *The Oracle told me different, man of Kirisan. But if you truly take me to the Temple, I will go with you.*

"We must wait for the others to get farther ahead." The Soothsayer dusted his hands, then pulled the owl stone circlet out of his bag. "While we wait, I want you to use the power of this stone."

"No." Dakhma glared at him and clenched her little fists. "That stone is not for me. And do not brew me any more of your herbs. I will not drink them." Her chin came up in defiance.

"How do you know this stone is not for you?" The thin mouth went tight.

"I can feel its life-force. It is not for me." Her mouth grew as tight as the Soothsayer's. "If you want its power, you use it, if you dare."

The man stared at her, eyes narrowed in anger. "I will," he said as he placed the owl stone circlet on his head, adjusting the stone until it lay on the center of his forehead.

The Soothsayer closed his pale eyes and directed his energy toward the owl stone. A kaleidoscope of images flooded his inner vision. Swirling scenes of battles and deep emotions of ancient loves and hatreds poured through his mind. As he whirled and twisted in the onslaught of strange visions, he became aware of flickering images at the edges of his sight.

Focusing upon these, the Soothsayer went rigid with fear. Forms of Otherworld spirits clawed their way toward him, taloned hands grasping, fanged mouths open. He screamed and tried to move away; instead, he found himself paralyzed, caught in the spirit realm, unable to break free and return to his physical body. The demons swirled around him, their circling forms getting closer and closer. A taloned hand scraped his arm, drawing blood and leaving in its wake a fierce burning. He screamed again, but his voice was soundless within their realm.

Dakhma watched in horror as the Soothsayer writhed on the fir needle-strewn ground, his mouth open in a silent scream. Suddenly, four deep scratches opened on his arm, the blood running down his rigid hand onto the forest floor.

Remove the stone! The Oracle's voice was faint in Dakhma's inner senses.

The little girl scrambled on her hands and knees to the Soothsayer's side. As she hesitated above him, the man gurgled a scream deep in his throat. She snatched the owl stone circlet from his brow, throwing it to one side.

The Soothsayer's body shook from head to foot as if with a terrible fever, but the paralysis of his arms and legs was gone. She ducked as he flailed out, gasping for air. His terror-filled pale eyes snapped open, and he looked around wildly.

"Are they gone?" The Soothsayer scrambled to his feet, staggered, and went to his knees.

"I do not know what you saw, but there is no one here but me." Dakhma backed away from him, fearing his wild eyes.

"The demons. . . ." He became aware of his bleeding arm. "See what they did!" He jerked out his supply bag, fumbled in it for a pouch, and sprinkled powder from it onto his wound with shaking hands. "The owl stone is accursed!"

"No." Dakhma stood with her back against a tree, looking at him with calculating eyes. "The stone is not evil. It is not for you and it is not for me. It is only for the Dream Warrior."

"Where is it?" he demanded, then scrambled for the circlet among the needles when the girl pointed it out. "Farblood and those at the Temple will want this." He stuffed it back into his bag. "Come, Dakhma, it is time for us to go to Kystan." *If Farblood and those in the Temple want this owl stone, they will have to meet my demands for entrance there.*

Corri was tired. She knew she had no tracking skills such as those of Imandoff and Takra, and she feared that the Soothsayer might have gone on another trail away from Kystan. All day she had ridden on their trail, hoping that the hoof prints she followed were the right ones. When the marks of two other horses joined theirs, Corri swore in frustration. She could not hope to tackle three opponents to get the child back.

Mouse threw up her head and snorted, pulling at the reins. Corri looked around but saw nothing. The horse tugged to one side, away from the trail. Knowing Mouse's instincts, the girl let her go. The horse scrambled down a slight bank along the trail and into the trees. In a short time, she stood with her muzzle deep in a hidden spring.

Judging the approaching darkness, Corri dismounted. She unsaddled Mouse and mind-talked with her to stay close. Then she splashed water over her own dusty face, sighing at the cooling touch of the clear water. As she spread her blanket, Corri decided against a fire. Any flame would be clearly seen by anyone traveling along the trail above, a risk she dared not take.

She watched Mouse for a time, but except for a flick of the ears and a swish of the tail at the circling insects around the spring, the horse showed no sign of alarm or wariness. Corri chewed at her journey bread, wistfully dreaming of the food she had shared with Norya.

I wonder where the shakka is now. And Takra and Imandoff. I must dream-fly to tell them where I am. It will be difficult without the owl stone, but I must try.

She tested her thoughts of Tirkul gingerly, as if exploring a sore tooth. The anger at his last words with her still rankled, but the hurt was less than she expected. *Does this mean my love was never real? Perhaps my feelings for Tirkul were as Takra once said, only a first love attraction that should have stayed a friendship.* She thought back to the moment when he had said the heart oath words before Halka's tent-wagon. *He pushed me to be his even then. I never gave thought to anything serious until I lay in pain after the battle in the Taktos. I made a mistake. I had no knowledge of the feelings between men and women, and he persuaded me to feel something that was not real in my heart. It will never work out for us, but how can I tell him?*

The full moon slipped above the mountain peaks, casting ghostly beams down through the thick trees, turning the tiny spring into a shimmering silver disk. Mouse, content to crop the thick grass, showed no signs of wandering. Corri's muscles ached as she stretched out on the blanket. It did not take her long to slip from her physical body and float above the treetops.

I will seek Imandoff, she thought. *I still have to find you, old man. Why must you go a-wandering when I need you most?* Instantly, she felt a tugging sensation toward the grasslands. *Are you already on my trail? How could you know?*

As soon as she moved forward toward the grasslands, Corri was caught in a stream of force as strong as the tides that washed the beaches of Asur during a storm. She fought against it, but it sucked her into a spinning tunnel of darkness, dragging her away from her goal.

No! Lady, help me! Her voiceless cries went unheeded. *I will not go to Frav! I will not see Minepa!*

Like a leaf in a gale, Corri whirled down the black tunnel, spinning out of control, until she hung, suspended in air, near the ceiling in the black-walled room of the Fravashi priest.

Why is this happening? she thought frantically. *I do not seek this Minepa, yet each night I am drawn here as if called.*

The Fravashi priest and Kayth sat at the dark table facing each other. Minepa's long-nailed fingers curled around a goblet, his matted hair falling over his shoulders and around his skull-like face. Kayth lay back in his chair, a smile of satisfaction lifting the corners of his mouth. "Do you still challenge me?" Kayth's voice was low and smug. "Or do you wish to see more of my new powers, Minepa?"

"I do not challenge you." The priest's fingers tightened around the goblet. "I am no fool. But you are not Jinniyah. There are certain signs, by those I would know!"

"True." Kayth ran one finger idly through the circle of moisture left by his goblet on the smooth surface of the table. "Not yet am I Jinniyah, but soon I shall be. I, and only I, can translate the last of the Books of Darkness, those written centuries ago by Jinniyah himself. The loss of my star ship was of little matter." Kayth snapped his fingers, and the priest stared up at him with feral yellow eyes. "You feel how much my powers have grown. I know the secret Jinniyah hid, even from your ancestor, the Minepa who was at his side."

"Tell me," Minepa said, his voice thick with eagerness.

"Why not? It is of no use to you, Minepa, for you cannot read what is written there, however much you try." Kayth stared smugly at the sharp face across the table. "Jinniyah learned the ancient secrets of enhancing psychic powers. And he told how to use those powers to draw forth demon spirits from the abyss of the Otherworlds, calling them forth and making them do his bidding."

The intake of the priest's breath hissed through the room. "Why do you not share this knowledge? When you die, it will once more be lost!"

"No, for I will sire children strong in natural-born powers and raise them in the knowledge. They will rule Sar Akka with all Frav and the priesthood behind them." Kayth smoothed his finger down the side of the goblet. "In this manner, I shall rule over Sar Akka forever, and your family, Minepa, shall be at my side."

Minepa's thin hand dropped slowly to his belt. In the blink of an eye, the hand came up, throwing the knife he had drawn. Kayth simply held up his hand, and the knife changed course and flew into the stone wall, snapping the blade at the hilt.

"Do you now believe?" Kayth smirked as the priest drew back in fear.

"I believe." Minepa bowed his head. "I will follow you."

Kayth's head suddenly turned, as he stared about the room. His nostrils expanded, like a dog that comes across a new scent. "Someone is here," he whispered.

"No one in the flesh," Minepa answered, staring straight at Corri's invisible form. "But the feeling of being spied on has come to me night after night."

Kayth's eyes widened, then he laughed. "Daughter, I command that you reveal yourself." He slipped into a strange language, its syllables crashing against Corri's dream-form.

She struggled to leave, yet found herself bound fast as a fly in honey. In terror, she realized that she was slowly becoming visible to the two men staring up at her.

Back! Go back! she ordered to her dream-form as she fought against Kayth's powers. But she had no control over her going or staying. *Imandoff, help me!*

"I have you at last." Kayth stood up, stretching his hand in a grasping motion toward her.

Corri felt as if her soul were moving toward the outstretched hand. She was totally helpless. Just as she felt her dream-form yield to the pull, she became aware of another force dragging her back. For an instant, the face of the Green Man she had met in her flight over Deep Rising with Imandoff stood clear in her mind. She felt the power of his mind lock onto her, as if dragging at her arm. With a pop and a sickening sensation of falling, she shot from the room, back through the tunnel of darkness.

"Be silent!" The whispered voice next to her ear sliced through her pounding head as she struggled to sit up. "Lie still. There is danger near."

It is the Green Man Imandoff called Gadavar! Corri still felt the linking of their life-forces from the man's struggle to free her from Kayth. She lay still, suddenly very aware of his muscled body pressed against her, the smell of leather and pine on his clothing, the masculine scent of his body. *I wonder what it would be like to kiss him.* A blush, unseen in the darkness, heated her cheeks.

Above her, moon-glow highlighting his nose and cheekbones, his eyes glimmering in pools of shadows, crouched Gadavar. In the wan light his clothing appeared in shades of grays and blacks. A dagger winked in his free hand as his eyes slowly raked the shadow-pooled forest around them.

Corri relaxed under his grip, then felt the callused hand slide away from her mouth. She slowly turned her head to where Mouse had grazed at the spring and saw the horse, ears pricked forward, stone-still in the dappled light of the moon.

"They will pass by us soon." The whispered voice and the man's soft breath brushed her ear. "There are too many to challenge."

Corri heard the soft plop of horse hooves on the trail above, the murmur of male voices, the jingle of horse brass and the clink of weapons against chain mail. She lay in the man's shadow, his hand on her shoulder, willing her heart to slow from its frantic pounding.

The minutes dragged on until, satisfied that the men were beyond hearing, the Green Man stood up and sheathed his dagger. He held down a hand and pulled Corri to her feet.

"You did well not to have a fire," he said softly. "What did you dream, Farblood, that made you thrash about so?"

"So you remember me?" Corri peered up at the shadowed face. "I did not expect your help in my dream-flying. In the name of the Goddess, how did you find me?"

"I received a message from the feya women and followed." The Green Man strode to Mouse and patted her neck as she nuzzled against him. "There are many dangerous men about Deep Rising now, those who once worked for the Master Thief of Hadliden, and some who spy for Frav. I feared for your safety. When I cut across the hills to the trail above, I heard the mind-talk of your horse and had no difficulty finding your camp. By the Lady, why did you allow your dream-self to wander into Frav?"

"I just found myself there and could not retreat. Thank you for saving me."

"I could not leave you to such a fate," Gadavar answered. For a time they stood in silence, looking into each other's eyes until Corri spoke.

"Have you word of the Soothsayer?" Corri felt small standing beside him, for he was taller then Imandoff. "He passed this way with a girl-child, probably on his way to Kystan." *What is this strange attraction I feel for you?* she thought.

"The Green Men knew of his passing." Gadavar turned to give Mouse a last slap against her back, then sat down and leaned against a tree. "We have been hard-pressed to control the bands of cutthroats and criminals who now try to make Deep Rising their lair. We did not know in time about the Soothsayer's deeds. He is at least a day and a half ahead of you, almost to the main roads, where we have no power."

Perhaps I read him wrong and this feeling only comes from me, Corri thought as she watched the Green Man. But when he lifted his eyes to meet hers, she held her breath at the fire-like thread of intense emotion that passed between them. *No, he feels it also.*

Gadavar ducked his head as he stretched his long muscled legs and tightened the laces on his knee-boots. "There are also many dangerous high mountain animals that have come down to the lower slopes. I fear it is a sign of an early and hard winter."

"But it is barely summer," Corri said. "How can you tell so soon?"

"There are signs for those who know how to read them. You have changed," Gadavar said as he stared at her across the little fire. "Has so much happened to you since we last met in Deep Rising?" The Green Man pulled a pipe and smoke-leaf pouch from his belt. He continued to watch her face as he tamped the leaf into the pipe and lit it.

Corri nodded. "A great many things, most of them unpleasant."

As they sat waiting for dawn, Corri told him of her long journey across Kirisan, the fight in the Takto Mountains with Kayth, and her troubles with the Clan of the Feathered Spear.

"And this vision your dream-self had when I found you, what troubled your mind to create that?" Gadavar flexed his broad shoulders and leaned forward, resting his arms on his drawn-up knees. "You were in Frav, I know, but in a place of terror more than just Fravashi. Your body fought so hard I feared you would cry out despite my efforts to keep you quiet."

"It was not a vision." Corri searched for words to explain. "A real part of me was there. I have always known how to dream-fly." She saw Gadavar's nod of understanding and plunged on. "My dream-form was drawn against my will into Frav. This has happened many nights lately. Always I see Minepa and sometimes Kayth." She clasped her shaking hands together. "I do not understand. I do not seek them, yet each night I am drawn there."

"The Green Men have heard rumors of stones used by the spies of Frav to communicate with their masters. Surely you do not carry such a thing."

Corri felt her cheeks grow hot. "Perhaps I do, not knowing its full power. It was innocently given to me as a gift. I know it once belonged to Malya." She hurried on. "But I have it wrapped in moly. I thought to give it to Imandoff."

"Let me see it." Gadavar held out his huge hand.

Corri brought the red stone out of her belt pouch and dropped it into the outstretched hand. The moly around it, which would stay green for months after being cut, was black and tinder-dry to the touch.

"This must be destroyed!" The growing light of dawn touched his leaf-brown hair, his slender tanned face, revealing an upright line of concern between his brows. "The Green Men discovered two such stones on the bodies of spies we killed in the mountains."

"Bury it then or burn it!" Corri grabbed at the winking red stone, but Gadavar held it out of her reach.

"Fire has no effect. We tried fire. We tried burying them." The Green Man's mouth drew tight. "Nothing worked until we crushed them under a boulder."

"Then do it!" Corri felt a sense of uncleanness from carrying the stone so long. "Because I carried it, will I now be open to the Volikvis and Minepa?"

"We found no such effect," he answered. "I do not sense any Fravashi evil in you, Corri Farblood. Rest easy." He slid the stone into his own pouch, rose and stretched in the faint rays of dawn. He paused and started to put out his hand to her, then drew it back.

What is this? Corri felt her heart beat hard at the glance of those dark eyes. *I feel such a strong, warm feeling coming from him, a feeling that matches my own. Yet he fears to speak of this.* Her own fear of being a fool if she spoke the wrong words kept her quiet.

"I will ride with you as far as I can toward Kystan. Along the way there is a rockslide to one side of the trail. It will take little effort to bring a boulder down on this."

"But you have no horse." Corri looked around.

He laughed and whistled softly. "Nuisance is not far away. He knows how to stay hidden and not show himself until I call."

She heard the crackle of needles and twigs beyond the spring, the soft snort of a horse. Mouse's ears pricked forward, and she nickered softly. Out of the tree-shadows stepped a dark chestnut horse, nearly invisible in the patches of darkness.

"How far to the main trail to Kystan?" Corri asked as she saddled Mouse.

"Three days' journey. We dare not press too fast, or we might overtake the men who passed by." Gadavar tapped out his pipe and carefully ground the smoke-leaf into the bare ground. "You should take the trail around Leshy, for that is surely where they go."

"Does Malya hold power at Leshy?" Corri thought of the unpleasantness she endured when last she was in that Mystery School.

"No, we have heard that the School at Leshy cast her out." Gadavar led the way as they walked the horses up the bank to the trail above. "But rumor says that she still frequents the town and that certain men meet her there."

"Have you any news of Imandoff the sorcerer and a Tuonela warrior woman in Deep Rising?"

"We have not seen them." Gadavar mounted and waited for Corri to ride up alongside him. "If they follow you, perhaps they chose another way, closer to Kystan."

"Perhaps. If they got my message." *Where is Takra? I know she must have gotten my message by now. And Imandoff, is he still missing?* Corri cast a sidelong glance at Gadavar and felt her face flush. *What is this attraction I feel toward this Green Man? I never felt this way about Tirkul. I dare not show my feelings, for he might not look at me as other than friend.*

They rode together down the dusty trail in the breaking dawn, Gadavar's senses alert, while Corri mulled over her plans and what she would say and do when she got to the Temple. By late afternoon, Gadavar called a halt, pointing to a fan of rock on the slope below them. A boulder, nearly as tall as the Green Man, hung precariously at the top.

"This should work to destroy the stone." He dismounted and scrambled carefully down the bank, planting the red stone about halfway down. Rocks turned and scattered from under his boots as he fought his way back to the top.

"Hold the horses," he ordered. "The noise may spook them."

Corri clutched both reins tightly in her sweating hands as she watched Gadavar lean his broad shoulder into the boulder. He braced his long legs and pushed, the muscles showing through his dark green trousers and brown shirt. The boulder teetered from his efforts, then slowly wavered over the lip of the bank. With a roar of gravel, it fell with a crash that echoed through the surrounding trees and hills.

Gadavar jumped quickly back, grabbing the reins as both horses reared, their eyes wild. "Easy, my pretties. You are safe," he crooned. But he kept his strong grip as the boulder bounced down the scree.

The boulder struck the red stone as it gathered speed. There was a violent flash of light, a sound like the crack of lightning when it strikes the earth. Then there was only the sound of the rolling, bouncing boulder as it continued down the slope.

"Now you are free." Gadavar looked down at Corri, who stood by his side, her shaking hands beside his on the reins. "I wish times were different," he said. "I could show you such wonders in Deep Rising as you cannot imagine."

"I would like that." Corri gazed up into his brown eyes, wondering at the emotion she saw there. "Your tie has come loose." She reached up to where his shoulder-length hair had half-slipped from the leather band that kept it back from his slender face.

"Corri."

The single word held her breathless. Gadavar dropped the reins, gathering her into his strong arms. She leaned into his muscled form, her face raised to meet his kiss.

What I felt with Tirkul was nothing compared to this. But how can I tell Tirkul that I love another?

When she finally drew back, Gadavar cupped the side of her face with his hand. "I have felt this for you since first we met," he said in a low voice. "A Green Man has little to offer, other than life in the mountains. No fancy town clothes, not much company except for the families of other Green Men. But I can offer you freedom, for I would never seek to bind you fast. You have a free spirit, Corri Farblood. No one should ever cage it."

"I cannot make any commitment, Gadavar." Corri's mind whirled in confusion. "The Goddess has called me to be Her Dream Warrior. The war draws closer, and I must be in the midst of it when the time comes. I may not live through this war. In fairness, I can offer little to any man."

"I understand this." Gadavar smoothed her hair, letting his hand drift on down to the small of her back. "I do not ask that you make any commitment to me. Any man who truly loves you will leave you free to do whatever you want. Even if you should love another, I would be content to take what is left over. If ever you have need of comfort and quiet, come to me in the mountains. My love will always be there for you."

Corri looked up, deep into his brown eyes, seeing there the truth of his heart and spirit. *Why must I choose between them?* she thought, her throat tight. *Why could not the best of both Gadavar and Tirkul be in one man? And what do I really know of Gadavar?*

Another part of her mind answered: *What does it matter, when he loves you? Look at his heart in his eyes. The best of Tirkul is within this man.*

Tirkul broke heart oath, but I do not know how to erase the last of my feelings for him. What if Imandoff and Takra think I am given to following strange whims of fancy without any thought? Tirkul's feelings for me changed from loving to controlling, and that I cannot tolerate. But how do I tell him there is no hope of rekindling the love that once was between us?

"Your troubled thoughts show in your eyes, Corri. I will not push you where you do not want to go."

"I am where I want to be," she answered softly.

Gadavar gently pulled her close and bent to kiss her. They clung together, oblivious to their surroundings until Nuisance nudged the Green Man sharply with his nose, pushing him out of Corri's embrace.

"I know," Gadavar said with a laugh. "We must move on."

They mounted again and rode off toward the main roads leading into the Kirisani towns. For two more days, Corri and Gadavar talked of their childhoods, their personal experiences, and their hopes and fears of the future as they rode down out of Deep Rising.

"How much alike our lives have been," Gadavar said as they paused at the edge of the trees near the road into Kystan. "I was orphaned young and raised by a Green Man, Amintyr, friend of my father. Before he came for me, I had to live on scraps in the streets of Kystan, sleeping in stables at night, and taking more than one beating from merchants who disliked beggars. An old priest from the Temple saw me one day and stopped to talk. He took me with him until Amintyr could come for me."

"But if your father was a Green Man, why did the others not know of your plight?" Corri asked.

"My father was not a Green Man, but a trader who knew the Green Men from his travels through the mountains." Gadavar stared at the traffic on the road beyond. "My parents both died the winter of the great snows. I was only nine."

"That was the year my father left me with Grimmel. My old nurse told me how I was fortunate to be alive, when so many people died from the lung sickness that winter." Corri reached out to touch his arm. "But you have made something of your life, Gadavar. You are a Green Man, while I am only a thief."

"Was a thief," Gadavar corrected her. "Now you are Corri Farblood and still discovering who you really are."

Yes, I am still seeking, she thought, watching the open expressions of love in his eyes. *I think I love you, Gadavar, but how do I know if what I feel is true love or simply more of what I thought I felt for Tirkul?*

It is different, a part of her mind said. *Wherever you go, whatever happens, you know deep within your soul that a thread will always exist between the two of you. This is real, not a fantasy born of a night's wishful thinking. This is love.*

But I cannot tarry to experience love with him. Corri felt a tightness in her throat and swallowed hard. *However much I wish for it to be, I must center my thoughts only upon the task ahead.*

Corri felt a soft warmth creep over her troubled thoughts. She turned to find Gadavar smiling at her. The debate within her died away when she looked into his eyes. As if there had been no pause in the conversation, Gadavar coaxed her into more reminiscence.

By the time he left her near the road leading off toward Kystan, they were entirely comfortable with each other, each knowing the other's thoughts almost before they were put into words.

"I will watch for you," Gadavar said, as they stood side by side, looking down at the cultivated fields beyond the last fringe of trees. "If ever you need me, or simply want to come to my home in the mountains, the feya women know how to contact the Green Men."

"I will remember." Corri kissed him one last time, then mounted Mouse and rode down into the valleys, silent tears streaming down her face.

No word of Farblood's being here." Takra Wind-Rider leaned against the wall of the inn and watched Imandoff as he washed the dust from his face and beard. "She must have gone another way."

"The High Clua has heard rumors of the Soothsayer." Imandoff shook the water from his beard. "According to the mountain feya women, he used Dakhma to take a foreseeing crystal from his mother's grave near Springwell. The High Clua did not know why Corri was not with them."

"The High Clua?" Takra's hand dropped to her long dagger in her belt. "What controlling old woman did they choose this time?"

"One of gentleness and honor for a change." Imandoff grinned at her. "And she is not that old, Takra. Jehennette is an excellent healer and not one given to imprisoning people against their will."

"You are too trusting," she growled as Imandoff threw his arm about her shoulders.

The sorcerer laughed and kissed her cheek as they walked through the common room to the stairs that led up to their room.

Dawn light cast a grayish glow through the open shutters when Imandoff woke suddenly from his sleep. He lay for several moments, Takra's head heavy on his arm. Easing her head aside, he sat up and touched her bare shoulder gently.

Takra's amber eyes snapped open, but she lay silent under Imandoff's hand, watching the sorcerer tip his head to listen to voices in the hall outside their door.

"What is it?" she whispered.

"Malya, I think, and Roggkin." The sorcerer's voice was barely audible. He pressed Takra firmly back against the rough blankets when she tried to sit at the mention of the names. "They do not know we are here."

"Then we must be gone." Takra eased herself out of the blankets and reached for her clothes.

"Agreed." Imandoff listened until the voices died away down the stairs. "But there is another problem. I heard Corri cry out to me in my sleep. If the Soothsayer rides out of Deep Rising with only the child, where is Corri?" He tugged on his trousers and tunic and slid his feet into worn boots.

"Has he harmed her?" Takra asked, as she belted on her dagger.

"I do not feel her life is in danger. If the Soothsayer goes to the Temple, and I think he will, then Corri will follow him. We will head for Kystan." He grabbed Takra's arm as she rose to face the door. "Not that way. They went back down to the common room."

"You mean to go out over the roof?" Takra stared at the open window.

"There is no other way." His smile was visible in the faint light. "Come, Takra, surely a Tuonela can climb."

"Climbing rocks is one thing. Breaking my neck falling off a roof is another," she growled as she slung her sword over her back and tied her boots to the sides of her belt. She picked up her saddlebags and crept to the window, looking down at the quiet inn yard.

"We will go slowly," he said quietly as he came to her side, his sword also slung over his back, saddlebags in hand. From one bag hung a corner of his faded blue robe. He leaned out of the window and peered at the roof in both directions. "If we go to the right, we can use the ledge to get to the kitchen roof, then down the back to the stables."

Takra grunted her disapproval as she thrust her long legs over the sill and felt for the ledge with her toes. As soon as she moved off cautiously along the narrow ledge, Imandoff slid out. Inch by inch they worked their way along the ledge, past open shutters, snores coming from within the dark rooms. The thatch of the kitchen roof crackled under their cautious movements as the two gingerly crawled to the edge.

"There is a rain pipe there." Imandoff pointed below, then swung himself over, catching the pipe and sliding to the ground. Takra followed him, her hands slick with perspiration. Just as she prepared to jump the last few feet, the pipe gave way, and she fell backward. Imandoff's strong arms caught her before she hit the cobblestones. The pipe crashed into the darkened yard, sending a squalling cat streaking around the building.

They pressed themselves into the shadows of the stable wall, hands on daggers and listening intently as the inn door flew open to reveal the cat, back raised and hair on end.

"A cat!" Roggkin's voice dripped with disgust. "You shy at shadows, Malya." He slammed the door.

Imandoff let out his breath with a sigh. "We will lead out the horses," he murmured. "We dare not ride until we are some distance from here." He buckled the sword belt around his waist.

"I still think I should put an end to that Tuonela traitor." Takra's long dagger was half out of its sheath.

"We cannot take the risk." Imandoff's hand clamped firmly over hers. "Corri needs us."

"Agreed," Takra said through clenched teeth. "But I would feel better if those two were not at our backs." She adjusted her sword sheath, then slid her slender feet into her boots while constantly scanning the inn yard.

Silently, they led Sun Dancer and Lightfoot out the back of the stable into the quiet street beyond. A plodding, clopping line of donkeys rounded the corner and approached the inn.

"Their noise will cover the horses," Imandoff whispered as he led Sun Dancer past the caravan of incoming merchants, toward the southern road leading to Kystan.

Takra followed, one hand always near her dagger, her amber eyes alert as they passed dark alleys and the first merchants of the day sleepily opening their shops.

Where is Corri? Takra thought as they passed through the city gates. *And where is Dakhma? There must be something about the child I do not know for Corri to protect her by taking the girl to Kystan.*

By the hell fires of Frav! Imandoff stared at the forested hills along the side-path into the mountains. *I wasted time in Nevn when I should have been with Corri and Dakhma. The child is important to the events to come, in some way, and my stupidity may have endangered us all.*

When the first full sunlight slid over the eastern mountains, the two were riding along the dusty road south toward the Temple of the Great Mountain in Kystan.

"Is it much farther?" Dakhma's piping voice roused the Soothsayer out of his daydreaming.

"There it is." He pointed ahead to a high flat-topped peak rising up out of the Kirisani farmlands. "The Temple sits in the middle of a lake in the center of the city."

The Oracle will protect me when you take me there, Dakhma thought. *Whatever you plan, she will protect me from you.* But the little girl said nothing to the Soothsayer.

Now we shall see if you refuse me again. The Soothsayer smiled to himself. *If you do not admit me to the Temple, you do not get the child. You will admit me to the Temple this time and it will be on my terms.*

Chapter 6

$\mathcal{S}$he will sleep until I return," the Soothsayer said as he brushed the travel dust off his clothes. "You need do nothing but see she stays in this room." His temper was frayed from getting Dakhma to eat the drugged food.

"Do you really believe the Jabed and the High Priestess will admit you to the Temple?" The woman sitting at the foot of the bed stretched, her painted eyes watching the Soothsayer as he viewed himself in the long mirror. "They sent you packing last time like a cur dog." Her reddened lips curved in a mocking smile.

"If they want this child, they will." The Soothsayer turned and stared at her, his pale eyes cold. "My powers have strengthened since I last stood in the Temple."

The woman curled away from him, her eyes wide, the tip of her tongue sliding across her lips in nervousness. "The child will be safe with me," she stammered.

"See that she is." The Soothsayer swept his cool gaze over the room. "No one should come here seeking her. Who would think I would leave the child in a whore's house?" His mocking laughter followed him down the stairs.

"Poor little thing." The woman bent over Dakhma, smoothing back the child's hair from her sleeping face. "How did you come to fall into that one's hands? If I dared, I would take you to the Temple where you would be safe. But I dare not interfere with the Soothsayer."

The Soothsayer hurried through the meandering streets of Kystan, his destination always downward toward the glistening, wind-ruffled waters of the lake that surrounded the shining Temple like a moat. The narrow band of waters, separated from the city by a wide promenade and a low stone wall, sparkled in the sun. The man strode quickly along the promenade until he reached one of the two bridges that stretched across the lapping waters to the white stone buildings. At the land end of the bridge stood two white-clad women, sheathed swords at their sides.

The Soothsayer passed between the guards and over the bridge without a word; neither did they challenge him. The great gates to the Temple stood open, the wide courtyard beyond empty at this hour. The Soothsayer crossed the cobblestone yard, climbed the wide steps leading to the main building and entered the cool interior of the porch to the audience hall. In the square alcove of the entrance stood a huge metal gong, the sunlight filtering in through the stone-latticed windows and bouncing off its smooth surface.

He took down the mallet and struck the gong a solid blow. Its clarion call boomed through the alcove, bouncing through the open door and into the courtyard behind him. The Soothsayer smiled as he replaced the mallet, then folded his arms, and waited.

A young priest pulled open the inner door, then stopped, his eyes wide and mouth open. He turned and whispered hoarse instructions to another priest, who ran to get the Jabed.

"I claim the right to stand before the high seat of the Temple." The Soothsayer looked down his nose at the nervous priest. "Do you deny me this right?"

The young priest shook his head as the Soothsayer pushed his way past and into the audience hall. The slap of his boots on the smooth floor was the only sound as he strode the length of the hall to stand before the high seat.

The walls were all of white stone with colored murals of the history of Kirisan painted on them. Bright pictures of the ships bearing the Peoples to the new land flowed down one wall; another wall portrayed the last war with Frav, with sorcerers casting the ancient spells to seal the border. Tall pointed windows, latticed with carved stone, marched in a line down one side. Graceful columns, alternating black and white, made two rows from the door nearly to the foot of the single high-backed chair set on a dais.

The Soothsayer waited at the foot of the dais, his arms folded, his thin mouth drawn tight in impatience. It was only moments before the dark purple draperies behind the seat moved, and the High Priestess walked through. She sat in the high-backed chair without a word, her hands lying along the carved armrests. The Jabed came to stand near her left shoulder.

"I ask for admittance to the Temple, High Priestess Vairya." The Soothsayer bowed his head briefly to the High Priestess, ignoring the older man who stood behind her. "My powers have strengthened since our last meeting."

"And how have you done that?" The Jabed's voice was thick with dislike. His plump fingers rubbed at his chin and the corners of his mouth, which was bracketed with lines of sour discontent. "Your powers were deemed to be of small importance to the Temple. You were also judged too prideful and ambitious." The Jabed's hard, little eyes were full of self-right-eousness as he reached up to push back a strand of gray hair from his forehead.

"Your hatred of me clouds your judgment, Jabed." The Soothsayer held the priest's stare until the man turned his eyes away. "I thought you were beyond personal vendettas." The Jabed frowned at the accusation and turned his face away.

Vairya held up her hand for silence. "And is this the only reason you come here?" she asked, her voice soft but carrying in the quiet room.

"I also know of a child, one with untested powers, but with promise of great talent." The Soothsayer's smile touched only the corners of his mouth.

"Not untested." A thin figure in a violet robe, her face nearly covered with a matching veil, stepped from behind the draperies to stand at Vairya's side. The forceful words, dropped into the stillness of the tense hall, startled the three. "She can call things to her, through distance or walls. A child whom he stole away from her rightful guardian."

"Not true, Oracle!" The Soothsayer glared at the slender woman concealed in her veils. "The child was placed in my hands to bring into Kirisan. Her own people turned her out!"

"Did you not force the child to bring your mother's crystal out of her grave?" The dark eyes stared at him over the edge of the concealing veil. "She is not with you, Ayron. You came to bargain for a place in the priesthood, thinking to use her as a lure."

"And why not?" the Soothsayer growled. "The Jabed turned me away even though he admitted my powers were strong enough to gain me entrance here. He held out promises that if I did this and that, he would allow me to enter the priesthood. They were all lies."

"If such promises were given," the Oracle turned to look at the Jabed, who lowered his eyes, "then it was done in ill-faith and wrongly. No one of this Temple is to use his or her position to aid any talented person in entering, nor keep any such person out. It is also law here that any priest or priestess who lies, steals, carries malicious gossip, or foments dissatisfaction with the rule of the Goddess must be cast out. These are the ancient laws. Have they been twisted to satisfy whims, personal likes and dislikes? If this is so, then the laws also state that whoever is Oracle must sit in judgment and decide upon the penalties."

Vairya half-turned in her chair to look at the Jabed. "If this was done, Oracle, it was done without my knowledge and outside my hearing."

"I do not lie. It was done even as I said!" The Soothsayer clenched his fists at his sides.

"At least there is truth is these words of yours. This accusation fits with other things I have heard, such as your speeches to certain priests that the Temple should not be ruled by women or the Goddess any longer. Jabed, your time at the Temple is finished. I have spoken." The Oracle motioned with a moon-pale hand. "I care not whether you stay in lesser priestly position or go, but from this time forward you no longer have any power here."

The older man stammered silent words, then staggered as if from a blow when the young Oracle pointed a thin finger at him.

"You talk of wrong use of power, Oracle, and then use it on me!" The priest could not move forward against the Oracle's will, although he tried. "There are those here who see things as I do and who follow me, not you!"

"Then take them with you. I no longer give you a choice, Jabed. You will leave the Temple and never return."

The gray-haired priest shuffled slowly back through the dark draperies, his eyes sending spears of hatred at the Oracle as he disappeared.

"And you, Ayron, who call yourself the Soothsayer, you may use all the right words but most of the truth is still hidden." The Oracle came to the edge of the dais and looked down at him. "You would use the life of this child to bargain for power here. I tell you, you will never stand as a priest in this place. Your mind hatches plots like insects hatch eggs, without regard to the consequences or outcome."

"So be it." The Soothsayer set his jaw. "You will never see the child now."

He whirled on his heel and stamped out of the hall. He looked neither right nor left as he marched back across the bridge into the city. Pedestrians drew back from his dark aura of rage as if he carried a bared blade.

You must have gotten word to them, Farblood. And for that you will pay. I did not turn traitor before, but now I will see that Malya finds you.

"Why, Ayron, you look like a bull defending his pasture." A silky laugh sounded at his elbow.

The Soothsayer looked down at Malya walking beside him, her dark hair glowing red in the sun. "I do not wish to speak with you." He turned away and kept walking. "Farblood has ruined my chance to be entered at the Temple. You told me before that you wanted her. Why then are you not dragging her back to Frav for your father?"

"Farblood! Is she here in Kystan?" Malya's dark brows crinkled in thought. "Tell me where she is."

"I only know she followed me and, by this time, must be within Kystan. Beyond that, find her yourself, woman." His eyes flashed when Malya grabbed at his arm.

"I came to see you, Ayron, to buy the child you smuggled into the city."

The Soothsayer stopped suddenly and glared down at her. "I will never sell you the child, nor give her to you. She is wholly of the blood of the Peoples. Farblood is not. Like you, Farblood is tainted with an ancestry not of Sar Akka. Go find this kinswoman of yours, Malya, and leave me be!"

The tall man shoved her, sending the woman reeling back against a wall. Without another word, he strode quickly around a corner and was lost in the crowd.

"You will pay, Soothsayer!" Malya's soft words hissed like an infuriated cat. "No man treats me like this and lives!"

*H*ave my belongings moved from the cavern rooms to the Jabed's room near the sanctuary. It is time I stopped hiding from the world." The Oracle leaned back into the embrace of the high seat, her thin hands lying along the carved arms. The violet head-veils lay in soft folds about her thin shoulders. Her brown eyes, almost black in the gloom of the audience hall, were underscored with blue shadows of deep fatigue. "I prayed for peace, knowing within my heart that it would not be so. Now we must prepare for war."

"Who will replace the Jabed?" The High Priestess Vairya looked down at the slender girl, worry lines wrinkling her forehead. "It is the Jabed's duty to train the warriors."

"Do you think, Vairya, that the old Jabed could or would have done this without great argument and private conspiracy?" The Oracle lifted her head to look up at her, the heavy coils of her black hair sliding against the ancient wood of the chair.

"No, I do not." Vairya's hand brushed the sword slung at her side. "I have long known that he thought the position of the Jabed should be the highest in the Temple." She smoothed her white robe nervously. "Oracle, I know that my talents are small. I have only a little talent to far-see or prophesy. But I do know the way of the sword, although my skills need sharpening. Let me choose those priestesses willing and able, and once more raise up the band of the Moon Sickle, the troupe once called Her Own."

"Yes, the women warriors should never have been disbanded." The thick lashes closed over the dark eyes in weariness. "For too long have the priests of this School, especially the Jabeds, undermined the importance of the priestesses. And we have allowed it. The position of Jabed will not be filled until we find a man who places great value on the Goddess and Her women."

"That may not be for some time," Vairya answered, her mouth pursed in thought.

"Perhaps never. Do you think we will fail without a Jabed?" The dark eyes opened to stare up at her.

"I think we will do better without one." The High Priestess smiled, one hand on her sword hilt.

"I need two trusted warriors to carry out a task."

"The best of the Kaballoi, Oracle, are Odran and Hindjall. These men are great swordsmen and greater shape-shifters. And they follow the old ways of the Goddess. I trust them completely."

"Send them at once after the Soothsayer," the Oracle answered with a sigh. "We must get the child from him."

"It shall be done."

"And Vairya, select your women warriors at once and begin their training." The Oracle absently tugged at one of the dark curls near her brow. "Also select the best warrior priest here to weed out the dissenters in his ranks and train the others. He will answer to either you or me, no one else."

"Then you foresee war soon?"

"I see it upon us, but no time has been revealed. We must be prepared." The Oracle closed her eyes again as the High Priestess hurried from the audience hall.

Damn him! Where has he gone? Corri leaned against the low stone balustrade at the edge of the lake and stared across at the Temple. She was exhausted from her search of Kystan. *I can only hope he has taken Dakhma to the High Priestess.*

She turned to watch the promenading matrons as they minced along the stone-paved boulevard, their wealth displayed in rich clothing, their servants shading them with umbrellas to protect their pampered skin.

"Corri!" A deep voice penetrated the noisy crowd.

Corri whirled and looked around, then broke into a wide smile as she saw Imandoff and Takra striding toward her.

"Where have you been?" she gasped as Imandoff crushed her in his embrace.

"Trying to find you." Takra hugged her close, then looked sharply at her. "What evil has happened? I can see it in your eyes."

"A long tale," Corri answered, "but that must wait. We have to find the Soothsayer and get Dakhma away from him."

Imandoff raised his eyebrows in question. "The Soothsayer has gone renegade?"

Corri shrugged. "I do not think he works with the Fravashi, but I know he ill-uses the child for his own gain. His mother's crystal. . . ."

"We heard." Takra's hand dropped to her sword hilt as her amber eyes watched the milling crowds on the promenade. Her mouth pursed in disapproval as she eyed the sheltered women.

"Come. We must seek audience with the Oracle." Imandoff motioned toward the Temple with his staff. "There is news beyond the Soothsayer the Oracle must hear."

He nodded to the silent guards as they passed onto the bridge. "The time will come," he said to Corri, "when no one will cross this bridge without challenge."

The Temple courtyard was a mass of activity when they passed through the great gates. Solemn ranks of white-robed priests and priestesses stood, hands on the traditional swords, watching a small group of men coming from the personal quarters. The Jabed, a scowl on his face, led the group.

"Out of my way, sorcerer," he ordered, pushing against Imandoff with a stiffened arm. The sorcerer scarcely rocked from the shove, but the Jabed recoiled as if he had touched a snake. "Take care, or you may not live to regret it." Imandoff's gray eyes were as cold and penetrating as a grasslands' ice storm.

"Get you gone, law-breaker!" Shouts came from the massed ranks. "The Goddess rules here!"

Imandoff guided Takra and Corri back to one side with his staff as the Jabed and the little band of priests hurried through the gates toward the city.

"What hornets' nest have we stepped into, old man?" Corri asked as he led them through the shouting initiates.

"I thought Mystery School initiates were solemn and not given to excitement." Takra grinned at Corri as they followed Imandoff toward the audience hall, where the Oracle and the High Priestess stood at the top of the marble steps. "Someone surely stirred them up."

"Greetings, Imandoff, Wind-Rider, Dream Warrior." The Oracle's dark eyes went to each of them. "You witness the cleansing of the Temple, a thing long overdue." Her eyes returned to the sorcerer. "You bring strange tales. Come, we will talk in my quarters."

"Not underground again," Takra groaned. "That place makes my skin creep."

"And the snake," Corri murmured.

"The Oracle has taken quarters near the sanctuary now." Vairya fell in step beside them, her hand resting on her sword. "She has taken control of the Temple. What you witnessed was the outcasting of the Jabed and those priests who followed his will."

"The Soothsayer, has he been here?" Corri glanced up at the tall regal woman at her side. "Did he bring a girl-child?"

"He came alone, thinking to use the child to gain position here. When the Oracle rejected him, he left. Even now Kaballoi warriors seek him. They will bring the child to the Temple."

"If they find him," Corri answered. "The Soothsayer is tricky like a fox. I followed him all the way from the peaks of Deep Rising and have yet to catch sight of him."

They followed the Oracle into her new rooms, seating themselves in chairs drawn around a central table. Takra lifted her fair eyebrows at the sight of two men guarding the door.

"We have returned to the old ways," Vairya murmured. "The Oracle even has commanded the retraining of the Moon Sickle."

"The Goddess' band?" Takra let her breath out slowly. "Her Own has not existed for many years."

"It does now." Vairya sat with one hand still touching her sword. "I lead it. The way of the spiritual sword has returned to the Temple."

"You bring news for me, Imandoff?" The Oracle leaned back in her chair.

"I discovered something very surprising at Nevn," Imandoff said, leaning toward the Oracle. "Some Fravashi traders are able to cross the spellbound border. In fact, they have crossed it for generations."

The room was so quiet Corri could hear the rustle of the wind among the trees outside the open window.

"Spies?" The Oracle clasped her thin hands together. "I know only of the comings and goings of spies from Kirisan and Asur."

"Not spies, but traders." Imandoff leaned back in his chair, watching the Oracle through half-closed eyes. "A family who does not love the Volikvis and who has reason to fear Kayth and Minepa. Innocent people, Oracle, who want nothing more than the right to trade and live in peace."

"There have been rumors of this for a long time, but no one really believed. Tell me!" The Oracle's face was drawn with lines of little sleep and deep concern, but her eyes were bright with curiosity.

"The Fravashi I spoke with were not too clear about how many generations back it began. They only know the secret of crossing the border was discovered by an ancestress named Balqama, who fled from a Volikvi priest." Imandoff smiled grimly. "The stories we hear of the Volikvis' use of women is true, according to the traders. Balqama fled into the Mootma Mountains with the Volikvi hard at her heels. Before she realized what happened, she found herself on the Tuone side of the border, the Volikvi unable to follow."

Imandoff absently took out his pipe and bag of smoke-leaf. He stopped, hand curled around the bowl, and looked at the Oracle.

"Smoke it," she said with a quiet smile. "It will remind me of my father and happier times."

Imandoff tamped the leaf into the pipe, lighting the pipe with a snap of his fingers. "Her brother Sazerac, who had followed her, killed the priest and hid the body. Then he too tried to cross. After several attempts, the family discovered that the mind and its beliefs hold the key. They have kept this secret for generations, small groups of the family slipping across the border from time to time to trade with Tuone and Kirisan, even a few times going as far as Asur."

"Why did they not all cross and stay?" Vairya tapped her fingers against the chair arm in thought.

"Some of the family simply cannot believe it can be done." Imandoff blew a smoke ring at the ceiling. "Belief is the key. This family of Sazerac has offered to help the Peoples against Frav when the war comes."

"Why?" Takra frowned as she stretched her long legs. "What do they hope to gain?"

"Freedom. It seems that many people in Frav do not appreciate being forced to worship Jevotan. It seems, Takra Wind-Rider, that many of the common people in Frav secretly worship the Goddess."

"An enemy within their own walls!" The High Priestess smiled, her dark eyes lighting up with understanding.

"It will not be that simple." Corri shook her head, and the Oracle nodded in agreement. "It is good to know there are those within Frav who will fight against the Volikvis, but you are forgetting about the Prophecies and Kayth."

"You have read it right, Dream Warrior." The Oracle leaned against the back of her chair, her eyes filled with deep weariness. "We know the dangers posed by Kayth and Minepa, but who is the Soothsayer of the Prophecies?"

"He was the Soothsayer who came here." Corri looked at Takra, who nodded.

"I do not know that for certain." The Oracle sighed. "We look for the obvious. The Prophecies have never dealt in the obvious. However, we must not take chances. The Kaballoi should soon find him and the child."

One of the guards threw open the door to admit an extremely tall warrior. The man held his helmet in the bend of his arm as he came five steps within the chamber and bowed his head to the Oracle.

"Odran and Hindjall follow the Soothsayer toward the south," he said. "What are your orders, Oracle?"

"Secure the gates and the bridges. None may now enter without challenge, unless they know the password." The girl frowned in thought, then added, "The healers will meet each morning on the city's promenade for the benefit of the sick among the people of Kystan."

Corri watched the warrior in fascination. His long black hair was bound up in a knot at the top of his head. Light gleamed off the helmet under his arm, shaped like the head of a barsark, the ferocious bear-like creature she had seen in the Valley of Whispers. The warrior bowed his head again, turned with a swish of his fighting kilts, and strode out.

"That is a Kaballoi?" Takra's eyes were bright with interest. "Never have I met one. What an opponent he would be! He is truly Nu-Sheek?" she asked Imandoff.

"All Kaballoi must be Nu-Sheek," Vairya answered. "That much of the old ways we have kept. Perhaps we will discover Nu-Sheeka among the priestesses who train for Her Own."

Corri leaned over and poked Takra's arm to gain her attention. "What is a Kaballoi and what is Nu-Sheek?"

"A Kaballoi is an expert horse-rider," the Wind-Rider answered. "Perhaps even as good as the Tuonela. And Nu-Sheek, it means he can put on the form of an animal when he fights."

"Not physically become an animal, Corri." Imandoff puffed thoughtfully at his pipe. "Rather he takes on the animal's fighting spirit, forgetting he is human for a time." He turned to the Oracle. "Are there many such here?"

"Not enough, sorcerer. The requirements are stiff, and not many can meet them. But we do have a full band of Kaballoi."

"Wait! He said they followed the Soothsayer to the south." Corri sat bolt upright in her chair. "He will not go to the south, I know it!"

"Where, then?" Imandoff watched her face closely.

"To the west, back to the mountains." She slapped her fist against her knee. "Like a fox, I said he was. He will run to a safe hole where we will be hard pressed to find him or smoke him out."

"I have very limited contact with the child," the Oracle said. Vairya looked at her in surprise. "We lived together in other lives. However, when Dakhma shields her thoughts from the Soothsayer and others, I cannot reach her either." The Oracle stood, hands clasped together. "My mind-contact with her is difficult, for her training is lacking. Dream Warrior, I know your heart, and in this it follows the will of the Goddess. Seek the child, and take her from the Soothsayer. Then bring or send her here where she will be safe and can be properly trained. My heart tells me she will play an important part in the Great War that is to come."

As Takra, Imandoff, and Corri made their way back through the meandering streets of Kystan to the inn where the horses were stabled, the sorcerer wondered aloud about the Soothsayer.

"I have known Ayron since he was a boy," Imandoff pondered. "Like Dakhma, he has always been able to mask his feelings and thoughts, but I did not think his powers were very great."

"You should have guessed, old man," Corri said as she hurried to keep up. "With Grimmel as his father. . . ."

"What?" Imandoff grabbed her arm and pulled her to face him. "Are you certain?" Corri nodded. "What else have you discovered about Ayron? Tell me, girl. It may be important."

"I know that he takes draughts of fenlix spores and wermod. He told me himself."

"So!" Imandoff's breath hissed through his teeth. "We now must trail not only a man who has some powers of mind-concealment, but one who can suddenly become very dangerous."

The sorcerer hurriedly purchased what supplies he could, rushing the women to saddle the horses and be out of Kystan within an hour.

As they rode down the long stone ramp from the city to the valley below, Corri puzzled over something, finally asking Takra, "How did you know where I stabled Mouse? There are hundreds of inns, large and small, in Kystan."

Takra grinned and shrugged her shoulders. "Imandoff just told Sun Dancer to find her. And he did."

They rode through the valley under the late afternoon sun, finally turning from the main road onto a branch leading back into the thick forests of Deep Rising.

Soothsayer, beware if you harm Dakhma further. Corri rode with her eyes on the forested foothills ahead. *I do not know about burning you at the crown, as it says in the Prophecies, whatever that is, but I do know that you will not live to come down from these mountains if the child is harmed.*

*H*ow could you lose him?" Malya's sharp words sliced right and left as she rode with three men up the mountain trail. "Now he is at least half a day's ride ahead of us."

"We can catch up with him by morning." Roggkin scowled at her.

"Not likely. The Soothsayer has night-sight. He will ride on after dark, and we dare not." Malya set her jaw. "Menec, Shilluk, watch our back-trail for Corri Farblood. If she comes close enough, take her. This journeying about is getting tiresome." She impatiently tapped her fingers against her bent knee, hooked over the horn of the side-saddle. "I must get to Frav as soon as possible."

"Perhaps he goes back to his village." Roggkin's dark eyes constantly moved over the forested hills on both sides of the trail.

"No, the Soothsayer has been outcast." Shilluk's broken-nailed fingers scratched at his day-old beard. "He knows they will take the child and stone him out of Springwell."

"I heard once that he has a secret place higher in the mountains." Menec cleared his throat and spat. "Likely he plans to use the child for some of his dark magic. You know what I mean?" He grinned, exposing his stained and broken teeth.

"You Kirisani imbecile." Malya turned her head to glare at him. "You know nothing of the Soothsayer. He may skirt the edges between light and dark, but he is no child-lover."

"But the villagers do talk of a secret place he has," Shilluk insisted. "I heard it was near a place of great power." He scratched his stringy hair in thought. "Perhaps near that Valley of Whispers they always talk about."

Malya's pale blue eyes widened. "Of course, he would choose a place of power. Do you know where this valley is?"

Shilluk shook his head. "I would guess a place where the Green Men seldom go, else those trail-runners would have ousted him long ago."

"Where do these Green Men seldom go then?" Roggkin twisted in the saddle, his brown eyes snapping with impatience. "Do you know even that?"

"I know of a place the Green Men allow no one to enter," answered Menec. "Up on the border between Kirisan and Asur."

"Then we go there." Malya tapped her mount with her slippered heel. "Shilluk, you and Menec keep a close watch for Farblood. If I can deliver Farblood, the child, and the Soothsayer to Kayth, he will realize my great importance to his work." She smiled to herself, as smug as a cat with a bowl of cream.

Roggkin watched her from the corner of his eye. *You will not stop my plans for Farblood. She is mine to use and then cast aside, Kirisani traitor. As I will use you, poisoned dagger or no.*

The Soothsayer and Dakhma rode late into the night, taking only a short rest before continuing as the first sunlight crept over the sharp peaks of Deep Rising. For three days they pushed the horses as much as they dared, taking to the trees whenever the Soothsayer's sensitive ears caught the sounds of other travelers. They skirted the trail leading into Springwell, and on the fourth day left the worn trader-paths to journey along a thin animal track up into the forests.

"When will we reach this secret place you speak of?" Dakhma drooped with exhaustion. The first day she had awakened, seated before the Soothsayer, and with an aching head. After that, the girl allowed him to touch her only when necessary to mount her horse.

"Not far now." The Soothsayer rode, back straight, alert to the shadowed trees and thick underbrush through which they passed. "Farblood will join us there."

"Farblood will follow us, but join you? Never!" Dakhma's small mouth drew together in disbelief. "The Dream Warrior works for the Peoples, Soothsayer. You do not."

The Soothsayer ignored her, instead pointing downward into a wide valley as they emerged from the thick trees at the top of high cliffs. "There is the Valley of Whispers, a place of the Forgotten Ones of long ago. If you look closely, you can see some of the temple stones still standing."

Dakhma followed his blunt finger with her eyes. Squinting against the setting sun and a wavering distortion within the valley below, she turned in the saddle to view the valley from one end to the other.

"This is a place of great power. I can feel it," she whispered.

"My cabin is not far." The Soothsayer pointed to the distant walls across the hidden valley. "Up there, deep among the trees. Do you know, Dakhma, that Qishua Tears are found up there? Just like the one you stole from the shakka."

The little girl hung her head. "I did not mean to keep it."

"But you took it." He turned his head, a mocking smile on his lips. "The Rissa also come here, the beautiful big cats seldom seen by men. I have made friends with them." He laughed at the child's frown. "Wait and see."

They rode around the valley rim, then up into the tall sheltering trees of the last forests where Deep Rising met the stark teeth of the Barren Mountains. A square cabin, walls of stone blocks and roof of timber, sat in the center of a mountain meadow. Beside it the poles of a corral and the shadowed outline of a lean-to shelter were plain in the dying sunlight.

"The walls of this cabin were built in the far past by Kirisani guards. You will sleep in a bed tonight," the tall man said as he lifted down the little girl. "Perhaps tomorrow the Rissa will come visiting."

And I will animal-talk with them, Dakhma thought to herself. *I will run away with them and get them to take me back to a village, far away from you, Soothsayer.*

*W*e are close to where the Barren Mountains meet with Deep Rising." Imandoff shifted in the saddle as he waited for Corri and Takra to ride alongside. "The village of Springwell is down that trail, and off that way," he pointed to the right, "is an ancient burial place. There are grave mounds of the Forgotten Ones at the end of the valley, but also the mounds of many of the Peoples who died during the last war with Frav. The villagers buried the Soothsayer's mother there."

"He took the child into that place?" Takra raised her pale brows, then drew them down in anger. She shivered. "If it makes me uneasy to think about walking among the dead, what did the child feel?"

"Do they really believe that burying the crystal with her will trap her spirit?" Corri asked, as she pushed back her tangled hair. "That is a strange thing."

"Yes, they believe that burying personal items with the body will keep the spirit from walking at night and disturbing the living." Imandoff shielded his eyes with his hand as he stared down the trail to the village, then at their back-trail. "But there are far older grave-mounds here. Many of the Peoples who died during the last war with Frav were slain by a plague, not the sword. Whatever disease was unleashed clung even to their possessions, so they were buried with all their belongings. Over many years, this story has become twisted in the minds of the mountain villagers, so that they believe without their belongings the dead will walk."

"Superstition." Takra shook her head, her long pale front-braids rasping over her leather tunic.

"Perhaps." Imandoff smiled grimly. "Many years ago a trader dug into one of the graves and brought out a jeweled bracelet. The villagers tracked him to the high pass into Asur, where they found him dying, the bracelet clutched in his hands. As far as I know, his bones and the bracelet are still up there."

"The prints of the Soothsayer's horse do not come this way." Takra ran her hand down the smooth spear shaft near her left boot, her amber eyes intent on the shadows under the trees. "They go off to the north."

Imandoff turned Sun Dancer back onto the main trail. "Yes," he said softly. "I think he rides in the direction of the Valley of Whispers."

"Would he take Dakhma into that place?" Corri shivered as she thought of the strange forces she had experienced there. "Her mind could not withstand the Whisperers."

"Nor, I think, could his." Imandoff clucked to Sun Dancer, who danced along the pebble-strewn trail in the fading sunlight. "Come, the valley is not far from here."

The three pushed on as long as the light lasted. When they stopped to camp for the night on the rim of the valley cliffs, they found faint evidence in the dry soil that the Soothsayer and Dakhma had passed that way. A small breeze whispered from the peaks to the west, blowing down their back-trail.

Takra built a small fire to cook the fat mountain quail she had bagged along the last part of the journey. As she hung them on green sticks over the low flames, she constantly eyed the darkness closing around them.

"I think you should not dream-fly here, Corri," Imandoff said as he leaned forward to trace a sign on the girl's forehead. "Little is understood about the power in this valley. Perhaps it is a power you can use, perhaps not. Better not to chance it."

"Wait!" Corri's voice was barely audible as she reached for Imandoff's arm. "Look at the horses!"

Sun Dancer and Lightfoot snorted and pawed at the ground, while Mouse backed to the full length of her tether, ears back. Takra leaped up, drawing her sword, her eyes wide in the flickering firelight. There was a faint rustle in the underbrush, then silence. The horses eyed the darkness with suspicion, blowing and stamping.

"Whatever it was is gone." Takra listened intently, the long sword ready in her hand. "But I still feel spied on."

"Well you should, Wind-Rider." A man stepped slowly from the shadows, long bow in hand. "Dangerous animals are abroad now in these mountains, besides the cutthroats who search for a hiding hole."

"I wondered when we would find you." Imandoff raised his hand in greeting. "What happens in these mountains, Gadavar, that the Green Men are out in force? I saw your signs all along the upper trails."

Gadavar's eyes met Corri's, and his mouth curved in a smile.

I can no more turn aside my feelings for this man than I can change the course of a storm off the seas, Corri thought as she smiled back. *My heart sings whenever I look at him.*

"These mountains are always dangerous, but more so now." Gadavar sat down by the fire, his bow on the ground beside him. His leaf-brown hair, tied in its leather thong, slipped over his broad shoulder as he smiled again at Corri. "I would have come sooner, but the Green Men had need of me. Bands of cutthroats roam these mountains, trying to establish lairs. And many of the dangerous high peak animals are coming down. This is not a time to be wandering about, sorcerer."

"We seek one called the Soothsayer." Takra sheathed her sword and squatted beside him. "We trailed him and a Tuonela child up here."

"Ayron of Springwell? Last I heard he was headed for Kystan, and now he returns." Gadavar looked over his shoulder and listened to the night sounds, then turned back to Imandoff. "The Green Men want to know what that one does up here. I was sent to help you find him."

"Why do the Green Men take an interest in the Soothsayer?" Imandoff asked, taking out his pipe. "His powers are those of any village feya woman."

"His powers are changing, sorcerer." Gadavar folded his arms across his bent knees. "Not only are they growing stronger, they are changing in a manner that puzzles us. We need no more spies, if that is what he has become, lurking about these mountains."

Imandoff looked straight into the Green Man's eyes, his pipe forgotten in his hand. "You have the power to smell out evil."

Gadavar nodded. "Not anything great, Imandoff Silverhair, but I can smell out those who lean toward Frav. And the Soothsayer puzzles me, for his scent is neither one nor the other."

"What caused the horses to react as they did?" Corri looked from Takra to Gadavar. "They were upwind of Gadavar."

"Probably the passing of some night creature, although I saw and heard nothing." Gadavar whistled softly; his horse Nuisance stepped daintily from the darkness to stand by the other mounts.

"It was not his mount they scented," Takra said as she watched the Green Man tether his horse with the others. "Neither would Lightfoot have readied to fight him."

"I think we should set a guard tonight." Imandoff snapped a spark from his long fingers and lit his pipe. "Someone or something spied on us." He handed his smoke-leaf bag to the Green Man when he came back to the fire.

Gadavar tipped his head slightly as he looked at his horse. "Nuisance says it was a large animal, one that spied with purpose before leaving." He tamped his own pipe with leaf, then lit it with a twig. "Events are moving fast now. I feel it here." He tapped his chest with a sun-browned hand.

Takra moved to Corri's side and spoke softly. "We heard of the whipping. I would see what Melaina did." She pulled up the back of the girl's tunic, then gently brushed her hand across the pink-stitched scars. "By the hell fires of Frav! I let her off too lightly."

"It is healed now." Corri tugged the tunic back in place. "Some time there will be a further reckoning between Melaina and me, but for now there are more important tasks."

Corri sat, her chin on her knees, and stared into the glowing embers. *We must find Dakhma soon. If the war draws nearer,*

I need to return to the border. I cannot leave the child to the Sooth-sayer. Lady, let this man be the one of the Prophecies. Then there will be one less part for me to fulfill. She sighed and laid her face on her folded arms.

None of the travelers clustered around the small fire saw or heard the stealthy movements of the great cat as it settled into its position downwind of the horses to watch. Its silver-gray eyes narrowed as it reached out with its mind and touched Corri's sleeping thoughts. The girl yielded to the gentle pressure as the cat sensed what she was and what concerned her. With a flick of its long tail, it made a wide pass around the horses and ran in bounding leaps up the mountain toward the Soothsayer's cabin.

Chapter 7

False dawn spread gray fingers over the mountain cabin, leaving prints of misshapen shadows under the crouching trees. The few birds that made their homes in the high peaks muttered sleepily in the predawn chill. The horses in the pole-bound enclosure blew misty clouds of breath, nickering softly as the Soothsayer filled their water trough.

The big cat stretched, its fanged jaws open in a wide yawn, the tongue curling out over the sharp teeth. Sniffing the morning breeze flowing down the slope from the horse-pen, it flicked its tufted ears to catch the Soothsayer's soft words as he threw armloads of fresh-cut owl clover into the corral. The cat stretched again, this time lifting each hind leg in turn, and began to purr loudly.

The Soothsayer turned, his eyes seeking the cat among the dappled morning shadows. "Come," he said softly, holding out his open hand. "There is someone else here to see."

The cat regally made its way along the wall of the cabin, ignoring the horses that blew and stamped their feet, certain that the animal might be dangerous but unable to catch its scent. The Soothsayer braced his feet as the cat gently pushed against him, its back thigh-high to the tall man.

"What have you seen?" The Soothsayer looked down into the silvery eyes. "Yes, that one is of importance to me," he said in response to the telepathic message. "Let the Dream Warrior come to the cabin. And the Green Man is no threat. He will likely go about his business elsewhere. The others I shall prepare for."

"Soothsayer?" The cabin door opened, framing Dakhma in sunlight and dark. The child backed up slowly, her eyes wide, as the cat turned to stare at her.

"This is a Rissa, Dakhma." The Soothsayer stroked the cat's big head. "They live up here in the mountains. He will not harm you, for I have told him you are a friend."

Dakhma blinked in surprise as mental pictures flowed through her mind, then smiled. "He can animal-talk!" She held out her small hand and cautiously walked toward the cat. The Rissa delicately sniffed the offered hand, then rasped its long tongue across the palm. The girl laughed, running her hands along the golden brown sides and through the dark brown-tipped fur on the back.

"He is so big!" Dakhma threw her arm up over the Rissa's neck and buried her face in the lush fur.

"If strangers come, the Rissa will protect you. He is my friend." The Soothsayer braced himself as the huge cat set its plate-sized paws against him to look straight up into his eyes.

"I have seen her before," Dakhma said as she caught the image of a woman pass from the Soothsayer to the cat. "The shakka drove her from the Clan. A Tuonela warrior was with her. They are not good people."

"Do not fear. The Rissa has not seen them." The Soothsayer took the child's hand as the Rissa disappeared into the trees and rocky slopes, headed up the mountain. "We will eat now. Then we will forage for herbs on the slopes below."

"Farblood will come for me." Dakhma set her jaw as she watched the man stir up the coals on the wide heath. "You know she will, Soothsayer. I will not let you harm her."

"Why should I do that?" He hung a kettle of water over the growing flames and stirred in ground grain. *There will be no need,* he assured himself. *Malya is somewhere in these mountains, not far from Farblood. I know it, even if the Rissa has not seen her.*

Dakhma's eyes narrowed as she watched the Soothsayer's back. "Farblood will come for me and for her owl stone. You will not want to give up either."

The horses in the corral nickered suddenly, the sharp sound shattering the morning stillness. The Soothsayer dropped the ladle into the simmering kettle and pressed his face against a crack in the shuttered window.

"Quick! You must hide." He whirled, grabbing the girl's thin arm in one hand, while the other scooped up the bag containing the owl stone circlet and the crystal. "Do not make a sound." He kicked aside a small rug and levered up a trap door in the wooden floor. "Inside, and do not come out until I tell you."

Dakhma slid through the hole into the blackness below. The Soothsayer dropped the bag after her, pressed the trap door into place, and straightened the rug over it. When the cabin door flew open, he stood beside the fireplace, dagger in hand.

"Where is the child?" Malya ordered, her stare raking around the small cabin. "I know you brought her here."

"I am alone." The Soothsayer's pale eyes were icy in their contempt. "Did you think I would let you take her to Frav? Come, Malya, I think you did not forget what I told you when last we met."

Roggkin and the other men pushed by Malya, arranging themselves on either side of the woman. "Tell us, Soothsayer, what we want to know, or . . ." Roggkin slipped his long Tuonela dagger from its sheath and flourished it in his strong hand.

"The child is not here," the tall man repeated. "But Farblood comes this way." His mouth pulled up at the corners in a mocking smile. "I have ways of knowing. I have known you since childhood, Malya. Your heart has always turned to Frav. Take Farblood and go there. Leave me in peace."

"Peace?" Malya sneered. "There can be no peace for you, Ayron. Farblood seeks you for the same reasons that the Kaballoi ride on your trail. You have stirred the Temple like a maddened anthill. Do you think they will leave you in peace?" She smiled sweetly as she moved closer. "Come with me to Frav. There your powers will be appreciated."

"I may be many things, daughter of Darkness, but I am not a traitor to Kirisan." The Soothsayer looked down his nose, disgust clear in his voice.

"Then die." Malya's dagger, its tip darkened with tujyk poison, flicked toward him. "We will find the child and take her without your aid."

In the blink of an eye, the Soothsayer's dagger scored across Malya's shoulder and down her breast, the blood splattering in thick red drops onto her white gown. With a cry, she slashed out, the poisoned blade slicing into the Soothsayer's forearm. He drew back against the wall, aware of the deadly poison taking hold in his blood.

"Someone comes!" Shilluk stood poised for flight in the open door, Menec beside him.

"Search the cabin," Malya ordered as she pressed her hand against the wound in her breast. "The child must be here. Make the Soothsayer reveal her hiding place."

Shilluk and Menec raced out the door to the waiting horses, leading the mounts to the door. "There is no time!" Shilluk cried. "They see us!"

Malya stumbled out, blood pouring over her hand. She fumbled in her saddlebag, dragging out a mass of herbs and dried moss, and pressed them against the wound. The bleeding slowed to a thin trickle as she gasped with pain.

Inside, the Soothsayer fell to his knees, pain etched into his face. His dagger dropped from his numbing fingers. Roggkin watched him, a cruel smile on his mouth.

"Hurry!" Shilluk's cry broke through the Tuonela warrior's thoughts. Roggkin stepped behind the Soothsayer and buried the long dagger in the man's back. The blade grated against a rib as Roggkin jerked it back out.

"You will tell Farblood no tales of us," he sneered, then turned to race through the cabin door.

Malya managed to pull herself up onto her horse, where she leaned over the saddle-horn, eyes closed in pain. Shilluk and Menec were already riding up the mountain toward the Asur border. Roggkin leaped on his horse and leaned over to take the slack reins from Malya's hands.

"Take me to Sadko," the woman said through gritted teeth. "They are healers and turn away no one." She raised her dark head to stare at Roggkin. "Go to Sadko, up in the mountains near the Metal Mines. We will be safe there."

Roggkin kicked his mount forward, Malya's horse following. They were soon up the grassy, rock-strewn slope and among the trees, hidden from the riders on the trail below.

*D*akhma cringed in the darkness when she heard the demanding voice of Malya in the cabin above. She crouched, hands over her head, on the cold dirt. The quarreling voices filled her mind with fear for both herself and the Soothsayer. An image of the Rissa popped unbidden in her mind. Cautiously raising her head, the child followed the stream of thought-pictures, feeling the silent entreaty to leave her hiding place. Malya's scream galvanized her into action. She crawled toward a crack of light, dragging the bag with the owl stone behind her.

A huge paw, razor-claws extended, hooked into the thin block of stone covering the exit-hole, and dragged it aside. The Rissa stood, teeth bared in a silent growl, eyes narrowed at the corner of the cabin, as Dakhma wiggled through the hole into the daylight. Clutching the bag in her sweating hand, she followed the Rissa away from the Soothsayer into the underbrush and concealing trees of the mountain slopes.

They rode out alone," Imandoff cried as he urged Sun Dancer up the last part of the slope to the stone-walled cabin. "Search for the Soothsayer and the child!"

Takra and Gadavar, dropping the reins of their mounts and leaping down, reached the open cabin door first, swords in hand.

"He is here, but Dakhma is gone." Takra motioned to Imandoff and Corri.

Gadavar sheathed his sword with a snick as he strode across the planked floor to where the Soothsayer sat, back against the cold wall, face twisted in pain. The others crowded close.

"Where is Dakhma?" Corri asked as she squatted on her heels near the dying Soothsayer. A sticky pool of blood oozed across the uneven floor from where the man leaned against the stone wall. A strange scent of bitterness mixed with a nose-clogging sweetness hung over the man.

The Soothsayer opened his pale eyes. "She is safe with the Rissa." His voice was a thin thread of sound in the stillness.

"There is too much blood to have come from only this scratch." Imandoff bent over the bleeding arm, then quickly drew back his fingers. "Tujyk poison!"

Gadavar's nostrils expanded as he sniffed the air. "Yes, I smell its odor. Who arms their dagger with such? You are right, sorcerer. This blood, it cannot all be his, for a trail of it leads outside."

The Green Man pointed to the splattered line of blood, smeared by their boots and Roggkin's retreating steps. The sharp coppery odor, suppressed by the mountain chill, hung as a faint nerve-rasping smell over the crimson puddles that led across the cabin and out the door.

"Malya did this, but I marked her." The Soothsayer's body twisted with pain as the poison sank deeper into his organs. "I have little time. Imandoff Silverhair, I beg you to protect my son from that evil woman."

"Son?" Imandoff bent closer. "Where is your family?"

"I did not marry Eszti. She is now married to Franzel, a farmer in Kirisan. He thinks the child is his. But Athdar is my son." The Soothsayer struggled to catch his breath. "Ayron, one born from sorrow. A fitting name, is it not?" A blue tinge colored the flesh around the gasping mouth. "Dream Warrior, the owl stone is safe with Dakhma. I truly never meant to harm the child. Forgive me for taking her, and forgive me for my jealousy of you. We were both Grimmel's victims, you and I."

"Yes, we were both victims." *How can I hate this man who suffered as I did? I understand his grasping for something to call his own in this life, for I have done the same myself.*

"Farblood, give my mother's crystal to the child." Ayron gasped for air with each word. "When she comes into her power, when she is older, when she has trained at the Temple. . . . "

"I will do it." Corri brushed the sweat-damp hair back from the man's face. *He may be Grimmel's son, but the Soothsayer is nothing like his father. And if it had not been for Imandoff, I could have been like Ayron.*

"The Soothsayer of the Prophecies, that is not me. There is another." Ayron's frantic gasping for breath filled the cabin. A bloody froth coated his blue lips as the snake poison caused his blood vessels to burst within him.

Imandoff gently drew Corri back from her place at the man's side. "You are dying, Ayron," he said as he knelt beside the Soothsayer. The pale hazel eyes looked up at him, pleading in their depths. "All I can do is give you sleep and let you pass Between Worlds without pain."

The man nodded, then twisted in agony as the poison bit deeper. "Do it." The words were almost inaudible.

Imandoff touched the center of the man's damp forehead with his fingers, his eyes closed in concentration. The pale eyes closed as the deep lines of pain smoothed away. The breath rasped slower and slower until only silence filled the room.

Takra turned away to douse the hearth fire with a bucket of water nearby. "He prepared a meal for two," she said as she looked into the cooking pot.

As Gadavar and Imandoff lifted the body to wrap it in a blanket, the Green Man's brows raised in surprise. "He was stabbed in the back! A coward's blow! The poison was already in his blood. He could not have defended himself."

"Roggkin!" Takra spat out the name. "He is a coward, and that is his way of fighting."

"So Roggkin and Malya still travel together. A deadly combination." Imandoff leaned against his staff in thought as the others piled stones over the Soothsayer's grave near the trees in back of the cabin. "The child escaped through there." He pointed to the loosened stone in the cabin's foundation. "At least Ayron protected her in the end."

"The Rissa took her this way, into the trees, toward the higher peaks." Gadavar followed the faint pug marks across the clearing to the edge of the trees. "Do we follow them tonight?"

"We must. Dakhma will be frightened." Corri frowned as she stared up at the stark teeth of the Barren Mountains, visible in the distance.

"So he has a son," Imandoff said as they led the horses up the mountain, Gadavar searching the ground before them for tracks. "I wonder how much of the father is in him."

"Hopefully, none." Takra's amber eyes narrowed as Gadavar silently motioned for them to join him at the foot of a rocky, shrub-dotted hill.

"At the end there was little of Grimmel in the Soothsayer." Corri mulled over the man's last words. "What did he mean, Imandoff, that there is another Soothsayer?"

"If he knew the answer, it died with him. Only time will reveal it to us now."

"We cannot take the horses any farther." The Green Man handed Nuisance's reins to Imandoff as he looked up at the steep slope of rocks and ledges before them. "We cannot all go, or the Rissa will take her deeper into the mountains and we will never sight them. Can you mind-speak to animals?"

Takra shook her head, and the sorcerer murmured, "A little."

"I will go." Corri handed Mouse's reins to Takra. "Dakhma will be frightened, perhaps enough to stay silent and mind-shielded. She will recognize my voice."

"If the child is frightened, the Rissa may react with anger," Gadavar said. "She must have established a mind-link with the big cats; an unusual thing, but not impossible if she has strong abilities to animal-talk."

"Speaking with animals is an ordinary thing for her. And she has a very strong mind-shield, strong enough to avoid detection by any of us if she does not wish to be found." Corri held Gadavar's gaze, defying him to say she could not go.

"How big are these Rissa?" Takra's hand rested on her sword hilt as she scanned the rocks above.

"Not too big." Imandoff gestured with one hand a little below his hip. "Smaller than a barsark." He grinned at her startled glance.

"Come." Gadavar touched Corri's shoulder, then scrambled up the slope with her as close behind as his shadow.

The two moved from outcrop to outcrop, climbing between the stunted trees that clung in the shallow soil around the larger boulders. The ledges, little more than boot-wide, were dotted with krakeberry bushes, scratchy juniper, and once, a thick patch of purple phlox.

Corri paused and wiped the sweat from her face as she climbed up beside Gadavar on a wide ledge leading at an angle from the clearing far below, up into a maze of stunted yellow-bark pine mingled with dense firs.

As the Green Man held out a hand to help her to a safe spot, their eyes met, and Corri felt an intense warmth kindle in her abdomen. *Does he feel this attraction as I do?* she wondered. The look in his eyes told her he did. *I want to explore this feeling with him,* she thought, *but first we must get Dakhma to safety.*

"Where now?" she asked, every inch of her body aware of his closeness on the ledge.

"The Rissa probably brought the child up along this ledge," he said softly. "It is easier than the way we came, but longer."

"Where did they go?" Corri whispered as she looked around. She could see no sign that anyone had come along the ledge.

"See?" Gadavar bent down to trace a faint disturbance in the thin soil. "A boot mark. And here, an indentation where the Rissa stepped from one rock to another."

"If the cat hides its trail so well, how will we know where it took Dakhma?"

"They den in caves near water. There is a spring up higher. We will start our search there."

Gadavar climbed on into the thick pocket of forest with Corri at his heels. Several times he stopped, appearing to listen. Corri caught the faint ripples of mind-seek coming from the Green Man as he sent out appeals to the unseen Rissa.

Dakhma, it is Corri Farblood. You are safe now. Come to me. Corri threw out her own seeking, her inner senses straining to catch some sign of the lost child. *The Soothsayer is dead. The others are gone. Tell the Rissa the Green Man and I are friends.*

A flash of fear swept through Corri's mind, then vanished. She grabbed Gadavar's arm, pulling him to a stop.

"I felt something, but I do not know who sent it."

"I have contacted the cats. They are up ahead."

Gadavar pushed his way through a last barrier of juniper into a tiny clear spot. A cliff of rock, dusted with green moss growing in its damp cracks and with a seeping spring near its base, rose only four paces from the brush. The Green Man tipped back his head to stare up at a dark opening in the cliff.

The hair on Corri's neck lifted as she heard the nearly silent warning growl of the big cat. She moved a step behind Gadavar when she saw the cat watching them, its body so close to the ground and its color so nearly that of the rock ledge itself that her gaze had passed over it until the cat flicked its tail.

Gadavar held out his empty hands, his green eyes locked on the animal above them. A flurry of pictures shot through Corri's mind.

I must get to Dakhma. Corri closed her eyes and built up the picture of the child and her as they sat in the shakka's wagon. *How do you picture a friend?* she thought. Instinctively, she let her affection for the child pour forth, allowing the big cat to reach into her mind. There was a gentle push, a tingling, then a withdrawal.

"The child is unconscious in the cave." Gadavar looked down at Corri. "She is terrified to be found, so she has retreated within herself. The Rissa are upset."

Corri blinked in surprise. "There is more than one cat?"

"A pair. The other is right behind us."

Corri felt the soft, wet touch of a nose against her hand. Slowly, she turned her head, her eyes going wide as she looked down into the silvery eyes of the second Rissa. The cat rumbled deep in its throat as it pushed against Corri's leg.

"The Rissa up there," Gadavar pointed to the cave, "is the female. She will not let us go up, for she has a cub." He braced his muscled legs as the other Rissa leaped against his chest, staring up into his eyes. "This one, the male, says he will bring down the child."

The male Rissa loped up a steep ledge, nearly invisible among the shadowed rocks, and disappeared into the dark cave.

"Most unusual." Gadavar frowned as he watched the Rissa, its teeth locked in Dakhma's leather tunic, pull the child down the ledge. "They see the child only as a young one who needs protection, and who can speak with them. But you," he turned his head to look at Corri, "you they recognize as the Protector, their interpretation of Dream Warrior."

"You talk much with these Rissa?" Corri knelt beside Dakhma as the big cat once more returned to the cave. "You have the knack of it."

Wake up, Dakhma. It is Corri. You are safe now. She tried to send her thought-message into the girl's mind, but met with a shield she could not penetrate. *Do not be afraid. You are safe now.* Corri stroked Dakhma's hair.

"I have only mind-talked with them from a distance before. The Rissa rarely let humans near them." Gadavar squatted on his heels, checking the child for head wounds. "She has no injuries. If this is truly a sickness of the mind, I have no skill in that area. You cannot reach her mind?"

"No, and I have no healing skills either." Corri watched the big cat as it deposited a worn leather bag near them, then sat on its haunches to stare with unblinking eyes. "Can we leave now?"

"What is in this?" Gadavar drew the bag to him.

"Perhaps the crystal she called for the Soothsayer. But we have no time now to find out." Corri's voice was full of concern as she stroked the little girl's face. "We must take her to a healer at once."

Gadavar studied the Rissa for a few moments, then nodded. He held out his hand; the Rissa touched it gently with its tongue.

"The Rissa says to take her to Sadko. The healers there can help the child. And the Goddess knows, it is closer than even one of the feya women."

Imandoff and I passed the Mystery School of Sadko when we fled Hadliden, Corri thought. *I did not realize it was so close to the Valley of Whispers.*

Gadavar gathered Dakhma up in his arms, leaving Corri to pick up the bag and follow. She looked back once, just as they entered the shadowed trees. The Rissa on the ledge, and the one by the spring, both sat staring after them, only the tips of their long tails moving at all.

The journey down the steep, rocky slope was difficult for Gadavar, burdened with the limp form of Dakhma. He slipped and slid the last few yards, leaving long streaks of dirt on his green trousers. Corri fared little better.

"Is she hurt?" Imandoff lifted the child from Gadavar's arms.

"Not of the body." Gadavar was breathing hard as he adjusted the leather band on his hair. "The Rissa say to take her to Sadko. Sorcerer, what do the Rissa know of Sadko?"

"Old legends say that the Rissa belonged to the Forgotten Ones." Imandoff sat with the child cradled in his lap. "And all the buildings of the Mystery Schools were here when the Peoples came to this land. It may be that they can call upon a racial memory, something we know exists but few humans can use." He stared up the slope, his eyes bright. "Do you think they would mind-speak with me?"

"Not now, old man." Takra tapped his shoulder and pointed to the horses. "It will be dark soon. I would feel better if we moved on, at least to a place where there is water and better cover than this." She swept her hand around at the open rocky area.

"If we ride after dark, we can reach Sadko by midnight." Gadavar held the child while Imandoff and Takra mounted, then lifted her into Takra's arms. "The trail between here and Sadko is not too dangerous. Can you call light to help us see?"

Imandoff nodded. "But not for long periods at a time."

For a while their trail was lit by the dying rays of the sun, but as that brightness fell behind the mountains, they had to depend on Imandoff's magically called balls of pale light. The sorcerer sent the light before them, low to the ground to keep from blinding the horses. Exhaustion soon deepened the lines on his face as he fought to keep the balls of light glowing.

Corri often found her thoughts, and her eyes, on Gadavar as they rode. *I can still feel his kiss on my mouth, his body molded against mine. Does he remember also?* She felt her face flush whenever Gadavar turned as if feeling her thoughts against his back. From his smile and the brightening of his eyes whenever he looked back at her, Corri sensed that Gadavar also remembered.

Even with the frequent rests they took to spare both the horses and Imandoff, they heard the School's bells toll midnight before they rode out of the mountains. Corri shivered with the cold as they stopped before the great iron-bound gates of the Mystery School.

Imandoff dismounted and pulled the rope attached to the huge gate-bell. Its deep-throated call echoed across the little patches of tilled fields, bouncing back from the sharp mountains. "Open at once!" the sorcerer cried. "Bring the Tamia Zanitra, for Imandoff Silverhair is here with a sick child." He jerked the bell again, its loud voice shattering the stillness.

As they waited in the cold darkness of the mountain night, Gadavar brought his mount close to Corri. "Take care when we are inside," he murmured, leaning close to her. "These healers are not like the ones in the Temple. They are mum-tongued about their doings, drawing together against the uninitiated. But they take in all who are in need of healing." His face was hard as he stared at the gates. "Even those who are criminals. I do not know who we may see within these walls."

"Back at the cabin you said there was blood that was not the Soothsayer's," Corri whispered. "And he said he marked Malya. Would she come here?"

"I think so. From the amount of blood in the cabin and on the ground outside, one of those attacking the Soothsayer took a deep wound. Before night fell, I saw several splotches of blood along the trail, leading in this direction. It would be no surprise if the Soothsayer's killers are here. If they are, the healers of Sadko will let us do nothing."

One leaf of the great gate opened, and a very tall woman draped in a white robe held up a lantern. Her long black hair spilled loose across her shoulders, falling far down on her breast.

"Who calls for the Tamia Zanitra?" Her deep velvety voice challenged them.

"Who else, sister, but Imandoff Silverhair." The sorcerer slid down from Sun Dancer and held out his hands. "We bring with us a sick child, one who has retreated from the world inside her mind." He stood, hands outstretched, as the woman stepped closer.

"It is you!" The woman handed the lantern to a robed figure hovering behind her. "Where have you been all this time?" She threw her arms around the sorcerer, who folded her into his embrace.

"This is Takra Wind-Rider and the child." Imandoff reached up to take Dakhma from Takra's weary arms. "And Gadavar of the Green Men, and Corri Farblood."

An initiate stepped forward to take the child, disappearing through the gate with a swish of robes. Corri's legs trembled as she slid down from Mouse. Takra and Gadavar eyed the initiates now peering around the open gate with distrust.

"And this," Imandoff threw his arm once more around the tall beautiful woman and smiled at his companions, "this is my sister, the Tamia Zanitra."

I do not like this place, or these people." Takra paced back and forth across the room like a caged animal. Every line of her body expressed distrust and a desire to be gone. "All this constant praying and chanting rakes my nerves. One cannot pray to the Goddess by rote at each hour. This place reminds me too much of Leshy."

Corri splashed cold water from the basin on her face as she listened to the tenseness in Takra's voice. "I have no intention of being put off any longer." She dried herself on the coarse towel, then threw it on the floor in anger. "I think it is time we created some unpleasantness in Sadko." She grinned at the answering glow of agreement on the warrior woman's face. "I want to talk to Imandoff and this sister of his."

"I am with you on that. And if any are foolish enough to try to imprison us, as they did you in Leshy, I say we fight our way out." Takra's pale brows pulled down and her mouth set, while one hand caressed the hilt of the long sword at her side.

Corri gathered up the bag with the Soothsayer's crystal ball and motioned toward the door. "I sense a guard at the door," she said softly. "Shall we teach him about the Tuonela?"

Takra grinned, yanked open the door, and stood face to face with a white-robed initiate. A tall woman, Takra looked slightly down upon the man. He froze, his mouth stammering silent words. She shoved him to one side and strode out into the stone-paved hall, Corri behind her.

"You must not wander about!" the initiate said, grabbing at Corri's arm.

She whirled, her belt dagger in hand, bringing the knife quickly up under his chin. "If you like the sight of blood, especially yours, I can oblige you."

The initiate jerked back his hand as if it had been burned. "There is no need for threats. By our law, the uninitiated are forbidden to leave their rooms without escort." The man retreated as Takra drew her sword.

"We spit on your law," the Tuonela woman growled. "We demand to see Imandoff and Zanitra now."

"But the law . . ." The man flinched at Corri's hard stare.

"I tasted such laws before." Corri's voice was low and threatening. "And I have no intention of being trapped by them again. Take us to Imandoff and Zanitra now, or we will go through every room in this place until we find those we seek." She stalked the man, dagger pointed at his heart.

"They are in the healing center," the man stammered as he cautiously edged around the women. "I will take you. But our law says weapons are forbidden here."

"I told you we spit on your law." Takra emphasized her words with a whack on the man's leg with the flat of her sword as he scuttled past.

The initiate led them through the building and out into the open courtyard, his crab-like walk allowing him to keep an eye on them. By the time they entered the separate healing building, Corri was hard pressed to keep a straight face at the man's nervous contortions.

The healing center was a long, narrow building near the rear wall of the enclosure of Sadko, its gray stone face fronted by a roofed and columned porch running the full length. Inside, long narrow windows set high in the walls dimly lighted the main room of the healing center. Below these windows were curtained alcoves, their stone walls jutting out into the room and rising higher than the reach of a tall man. The draperies of most of them were open, showing empty beds. A few of the curtains were drawn shut, containing, Corri guessed, the sick who came here for healing.

As Corri and Takra hesitated just inside the door, Imandoff opened one of the curtained alcoves. His brows lifted in surprise, then he beckoned to them. The initiate scuttled past and into the alcove Imandoff had just left.

"Dakhma is better," the sorcerer said softly, "but she still needs much healing." The filtered sunlight cast silver glints in his black hair and beard as he glanced back at the closed curtains. "Zanitra cares for her, and she is the best healer among all the Peoples."

"Where is the Green Man?" Takra's narrowed eyes raked the long room.

Imandoff shrugged. "About somewhere."

"Can I see Dakhma?" Corri held up the leather bag. "I made a promise to the Soothsayer about his mother's crystal. It is to be hers."

Imandoff nodded and lifted the curtain while they went inside the little cubicle. Zanitra sat on a plain stool beside the small form on the narrow bed, holding the sleeping child's hand. Her black hair was twisted into a tidy bun low on the back of her head, but her robe was creased from sleep. The initiate scowled from the corner where he sheltered behind the healer.

"She cried out for you during the night," Zanitra said, her dark brown eyes intent on Corri. "The hour was late and the child too excited, so I thought it best to wait. Now she is sleeping under the influence of a healing draught. My brother has told me some of what happened. I myself will take her to the Temple as soon as she is well enough to travel."

"We come for another reason." Takra fingered her sword hilt as her amber eyes stared at the initiate.

"You know about the Soothsayer?" Zanitra nodded at Corri's question. "He entrusted this crystal to me. It is now Dakhma's, according to his wishes." She held out the leather bag.

Zanitra reached into the bag and took the crystal in her long-fingered hands, turning it round and round. "A thing of great price. A crystal this flawless is rare. I will take it to the Temple along with the child. When her training reaches the proper stage, the Oracle will see that she receives it." Zanitra slid it back into the bag, hesitated, then drew out the owl stone circlet. "Surely this is not for the child!"

"I thought it was gone forever." Corri gave a sigh of relief.

"That belongs to Corri, this one who is called the Dream Warrior." Imandoff laid his hand on Corri's shoulder.

"The Soothsayer had Dakhma steal it through her mind powers." Corri took the smooth metal in her hands, running a finger over the yellow-eyed stone. "I do not know if he forced her to use it, but I think not."

"The power of that stone would have damaged her mind beyond what I can heal." Zanitra stroked the child's cheek. "I feel within her only a desire to withdraw from the terror and sorrow she has felt, not a damaging of the mind itself."

"We wish to stay for a time, until the child is better." Imandoff folded his hands over the blue stone buckle at his slender waist. "It has been long since you and I talked, Zanitra. You have never been out of my thoughts."

"Nor you from mine. With children of one birth it is always this way." The healer smiled up at him. "I look forward to hearing of your mighty adventures. And do not tell me you have had none. Before I entered Sadko, you were always wandering about the land, seeking old knowledge and the older ruins of the Forgotten Ones."

"He has not changed," Takra said with a grin. "But he never told us he had a sister, let alone one from the same birth."

"Indeed?" Zanitra rubbed her shoulder muscles, then stood and stretched. "Stay with the child until I return," she said to the initiate as she motioned for the others to leave with her.

"It has been a busy night," Zanitra added as they stood on the columned porch. "Another party came down from the mountains before you, bringing with them a wounded woman. Healing her body presents no problem." The healer sighed. "However, healing her sharp tongue and acid thoughts is beyond my ability."

"Were there others with her?" Imandoff asked.

"Three men brought her to Sadko, but they rode on." Zanitra looked from Imandoff to the others. "This woman, she is bound up some way with the child Dakhma and the death of the Soothsayer?"

"She killed him with tujyk poison." Imandoff took his sister's hand. "Zanitra, she must not be allowed to speak with the child or be anywhere near her. This woman is a spy for Frav!"

"Is her name Malya?" Corri asked, one hand fingering her amulet on her breast.

"Yes, that is the name the men called her. She is truly a spy for Frav?" Zanitra's face paled at Imandoff's nod.

"Why not outcast her from Sadko?" Takra frowned at Zanitra's shake of her head.

"We are sworn to accept any who are sick or hurt. I cannot outcast her. I will have the child moved at once to my quarters for safety." With a swish of her white robe, Zanitra went back into the healing center.

"Takra, go with them," Corri said softly. "I will stay behind. There are things to be settled with this Malya who keeps following me everywhere I go."

"Will you be safe alone with her? She is a cowardly fighter."

"I do not think she will kill me. She seems to have something else in mind, and I plan to have it out of her."

Corri slipped behind one of the porch columns as Zanitra, followed by the initiate carrying Dakhma, came out of the healing center. The girl watched them cautiously as the healers, accompanied by Imandoff and Takra, crossed the empty courtyard. Then, her half-boots making little sound, she slipped back inside.

You should have heeded my warning the last time, Malya. Corri stood just inside the door, listening with all her senses to the silent building. *Now you will tell me what game you really play and why you keep following me.*

Chapter 8

Corri stood motionless in the dim silence, listening intently for any sounds within the long room. Slowly, she placed the owl stone circlet on her head, centering the stone. *I know you are here, Malya. Do not think to play any more games with me.*

She concentrated her thoughts on the strange stone, letting her heightened senses pour through it and out into the room about her. A spark of life-force, the faint sound of breathing and the rough feeling of whispered magic-filled malice as it settled on her skin drew the girl down the aisle until she stood before one of the close-curtained alcoves. She released her concentration on the owl stone as she whipped back the drapery and stepped inside.

Malya lay on the narrow bed, propped against the wall, her eyes closed. Corri saw the lumpy outline of bandages on the woman's left shoulder and breast through the loose robe.

"At last we meet again." The pale blue eyes snapped open, staring into Corri's blue-green ones. "And you have with you the ancient stone. Good." Malya eased her position, never taking her eyes off Corri. "I assume you want to talk."

Corri mentally shoved aside the impulse to move closer to the bed. *That magic will not work on me.* The corners of her mouth lifted in satisfaction at Malya's surprise.

"Are you not the least bit curious about me?" Malya said sweetly. "You should be, Corri Farblood, for we are half-sisters."

"This belief of yours does not interest me." Corri folded her arms across her chest. "Even if it were true, why do you keep following me? Not out of sisterly affection, that is certain." *I should have guessed there was a blood-bond,* Corri thought, *but I will never call her sister. True sisters come from the heart, not the blood.*

"You misunderstand me." Malya's soft fingers wove intricate patterns across the blanket. "I wanted to meet my sister, nothing else."

"Liar! You have dogged my trail from Kirisan into Tuone and not out of curiosity or friendship," Corri shot back angrily. "Your own words that night among the Clans make plain your lie. Do you deny that you sought to force my return to Grimmel? Come, Malya, your true self is known by the company you keep. And you spy for Frav!"

"Who are you to condemn me?" Malya's eyes burned with deep angry fires. "You who were a skilled thief for Grimmel, you who lived in luxury and know nothing of doing without, you who deny the very blood of our father that flows through your veins. How dare you criticize me!"

"I am no follower of Kayth or Frav." Corri's voice was soft and cold. "Nor do I company with any who are. As for Kayth, he never was, nor is he, any father to me. He is a mad dog, frothing at the mouth, who must be hunted down and killed for the good of Sar Akka." She took a step closer, her right fist threatening the woman in the bed. "I care not whether we share blood, as you say. You and Kayth are already counted among the dead. His fantasies of ruling Sar Akka are only drug-dreams."

"Ignorant peasant!" Malya's mouth lifted in a sneer. "Kayth will soon be too powerful for you or anyone to stop him. And I shall sit at his side and bear his dreamed-of child. If you do not submit to his demands, your broken body will be cast aside and left for the wild animals. As Kayth's consort, I will have the power to punish all who opposed me in the past and those who still do so." *And if I can steal the sedja balls from this place,* she thought, *Kayth will be even more pleased. None here know how to use the great power those crystals hold, but Kayth will force them to his use.*

"One man lies dead because he demanded that I bear him a child. If this idea has now sprung in Kayth's mind, he is more evil than I thought. And you are a besotted, mind-sick wench with a child's dreams of revenge against those who thwarted you. Beware what you desire, Malya, for you might get it, to your sorrow."

"Then you do think that Kayth will win." Malya grimaced as she moved her injured shoulder.

"No, Kayth will lose. And you will fall with him. Your plans at Leshy failed, did they not?" Corri smiled grimly. "The Tuonela Roggkin and your Kirisani henchmen left you here and rode off, did they not? You are alone, Malya, and unprotected, except perhaps for your poisoned knife with which you killed the Soothsayer."

"He was nothing." Malya dismissed the death with a slight wave of her hand. "Besides, he received what he deserved. I will bear the scars of his knife until I die. The Tuonela child would have been of use to Kayth because of her calling powers, but Ayron was nothing. It is unfortunate that he chose as he did, but his bloodline may still prove important."

"We know of his child. Both Dakhma and Ayron's son are now out of your reach, safe within the walls of the Temple of the Great Mountain." Corri shielded her thoughts from

Malya's weak probing. "The Soothsayer of the Prophecies is dead. In spite of your efforts, thus far I have won."

"Won?" Malya smiled sweetly. "You have not won, Corri. Ayron knew he was not the Soothsayer of the Prophecies. The true Soothsayer is more powerful than Ayron could ever be, even with his drugs and dreams. I know, for I have seen the real Soothsayer."

Corri shrugged. "Man or woman, it does not matter. Whoever the Soothsayer is, that person is as good as dead. I will be the Soothslayer for the Goddess when the time is right. And do not send your night-creeping minions on my trail, for my friends have declared blood oath against Roggkin and the others." *I think you babble too much, Malya, but every piece of information you reveal can work against you, so babble on.*

"Roggkin had importance before his outcasting. Now he is valuable only for his sword-arm. And Shilluk and Menec, I use them for their knowledge of all the back trails through these mountains." Malya smoothed back her dark hair that glinted red in the sunlight falling from the high window. "Perhaps it is better that you do not wish to fulfill Kayth's wishes for a child. If you had, I planned to kill you as soon as the child was born, thus ruling at Kayth's side and controlling both children. Kayth needs children who are strong enough to follow his ways."

"His ways lead straight onto the life-wheel of Between Worlds, where those who follow him will be forced to return again and again into lives of pain and misery until they repent of their past deeds." A flush rose on Corri's face as Malya laughed. "I choose to follow the strength and purity of my mother's blood. I sever all ties with you and Kayth."

"Your mother was nothing, as is mine, even though she calls herself a feya woman." Malya's good hand slipped under the blanket to draw out the poison-tipped knife. "Yes, the weaklings here did not find all my weapons. I choose my father's blood. Both your mother and mine were afraid to reach for power. I am not!"

"When the Temple warriors come for you, that will do little good." Corri pointed at the poisoned blade, then dropped her hand to the worn wire-hilt of her belt dagger. "Then it will be you wailing the loss of your freedom, not me, Malya!"

Corri whirled and pushed through the curtain into the aisle, her jaw and her face hard, while Malya's laughter echoed through the healing center. She nearly ran into a white-robed initiate who waited outside the curtained doorway.

"Out of my way, shadow-skulker." Corri stiff-armed the man to one side, her belt knife half-drawn. "Take me at once to Zanitra."

The initiate opened his mouth to speak, then thought better of it. Corri watched with an inner amusement as he turned and stamped out, every step expressing his dislike of these uninitiated ones who disrupted the quiet of Sadko. She followed him across the courtyard, her hand on her knife.

Zanitra's spartan rooms were warm with the sun coming through the open shutters. She dismissed the initiate with a wave of her hand, then beckoned Corri to sit with Imandoff and Takra. Gadavar leaned against the stone wall behind Corri's chair, his arms crossed. He gave a half-smile to Corri, then his face closed to any sign of emotion.

"The child is sleeping." Zanitra pointed through the connecting door to the bedchamber where Dakhma lay on a narrow pallet. "She improves with each hour. I shall take her to the Temple as soon as she can ride."

"You must expel Malya from Sadko," Corri said, her eyes sparking. "She is a great danger to Sadko, to Sar Akka itself. Kaballoi warriors from the Temple even now seek her. Release her into their hands!" She jerked off the owl stone circlet, sliding it through her belt.

"According to the laws of Sadko, all who come here for healing have total sanctuary." Zanitra sighed and clasped her long fingers together. "I would be willing to do this, for I have seen a little of her true self. But I do not think the other initiates will go against the laws."

"What she is saying, Corri, is that criminals who come to Sadko will not be turned over for punishment." Gadavar's mouth was set in a bitter line as he stared at Zanitra.

"You mean, the scum of Sar Akka can come to Sadko and be safe?" Takra looked from Zanitra to Imandoff.

"Unless the entire council of Sadko agrees, no one will be cast out. And such a ruling has never happened." Zanitra closed her eyes wearily. "I shall petition for a council meeting tomorrow at sunrise. But I tell you, I do not have any hopes that the answer will be what you wish."

"We will await the council's decision." Imandoff gently touched his sister's arm. "However, tonight we would have our rooms side by side in the same building."

"That will certainly lift eyebrows," Zanitra said with a smile, "but it shall be as you say."

"And keep your man away from my door," Takra growled. "Next time I catch him eavesdropping, I will tattoo him with my dagger." She patted the long knife at her side.

"Eavesdropping? Not by my orders." Zanitra frowned. "This does not bode well." She tapped her knee with one finger. "There has been talk lately that we should keep apart from any war with Frav and accept whatever comes, even if it is the rulership of Frav. If the council decision goes as I think it will, I will take the child, and any others who wish to leave, and go at once to the Temple."

They left Zanitra in deep thought, as they prepared to move their few belongings into adjoining rooms nearer to the great gates of Sadko.

Corri sat cross-legged on the floor, listening to Takra's quiet breathing of deep sleep. Outside, the bells tolled midnight. Slowly she placed the silver circlet across her brow, centering the owl stone on her forehead, stilling her thoughts and sinking down into the deep quiet of meditation. In the next room she sensed Imandoff and Gadavar, both stirring restlessly on their pallets. Fighting against the turmoil of emotions aroused by the Green Man, Corri forced herself to relax, muscle by muscle. She felt her dream-form loosen and rise free of the physical limitations of the body.

I will seek Tirkul. My heart leans toward Gadavar, yet I have this sudden urge to see Tirkul. Why is this? My heart has resolved that Tirkul can only be a friend. She felt a great uneasiness as she compared the two men, Tirkul with his parting demands but steadfast heart, and Gadavar who seemed to hold out unrestricted freedom to do what she wanted. *What will I do if Gadavar walks away?* The emotions warring within her mind threatened to slam her back into her body. *I will dream-fly to Tirkul. I can ask him about what happens at the border. And perhaps I can make him understand that there is no longer love between us, just friendship.*

With her decision made, Corri relaxed and floated free. She looked down upon Sadko, a mosaic of light and dark under the brilliant moon. For an instant, she saw a deep red flash, a thin line of power, shooting from the healing center straight toward the north. Then it was gone.

So you have ways of contacting Kayth. We shall see who wins, Malya. Corri faced the north, fastening her thoughts upon the Tuonela warrior she sought. Instantly, she sped in a blur of scenery over the mountains of Deep Rising, across the rolling grasslands of Tuone, to the border with Frav.

Tirkul? The Tuonela camp below was quiet, the guards walking their silent rounds, the horses drowsing in their rope enclosure. *He is not here,* she thought, her mind seeking among the life-forces in the camp. *He must have been sent to guard another place.*

She hung in the air, opening her mind to widen her search. The moonlight splashed over the sharp rocks and deep-shadowed trees below. Her questing mind caught a flicker of energy to the west. *Tirkul. Why is he so close to the Fire Temple?*

Her dream-body sped along the spellbound border, the black crack of the Kratula Gorge visible below. In the blink of an eye, Corri saw the natural land bridge over the Gorge and, below it, hidden among the trees and rocks, the bright spark of Tirkul's life-force. The Tuonela warrior lay sleeping, Hellstorm nearby. The great horse blew and moved restlessly as Corri dropped lower.

Tirkul, it is Corri Farblood. Give me news of the border troubles. She reached down to gently touch the warrior's forehead, but he seemed sunk in a deep, dreamless place where she could not find him. *What is happening? This is not right.*

A prickling sensation at the nape of her neck alerted all her instincts. She saw nothing, either in the physical or in the dream-world, but the feeling of being spied on continued. As she turned her concentration to the spellbound border, trying to identify the source of her unease, her senses sounded danger like the tolling of a great bell. From the priest-city of Vu-Zai, across the land bridge at the foot of the Fire Mountain, arose a column of roiling black, a cloud that flicked in and out of Corri's vision. She moved between it and the sleeping Tirkul, her inner senses fighting to learn its powers without being caught in it.

Out of the black cloud came a flash of power, a deep red tentacle the color of old blood. It flung itself through the night skies, over the spellbound border, coiling, then striking like a great snake. Corri threw up her hands, instantly calling upon the power of the owl stone on her forehead. A brilliant streak of energy shot from her hands to burst into a thousand star-bright points against the striking tentacle. It hesitated, then grew thicker as it absorbed the power used against it.

Corri launched her dream-form straight up into the air, the tentacle following. A small part of her mind was aware that Tirkul cried out in his sleep, that Hellstorm now stood guard over his master, teeth bared and eyes wild as the great horse sought the presence of a physical attacker. From the west she saw thick storm clouds gathering, rolling over the far seas toward the land.

Enough, Kayth. If you wish to do battle with me, then show yourself! Corri threw another energy ball from her hands and watched the tentacle feed upon it.

Well, daughter, I feel your surprise. Kayth's face hung in the dark air above the Fravashi Fire Temple, a magnified form coruscating with a magical energy unfamiliar to Corri. *My powers have strengthened greatly since last we faced each other. You know I speak the truth, for you have seen a little of what I now can do.*

I know your soul has blackened even more, Kayth. And I know that Minepa aids you, for I smell his stench. But my answer remains the same. I will never join you. Corri kept a tight barrier across her mind.

I no longer ask you to join me, daughter. When the time is ripe, I will take you and your powers whether you wish it or not. Kayth smiled, and the blood-red tentacle whipped closer to Corri's dream-form. She formed a mighty sword in her hand, slashing at the attacking entity. It coiled about the flaming sword, sucking off its energy until the weapon disappeared.

Frayma! Corri's mental shout echoed through the night.

No Goddess answers you, Kayth sneered. *There is only me and the deep power I wield. This time you will not escape.*

Corri dodged the whipping tentacle, an extension of Kayth's mind. As she rose higher, she became aware of the swiftly moving storm, now almost overhead.

If one kind of power will not work, perhaps another will. Instantly, she concentrated on the storm, coaxing its hidden lightning from the depths, channeling its raw potency through the owl stone on her forehead. *It may well burn through my skull this time.*

Corri cast aside the thought of danger and sent the lightning like a spear through the ancient yellow-eyed stone, straight into the tentacle. As it struck, she gathered the mighty force in her hands, throwing it as she would throw stones, directly toward Kayth. The tentacle withdrew, but the lightning ran down it, exploding the foul energy as it went. The lightning balls lit the night like first dawn as they crashed against Kayth's projected form.

It is not my dream-form you see, Corri. Kayth laughed. *My power goes far beyond your simple dream-flying into the realms of magic that you cannot understand. You cannot harm me.*

I think you lie. Corri kept her connection with the storm, but released her tight control over the lightning. *Magic is magic. Whether it is good or evil depends on the intent of the user, this much I know for certain. Without Minepa's aid you would be unable to withstand me. Therefore, Kayth, your power is not as great as you say, for what you do, you could not do alone.*

You dare to question my ability! The projection of Kayth's face wavered, flickering in and out of sight. *You are my daughter, of my blood, and when I call you will come!*

Never! I am my mother's daughter only, and nothing of you. Corri's anger burst through her control. *You have willingly taken into yourself an evil power, a power that matches the evil thoughts you had when you came to Sar Akka. Now you reek of filth!* Norya's face momentarily rose in Corri's mind. *I cast you out! I cast you out! I cast you out!*

She snatched at the lightning in the rumbling clouds overhead, directing it in eye-blinking swiftness at the priest-city beyond. It struck with devastating force, smashing into temple walls and buildings, exploding great holes in the structures. Some of the energy struck the nearby city of Vu-Murt. Residue of the energy ricocheted off them to blow rocks from the sides of the Fire Mountain.

Kayth's face snapped out of existence in the air before her, but Corri felt the powerful force of his mind reach out to smother the fires in Vu-Zai and Vu-Murt. She hung there, watching the screaming people milling about the Fravashi cities, aware when Kayth's magic calmed the fear. She waited, expecting Kayth to return to the attack, but he did not reappear.

She glanced below and saw Tirkul standing beside the nervous Hellstorm, looking in bewilderment across the border. The warrior shivered and looked about him, then shook his head.

Tirkul? Corri tried to establish communication but found the warrior's mind barred to her message. *This is strange. Never before have I been unable to reach him. Perhaps the anger at our parting broke the tie.*

Something tugged at her form. She resisted the pull, her eyes still angrily focused on the Fravashi temple. The weak tugging receded to the back of her thoughts.

"I cannot wake her!" Spoken words whispered faintly at the edges of her concentration.

Corri felt Kayth speaking magical words, heard them as a distant murmur, saw the magic begin to take shape again. She braced herself, reaching out to draw the storm clouds closer.

I must stop him, she thought. *He has grown in power. I am the only one who can stand against him now. And if he continues to grow in strength, at some future time my will and power may be no barrier to him.* Corri prepared to meet Kayth again, as his face began to shimmer above the city of Vu-Zai.

"Awake!" Imandoff's deep voice sliced through her concentration. "By the name of the Goddess, I command you to awake!"

No! Corri cried as she felt the owl stone jerked from her forehead. She felt her dream-form whipped back across the Tuonela grasslands to the Mystery School of Sadko. She fought against the pull, struggling to return to the battle with Kayth, but she was unable to resist the power that sucked her back to the small stone-walled room.

"Where did you go?" Imandoff bent over her, the circlet in his long-fingered hand. "And, more importantly, what did you do?"

"The headband, it is burned nearly through!" Takra knelt beside her. She gently pulled off the leather band, holding it before Corri's eyes; the girl saw the leather blackened and thin. "And your forehead is red where the stone lay."

"Only a slight burn." Imandoff helped Corri to her feet.

"Sadko is buzzing like a hive at honey-gathering time."

Gadavar stood in the doorway, sword in hand. "Whatever you did, Corri, it rebounded on the healing center. These mum-tongued initiates are even now putting out fires there."

"Too bad it did not get to Malya." Takra's eyes narrowed. "That one is dangerous."

"It nearly did." Gadavar smiled, his eyes never leaving the hall outside. "The curtains around her bed burst into flames. She came out spitting like a scorched cat."

"Nearly is not close enough." Takra tossed the burned headband aside. "Do you think we will need to fight our way out of here, sorcerer?"

"The initiates of Sadko have no training in weapons," Imandoff answered. "But this night's happenings will certainly not help our petition with the council."

"Which will meet soon," Gadavar answered. "Dawn is only an hour away." Worry-lines crinkled in the corners of his eyes as he glanced at Corri.

"What I did was necessary." Corri sat on the narrow bed, head in hands. "Somehow Kayth's powers have grown. I cannot understand it, for I see him when I dream-fly, yet he claims he is beyond such a method of travel. And Malya in some way still communicates with him. Tonight I saw the energy of that communication come from the healing center and go toward Frav."

"We do not know what knowledge the Fravashi have." Imandoff stroked his beard as he thought. "The original books of Jinniyah, the great Books of Darkness, were supposed to have been destroyed. Those were the terms agreed upon at the close of the last war with Frav. But now I wonder."

"What concerns us now, sorcerer, is whether or not we can convince the council of Sadko to release Malya to the Kaballoi from the Temple. And I, for one, do not think they will." Gadavar motioned with his hand. "Someone comes," he whispered.

"Gather your belongings and take them with you," Imandoff ordered. "For my instincts tell me that we will not be
allowed to return to these rooms. They will want us gone as
soon as the council is over."

The messenger from the council hesitated at the door, wary
eyes on Gadavar's sword. "The council of Sadko awaits." He
led them down the hall, shoulders hunched against the danger he believed to walk at his back.

*Y*ou must not allow her to stay here." Corri clenched
her teeth in frustration. "She will bring evil down upon you,
the evil of Frav and all the scum who choose to follow Kayth
and Minepa."

"The answer is still no." The old man frowned up at Corri
and her friends from his seat along the far side of the circle of
initiates. "This woman Malya has caused us no trouble. We
cannot say the same for you."

Zanitra rose from her seat to stand beside Imandoff. "Tamia
and Taymin, we must face the truth. We dare not turn our
backs to the danger that arises from those who spy for Frav.
We must stand with the Peoples."

"We have heard these words from you before." The old
man's mouth twisted as if he tasted something bitter. "It is the
decision of the council to take no sides. By remaining passive
we can work to reform the Fravashi, should they invade our
land. We can help them to return to the worship of the Goddess. By our example they will turn from their evil ways to the
light."

"How long do you think the Fravashi priests will allow you
to live, Taymin?" Imandoff asked quietly. "For centuries,
beyond the coming to this land by the Peoples, the Fravashi
used the sword to force people to worship their god. Those in
control have no use for the Goddess. And you know they do

not allow anyone who shows signs of power to live outside their exclusive priesthood."

"The only power we have here at Sadko is that of healing," snapped the old man. "These other so-called powers are only illusions, lies concocted by men and women for personal gain. We at Sadko have the only true power!"

Most of the council nodded in agreement, but Corri saw several of the initiates look at each other, shaking their heads in disagreement.

"So you believe, old man, that the fire this morning was caused by an 'illusion.' Explain that to me." Takra rested her hand on her sword hilt as she kept a wary eye on the circle of initiates.

"Do not split philosophical hairs with me, Tuonela!" A fleck of foam dropped to the old man's chin in his anger. "The fire was the logical result of lightning."

"There are no storms in the sky." Gadavar rested his hands over his belt buckle, feet apart, eyes alert. "And there is no mark of lightning on the stones of the healing center."

"Enough!" The old man rose and shook his fist at the group in the center of the circle. "It is the decision of this council that you nevermore be allowed within the walls of Sadko. Leave at once!"

"There was no council vote." Zanitra stepped forward, looking around the circle at the initiates. "Each initiate of Sadko has an equal voice in the council. That is the law. I did not vote on such a thing."

"It saddens me, Tamia Zanitra, that you do not stand firm with us," said a younger woman. "We knew you would not, so we did not call you to the meeting last night when we changed the law."

"Changed the law? How?" Zanitra's brows came down in anger.

"We chose a second and higher council composed only of third degree Tamia and Taymin who will determine all the policy for Sadko from here on." The woman indicated herself, the old man, and two others who sat close by. "You are not included."

"You hypocrites!" Corri spat. "You mouth words about goodness and neutrality, when what you really mean is you do not want to become involved in anything that might threaten the power you have amassed for yourselves here. How dare you pass judgment on me or my friends? You narrow-minded walkers of the dark path, you have shown your true selves by this action. The Goddess will surely turn Her face from you!"

"Be gone!" The old man shook his fist at them again.

"What will you do, kill us?" one of the initiates asked, a self-righteous smile on her face.

"I would not dirty my sword." Takra half-drew the shining weapon, then slammed it back into the sheath with an ugly snick that made several of the initiates jump. "But do not think to stop us from taking the child, or I surely will kill any who stand in my way."

"We will go." Zanitra's soft voice was edged with anger. "I will take the child to the Temple at Kystan. Any who wish to ride with me, gather your belongings at once."

Nine men and women rose from their places in the circle and hurried out the door. Zanitra turned without another glance at her fellow initiates to follow the defectors. Imandoff, Gadavar, and Takra backed out last, their hands near their weapons.

One initiate tried to keep them from taking their horses but turned and ran when Takra advanced, sword in hand. Zanitra sat, straight-backed, on her horse, her eyes watching every movement of the initiates who remained behind. Two leather saddlebags bulged under a hastily folded blanket across her horse's rump, bags which Imandoff and Zanitra had taken great pains to smuggle out unseen. Sunk in a drowsy sleep, Dakhma sat before Zanitra, safe in the shelter of her arms. The little band quickly loaded the donkeys with the initiate's packs, mounted and rode through the great gates of Sadko two hours after dawn.

Imandoff and Takra led the plodding line of refugees up the trail, passing from the rocky peaks of the Barren Mountains into the forested slopes of Deep Rising; not one of the initiates looked back at Sadko. Gadavar and Corri rode at the rear of the line, eyes and ears alert, until they were well up among the resin-scented trees.

"What will you do now?" Gadavar asked as they rode on. "Zanitra will take the child to the Temple, along with the people who came with her. There is no need for you to return there."

"I do not know." Corri brushed a curl off the reddened scar on her forehead. "I will not return to the Clans. There is trouble brewing on the grasslands as well as in Sadko. Yet it is not time to go to the border for the war."

"Come with me then." Gadavar looked straight ahead, his tanned face troubled. "You will be safe in the forests of Deep Rising among the Green Men until you are needed at the border."

I want to know Gadavar better, much better, Corri thought as her eyes met those of the Green Man. When he reached out to touch her hand, both their eyes went wide at the sexual electricity they felt. *He does feel it! But will it last, or is it merely a fleeting thing that will die if I come to his bed?* The trail forced their hands to part.

Does love come in different forms? Corri bit her lip as old memories came flooding back. *Tirkul said he loved me, yet when I would not bend to his will, he became angry. I think his breaking heart oath was a kind of punishment. Will you change, Gadavar, if I choose not to follow your wishes? I know the kind of love Tirkul feels, even though I do not like it, but what is your idea of love, Green Man? The love Imandoff and Takra seem to share is what I seek.*

"I will think on it," she finally answered. "The Goddess knows I have nowhere to call home."

Gadavar turned to her, his smile clear in the shadows of the trees. "I love you, Corri. I will always love you. My home shall always be your home. Remember that, wherever you must go."

Oh Goddess, she thought. *How can I tell him what I feel when this fear of being trapped still gnaws at me? I can offer him so little. How can Gadavar choose to love me? Why is it so difficult for me to see the way I must go?*

As the line of travelers plodded to a stop, Gadavar shielded his eyes with one hand to stare ahead. "Green Men! Something is afoot that they should send a band to meet us. Wait while I talk with them."

He edged Nuisance past the other horses till he came to the front of the line, where Imandoff and Zanitra were in deep conversation with four men dressed much like Gadavar and mounted on horses who blended into the forest shadows. Zanitra waved to her fellow initiates, then turned her horse to follow three of the Green Men down the trail.

Corri urged Mouse forward until she sat beside her friends and the remaining Green Man. "What has happened?" she asked the sorcerer.

"Two of the Kaballoi are waiting just beyond to escort Zanitra and the child to the Temple," Imandoff answered. "Two others have gone by another trail to Sadko to try to get Malya."

"A task they will not complete." Gadavar shook his head, his long leaf-brown hair whispering across his shoulders. "That den of sharrock will not let them in the gates."

"I bear other messages for you, Imandoff Silverhair." The strange Green Man drew out a small rolled parchment, handing it to the tall sorcerer. "This is from the High Clua at Leshy. The other message is from the feya woman Uzza at Springwell. She wants to speak with you as soon as possible."

"Do you know why?" Imandoff asked, but the man shook his head. Imandoff unrolled the parchment, quickly read it, then tucked it into his belt. "The High Clua wishes to speak with us when we pass that way, but it is not a matter of urgency. I think we should first turn aside and see Uzza."

"The feya women seldom involve themselves with outsiders," Gadavar said, rubbing his chin. "Any news from the Fravashi border?" He turned to the other Green Man.

"News comes that the border clashes are more frequent, that it has become difficult to keep out every little band of Volikvis and their soldiers. The Green Men held council three nights ago. We feel the time of the great war draws nearer. When it comes, the Green Men will guard the mountains, even go into the valleys if necessary, to protect the Peoples against those who favor Frav."

"A wise choice." Takra looked up the forested slopes around them. "If any Fravashi-loving bands get in these mountains, they can go into hiding. From here they can strike at the valley settlements, quickly and easily. It will be bloody warfare if any get a foothold here."

"Send word to the High Clua that you found us and we go first to Springwell." Imandoff pulled at his beard. "Do you ride with us, Gadavar?"

"I ride with you until you leave the mountains," Gadavar replied. He raised a hand in salute as the other Green Man nodded, then turned his horse back up the trail. "I, too, am curious about Uzza's message."

"Uzza is Malya's mother. I knew her and Cassyr well." The sorcerer tapped his fingers against the saddle as he stared into the distance. "Perhaps she has had a foretelling vision. We cannot afford to pass by any information that may aid us in the coming days." He turned to smile at the others. "Those at Sadko are in for an unpleasant surprise soon. It will not take long for them to realize that they no longer possess the sacred sejda. Zanitra smuggled them out with her."

"She took the sejda?" Gadavar threw back his head in a laugh. "Sadko must be buzzing like an overturned hive of angry bees by now."

"What are sejda?" Takra looked from Gadavar to Imandoff. "The sejda are four perfect balls of crystal, each as big as two of my fists." Imandoff held up his clenched hand. "They are sacred stones of great power that were in Sadko when the initiates took over the ancient buildings of the Forgotten Ones. Zanitra takes them to the Temple in Kystan. My sister feared their power would be misused by those who now rule the Mystery School."

"But no one has ever discovered what their power is or how to use them." Gadavar wrinkled his brow in thought.

"Zanitra has discovered a little of their power, enough to fear their falling into Fravashi hands." Imandoff urged Sun Dancer on behind Gadavar's mount. "When Malya spoke of the sejda, I sensed her fear."

"Their existence has been known only to the initiates!" Gadavar's tanned hands tightened on the reins as he turned in the saddle to look at the sorcerer. "I know only because you yourself told the Green Men so they would understand why Sadko needed watchfulness and protection. How did Malya know of the sejda?"

Imandoff shook his head. "No initiate or Green Man told her, of that I am certain."

Kayth must have learned of the sejda and spoke of them to Malya! Corri stared unseeing at Mouse's neck as she thought. *But Malya would only fear them if Kayth did, and Kayth would only fear what he knows would cause him harm. What role will the sejda play in this battle?* She sighed. *Zanitra must learn, for no one else has the understanding.*

Takra dropped back to ride beside Corri as they moved on, Gadavar leading the way into a fork of the trail, which wound away from the path toward Kystan.

"You are troubled, sister-friend." She leaned toward Corri, her long pale braids swinging. "Was it so terrible last night? You did light a fire under Malya." She grinned, the blue tattoo on her cheek pulling at the thin scar that ran through it.

"There is another thing that troubles me." Corri looked into the amber eyes and blushed. "Takra, what if two men say they love you at the same time? How can you know which one to choose? And how do you know what true love is?"

"So, that is it." The warrior woman's face was solemn. "If the two men are willing to share, I cannot see why one should have to choose. Even though he is brother-kin to me, Tirkul is too controlling. On the other hand, Gadavar is a fascinating man, much like a Tuonela warrior in his ways. But who am I to give advice? I have only met one man in my life who is willing to give me my freedom."

Freedom. Corri rode down the tree-swept path in deep thought. *That is the key. I will not give up my freedom to be what I am, to come and go as I must. Tirkul promised me freedom once and then took back his promise. Will Gadavar do the same?* She sighed and urged Mouse on. *I want a promise on that, yet I fear to speak such words to him. Could I believe the words if they were spoken?*

She thought of Grimmel and his golden chains, the deceptive words that lulled her into a false sense of being free. Then her mind jumped back to the news of the border clashes, the inevitable war hanging black on the horizon.

The future is uncertain. How can I ask for a promise when I can promise nothing in return, when I know not if there is even a future for me? And I do not think I could believe in a promise if it were given. Her heart leaped as her eyes lifted to Gadavar's broad back. *Imandoff and Takra feel this uncertainty, even though they love each other, so they share love without thoughts of tomorrow. Perhaps I should take what companionship I can now, for there may be no future.*

Corri felt a kind of peace settle over her confused and churning mind. *When this journey began, I fought against the Lady's setting me this task. Now I go forward willingly to meet whatever the future holds. All the hardships have only strengthened me. If there is to be love with Gadavar, I trust Her to open the door at the right time and place.* Corri felt the weight of her purpose as the Dream Warrior settle in hard folds about her soul as if she donned armor. *Even though I may be afraid, Lady, I accept my place as Your Dream Warrior. Just be with me in the great battle to come.*

Chapter 9

Imandoff turned Sun Dancer off the main trail to Springwell onto a little-used path that led down into a narrow valley. This hidden dip in the mountains ran back into the higher ranges of the Barren Mountains between Asur and Kirisan.

"Why does the sorcerer go into that place?" Gadavar asked, his eyes alert to the forested slopes around them.

"Whatever lies this way makes my skin crawl." Takra shivered, one hand moving restlessly across her sword hilt. "Did Imandoff say this was an ancient burial place?"

Corri shivered. "I can feel the power coming from the very ground." Corri looked at the Green Man, who nodded. "Not like the Valley of Whispers. That is ancient power of the Forgotten Ones. But this, I do not understand."

"Only the feya women will come here. Others shun this place, most not understanding why. Perhaps those who buried the Forgotten Ones at the rear of the valley cast a warding spell. But there are others buried here from the last war with

167

Frav." Gadavar's eyes never stopped their piercing scan of the surroundings. "The mountain people say that to open any of these burial mounds is to court death."

"Imandoff told us of one who robbed a grave here and paid the price." Takra jumped as Lightfoot's hoof sent a stone rattling down the trail.

The bare finger of valley opened before them, not a single tree from the steep forested slopes intruding onto the valley floor. Tall mounds carpeted with green grass stretched from one end to the other; meandering trails, dotted with the white and blue of spring flowers, wandered off between and around the mounds. The only sounds were the jingle of horse bridles and the echoing clatter of shod hooves as they dislodged small stones from the narrow path.

"The old man said that Ayron's mother is buried in this place," Corri said. "Perhaps he thinks to find the feya woman Uzza here."

Mouse went single-file behind Lightfoot among the mounds, which were higher than a rider. Imandoff rode ahead, the bronze-capped staff now in his right hand, while behind came Gadavar, his eyes never still.

Imandoff reined in Sun Dancer and slid down to stand beside a low hump covered with grass and wild flowers. He dropped the reins to trail on the ground while he bent to look at the charcoal remnants of a fire.

The others dismounted, Takra and Corri moving to stand beside the sorcerer, while Gadavar kept watch on the back trail.

"This is where he brought the child," Imandoff said softly. "Wermod leaves." He stirred at a black mass near the charcoal with the end of his staff. "A charlatan's method of working with what little power he has." He ground the blackened leaves with his boot heel.

"Why are we here, old man?" Corri's unease grew the longer they were in this death valley. "I see no feya woman or any house."

"Curiosity." Imandoff smiled and shaded his eyes against the late afternoon sun as he looked at the mountain slopes to the western end of the silent dale. "Most of these graves date from the last war with Frav, when people died by the hundreds, families and villages all at once. This is not the only burial place; there are mounds at the far edges of other Kirisani lands as well. I believe the Volikvi priests discovered some way to loose a plague upon the Peoples during that battle, although, according to rumors, they suffered as much as we did. No one could persuade me to dig into any of these graves."

"But the mounds of the Forgotten Ones tempt you." Gadavar's face was grim. "Beware, Imandoff, for we do not know why the Forgotten Ones buried these few of their people here. Perhaps they also died of some disease. Thus far, these are the only burial mounds of the Forgotten Ones we have found."

"Perhaps. There is danger here, I know, yet hidden knowledge also." Imandoff reluctantly mounted Sun Dancer and led the travelers back up the trail out of the death valley.

One waits ahead," Gadavar murmured as he rode close beside Corri. "Up ahead, under the deep shadows of the fir at the trail bending."

Corri's sharp eyes barely could distinguish the woman's silhouette from the darkened patterns under the swooping branches of the evergreen. Even though she knew a person waited there, she still was startled when the old woman stepped from under the scented branches into the dying sunlight. The feya woman wore trousers bloused into the tops of her calf-high boots; from her leather belt hung a dagger and a woven pouch, its design and texture matching the larger strapped bag hanging across the woman's shoulder.

"Greetings, Imandoff." The feya woman raised one hand in greeting, the other gripping a tall staff. "It has been long since we last met."

"May the Goddess smile upon you, Uzza." The sorcerer solemnly raised his hand, then smiled. "We came as soon as the Green Men brought your message."

Corri suddenly shivered and ducked, then glanced skyward. Takra's dagger was out as she turned in the saddle, her amber eyes narrowed against their back-trail. Gadavar nervously turned his head from side to side, searching the forested slopes around them, while Imandoff and Uzza both instantly stared upward at the sky, empty of all except a few tattered red and orange clouds.

"What was that?" Corri's voice was low, filled with tenseness.

"What did you feel?" Gadavar looked at her, a frown drawing down his brows.

"A coldness, as if a great shadow passed overhead." She shivered again. "But nothing was there."

"I sensed a presence, like a giant bird of prey." The Green Man rested a hand on his dagger hilt.

"Quickly! We must get under cover at once." Uzza pointed down a narrow side-trail that led back among the thick trees, then hurried before them.

Like the house of Thalassa, the feya woman of Tree-Home, Uzza's cabin was built of logs alongside a bubbling creek, deep in a grove of meppe, pine, and fir trees. After caring for the horses, the travelers sat before the low-burning fire while Uzza dished up the ever-present mountain stew, rich with chunks of venison and wild tubers.

Imandoff sat, his hands cradled around the bowl, his gray eyes staring at the red coals in the fireplace. "I do not know what stalked us back there, but it was an evil presence, that I do know."

"I felt a coldness, then something like a huge shadow pass over me," Corri said, hunching her shoulders as if the shadowy being still menaced.

"I thought to see some giant bird of prey swooping down upon us." Gadavar looked at Takra. "What did you feel, Tuonela?"

"Great danger, as when you turn to find someone with a knife at your back." The warrior woman shook her head, bewildered, her pale braids swinging. "I do not understand. Always that sense of danger has proved true. But I saw nothing."

"You looked for something in this world," the feya woman said. Her yellow-brown eyes flicked across each person gathered at her hearth. "It was dangerous, Tuonela, in that you are right. But I think it is not of this world." She brushed her long braids from her face with a tanned hand.

"A shadow-seeker?" The flickering fire sparkled on the silver threads in Imandoff's black hair and beard as he stared at Uzza. "That is beyond the powers of anyone I know, even those of the Mystery Schools. There are stories told from before the Great Journeying of Fravashi priests who could do this thing, but we have always believed that knowledge to be lost."

Uzza stared down at her brown hands that lay folded together across her knees. "Then it has been rediscovered, not by weak Fravashi priests who follow the bidding of Minepa, but by one strong enough to harness this Otherworld power and command it without being swallowed up." She raised her lined face to meet Imandoff's eyes. "It would take one who delights in walking with darkness, one who has no fear of the shadow-self."

"Kayth." Corri's murmured word shattered the silence. Her companions turned to stare at her with intent eyes.

I cannot tell them how I know, that I have been many times within Minepa's den and heard both him and Kayth speak of these things.

"I cannot tell you just how I know, but I do. Kayth seeks for this kind of power," she continued, turning her spoon round and round nervously. "He desires to become Jinniyah and works even now to translate the Books of Darkness."

"Just as I thought, the Books were not destroyed. Kayth will not hesitate to use such knowledge to gain control over Sar Akka." Imandoff watched the girl, his eyes narrowed as he thought.

"Kayth Farblood, this is the Kayth of whom you speak?" Uzza sat bolt upright, the lines at the corners of her mouth expressing dislike. "How do you know of him, girl?" she demanded.

Corri looked up at Imandoff, pleading for his help with her eyes.

"He is Corri's father," Imandoff answered.

"Kayth may have got me on my mother Ryanna, but he is no father to me!" Corri said, cheeks flushed with anger. "I have severed all blood ties, taking only those of my mother. This I told Malya at Sadko."

"Kayth Farblood and now Malya." The feya woman carefully stirred the coals before laying on fresh wood. "What else should I know, Imandoff Silverhair?"

"That Corri is vitally important to the outcome of the future battle with Frav," he answered.

"Corri is the prophesied Dream Warrior." Takra set aside her empty bowl and leaned back in her chair. "That there is blood bond between us. That she nearly burned Malya out of Sadko when that Fravashi spy took refuge there." The Tuonela hooked her thumbs in her sword belt, her amber eyes daring the feya woman to contradict her. "She battled with Kayth once before and beat him."

"Malya was in these mountains, at Sadko?" Uzza frowned. "I warned her to stay clear of here. I will not have her stirring trouble among the mountain people. Ever since Kayth came to see her, she has followed after him like a female dog in heat." She shook her head, her gray-streaked braids sliding down her thin shoulders. "I know my daughter well, Tuonela. I fully know the evil that breeds inside her. Like speaks to like, and when I discovered that her desires matched Kayth's, I turned her out and drove her from Springwell. It is unfortunate, Corri Farblood, that you did not succeed in getting her removed from Sadko."

"Why did you send for me?" Imandoff settled back in his chair, clay pipe in hand. "I have never known a feya woman to act without purpose." He tamped in a smoke-leaf and lit the pipe with a snap of his fingers.

"I received a message from one dead and buried," Uzza answered. "I wanted to ask if you knew of the Dream Warrior. Instead you bring her with you."

Imandoff blew a smoke ring toward the ceiling. "Would the message be from the mother of Ayron, also called the Soothsayer?"

"It is. Cassyr told me her son is now dead. She had rested easy within her grave mound until Ayron used the child to call out her crystal." Uzza rose to fetch mugs and an earthenware bottle of dewberry wine. "Now she comes to me, night after night, with a message for this girl." She passed the mugs and bottle around.

"Why me? I did not know her," Corri protested.

"I think I see the pattern." Gadavar poured wine into his and Corri's mugs. "You and Malya are both children of Kayth. Ayron was the son of another not of Sar Akka. Were there others born to these strangers, others of whom we know nothing?"

"I know only of the three children," Uzza answered. "Both Ryanna and Cassyr are dead. I have no intention of dying soon." She tipped up her mug and drained it. "All three children were born here in Springwell, and all three women knew each other."

"Will you let Cassyr speak?" Imandoff's words brought surprised glances from his companions. "If she speaks to the Dream Warrior, will that allow her spirit to rest?"

"Yes. I will do the trance an hour before dawn, the time she usually comes to me." Uzza set down her mug. "It would be wise for you to stay close to my cabin, or sleep within. The mountain villagers have grown wary of outsiders. Troubles at the border make them suspicious of strangers. Two villages have stoned outsiders from their lands."

Gadavar spread out his blankets on the floor near the door, while Corri chose a narrow bed-shelf under one of the unshuttered windows. Outside she heard the murmuring voices of Imandoff and Takra as they bedded down close to the tethered horses.

"This shadow-seeker, can it harm me?" Corri asked the feya woman.

"The stories say it cannot harm you physically, child, only influence your decisions or plague you with bad luck." Uzza stood looking down at the girl, her face sharply contrasted with the dying firelight and deep shadows. "But how can I know that is true? For years beyond counting, no one has had the knowledge to call up a shadow-seeker." She hesitated, then went on. "Your mother's people live in Deep Rising, in a place called Rising Fort. I only knew Ryanna after she was left here by Kayth, but she was mountain born. My own hands brought you into this life."

Corri shyly touched the old woman's hair where it lay against her cheek. "I wish I could remember her."

"Kayth stole you off my doorstep when you were three," Uzza said. "If I had been more watchful, you would never have left Springwell. Where did he take you?"

"To Grimmel, Ayron's father, in Hadliden. Grimmel is now dead," Corri added.

Uzza sighed and shook her head. "Sleep well, child. In the morning you will hear Cassyr's message with your own ears. I do not know if it bespeaks good or ill, but look to the sorcerer for guidance. He will not lead you astray."

The old feya woman sat on her square of brightly woven carpet, long gray-streaked hair hanging loose about her wrinkled face. The hide drum throbbed a bone-jarring rhythm under Takra's hand as the old woman swayed her way into a trance. Soon she quieted, sitting very still with her head dropped upon her breast. Takra's hands fell on the drum-head in a final blow, then lay silent. Uzza took a deep breath, and on the second breath sat upright with open eyes.

"Imandoff Silverhair, where is the Dream Warrior?" The voice was totally different from Uzza's, that of a soft-speaking woman with a slight lisp.

"She is here, Cassyr." The sorcerer touched Corri's rigid arm.

The open eyes turned to look at her. "Yes, I can see now. One who is like him in appearance but whose heart is clean. Beware the Soothsayer, Dream Warrior! And beware of one close to you whose mind is captured, but whose heart rebels."

Corri clenched her fists. "The Soothsayer is dead!" she whispered. Gadavar laid a comforting hand on her arm, his lean face grave.

"Not so," came the lisping reply. "There is another. My son perversely took the name from the Prophecies, but he was never the true Soothsayer. When you meet him, and you will, burn him at the crown as the Prophecies say."

"Who is the one close to her, the one of whom you give warnings?" Imandoff leaned forward, all his attention on the feya woman.

"One close to the heart, one who is a traitor not by choice."

Corri watched in frightened fascination as the feya woman's face underwent subtle changes, as if another woman's face overlay that of the physical one before her.

I understand what she does, although I have never called upon the dead. Corri shivered slightly. *She takes her shadow-self from her body and allows a spirit of someone dead to speak through it.*

"Ayron did what was right at the end," the voice continued. "The child will use the crystal wisely. He did his best to protect her from Malya. He should have protected her from himself." Cassyr's words grew softer, as if they came from a great distance. "You must undergo the ordeal of the spirit, or this shadow-being will gain control over you." She paused, and Corri saw Uzza's body tremble with fatigue. "Now I can rest easy. Trust in the Goddess, Dream Warrior."

Imandoff leaped forward to catch Uzza as she sagged into his arms. "Bring water," he ordered. "And keep quiet until she regains her body." He took the cup Takra offered and held it to the feya woman's lips.

"I am back," she finally whispered. "There was great difficulty. The shadow-seeker tried to stop Cassyr from speaking. If it had been stronger, I might not have returned."

"What did she mean by the warning about one close to the heart?" Takra set the drum back on its shelf, her brow wrinkled in concern. "And what is the ordeal of the spirit?"

Corri's breath caught in her throat. *I think I know some of the interpretation,* she thought. *But I am not certain who is meant. The cold feeling in my gut says I am right. Those close to my heart are Takra, Imandoff, Tirkul, and Gadavar. One of you will be captured, but which one?* She could not bring herself to look at any of those about her.

"Only time will reveal the meaning behind the warning." Imandoff helped Uzza to her chair by the hearth. "As to the ordeal of the spirit," he paused, chewing on his lip, "that is the greatest of ordeals known to the Mystery Schools. For that we must return to Leshy."

"Leshy!" Takra whirled, her hand dropping automatically to her sword hilt. "Those mum-tongued deceivers!"

Gerda was no deceiver, but a dear friend. Corri thought back to the days she spent in Leshy, healing her broken arm and learning all she could about the dream-flying. *Surely there are others at Leshy with as good a heart and soul as Gerda.*

"Jehennette now heads Leshy," Imandoff answered. "I trust her."

"Well, I do not," Takra mumbled.

"Where will you go now?" Gadavar stretched his arms and looked out the window at the new day.

"To Leshy." Imandoff looked at Corri and smiled. "But I think Corri wishes to enter the barsark's den and stop at Rising Fort on the way."

"Why would she wish to stop at a Kirisani stronghold?" Takra moved to Corri's side, putting her hand protectively on the girl's shoulder. "If there is danger, why go there at all?"

"It is the home of my mother's people," Corri answered. "I want to know more about her. What she was like, why she left the Temple for Kayth. I have chosen her bloodline as my true being. I would discover what that makes me."

"It is wise to leave sleeping barsarks alone." Gadavar leaned against the windowsill, his leaf-brown hair catching glints of the rising sun. "We make ourselves, Corri, not our bloodlines or family."

"Still I would go," she said softly.

"Your uncle Geyti heads Rising Fort now." Uzza's voice sounded tired and strained. "And expect no welcome from Cabiria of the sharp tongue. She may be your mother's sister, but there was no love between them."

"I must go." Corri looked up at her friends. "I must see them for myself."

Imandoff nodded. "We will leave tomorrow." He turned to the Green Man. "Gadavar, can you get word to the Temple and the other Kirisani forts that preparation for invasion according to the old laws must be undertaken?"

"The word will go out. Many of the forts have fallen into disrepair. The slopes are not cleared, the walls are not manned, food is not stored." Gadavar paced a few steps across the room, then back. "Some of the fort dwellers will not welcome such news, sorcerer. It will mean extra work on top of spring planting."

"If the order comes from the Temple, they had best obey." Imandoff's face was grim. "Tell the Oracle to send out the Kaballoi to see that the laws are carried out."

Gadavar nodded approval. "I will ride out now."

Corri followed the Green Man to the horses, where he saddled Nuisance.

"Take care, Gadavar. I do not know when or if I will see you again." Corri stood close beside the tall man, catching the scent of the sweetgrass and meadow-leaf he had used to bathe with that morning.

"I am sorry I must break my promise to ride with you through the mountains. Fate decrees I now take a different path." He sighed, stroking one hand down her hair. "Do not forget. I will know if you need me, and I will come. You need never fear that I will try to cage you with love and false promises, Corri. Such deeds would break your spirit." He pulled her into his arms, his kiss making her breathless and tingling. "Trust in the Goddess, Corri."

He swung himself astride Nuisance and rode up the trail.

I wish our time together could have been longer, Corri thought as she wiped at her tear-blurred eyes. *Perhaps your love could have given me the strength to defeat Kayth.*

Defeat? You know Kayth must die, or Sar Akka will never know peace, her mind whispered.

I know. Corri saw Gadavar turn to look back just before he disappeared around a bend in the trail. *But I feel that somehow Gadavar could have given me the determination to do that.*

That is Rising Fort." Imandoff pointed with his staff.

Before them, a stone-walled fortress crouched on a bare outcropping of mountain bone, the red tiled roofs of the taller buildings visible over the forbidding walls. On the terraced slopes below the fort Corri saw the moving figures of plowmen and oxen, the dark turned soil, and the women and children who trailed behind the men as they planted seed.

"I think we will not be welcomed here." Takra shielded her eyes as she stared at the fort. "The guard has seen us and sent a man to warn your uncle."

Corri hunched her shoulders and shivered as her inner senses felt the questing search of the shadow-seeker high overhead. The feeling of being spied on persisted until they rode through the open gates of Rising Fort.

"There are ancient spells woven into the making of these walls," Imandoff murmured as they dismounted. "No seer can read the minds of those within. Rising Fort is one of the places that already stood when the Peoples came to this land." He watched the stable boys lead the horses away to be fed and watered.

"Why did the Forgotten Ones leave?" Takra's restless eyes took in every exit, every possible ambush point, as they followed a servant across the stone-paved yard and into the great hall. "There are no signs of war on the buildings and walls they left behind."

"Who knows?" Imandoff shrugged. "We have found no records to tell us. Yet the Mystery Schools, the forts, parts of Kystan, Hadliden, and other cities all stood empty when the Peoples entered this land."

The servant swiftly crossed the planked floor of the great hall, leading them down a short corridor to one of the rooms at the rear of the building. He knocked at the closed door, then swung it open to reveal a sharp-faced man, blue-green eyes intently watching their every move. "The sorcerer, Imandoff Silverhair," the servant told the man.

The landholder of Rising Fort wore slick black boots and rust-red tunic and trousers, all speaking of wealth. The man's eyes widened as they rested on Corri.

"Who is this with you, Silverhair?" The man half-rose from his chair, then sank back clutching the carved armrests.

"Do you not know, Geyti of Rising Fort?" Imandoff strode to a chair next to the man and seated himself without invitation. "Come," he said, indicating the other stools with his staff.

"It cannot be after all these years." Geyti's face paled, and he rubbed a hand across his mouth. "We thought the child was dead."

"I finally found her a year ago." Imandoff's face was closed, his mouth drawn tight. "No thanks to your family, Geyti, that the girl is alive. Your father turned Ryanna away in her hour of need, with the birth close upon her."

"She broke her vows to the Temple." Geyti pulled at his graying mustache. "I would have helped her, but my father forbade it. On his death-bed, he spoke of his regrets."

"That did not save my mother's life." Corri stared into the eyes so like her own. "Neither did it spare me a miserable childhood under the control of the Master Thief of Hadliden."

"You are so like her." Geyti shook his head. "If your hair was black, I doubt anyone could tell the two of you apart. Even your voice is the same. Seeing you, hearing you speak, is like turning back time."

"Then you acknowledge her as your niece?" Imandoff touched Geyti's trembling arm.

"Yes. There is no question she is of my family's blood. I accept her as part of this family."

"But I do not!" The sharp, petulant voice from the open doorway brought all eyes to the woman standing there. "Ryanna broke her vows, leaving the Temple to lust after a stranger. The seed of that union has no welcome here."

The woman tugged at the widow's veil that covered her hair, then crossed her thick arms. Her blue robe strained over her plump figure, indignation in every line of her short form. A wisp of her mousy-brown hair slipped from beneath the veil. Her small blue eyes were pinched with constant discontent.

"You do not rule over Rising Fort, Cabiria." Geyti's voice was sharp-edged with old disputes. "I say she is of the family of Hakran. Look at her, woman, and tell me you do not see Ryanna sitting there!"

"Perhaps Cabiria dislikes Corri because of the resemblance." Imandoff's gray eyes assessed the robed figure and grew hard. "I remember well, Cabiria, that there was no love between you and Ryanna long before she left the Temple."

"She was a willful child who always got her way." Cabiria's mouth twisted bitterly. "Look at this girl. Dressed in dirty clothes like some man out of the hills. And she bears the evil red hair of that nathling who spawned her!"

Takra rose slowly from her stool, her hand on the long dagger at her belt. "Beware, woman, for you insult my sister-friend," she growled.

"Red hair does not make evil, Cabiria. Only the heart does that." Geyti leaned forward, a frown wrinkling his forehead and deepening the lines at the corners of his eyes.

"She has returned only for Ryanna's portion of Rising Fort," Cabiria spat. "Can you not see why she has truly come here, Geyti? Are you blind to her as you were to Ryanna?"

"The greed is clearly written in your eyes, aunt, not in mine." Corri's hand brushed against the worn wire-hilt of her dagger. "I wished only to know about my mother and her family. Now I see she had reason to do as she did. What did you do, Cabiria? Talk my grandfather into forcing her to enter the Temple against her wishes so you could be rid of what you saw as competition?"

The words struck home; Cabiria winced and turned her head away.

"My sister wanted the man Ryanna loved," answered Geyti. "Wanted him enough to turn our father's mind against his youngest daughter and force her into the Temple, even though her powers were not great. Then you married Ryanna's suitor, Cabiria, and what happiness did you gain? Baltir spoke Ryanna's name on his death-bed, proving that you never held his heart."

"I will never allow this woman to live in Rising Fort." Cabiria pointed at Corri, then turned on her heel and vanished.

"I did not come here for any inheritance." Corri turned back to her uncle, who sat, head down in weariness, in his chair. "It is as I said; I came only to learn of my mother. Then I ride on with Imandoff and Takra Wind-Rider." Geyti raised his head to look at her. "There are things I must do that cannot be accomplished here."

"Corri is the prophesied Dream Warrior." Imandoff's soft words fell into the silent room like a stone into a pond. "Her path leads far from Rising Fort, Geyti. It may well be her power that stands between the Peoples and the Fravashi when the war begins."

Geyti sat, straight-backed in his chair, his head slowly moving from side to side. "This cannot be. Ryanna had only a little power, nothing that was not stronger in others at the Temple."

"This is truth," answered Takra. "The Oracle herself named her thus."

"I cannot believe . . ." Geyti still shook his head.

"That does not matter, uncle." Corri sighed and stretched her legs. "We ride to bring warning that war with Frav is not far off. Every Clan and city and village must prepare, for war will come, as surely as the north wind sweeps down upon you in winter."

"I see you keep to the old laws," Imandoff said, laying his hand on Geyti's arm. "The approach is kept clear of brush, the walls are manned, you have deep wells within the Fort. Have you stored up food for a siege if it should come?"

"She speaks the truth?" Geyti's blue-green eyes narrowed in thought when Imandoff nodded. "I shall set guards on all the outlying trails and passes within a day's ride to protect the workers in the fields and warn us of intruders. How long?"

"I do not know, except it is close." Imandoff turned his head quickly, listening to the sound of approaching footsteps hurrying down the corridor. "Perhaps as early as next year."

A servant skidded to a stop in the open doorway, panting and briefly bowing his head to Geyti. "Lord, there is news from the Temple for you and Imandoff Silverhair." The man took another deep breath, then rushed on. "Zanitra and the child are safe, but the Jabed tried to raise rebellion within the city against the priestesses. Kystan has expelled him and his followers. They are moving through Deep Rising, seeking a fortified place of refuge. Already they have attempted to take control of two other forts, only to be driven off. The renegade band is growing as the Jabed travels through the mountains, taking in those criminals who wander Deep Rising. He comes this way!"

"The trails to Kystan and Leshy are cut off?" Imandoff stood, staff in hand, black brows wrinkled in concern.

"Yes, sorcerer," replied the servant. "As are the trails down into Tuone. Others are coming from the foothills to join with the Jabed. Only the mountain paths into Asur are safe now."

"Sound the alarm and send armed men to protect the workers in the fields." Geyti stood, pulling down his tunic with a jerk. "Send riders out to all the trails leading here so that they can bring warning if this band comes toward Rising Fort."

The servant left in a pounding run up the corridor.

"By the hell-fires of Frav, what do we do now, Silverhair?" Takra paced back and forth across the room, her hand clasping her sword hilt.

"We go back into the mountains and try to find a way around." Imandoff rubbed the side of his jaw. "The High Clua at Leshy will have to wait a while longer."

"Take what you need for supplies." Geyti clasped Imandoff's hand, then turned to Corri. "My father and Cabiria destroyed or sold all they could find of Ryanna's belongings. But I secretly took these, keeping them all these years." He reached into the pouch at his belt and withdrew two rings. "By birthright they are yours."

Corri's hand trembled as she took the rings from her uncle's hand. One ring, set with a large purple eye-stone surrounded by tiny pearly krynap eyes, she saw at once was of such value that its sale would keep her for the rest of her life. She carefully laid it back in Geyti's hand.

"I will keep this one, Uncle Geyti." She slid the other silver band on the ring finger of her right hand, staring through tear-misted eyes at the three small moss stones set in the silver. "Thank you."

"Can you not stay here at Rising Fort?" Geyti's words were choked with emotion. "You have yet to meet my wife and children. You will be safe here."

Corri shook her head. "My presence would only bring death down upon you when Frav attacks, and it will. We must go. The Oracle told me I am under a geas, a compelling to defend the border against Frav. Believe me, uncle, it is a task I cannot, dare not, turn away from."

"Remember me," Geyti said as he gently touched Corri's cheek. "Some day, when peace comes again, return to Rising Fort. There will always be a home for you here."

"I will remember." Corri smiled.

Geyti followed them out into the courtyard, listening intently to the suggestions Imandoff gave about defense of the Fort. He followed them as far as the gates when they rode out. When Corri and her friends reached the first trees along the trail, the girl turned to look back. She saw Geyti's small figure silhouetted in the sunlight of the stone-paved yard, watching her through the open gates.

"It is not here." Takra looked up at the sky.

"What?" Corri roused from her thoughts with a jerk.

"The shadow-seeker. Perhaps whoever sent it has given up."

"Not likely." Imandoff looked at them over his shoulder. "To my knowledge only Kayth or Minepa has the knowledge and power to send such a thing after us, and I cannot believe that either man would give up so easily."

"Do we take the mountain trail into Asur?" Takra's amber eyes constantly scanned the forest around them for hidden danger. "I have never been in that land of woman-users. Let one of those Asuran men look down his nose at me, and he will remember me for the rest of his life," she growled.

"We have no choice but to go through Asur," Imandoff answered. "But it is not to my liking either. It is as if we are being driven in that direction." He waved his hand toward the thick bushes crowding the edges of the road. "Someone comes. Quickly, into hiding."

They had barely concealed themselves when four men rode by. Corri's sharp eyes noted the mended chain mail, the straggling hair beneath the edges of the dented helmets. *They look like the kind of men Grimmel hired, men who would cut a man's throat for a copper.* When the leader's eyes passed unseeing over their hiding place, then flicked back to the trail, Corri knew Imandoff once more protected them with spells. *If men like these freely ride abroad, the trail into Asur will be dangerous, and the cities themselves even worse.*

Corri shivered suddenly, and Takra looked upward with a jerk of her helmeted head. A faint sense of panic passed through Corri's mind, then was gone.

"The shadow-seeker is back," the warrior woman whispered.

"It moves to the north," Imandoff murmured as he urged Sun Dancer back onto the trail. "It seems that its sender does not have all the power I thought at first or he would have revealed our hiding place to those outlaws."

"You both would be safer without my company." Corri kicked Mouse into a jolting trot until she rode boot to boot with the sorcerer.

"No!" came the reply from Imandoff and Takra.

Sun Dancer neighed shrilly, his hooves stamping up little clouds of dust, as a Green Man stepped suddenly out onto the road, bow in hand.

"Imandoff Silverhair, I have a message. The woman Malya left Sadko before the Kaballoi arrived. She and her men are waiting for you in the area of the Asuran passes. The Green Men cannot protect you. There are too many troublespots about to take flame in these mountains."

"Where exactly does she wait?" Imandoff leaned down as he talked to the man.

"She is in the area between Sadko and the Metal Mines. Each of her men is stationed within sight of one of the other passes. Only the old trail to the limna forests is free of watchers."

"Then we must go farther north and cross the border into Asur through the limna forests."

"Take care, for many dangerous creatures, human and animal, now roam the higher mountains. That trail is partially blocked by old slides, with much loose rock just waiting to come down. I would not take a horse over them. A man alone might be able to get through, if he were not caught in sudden rock slides." The Green Man raised his hand in salute and slipped silently back into the trees.

"I had hoped for an easier trail." Imandoff turned to Takra and Corri, deep concern on his face. "The mountain paths in that part of the Barren Mountains have turned more difficult than I like."

"Let us go where we choose and fight our way through Malya's men." Takra adjusted her leather helmet more firmly over her fair hair.

"Perhaps we could, but I would rather slip by unseen. If they see us, Malya will only send word to Kayth." Imandoff shook his head. "From now until we meet Kayth in battle, I would rather keep him guessing about what we do and where we go."

"Surely Malya will hear of our passing whatever we do and follow us." Corri patted Mouse's neck. "There is bad blood between us now."

"There is a secret way I think she does not know." The sorcerer rubbed his cheek, his thoughts far away. "It may be more dangerous than the mountain trails themselves, but I feel we will be safe from human predators and spying eyes if we go that way." He roused from his thoughts to urge Sun Dancer on.

"Do you know of such a place?" Corri asked the Tuonela woman.

Takra shook her head. "Knowing Imandoff, it is likely a hole in the ground full of crawling things." She shuddered.

"Probably a place also inhabited by barsarks or some animal just as ferocious." Corri grimaced.

"Barsarks I can handle. The Goddess forbid there should be spiders or narrow ledges." The warrior woman set her jaw and rode on.

Chapter 10

Corri was bone-tired, her nerves stretched tight from days of constant watching and listening. She hunched her shoulders against the danger she knew rode somewhere behind them. Takra's eyes raked the tree-lined slopes of the trail for ambushers, while Imandoff rode seemingly unconcerned, as if they were not pursued by men who wished to kill them.

Their travel back past Springwell and up into the foothills of the Barren Mountains had been one of never-ending vigilance, wariness of every sound and traveler. The trail they now followed rose in twists and turns along the rocky tree-shrouded shoulders of the mountains, each switchback leading them closer to the bare wind-swept tops. They saw the last krakeberries and other small bushes at least a mile back, along with the colorful splashes of mountain wildflowers. Now there was nothing but rocks, evergreens, and the tough grasses along the trail.

Imandoff signaled a stop and slid down from Sun Dancer to look around. "We must lead the horses from here." The sorcerer pointed toward a ledge just visible through the massed trees to their right. "The hidden trail is along that ledge, around the shoulder of the mountain. You cannot see it from here. It has been a long time since I last came this way, but I recognize the area."

"First we need rest, and so do the horses," Takra said as she led Lightfoot to Imandoff's side. "Before we go that way, one of us should scout out this hidden trail. It may be closed by slides."

Corri held up her hand for silence as she looked back along the trail. Although she strained to hear any sound behind them, there was nothing except the whisper of wind through the trees. But the tightening in her stomach and the prickle between her shoulder blades gave warning enough. "Someone comes," she said softly.

"By the blessed Goddess, the scales of Natira are tipped against us!" Takra looped Lightfoot's reins over the saddle, then drew her sword. "I thought we outwitted Malya's men two days ago, before we took this last branching of the trail. Do we make a stand here, or run for it?"

"There is no better ground for a fight between here and the peaks. I do not want them following us into the hidden way, or even learning of its existence." Imandoff strode to her side, sword in hand, eyes intent on the tree-shadowed trail behind them. "I had hoped to be gone from sight before any could catch up with us."

The dull ring of a horseshoe on stone, the roll and rattle of small pebbles skittering down the bare trail sounded overloud in the waiting silence. Corri urged Mouse toward the other horses before drawing her dagger and moving cautiously out of sword-range.

Corri felt a trickle of perspiration between her shoulders as she set her back against a steep bank, covered with half-dead grass and studded with rocks. She stared at the bend in the mountain track just below them, half-hidden by the low sweeping branches of thick evergreens and the deep rocky folds of the mountains themselves.

"Imandoff Silverhair." The words, tinged with a snarling growl as if they came from the throat of a great cat, drifted soft and menacing on the still air. "We are Kaballoi from the Temple of the Great Mountain."

Imandoff frowned, tilted his head to one side as he listened to the approaching sounds of horses. "I feel danger, yet I think it is not directed at us. Show yourselves," he called.

Two armored warriors came into sight around the shoulder of tree-shadowed trail, leading their horses. Corri sucked in her breath in surprise, for the men were the tallest she had ever seen. Strange animal-shaped helmets covered their heads, the visors drawn over the upper part of each face, leaving only the chin and lower part of the cheeks bare. She moved to stand beside the Tuonela warrior woman.

"Kaballoi!" Takra whispered. She reached out to push Corri farther behind her. "Do not approach them. They have already begun their shape-shift. See their faces?"

Corri felt her skin prickle as she watched the two warriors slowly approach. She closed her eyes, then opened them again, shaking her head in bewilderment. The two figures were obviously men, but there was a strange overlay of a second vision, one not of men but of animals.

The Kaballoi who wore a helmet in the likeness of the head of a snarling Rissa held up a muscled, sword-scarred arm in greeting. The second warrior, feathered wings flaring from each side of the helmet, the wickedly curved beak of an asperel jutting over his face, repeatedly turned his head to look at their back-trail.

"Odran." The Rissa-helmed warrior jerked a thumb at his massive chest. He seemed to be fighting against the shape-shift, the deepening cat-grunt in his voice, as he struggled to give his message. "We are followed." The spiked fighting bracelets of mountain steel ringing his thick wrists gave off dull glimmers of light as his hands moved restlessly.

"Hindjall." The harsh croak of a hunting bird rasped the second man's voice. "Those we hunted now hunt you." His light green eyes glared like those of a fierce bird through the eye slits of the visor. The asperel talons decorating his leather tunic clicked together as he loosened the reins of his horse and drew his sword. "Go quickly, Silverhair. Odran and I will meet these shadow-skulkers."

Hindjall gave the coughing grunt of a hunting cat as he loosened his horse and moved to stand a sword's swing from Odran. Corri felt the hair on her neck rise as she stared at the Kaballoi warriors. She continued to see the forms of the men, yet overlaid was a wavering vision of a huge Rissa, teeth bared and tail lashing, and a giant asperel, its curved beak open and thrust forward to tear at its foes.

This cannot be, Corri thought as she moved backward, her eyes still on the tall warriors. *I should see either men or fighting animals, not both!*

"Hurry!" Imandoff grabbed her arm and thrust her toward the horses. "The Kaballoi are buying us the time we need to disappear. We must not let their efforts be for nothing."

Leading Mouse, Corri pushed her way behind the sorcerer and Sun Dancer through the thick underbrush and trees. Mouse nuzzled against her back, urging her on. The mountainside quickly shrank to a ledge wide enough for the horses, a high cliff of solid rock to the left, a deep crevasse to the right.

Corri took a deep breath and walked as close to the rock as she could. *This is no different than what I used to do, climbing over the roofs of Hadliden by moonlight,* she told herself.

She looked back over Mouse's brown rump to see Takra inching along the ledge, back to the rock and face white. Behind her ambled Lightfoot as if the horse had not a care in the world. The warrior woman swallowed hard as she forced herself to move along the mountain-clinging trail.

Goddess, I hope this is a short trail. Corri rounded another bend and almost ran into Sun Dancer. *Now where has Imandoff gone?* The trail widened, but seemed to end in a series of rock slides, broken trees, and loose soil. The sorcerer was nowhere in sight.

Mouse blew gustily into Corri's hair, then nudged her again. The girl pushed the mare's head away as she debated calling for the sorcerer. Sun Dancer pricked his ears toward the first tumble of rocks and dirt as Imandoff scrambled over the low wall, dirt-smears on his stained robe. "It is still open," he whispered. "I thought we might have to go back." He grinned as he took Sun Dancer's reins, leading the roan carefully over the lower portions of the slide.

Just as Corri began to worry about his getting over the higher parts of the slip, the sorcerer and horse skidded with a rattle of small stones and disappeared.

Corri felt her heart pound as she pushed forward. She climbed to the top of the low wall only to see Imandoff waving to her from a dark hole in the side of the cliff, a hole completely hidden from sight by the slide of dirt and rocks. She urged Mouse over the tumble of debris and sent her into the cave, then clawed her way back up the wall to wait for Takra.

The Tuonela warrior woman inched her way toward the slide, with Lightfoot nuzzling her every step of the way. Her lips moved in silent entreaty as she forced herself, step by step, to negotiate the narrow ledge.

From the dense trees far behind them came the ring of sword on sword, the scream of an enraged Rissa and the harsh hunting cry of the circling asperel.

"Hurry!" Imandoff climbed beside Corri and reached down to grab Takra's arm. He pulled the woman into the circle of his arm and dragged her over the barrier. "You are safe now, Takra," he whispered.

Corri and Imandoff, his arm still around the trembling warrior, hurried into the cave as Lightfoot slid over with a rattle of stones. The gray-speckled black horse nudged Corri's shoulders until she flattened against one damp wall to let the horse pass.

"Rest while I gather wood for torches." Imandoff's husky whisper in the darkness sounded as if he were speaking from a deep well. "We will grain the horses and eat a little ourselves before we go on."

Corri felt the sorcerer's robe brush against her and watched his silhouette, as he went cautiously back outside to gather certain limbs from the slide debris. She felt along the cave wall until she found Takra sitting, back against the rock, head on her knees.

"The worst is over," Corri said, sliding her arm across Takra's shoulders. "With torches, this tunnel will be easy to travel." *At least I hope there is nothing worse,* she thought.

"I would not have you think me a coward." Corri heard Takra swallow hard several times. "I do not like heights, but I can traverse them when necessary." The long braids rasped over the chain mail as the Tuonela warrior woman turned toward Corri. "I was trying not to spew my stomach all over the hillside."

"Are you ill?" Corri tightened her arm around Takra's shoulders. "I will tell Imandoff and we . . ."

"No!" Takra's whisper was tense. "I am not ill, and I will tell Imandoff in my own time. Promise me!" She gripped Corri's knee hard. "Promise me, sister-friend!"

Corri turned to watch the sorcerer gathering limbs near the cave entrance. "I cannot promise without knowing what is wrong."

"I am pregnant." Takra paused, then went on. "If we were on the Tuonela grasslands, I could brew a drink of tesselberry leaves to keep away the sickness and strengthen the child. But we are not on the grasslands and we must continue our journey without delay. Promise me that you will say nothing, Dream Warrior, until I decide what to do."

"I promise." Corri hugged the woman. "Will you carry the child?"

"Yes, I will keep the child." Takra swallowed hard again. "Before this war is over, the child may be all I have of Imandoff."

Takra pushed away and vomited. Imandoff hurried back at the sounds, arms full of twisted limbs.

"What is wrong?" he asked, his voice full of concern. Neither woman answered.

Imandoff dropped the limbs, took up one and snapped fire from his fingers to light it. As the ruddy glow poured through the cave, he turned to comfort Takra.

"Just walking the ledge." Corri moved between the sorcerer and Takra to get a waterbag from Mouse's saddle. "You know how she is about heights." She handed the water to Takra without a word; the Tuonela rinsed out her mouth and spat.

"She did not do this when we took to the roofs in Leshy." He looked sharply at Corri.

"Rooftops are not mountain ledges." Corri divided the limbs and bound some to the saddle of each horse. "Let her be. You know how proud the Tuonela are." She held out two limbs for Imandoff to light from his torch.

Takra pushed to her feet, handed the waterbag to Corri, and took up a torch. "We are wasting time, sorcerer. We need to get through this hidden way of yours and out into Asur, then back to either Leshy or the grasslands."

"You are truly not sick?" Imandoff moved closer to look down into Takra's amber eyes.

"I am not sick," she answered firmly, her glance never wavering. "But I shall be very upset if you are leading us into another nesting place of black jumpers."

"I cannot say what is within this tunnel." Imandoff smiled. "Perhaps a barsark dens here, or a sharrock."

"Those I can handle." Takra gathered Lightfoot's reins in her free hand. "Lead on, sorcerer. Show us this marvelous hidden way of yours."

*T*here was no way to count time within the mountain tunnel. They rested when tired and ate when hungry. Except for the sudden flurry of little bats near the entrance, they saw no animals or spiders. An almost imperceptible current of air moved through the darkened underground ways. The tunnel wound back and forth at a gentle grade, always leading upward. Twice they passed through enormous caverns with stone pillars in colored ranks, reminding Corri of the Oracle's cavern beneath the Temple of the Great Mountain. Several times they found tiny streams of pure cold water pouring from a rock, only to disappear in a short distance into a crack in the floor.

"Your stomach is better?" Corri whispered during one of their rest periods. Imandoff was gone, scouting the tunnel ahead for any cave-ins or slides.

"I had one small piece of tesselberry root." Takra touched the bulge in one cheek. "I waited as long as I could to use it, not knowing if I could find more."

"Then you knew before we left the grasslands."

Takra nodded. "But no Tuonela woman lets a coming child slow her down. That is only for the soft women of Asur and Kirisan."

"When will the child come?" Corri broke off a piece of journey bread and handed it to Takra.

"In the deep of winter." Takra spat the tesselberry root into her hand, holding it while she gnawed at the tough bread. "I do not think Frav will be brave enough to attack before the next spring thaw. Plenty of time to take the child to the Temple where he, or she, will be safe."

"Do you wish for a son or a daughter?" Corri leaned back against the cold stone, trying to imagine Takra with a child on her hip.

The warrior woman shrugged. "Whichever the Goddess sends," she answered. "A child of the bonding between Imandoff and me will be a child born into love."

The rattle of pebbles alerted them to the sorcerer's return. Imandoff sank down against the wall next to them and took his share of the bread. "I may have to use sorcery to light our way before we reach the tunnel's end," he said, chewing on the sustaining journey bread. "We have torches enough only to reach the next cavern."

Takra frowned as she stood to dust off her trousers. "At least we have encountered no crawling things in here." She deftly palmed the tesselberry root into her mouth as she turned to look back down the tunnel.

"Or barsarks," Corri added as she rose to put what was left of their food back in the saddlebag. "Of course, if we meet a barsark, we could leave Imandoff behind to dazzle it with his magic."

"I do not dazzle barsarks," the sorcerer answered as he pushed himself to his feet. "Only fair Tuonela women." He grinned at Takra, then caught Sun Dancer's reins as he led them on up the tunnel.

"See, I told you, Takra. Nothing is here." Corri fell in behind Lightfoot.

"Nothing yet," Takra said over her shoulder. "Nothing yet."

They followed the twisting upgrade of the damp-walled tunnel for another two hours before they came out into another cavern, one vastly different from those behind them. The walls were slick with glassy rock, as if a tremendous force had melted the stone, leaving it to coat the walls and run in flattened puddles in places on the floor. Near one wall stood a long block of stone, chipped and polished from the glassy rock, and at each end a stone chair of the same material.

This was a place of ancient worship, Corri thought. *Surely Imandoff would not have chosen this way if there was danger.*

As they picked their way through the forest of stone pillars, Corri saw a rock-fall completely filling one corner of the cavern. She stumbled, hesitated, as her mind registered what it saw. From the bottom of the rock-fall protruded ivory-colored bones, the aged remains of a human hand. She felt the hair on her neck prickle, as if someone unseen stared at her from behind. She turned quickly and saw nothing but shadows and patches of light reflected from their torches. Takra and Imandoff showed no signs that they felt anything different or strange.

Something or someone is here! Corri thought. *It felt like this in the Valley of Whispers.* She shivered as a cold gush of air whipped past her. A faint buzz of sound brushed her ears.

Takra threw up a hand as if to ward off an unseen foe, then crumpled to the rocky floor. Lightfoot laid back her ears, bared her teeth as she stood guard over the Tuonela woman, looking for an enemy.

"Imandoff!" Corri shouted, the word ringing back and forth across the glassy chamber.

The sorcerer whipped around, hand on sword, until he saw that nothing visible threatened. He came at a run, dropping beside Takra, his long-fingered hand feeling for a heartbeat. The Tuonela warrior woman groaned and opened her eyes. Her face was a chalky white.

"What happened?" he demanded as Corri knelt beside him.

"Something flew past me." She struggled to find the words to explain. "Something unseen, but I felt it."

The sorcerer traced a sign with one finger on Takra's damp forehead, then helped her to her feet. When she swayed against Lightfoot, clutched at the saddle to keep her balance, he boosted her onto the saddle.

"I think we should hurry to be out of here. It is not far now," he said, worry wrinkling his forehead. "We will move swiftly and be done with this place soon." He turned to Corri. "This particular cave is called the Tomb of the Maidens in the legends, but never has it or this hidden way been said to hold evil powers. I felt nothing, nor were you harassed. Why should Takra faint?" He stood with one hand on the Wind-Rider's thigh.

"I am not a feya woman to find answers to such questions. This place is too much like the Valley of Whispers to suit me," Corri answered. "Get us out of this place, Imandoff!"

Corri and Mouse fell into the rear position as the sorcerer led them out of the cavern and up what he swore was the final length of the tunnel. As the torches failed, one by one, Imandoff called into being a ghostly ball of light and sent it floating before them. Another ball he caused to hang over Takra, bathing her in a strange blue-white glow.

In the semi-darkness of the surreal magical light, Corri flinched at each wavering shadow, each pool of blackness that huddled in cracks and deep hollows along the tunnel walls. The hair on the back of her neck pricked as she felt the presence of unseen forces gather behind her, staying just out of the glow of the light-balls.

The strange buzzing came again to her ears, this time forming into faint words: *The child. Let us see the child.* The compelling voices continued to sound in Corri's ears as she struggled along behind Takra.

No! By the Mother of Mares, you will not touch the child! Corri sent the mental message with grim determination. *The child is not for you. Go away!* She found herself suddenly unable to move, no matter how much she struggled to put one booted foot ahead.

We will not harm, only bless. The voices were those of women, many women. *The child is a gift from the Goddess. To know we speak the truth, put out your left hand now and you will find our symbol. What you find is our gift to the child.*

No! You could be evil spirits intent on harming the babe. Corri shook her head as visions of female faces darted through her mind.

If we were evil, we could not touch this. The Tuonela amulet hanging inside the girl's tunic moved slightly, forward and backward, as if someone had picked it up and dropped it again.

Corri forced one foot forward, then felt something trip her. She stumbled and threw out her hand to catch her balance against the tunnel's rough wall. Her fingers closed around a tiny object in the darkness. She found she could not unclench her fingers, so she drew it to her just as the sorcerer's lights failed.

She opened her mouth to shout a warning, but no sound emerged. Desperate, she staggered forward, tugging at Mouse's reins and blundering ahead with a splatter of pebbles. Corri felt the unseen women-spirits whip past her as they gathered around Takra's slumped form.

No! Do not harm her! Corri shouted within her mind. *Too late. What will they do to Takra and the baby?*

Then she heard the voices raised in song, a harmonious blend of women's voices, the chant rising and falling in such beauty that Corri caught her breath in wonder. A faint glow pulsed around Takra's bent form where she rode on Lightfoot. The chant echoed in Corri's mind as she felt the spirits pass her again, retreating back into the deep darkness of the tunnel.

Gasping for breath, the girl climbed the dark tunnel, guided by one hand against the wall, the other resting on the comforting roughness of Lightfoot's hide. A corner, then the gray of early dawn broke the blackness. She saw Lightfoot scramble up the grade to the dim opening, and tugged Mouse to follow.

As Corri led Mouse out onto the brushy mountain slopes, she remembered the object she clutched in her left hand. Opening her fingers, she stared down at a small worn statue of a woman, rough-chipped from glassy rock much like the stone that had coated the cave walls. The facial features were blurred with only deep indentations for eyes; the small image of a Rissa lay curled around the woman's feet.

"We are through?" Takra's tired voice broke the silence.

"High Limna, one of the limna villages is just below us," Imandoff answered as he helped the Tuonela to dismount. "How do you feel?" He stood close to Takra, looking at her pale face with worry in his eyes.

"I am fine now." The amber eyes held his without turning away. "For a time it felt like something in that blasted tunnel tried to pull me out of my body. Then I fainted, a disgraceful thing for a Tuonela warrior to do."

"I was worried." Imandoff smiled. "But it gave me an opportunity to rescue you, something rare when companying with a warrior woman."

Takra gave a half-smile and a shrug as she led her horse down the trail, but Corri saw the worry still etched in the lines on Imandoff's face as he watched her.

I will not give this to Takra until I know if it is safe. Corri tucked the little statue into her belt pouch. *If there is a feya woman in that village, she will know.*

Before true dawn broke over the Barren Mountains, the three were in the village of log cabins, listening to the news of the border clashes with Frav.

"What we hear is not good," the village headman said. "Willa, our feya woman," he indicated the silent woman at his side, "tells us that, although much we hear is garbled rumor, still much of the news is true. The Fravashi plague the border guards with constant hit-and-run attacks. But what worries us most is what we hear out of Asur." He leaned over to refill Imandoff's cup with ale.

"There is trouble in Asur?" The sorcerer's black brows pulled down in thought.

"The village Keffin and the Magni from the temples met in Hadliden. They agreed that Asur will take no part in the battle to come with Frav." The headman pursed his mouth in disapproval. "Do they think that if Frav conquers the Peoples, they will be allowed to continue life as they now live it? The Volikvi priests will tear down their temples, destroy the Mystery Schools, and force the worship of Jevotan upon them. The Magni and the Keffin do not speak for those in the limna forests!" He smacked his hand against his knee.

Corri cleared her throat and addressed the feya woman. "How do the people of Asur feel about this decision?"

"Most will follow the will of the Magni, and the Keffin always defer to the rulers of the temples." Willa's sun-browned hand played with the herb bag hung about her neck. "However, those in the far north at Zoc speak against this apathy, as do a great many of the sailors and fishermen."

"What they need is to speak with someone who knows the truth and has seen the troubles firsthand." Imandoff tugged at his beard. "I think we must go into Hadliden to speak with these farers of the seas." He looked from Corri to Takra.

He is right. Grimmel is long dead, so what do I fear in Hadliden? Corri met the sorcerer's eyes, then looked away. *Warning the Peoples who will listen is part of my responsibility as the Dream Warrior. I cannot shirk the task because of old, hurtful memories. If I do not bury those memories, I can never really build a future, if there is to be one for me.*

The Tuonela warrior woman met his gaze with steadfast amber eyes, but Corri sat deep in thought until the sorcerer spoke her name. "It will be dangerous," she said. "Even though Grimmel is dead, there will be those who know us well, old man, especially me."

"You need not go, Corri," Imandoff answered.

"You cannot find your way about Hadliden without me. You would walk straight into danger, not knowing which men to trust and which to beware. I go with you. Besides, there are old ghosts to slay."

Imandoff gave a nod of understanding. "We will rest ourselves and the horses for a day, while we gather supplies. Then we will travel by night to the lower foothills, where we can journey with merchant caravans, thus escaping any notice. When we reach the outskirts of Hadliden, we can enter with the morning crowds. In that way, we should be safe enough." Imandoff set aside his ale mug and rose. "Now I think we need to sleep."

The headman stood to guide them to lodging for the night, but Corri held out her hand to Takra. "We will follow," she said over her shoulder to Imandoff. "We would speak with Willa alone."

Imandoff looked sharply at Takra, his brows raised in question, but she waved him to follow the village headman.

"What do you carry?" Willa asked Corri as soon as the two men were out of hearing. "I have felt its calling ever since you entered High Limna."

"This." Corri pulled the tiny statue from her belt pouch and handed it to the feya woman. Then she told of the strange apparitions in the cave-tunnel.

"You heard the Maidens. Their spirits dwell in the glassy cave." The feya woman reverently smoothed her fingers down the statue. "Long, long ago, during the time of the last great battle with Frav, the young priestesses training at Sadko fled the Fravashi priests and warriors when that Mystery School was overrun. For a time they made their home in the cave in the mountains, with only the feya women of the limna villages knowing where they were. But they were betrayed by one who broke under the tortures of the Volikvi priests. When the Volikvis and soldiers came, two of the feya women went to warn the priestesses. Trapped in the cave, and faced with the bodily desecration planned by the Volikvis and soldiers, the Maidens, under the leadership of a powerful priestess, gathered near their altar. They sang down the ancient power, dying under a fall of rock that entombed their remains. The two feya women were tortured to death by the Volikvis."

Willa sighed and handed the tiny statue to Takra. "This is truly a gift of wonder. It is a statue of their leader, a powerful priestess." She turned sharp eyes on Takra. "I see the signs of childbearing on your face, warrior woman. Perhaps the child you bear is this ancient one returned. If the Maidens have blessed the child you carry, Tuonela, you are greatly honored."

Corri bit her lip, knowing what she must do and how Takra would react. "You cannot go to Hadliden with us." She held up her hand to stop Takra's flood of protests. "You are too conspicuous. The Tuonela do not willingly enter the cities of Asur, believing as they do in the freedom of women. We would not get two streets inside the city before we would be under constant spying. We could never do what we plan."

"I am a warrior!" Stubbornness hardened Takra's voice. "I can dye my hair as you did. No one will know I am Tuonela then."

"They would know by the way you carry yourself." Corri spread her hands on her knees, then looked straight into Takra's eyes. "And the first time some Asuran man confronted you for not veiling your face, you would have your sword at his throat. I can pass as a boy, Takra. You cannot. Besides, if you vomited in public, you would be taken to at once to a healing center, where they would certainly find out you are a woman. If you do not stay behind by your own choice, I will be forced to tell Imandoff that you carry his child."

"You would do that?" Takra's nostrils flared with anger.

"Think of the babe, warrior woman," Willa said. "If the Maidens called this child special, then it is your duty to protect its life with all your power. We cannot know what part the child may play in the future of the Peoples. You do not have the right to endanger this babe of unknown abilities."

"You are right." Takra lowered her head. "But what can I tell Imandoff?"

"I will tell him that you are too conspicuous to go with us into Hadliden. That is true enough." Corri put her hand on Takra's shoulder. "And Willa can tell him that you are not recovered enough from your sickness. He will believe that without question, for he saw what happened in the cave-tunnel."

"Men, unless they have been fathers already, do not recognize the signs of a pregnant woman. I will say you suffer from an imbalance of stomach energies, a temporary illness that has much the same symptoms." Willa smiled. "You can stay with me until the sorcerer and this brave woman return."

"I will not always shirk from danger, child or no child." Takra frowned at Corri. "It is not the way of Tuonela warrior women to stand aside passively when there is danger to be faced."

"I will not ask it of you again," Corri promised. "This time, though, I feel you must remain behind."

"If I stay behind, you will not tell Imandoff I am pregnant?"

Corri nodded. "I will not tell. But you must tell him some time."

"I will choose the time," Takra said as the feya woman led them to her cabin for the night.

Corri tossed and turned on her sleeping shelf, her thoughts full of the dangers of a return to Hadliden. The soft, even breathing of Takra and Willa sounded over-loud as the girl tried to will herself to sleep with no success.

I wonder what happened with Odran and Hindjall when they covered our retreat, she thought. Her fragmented, busy thoughts rolled round and round in her mind, turning from the Kaballoi to Gadavar and the dangers of Kayth. *I will dream-fly to the mountains,* she decided. *If I know that the Kaballoi are safe, perhaps I will be more at ease.*

Corri turned onto her back, slowed her rapid breathing, and willed her body to relax. In a short time she found her dream-body hanging in the crisp air of the mountain night above High Limna. She recalled the helmeted faces of the Kaballoi as she last saw them. Swiftly she sped over the high Barren Mountains, the scenery a blur. Down the other side she flew, until she hung over a tiny wink of firelight set near the thick blackness of evergreen trees. She hovered lower until she could see the sleeping faces of the two Kaballoi.

They are well. If they suffered wounds, the wounding was small. Perhaps I should go to the border and try to contact Tirkul. It would be best to know what has happened there before we journey into Asur.

No sooner did she think of the tall Tuonela warrior than Corri found herself streaking across the wide grasslands to the mountains that divided Frav from Tuone. Unerringly, she was drawn back to the rocky camp near the bridge leading across the Kratula Gorge to the Volikvi city of Vu-Murt. The buckskin horse, Hellstorm, dozed near the sleeping Tirkul.

Tirkul? Corri tried to contact the mind of the sleeping warrior but found no spark of recognition. *What is happening? It is as if his spirit has gone traveling.* She sent out a wider sweep of thought, but found no trace of Tirkul's dream-body.

Without warning, Corri found herself once more whirling through the night, straight across the border into Frav. She fought against the pull as a fish would fight against the entrapping line, but still her spirit-body was drawn onward until she hung once again in the strange shadow-darkened room of Minepa.

At the long table sat the Volikvi priest and Kayth, their eyes intent on a still, shadowy form trapped in an ethereal ball of red-streaked light above a smoldering incense burner.

"I told you his thoughts would open him to my influence." Kayth smiled as he leaned closer to the encapsulated wispy form. "When his thoughts dwelt on my daughter and his regret of his hasty words, I had my opening." He leaned back and steepled his hands under his chin.

"But will he not remember you when he wakes?" Minepa's deep-set eyes burned with eagerness.

"He will remember all this as a dream, thinking he is still free of me."

"But you cannot say with certainty that you control anything this Tuonela thinks or does." Minepa turned a skull-thin
face to Kayth.

"We will know soon enough." Kayth stretched out his hand
and a stream of black-specked light shot from his fingers to
strike the center of Tirkul's forehead. The hazy form within the
globe of reddened light disappeared, the ball of light snapping
out of existence.

Minepa leaned back in his chair, his eyes narrowed. "You
have strengthened your powers," he said, his lips curved in
dislike. "Tell me how. I am a direct descendant of the first
Minepa. The Books of Darkness are mine to guard and use."

Kayth laughed, and Minepa's face flushed. "Think you that
I do not know these Books were once called the Books of Jin-
niyah? You of all people, Minepa, should know the full
Fravashi prophecy concerning the Books."

"I am the Soothsayer of Jevotan," Minepa said as he suddenly stood glaring down at Kayth. "I have known the
prophecies since I became a Volikvi and entered the Fire Temple. There is no one among the Volikvis greater than me!"

Kayth rose to his feet, a confident smile on his lips. "Open
your mind to what you see, Minepa, and remember all of the
prophecies. When the great Jinniyah returns, he shall be able
to call up the ancient magic used long ago when he led the
Fravashi. And Minepa will bend to his wishes." Kayth thrust
his arms toward the darkened ceiling. "I am Jinniyah reborn!"
he shouted.

Corri tried to retreat as she watched a graying of the air
around Minepa. *He fears Kayth,* she thought. *The energy
around him shows it. How much of what Kayth says is truth and
how much the raving of a mad man?*

"On your knees before me, Minepa!" The Volikvi struggled
against Kayth's power, but was forced to his knees, his head
bowed. "I, Jinniyah, say that this Tuonela warrior is under my

control and will be our key to the doorway into Tuone and all the lands beyond."

"As Jinniyah says, so shall it be." Minepa's whispered words brought a gloating smile to Kayth.

I must be gone from this place! Corri brought all her mind power to bear on retreating. *Kayth must not discover that I hear his plans. Out! I must return to Imandoff and warn him!* At last she broke the compulsion that held her in Minepa's chamber and fled back across the grasslands to her body in the feya woman's cabin in High Limna.

Corri shivered and sat up, clasping her arms about her shaking knees. Takra and Willa still slept. She clenched her teeth to keep them from chattering.

If I tell Takra and Imandoff what I saw, they will ride at once through all dangers to reach Tirkul, perhaps to no avail. She lowered her head to her knees as she thought. *There is nothing we can do to help Tirkul now. Before we return to Tuone, we must rouse the fighting men of Asur. After that, I know I must go to Leshy and undergo the Trial. O Goddess, must I keep this secret from them?*

You must, came the Lady's familiar voice. *I will tell you when the time is right to speak of what you have seen and heard. Trust in Me, daughter, and I will guide you.*

Corri thrust aside the blanket and, with boots in one hand, quietly crept out of the cabin. She sat on the bench by the door, staring at the clotted shadows about the village until the moon fell into the seas beyond her view and the sun glowed pink over the mountains behind her.

Chapter 11

"The Asuran decision to remain neutral in this coming war should be no surprise to anyone." The Kirisani merchant waved one hand to emphasize his words as he rode beside Imandoff. "They have always discouraged any man who showed an interest in learning the arts of warfare. They have had no army of their own since the last great battle with Frav, relying upon Kirisan and Tuone to defend them if the need should arise." The man lifted his lip in scorn.

"Surely now that they see Frav plans to overrun the Peoples once again, they will train an army." Imandoff's gray eyes intently watched the road ahead and the growing number of travelers on their way to Hadliden.

"Not so. Their answer is to pass mandates that all Asurans must worship in the temples at least twice daily, pounding the ears of their god Iodan with prayers for deliverance. As if false and forced piety will protect them." The merchant shook his head. "Have you not heard of the new laws? All women, even

those of the farmers, are forbidden to go out in public, unless
heavily veiled and accompanied by men of their families. They
can speak to no male in public at all. Whether they live or die
for some small infraction hangs on the whim of a husband,
brother, or father. The women of Asur have always had little
freedom. Now even that is gone."

"What of the fishermen and the sailor-merchants?" Imandoff glanced at Corri, who rode silently at his other side. Her
face was expressionless as she stared into the distance, her red
hair once more discretely covered by a hood.

"Now there is the boil on the soul of Asur. As well try to
control the sea winds as try to control those of the sea or the
limna villages." The merchant chuckled and shook his head.
"Their independence and refusal to enforce or follow these
stringent new laws must give the Keffin and Magni sleepless
nights." He laughed again.

"If the Keffin and Magni have tightened their control, what
is expected of strangers?" Corri's voice was low and calm.

"That is a touchy point, lad." The merchant leaned forward
to look across Imandoff at Corri. "If you question their treatment of women, refuse to worship in their temples, speak
against their new policies, or even suggest different ways of
doing things, you will be run out of Asur." He sat back in his
saddle, a deep frown on his face. "I have heard tales of public
whippings for speaking one's mind."

"Surely they do not dare to punish the fishermen?" Imandoff raised his dark brows in question.

The merchant smiled, baring his teeth. "Those of the sea
keep to themselves, more than usual. And no Magni or member of the Keffin dares to send his guards into the wharf area
to enforce their rules. I heard that one Magni tried it, and
never saw his guards again."

The caravan drew nearer to the great gates of Hadliden, the
huge doors open but guarded by several armored men. The
merchant raised a hand in farewell, then rode to the head of
the line of pack animals, leaving Imandoff and Corri behind.

"Are you afraid?" Imandoff asked, leaning close to Corri.

"I would be a fool if I were not," she answered in a low voice. "Do you know the punishment for running away from an Asuran husband, old man? First the woman is paraded naked in the streets, spat upon by everyone she passes. Then she is turned over to the husband or his family to do with as they please." She hunched lower in the saddle as they passed between the soldiers and through the gates of the city. "If there is no family to exact the punishment, the Keffin will do it."

"I think we should go at once to the Red Horse Inn and not wander about the city." Imandoff turned Sun Dancer away from the caravan and down a busy street. "It is close to the wharf area and easily reached at night."

"What if the innkeeper recognizes me?" Corri fell into her old habit of scanning everyone they passed, all the alleys and shop-fronts.

"He will recognize me, that is certain," the sorcerer answered. "I once gave him a rash so fierce he near scratched himself raw for causing me trouble. New laws or no, I think the innkeeper will not dare to notify the Keffin or Magni that we are in Hadliden."

The Red Horse Inn looked the same to Corri as it had on the night she tried to rob Imandoff more than a year ago. The innkeeper's mouth flew open when the sorcerer crossed the threshold but his eyes passed over Corri without recognition. He led them straight up to a second floor room, warning them in non-stop conversation about the new restrictions and begging Imandoff not to bring the wrath of the authorities down upon the Red Horse Inn during his stay in Hadliden.

"It smells the same," Corri said, wrinkling her nose as she thrust open the window. "Fish and garbage!"

"I take it you did not miss this city." Imandoff chuckled at her frown. "Perhaps your nose will be numb by tonight. When we go down to the wharves, the delightful scents will be even stronger."

"I have not forgotten." Corri pulled out her boot-knife and a whetstone. She sat on the bed while she sharpened the knife she kept hidden in her boot. "Unless there have been great changes since last I was there, we should seek out Kanlath and Gran. They led the fishermen and sailor-merchants."

"I think we should sleep until dark." Imandoff threw himself down on the opposite bed, folding his hands behind his head. "Until we know more of what happens in Hadliden, I do not think we should be out on the streets during daylight."

"Sleep if you want to, old man," Corri answered, still running the whetstone along the edge of the blade. "Unless you have a spell against bugs, I will not sleep on this bed. I saw three cockroaches come out of your straw mattress a moment ago. Likely there are more in yours and mine that are hiding, awaiting a chance to creep out while we sleep."

"They are harmless." Imandoff turned his head and grinned. "After all, they have all they can eat downstairs."

"No cockroach walks on me and lives," Corri replied, smashing her boot down on a bug that strolled across the floor.

The sorcerer chuckled, then stretched and yawned. Before long his breathing deepened as he drifted off to sleep.

Corri stood at the window, arms folded on the sill, when Imandoff awoke from sleep. Her thoughts were full of the life she had led under Grimmel's control, a life as the best thief in Hadliden. *I wonder how Dakhma does in the Temple at Kystan,* she thought. *Zanitra will care for her with the love of a mother and teach her all she needs to know.* As she smiled at the thought of Zanitra, she suddenly saw Gadavar's face in her mind. *He is thinking of me! How I wish I were with you, Gadavar.* As if in answer, the image smiled.

She turned back to the darkened room when Imandoff snapped fire from his fingers and lit a candle. A soft knock at the door brought her against the wall, booter in hand.

"I bring food," came a voice from the hallway.

Corri slid her hand behind her back to conceal the bared knife while Imandoff opened the door. A young man sidled into the room, clutching a tray. His light eyes flitted briefly across the sorcerer's face, then centered on Corri. The man's mouth dropped open and his face whitened. His hands shook as he set the tray on the table.

"You!" His voice broke with fear. "I remember you!"

Imandoff shut the door while Corri slowly drew out her knife. The young man's mouth opened and closed silently, his wide eyes watching Corri's every move.

"Do you know this person?" Imandoff asked, leaning back against the door.

"His name is Hamn. He trained under Grimmel," Corri answered, sliding the knife back and forth across her trousers. "He held promise as a thief."

"Please, I beg you, do not tell anyone who I really am." The man stepped backward, collapsing onto the bed behind him. "If the Keffin or the Magni find me, I will be killed."

"Why would they issue a death penalty for you?" Corri bent to slide the knife back into her boot. "You were only a thief, not one of Grimmel's assassins."

"Early this morning—at sunrise—two of Grimmel's men were executed in the marketplace for spying for Frav." Hamn gulped and twisted his thin hands together. "Now those in authority believe that all who once worked for Grimmel are paid spies of Tuone and Kirisan. The fishermen and sailors only take in those who are strong. They refused me, saying I would blow away in the first sea wind." He lifted his hands in a gesture of defeat.

"Kayth must be using those left of Grimmel's men to gather information and stir up trouble." Corri looked at Imandoff, who nodded.

"You know that name—Kayth! That was the name tortured from one of the executed men!" The young man ground his clutching fingers into the straw mattress. "You spy for Frav?"

"No! I know who and what this Kayth is, but I do not work for him, I work against him." Corri folded her arms and looked down at the white face turned up to her. "Where do your loyalties lie, Hamn?"

"Not with Frav! But no one would believe me." He brushed the hair back from his forehead. "They have issued a death penalty for all who worked for the Master Thief."

Corri sat beside the trembling young man and laid a hand on his shoulder. "Leave Hadliden," she said. "Go to the mountain village of High Limna and ask for sanctuary. There you will be safe."

"They will take me in, not turn me over to the Keffin?"

"They will take you in, and the Keffin will never hear of it," Imandoff answered. "But do no thieving there or you will lose your hand as punishment."

Hamn nodded vigorously, his hands plucking at the edge of his jerkin. "I know a secret way to get over the walls at night," he whispered. "Then I can get work in one of the caravans until I reach the mountains." The young man stood and smiled faintly for the first time.

"This secret way out of Hadliden you spoke of," Imandoff said as he stepped into the hall with Hamn, "tell me of it."

Corri dropped her head into her hands as the door closed. *Lady, what hornet's nest have we entered? The old Hadliden was bad enough, but this new one I do not know. Once in, can we get out alive?*

Imandoff closed the door softly when he entered. "We will eat, then go out over the roof and down to the wharves. I think we should stay in Hadliden no longer than we have to." He poured a cup of ale and pressed it into Corri's hands.

"Is there another way out besides the gates?" Corri asked as she took a gulp of the ale. "In all my thieving for Grimmel, I never heard of one. Imandoff, we must move swiftly with what we must do here, then be gone. All my old thief's senses are working again, telling me this is truly a dangerous place."

"I agree that Hadliden, indeed all Asur, is now a dangerous place for such as we. And yes, there is a secret way through Hadliden's walls. Remember the inn at Zatyr?" Imandoff flipped back the napkin covering the tray and centered a thick slice of ham on a piece of crusty bread. "After finding that bolt-hole, I wondered how many inns have such places, all unseen and seldom used except by the innkeepers for the smuggling of goods or escaping from authorities. It would not surprise me to discover many such escape routes."

"And there is one here at the Red Horse." Corri took a piece of bread and ham, staring at it deep in thought. "How is it that Grimmel did not know of this bolt-hole?"

"How many times did Grimmel send his people into stables to steal anything?" Imandoff grinned as Corri looked at him in surprise. "It seems this escape route is cleverly hidden at the back of the stable here, the entrance to it inside a small room built against the outer wall itself."

"I have a feeling we should go that way when we leave Hadliden, old man." Corri narrowed her eyes as she chewed. "My instincts say that we will be leaving in a hurry, the dogs of the Keffin and Magni on our heels."

They ate in silence, both listening to every footstep and voice that came from the hall beyond. After Imandoff extinguished the candle, they waited until their eyes adjusted to the dark before climbing out the window onto the narrow ledge that led off across the inn roof to the stable.

"You must lead the way," Imandoff murmured, his mouth close to Corri's ear, as they crouched in the deep shadows of the stables. "I am not familiar with the streets and alleys that lead to the wharves."

"Keep your dagger ready," she whispered back. "The way we must go is the safest from the city guards, but dangerous for unwary travelers. And we do not know what kind of welcome the sea-farers will give us."

They moved like ghosts through the inn yard, keeping to the shadows. Corri knelt to pick up several small stones as they neared the inn gates. The guard at the small door set within one of the gate-leaves lounged against the stone wall, half-asleep until the girl threw one of the pebbles against a metal pail. The man jerked awake, turning his head from side to side as he listened. Corri threw another pebble, rattling it round and round the inside of the pail. The guard left his post in a rush. Corri and Imandoff silently hurried through the small door and down the street toward the Adag River.

The alleys Corri chose were black and smelled of garbage. The two often slipped in the muck underfoot, banging elbows and knees as they caught their balance against rough stone walls. Drunken singing once reached them as they waited within the blackness of a side street while a group of sailors staggered past.

"This warehouse belongs to Kanlath," Corri whispered as she stopped, one hand on a door that opened into the alley. "Pray that Kanlath still holds power here. If he does not, we may be in deeper trouble."

Her breath went out in a whoosh as Imandoff suddenly slammed her against the wall. She heard the hiss-ching of his sword as it left the sheath.

"Kanlath still rules these wharves for the fishermen," came a rough voice from the deep blackness of the alley. "Who are you, that you come sneaking to find Kanlath?"

"I am Imandoff Silverhair, the sorcerer." Imandoff's tense body still pressed Corri between him and the wall. "I will tell Kanlath to his face what business I have with him. My words are not for some disembodied voice in the night."

The rough voice broke in a gruff laugh. "If you have that much fire and determination, sorcerer, you are not from the Keffin or the Magni. Tell your boy to open the door and go inside. Remember, I will be at your back."

Imandoff sheathed his sword as Corri's fingers found the door latch. They stumbled through into a short, dimly lit hall leading to the main warehouse. As Corri jerked open the second door, she narrowed her eyes against the glare of bright light flooding the area around the door. Within that area of light stood and sat a crowd of fishermen with Kanlath in their midst.

"What have you here, Mikel?" Kanlath stepped forward, his eyes taking in the weapons and dress of both Corri and Imandoff. "Wait, I know you!" The short, thin man grabbed Corri's hood and yanked it off. "You were the Master Thief's best!"

"She still is the best thief I have ever seen." Imandoff pushed forward, drawing the man's attention to himself.

"I stole nothing from you or your men, Kanlath," Corri answered, clipping her words in anger. "I held to my part of our bargain, even against Grimmel's desires."

"Aye, that you did, girl." Kanlath grinned, showing several missing teeth. "We heard of the way you were married to the old toad."

"Aye, and we grieved to hear of his death," called out another fisherman. The other men laughed.

"Too bad you did not open his gut on your wedding night," Kanlath said.

"There was no wedding night," Corri spat angrily, her hand clenched on her belt dagger. "Imandoff," she indicated the sorcerer with a wave of her hand, "broke me out of the villa and we went to Kirisan."

"Our women come to us willingly or not at all," Kanlath answered. "You need not fear any here turning you over to the authorities, girl." The men murmured in agreement. "But with the new laws so harsh in Hadliden, why did you return?"

"To tell you to prepare for war," Imandoff said, his body balanced on the balls of his feet, one hand resting on his sword hilt. "It will not be long until Frav breaks through the spell-guards at the border and rolls like a flood into Tuone and beyond." His gray eyes raked across the gathered men, who pushed closer. "We came to Hadliden to see if any except cowards still dwell here."

A deep murmur of angry words rolled through the warehouse. "The fishermen and sailors of Asur are no cowards, sorcerer!" Kanlath's callused hand fell to the fish-knife at his belt.

"Then I have truly found a treasure of the rarest krynap pearls," Imandoff answered, a wide smile crossing his face. "I feared perhaps our journey was in vain."

"What do you want of us, sorcerer?" called one of the fishermen. "We have waited long for a fight with the soldiers and priests of Frav."

Kanlath motioned Imandoff and Corri toward the semicircle of boxes where his men lounged. The fishermen gathered around them and listened as Imandoff told of the border troubles.

"Long have we had secret meetings with the fishermen of Frav," Kanlath finally said. "They want no war and have no more use for their priests than we do for ours. Mayhap we can join together to attack the coastal cities of Frav when the time comes."

"How will you get your ships across the barrier mountains to the Zivitua Sea?" Imandoff stretched out his legs as he watched Kanlath's face.

"No problem there," called out one of the fishermen. "Many a time we cross the hills between the two seas and join the Fravashi fishermen. We just leave our ships anchored in the Zuartoc Sea, cross the spit, and sail on their ships."

Kanlath nodded. "The merchant-sailors under Gran have done the same. They will join with us, I know. All these new religious laws eat at a man's freedom."

"Good. When the time is ripe, I will send a message saying 'The Dream Warrior arises.' By those words you will know to sail." Imandoff stood and clasped hands with Kanlath. "Fair winds and weather to you all."

Imandoff and Corri left Kanlath's warehouse and crept back through the black alleys toward the Red Horse Inn. Before they reached the cross-street leading to the inn, the sorcerer pulled Corri into a darkened side alley.

"First, I must see my friend who gave us shelter before," he whispered. "I must warn him to flee Hadliden."

"If he is still here," Corri answered. "The Keffin may have imprisoned him."

Imandoff felt his way down the alley, finally tapping a code on one of the doors. Corri heard the creak of stairs as someone crept down to the door. A lock rattled, then Imandoff pulled her after him into the blackness of a stairwell. Someone pushed past her to lock the door, then by her again to lead the way up the stairs.

"What do you do here in Hadliden, Silverhair?" The old man's voice from the darkness brought back memories of running and hiding from Grimmel the night the sorcerer had freed Corri from the Master Thief's villa.

"Our stay will not be long." The door at the top of the stairs opened, letting soft lamplight fall on the sorcerer's face as he stepped through, Corri right behind him. "What is this?"

Corri felt the blade of a knife touch the side of her neck and froze. The room was filled with what appeared to be young men, all concealed in hooded cloaks, their hands on belt daggers, journey bags at their feet.

"Let her go, Breela," the old merchant said. "These are friends of mine. They are surely in as much danger from the Keffin and Magni as you are."

The knife dropped, and Corri looked around, straight into pale blue eyes set in a determined face. She turned back to Imandoff, her glance once more raking across the assembled people in the room.

"These are not men!" she said. "These are women!"

"Yes, Farblood," said the woman beside her. "When the Master Thief was killed, and another took his place, some of us fled. We found other women of like mind, with a desire to be free of Asuran men. We dressed as men, found work, and bided our time. Unlike you, we had no sorcerer to spirit us out of the city." The woman's full lips twisted in amusement.

"You were one of Grimmel's pleasure-slaves." Corri looked closer at Breela. "Without your long hair, I did not recognize you."

"Nor does any other living man in Hadliden." Breela slipped the dagger into the sheath and hooked her thumbs into her belt. "The few who did no longer are among the living."

"These are the last of the women who came to me over the past year wanting to flee the strict laws of Asur," the merchant said as he slumped onto a chair. "I sent a few at a time with merchants to the Temple of the Great Mountain in Kystan. The first group should have reached the Temple a week ago. We leave tonight."

"We will fight for our lands and the Peoples," Breela said, setting her jaw as if expecting resistance to her words. "Asur is a land of gutless men who feel their power through control of their women."

"I chose only the strongest and those not married." The merchant gathered a pile of small leather pouches on the table, stuffing them into a saddlebag near his feet. "The others I found safe havens with the families of the fishermen and merchant sailors. They, and other less militant Asuran women, will gather information and send it on to Kystan by merchants. These," he indicated the cloaked women in the room, "will join with the others at the Temple to train for Her Own."

"How did you know the Oracle is rebuilding Her Own?" Corri asked. "Word could not yet have reached you of that decision."

"I dreamed." The old man stood, saddlebag slung over his shoulder. "We must leave at once. Just before you came to my door, we received word that the Keffin is on their way to raid my shop."

Corri and Imandoff followed the old merchant and his cloaked women out into the dark alley. The sorcerer whispered a few words with his old friend, then led Corri in the opposite direction. The two cautiously made their way through the night toward the Red Horse Inn, listening for footsteps, making certain that each street was empty before crossing it.

"They will be safely out of the city before the hour is done," Imandoff said softly as they stood watching the gates of the inn from the shadows. "The guard is leaving his post."

"It feels like a trap." Corri tugged at Imandoff's sleeve. "Something is not right."

"It is our only chance to enter the inn unseen. I will go first, then you follow." Imandoff slipped across the silent street and stood for a moment peering inside the open door in the gate.

Corri felt her skin prickle with uneasiness. The silence of the street and inn yard cut at her nerves. *It is an ambush*, she thought. *Beware, Imandoff!* Her mind-speech found the sorcerer, but there was no answer. As she reached for her belt knife, armed men poured through the gate-door. The sorcerer had no chance to draw sword but was slammed against the stone wall, quickly surrounded, his arms bound behind him.

A short black-clad figure walked sedately up to the captured sorcerer. Corri heard the crack of the little man's open hand meeting Imandoff's face.

One of the temple Magni! Corri's mind was instantly busy going over plans to free the sorcerer, rejecting each as it surfaced. She sighed. *I cannot free him by myself.*

"Take him to the temple prison," ordered the Magni. "There we will persuade this spy to tell us what he knows."

The man jumped backward as Imandoff's foot shot out, catching him a punishing blow in the thigh. The Magni limped to one side as the guards pummeled the sorcerer into semiconsciousness.

"I will see that this non-believing sorcerer gets my special personal attention." The Magni signaled for his sedan chair as the temple guards dragged Imandoff down the street. The black-clad man grimaced and rubbed at his thigh as the bearers carried him away.

Corri leaned against the alley wall, her nails grinding into the palms of her hands. *Who will help me?* She willed her breathing to slow, a semblance of calmness to govern her thoughts. *Kanlath! He and his men are my only chance.*

Heedless of who would see her, and confident that no one could catch her if they did, Corri sprinted back down the alley, across streets and other alleyways, finally gaining the safety of the odorous blackness of the wharf streets. Her eyes constantly raked across every doorway and shadow, her ears intent on any sounds of pursuit. She caught herself against the warehouse alley wall, gasping for breath. As she reached for the latch, the door opened and she fell headlong into Kanlath himself.

"What? Farblood!" Kanlath jerked her inside and slammed the door. "What trouble do you bring on your heels, girl?"

"None that I know of. Imandoff . . ." Corri paused to catch her breath. "The Magni . . ."

"The Magni have taken Imandoff Silverhair?" Kanlath growled like an animal at her nod. "Mikel! Bring the strongest ale we have and send word of an emergency gathering to our men. And send word also to Gran," he shouted as he guided Corri down the corridor to the warehouse proper.

Corri collapsed on a bundle smelling of dried fish and choked down a swallow of ale from the cup that Kanlath pressed into her shaking hands. As she looked around, she saw nearly a dozen silent fishermen watching her.

"Someone must have told the Magni of our meeting tonight." The thin man paced back and forth, his sinewy hands clenching and unclenching as he walked. "Toran, did anyone leave the warehouse after Farblood and the sorcerer were here?"

"Korud did." A fisherman dressed in knee-cut trousers, his long hair braided in a plait, stepped forward.

"Korud?" Corri choked on the ale. "You hired Korud?"

"Korud gave no trouble." Kanlath stopped before the girl, staring down at her. "What do I need to know about Korud, girl?"

"He was brother to Druk, one of Grimmel's best assassins. Druk followed me to Kystan to bring me back to the Master Thief. He died there."

"I saw Korud leave wharfside and go into the city," said another fisherman. "Seemed strange, but I thought mayhap you sent him on an errand."

The alley door burst open, and a milling crowd of fishermen and sailor merchants poured into the warehouse. Gran, a heavy-set man with one eye covered by a patch, pushed his way to Kanlath's side where he looked down at Corri with a surprised arch to one brow.

"What happens, Kanlath?" he asked, one hand on the curved blade stuck through his belt.

"The Magni have arrested Imandoff Silverhair. Are you with us in setting him free?" Kanlath frowned up at the taller man. "If I remember rightly, it was Silverhair who used a confusing spell and pulled us out of a bloody tavern brawl when we were younger."

A gold tooth flashed as Gran smiled. "Right you are. And Silverhair only a young apprentice at the time." He turned to Corri, his mouth pursed in thought. "Describe what happened and who took him, girl."

Corri quickly told of the ambush at the Red Horse Inn and the mincing Magni who ordered the arrest. Kanlath added his suspicions about Korud.

"It's certain the innkeeper was no turncoat," growled Kanlath, and Gran nodded. "Seems we have yet another spy to treat to our form of justice, mayhap more than just Korud. And the Magni, that must be Cleeman."

"A kick in the leg, you say, girl?" Gran smiled, his tooth flashing in the lamplight. "That sorcerer never did fight fair. Like as not, it was not the Magni's leg he aimed for."

"At least not the one he walks on!" shouted one of the men, and they all laughed.

"We go with you." Gran looked around at his men, who nodded in agreement. "We go armed in these times, so let us be seeking out this Cleeman and Imandoff."

Kanlath held up his hand for silence. "If any see a fisherman called Korud near the prison, bind him and bring him back here alive. We need to know who else spies for the Magni and Keffin on the wharves."

The fishermen and sailor-merchants broke into small groups, flitting down the dark alleys and side streets toward the prison belonging to the temple Magni. Corri, sandwiched between Gran and Kanlath, reached the deep shadows of an alley directly across from the prison gates to find no one in sight. She jumped when one of the fishermen materialized beside them, a serrated gutting knife in hand.

"The men be in position." The lamplight from the prison gates winked on the wicked blade as the fisherman tested it on his thumb.

The stone-walled prison, protected by great gates of thick iron bars, stood cold in the thin street lights. What windows there were on the upper stories were barred also.

"Now what?" Corri whispered to Kanlath.

"Do not worry, girl. First the Magni and his guards need a little diversion." Sounds of fighting echoed down the street from the wharf. "One of the nightly riots to draw off their men."

In a few minutes a large squad of armed men marched through the prison gates and down the street toward the fighting. Two guards remained on duty behind the barred gates.

"The wharfside pleasure women will be coming down the street any time now." Gran's gold tooth glinted as he smiled.

The words were barely spoken when a rough-looking group of women stumbled out of another alley and wove their way toward the guards at the gates. Calling out a vulgar invitation to an hour of pleasure, the women waved a jug of ale as they crossed the street. One stopped to adjust her gown, and Corri caught the brief wink of a dagger blade.

The guards swaggered toward the women, away from their post at the gate. The women swarmed around them. There was a brief scuffle, a gurgling sound, and the guards fell to the cobbled street as the women ran to the unguarded entrance. One by one they cast off their soiled garments and veils to reveal men in knee-cut trousers.

Out of the night-black alleyways and shadowed areas between the dim street lights poured a silent horde of armed men. The gate lights flashed on the wicked curves of gaffs, the serrated edges of gutting knives, and the straight lines of belt daggers as the men rushed into the unguarded prison.

"Stay here," Kanlath ordered, pushing Corri back into the alley.

"Never!" Corri shrugged out of Kanlath's hold. "Imandoff is my friend."

"Then at least stay behind me," roared Gran, one hand dragging her back. "I know where they take the new prisoners."

The prison was a swirl of angry fishermen and sailor-merchants when Corri followed the two leaders into the great stone building. The men raced through the building with stolen keys, releasing any prisoners they found. What remaining guards had resisted lay dead on the floors, their blood running over the cold floors. Corri gagged and turned her head.

"Down here!" Kanlath pointed to a dimly lit stairwell leading down into the bowels of the prison.

Corri followed the two men down the narrow stairs into a bleak room filled with strange devices. A metal bowl glowed with coals where an iron rod heated.

"Imandoff!" Corri pushed ahead when she saw the sorcerer chained to the far wall.

Gran yanked her back just as the Magni Cleeman swung a pair of heavy iron pincers at her head. The little man lost his balance, falling into the wall.

"Not so good with those, are you, when there are no chains to hold a man still?" Gran twisted the little man's wrist until he dropped the pincers with a shriek. "I have waited long to repay you for this, Cleeman." The sailor-merchant touched his eye patch with a callused finger. "The time has come for you to taste what you dish out to others."

He dragged the whimpering, kicking little man to the wall beside Imandoff and fastened the wall-shackles around the thin wrists and ankles. Fishing a key from the Magni's vest pocket, Gran tossed them to Corri.

"Loosen your friend and go," he ordered, rolling up his sleeves and reaching for one of the strange implements. "A girl should not see what will be done here this night."

Corri's fingers shook as she unlocked Imandoff's shackles. "Are you hurt?" she asked, looking up into the gray eyes.

"Only my ears at this point," Imandoff answered, taking Corri's arm and leading her back up the stairs. "The Magni likes to work himself up to the torture by talking, it seems."

Corri jumped and caught her lower lip with her teeth as a scream pierced through the stairway. With Imandoff on one side, Kanlath on the other, she was pulled quickly out into the street and into the alley where they had waited.

Kanlath waved his fist. A series of whistles came from those fishermen who stood at the gates and was picked up and echoed by others farther inside. Within minutes, the prison was empty. Gran came last, wiping his hands on his trousers as he ran to the sheltered darkness of the alley.

"Go!" he shouted, pushing at Imandoff. "The prison guards will be returning any time now."

The fishermen and sailor-merchants melted away into the night. Imandoff hurried off toward the Red Horse Inn, Corri at his heels.

"We dare not return," she whispered fiercely as he stopped once more before the inn gates.

"There is no prison Magni to set a second trap. Hurry, though, for the guards will be out as soon as they find his body."

The inn courtyard was silent as the two paused to listen at the door. A low whistle drew them to the stables, where they found the innkeeper with their horses saddled and bags in place.

"This way, quickly!" The rotund man motioned them to the rear of the stable, where he opened the door to a false room. At the far end of the room was a black rectangle leading through the city's walls.

"I can do no more for you, Silverhair," the innkeeper whispered. "My family even now waits for me along the road to Kirisan. Hadliden, all of Asur, is aflame with fanaticism. The Magni and Keffin are creating another Frav with their religious persecutions. No man in his right mind will choose to live here."

As they led their horses through the bushes on the other side of the wall, the merchant came through behind them, pushing shut the concealed door. A saddled mule was tethered just beyond the bushes.

"May fortune ride with you." Imandoff clasped the innkeeper's hand. "Take the mountain trails. They are safer."

The man nodded, mounted the mule, and kicked it into a trot.

"You are hurt!" Corri cried as she saw a dark stain on the neck of Imandoff's robe.

"Not enough to keep me near this place. Mount and ride."

Daybreak found them nearing the foothills on the same trail they had taken when they first fled Asur over a year ago. Corri kept a close watch on their back-trail. Once she saw the dull gleam of armor as a party of temple guards fanned out over the farmland, seeking them. But none discovered their trail.

"Imandoff, what do we do now?" she asked as they rested beside a mountain stream. She watched the sorcerer as he washed the dagger scratch on his side. He grimaced as he touched the scrapes and bruises on the side of his head.

"We have done what we can for Asur," the sorcerer answered. "The Goddess help them. Now they must do for themselves."

Corri shivered. "We will join Takra and then I must go to Leshy?"

The sorcerer looked up, his gray eyes troubled. "Yes, Corri, you must undergo the Trial. Although you are not Temple-trained, you will need the power that comes from the Trial to fight Kayth. And the Goddess protect you, during the Trial and from Kayth, for you will need it."

Chapter 12

$\mathcal{T}$hose at Sadko have refused to meet with us." The young Oracle's mouth drew down in bitterness. "They are defiant that they will not become involved in the war with Frav."

"They are fools." The High Priestess stood with one hand on her sword hilt, her long hair braided back. Her fighting kilts were dusty from the practice field.

"At least the Tamia Zanitra had the presence of mind to remove the sejda and bring them here." The woman seated by the Oracle absently caressed the pendant on her breast, its golden globe and silver wings flashing in the sunlight coming through the windows. "We of Leshy have no fighting skills, but we can and will offer all our knowledge of healing. Already our best healers prepare for travel to the battlefield."

"May the Lady bless you, Jehennette." The Oracle touched the sleeve of the woman's blue gown with one thin hand. "A few came with Zanitra, and women have arrived from Asur to fight in Her Own. But I fear healers will be much needed before this trouble with Frav is over. I wish this war could be averted in some way."

"You know it cannot," the head of Leshy answered, patting the Oracle's hand. "Tell me, what of this Tuonela child of whom we hear?"

"Zanitra is training Dakhma to control the use of her strange powers." The High Priestess motioned with her head toward the inner courts of the Temple. "And we have Ayron's young son here also. With the woman Malya, and now the Jabed and his men, roaming the land, we thought the child safer here in the Temple."

Jehennette looked startled. "Ayron had a son? What are his powers?"

"None that we can detect," said the Oracle.

"Not so." The High Priestess chewed on her lower lip. "This morning while Her Own practiced on the field, young Athdar nearly went into shape-shifting in his excitement. The head of the Kaballoi is even now testing him for that ability."

"How strange. The powers usually run true in family bloodlines." Jehennette frowned. "Do you know the family line?"

"Zanitra says his father was one of Kayth's men." The Oracle laced her long fingers together in her lap. "Strange currents have entered the bloodlines of Sar Akka through these other-world men. Some of it, as with the Dream Warrior, is to our good. Other lines are tainted, as with Malya. We can only wait and see."

"The Tamia Zanitra brought word that Malya is half-sister to Farblood." The High Priestess paced around the room. "We do not understand what twisted the mind of that one. But these new bloodlines must be carefully watched and the off-spring tested."

The sound of heavy footsteps in the corridor beyond brought the High Priestess' sword half out of the sheath as she faced the open door. She slid the weapon back as a helmeted Kaballoi stepped inside the room, one fist striking his armored chest in salute to the women.

"Word has just come from the Green Men. The Dream Warrior, the sorcerer, and their Tuonela companion journey through the mountains, on the road to Leshy. Odran and Hindjall, along with one of the Green Men, ride with them."

"Then I must leave at once." Jehennette turned to the Oracle, who nodded. "It is my duty to open the lower gates so that the Dream Warrior may undergo the Trial." She stood and bowed her head to the Oracle, then swept out of the room.

"Have you any clear foresight about the Dream Warrior and this Trial?" The High Priestess moved to the Oracle's side.

The young girl sighed and shook her head. "All I see are possible outcomes. Every path is clouded."

"If she fails?"

"If she fails, she will die, either in the body or in the mind," the Oracle answered. "One does not emerge from the Trial unchanged in some way." She shivered at her memories. "I know."

I do not understand," Takra said as she rode beside Odran. Deep Rising was behind them as they journeyed on the dusty road through farmlands on the outskirts of Leshy. "How can one put on and take off this seeming form of an animal or fighting bird? Does your mind remain that of a man or do you become the animal?" She pointed at the Kaballoi's Rissa-shaped helmet.

The tall man looked down at her, his green-flecked brown eyes intent as he thought. "When first I learned I could do this thing, I was very young and found it hard to control. Now I choose when I open my mind to the Rissa and let it pour into my form. When the shape-shifting is upon me, I feel Rissa, I fight Rissa, I think Rissa." He rubbed at his nose. "The Rissa-spirit does not leave me as long as the need for battle remains. It is this way with all Nu-Sheek."

"Do you know friend from unfriend?" Takra glanced once more at the eye-visor shaped like a snarling mountain cat.

"Aye. No animal ever attacks its own kind in battle." Odran's hand fell to the hilt of his extra-long sword slung at his narrow waist. "We have enough control to fight with swords, but if we are cornered while in shape-shift, each Kaballoi will fight with fang and claw as well." His spiked fighting bracelets of mountain steel winked in the sunlight as his hand came up to briefly cup the talisman hanging against his chest armor. "You do not have this ability among the Tuonela?"

Takra shook her head. "The men who followed us into the mountains, they did not live to carry word of our whereabouts to Malya, did they?" Takra smiled when Odran shook his head. "And the Jabed and his men?"

"They disappeared into the forests of Deep Rising, like the sneaky thieves they are. We think they will eventually ride north toward Frav."

"They come from the Temple, yet are followers of the Fravashi god?" Takra's amber eyes went wide with surprise. "Imandoff said the Asurans bend that direction, but I never thought it of Kirisan." She frowned at memories of Imandoff's ordeal.

"I do not think they follow that evil," Odran replied. "I have heard them say they believe that the Goddess should not be given the greatest honor, that women should be subject to the will of men. For those reasons they go north, thinking to make common cause with the Fravashi."

"By the hell-fires of Frav! Do they not realize that the Fravashi will use their powers, then cast them aside into slavery?" Takra's hands tightened on the reins.

"They think they can withstand the Volikvi priests when the war is finished." Odran pulled off his helmet to rub at his hair, braided into a cushion at the crown of his head. "It is strange that a Green Man would come down out of the mountains and willingly enter a city," he commented as they came in sight of the walls of Leshy. He stared ahead at Gadavar's straight back where the mountain ranger rode beside Corri.

"He does this for the Dream Warrior," Takra answered softly.

Imandoff held up his hand in a signal to stop, as Hindjall rode back toward the Kaballoi beside Takra.

"We must return to Kystan now," Odran said as his eyes once more held Takra's. "Doubtless, we will meet again on the field of battle. If you have need of me before then, send to the Temple."

Takra moved uneasily on Lightfoot. "Imandoff Silverhair will see that no harm comes to us." Her unconscious tightening of her knees made the horse dance.

Odran nodded, then without a word turned his horse to follow Hindjall on the road toward the city of Kystan.

"It appears the Kaballoi Odran found you more than passingly interesting," Imandoff said with a smile when she guided Lightfoot forward to ride beside him.

"It will take more than a Kaballoi to make me free you from heart oath, sorcerer," Takra said, a note of jest plain in her voice.

"I jested," Imandoff answered, the hint of a growl in his deep voice. "Any man, even a Kaballoi, would tuck tail between his legs and run if he so much as hints at such a parting between us."

Takra turned her head to look back at Corri and Gadavar, who rode side by side behind them. "Is this Trial of the Mask of Darkness a dangerous thing, Imandoff?"

"A very dangerous thing. Even Gadavar senses it." Imandoff scanned the people coming and going through the open gates of the city of Leshy. "I have never known a Green Man to willingly come out of his mountains to stay in a city. Yet he does so."

"He loves her," Takra answered. "Tirkul was a fool to cause a breach when he demanded that Corri withdraw from the trail set for her to ride."

"People in love often do stupid things," the sorcerer answered as he guided Sun Dancer down the street toward the great inner gates of the Mystery School. "We think that demands will protect loved ones from danger. It never does."

"It only causes the love to die, however long it may take us to acknowledge its death." *What a fool you were, Tirkul,* she thought. *I feel that Corri has at last buried her love for you and has opened her heart to another who loves her even more.*

The gates of the Mystery School opened for them to reveal the High Clua Jehennette waiting inside. No one spoke as the head of the Mystery School motioned for initiates to care for the horses, then led the dusty travelers across the courtyard to her personal quarters.

"Time is short," Jehennette said as she waved them to the table where a meal lay waiting. "News from the border is not good." She sat in a high-backed chair at the end of the table next to Imandoff.

"The Fravashi army has invaded Tuone?" Corri froze, her hands clasped around a goblet of fresh juice.

"No, but there are more attempts. Now word comes that strange night visions plague the Tuonela warriors holding the border." Jehennette turned her goblet round and round on the table. "I sent my message to you because I have found ancient records here at Leshy, records that are part of the Dream Warrior Prophecies. These records say that it is vital that the Dream Warrior undergo the Trial of the Mask of Darkness. You must undergo the Trial within three days, Dream Warrior. I fear you will soon be needed at the border to hearten the warriors. And perhaps to do battle in your own way," she added.

Gadavar's sun-browned hand fastened around Corri's wrist in comfort. The girl's hands shook as she set the goblet down on the table. "But I know nothing of the training given to initiates of the Mystery Schools."

Jehennette sighed and turned to Imandoff. "I will do what I can to help you," the sorcerer answered. "I would feel better if you had more time to prepare, at least prepare as much as possible. Only two people now living have undergone the Trial and survived—myself and the Oracle."

"Only two people have undergone the Trial?" Gadavar asked.

"Only two people have lived through it." Imandoff leaned back in his chair and looked straight at Corri.

"Then Farblood must not undergo this Trial!" Takra's fist smashed against the table, jarring the goblets and dishes set there.

"She must!" Jehennette answered. "The Oracle agrees. The Dream Warrior will need all the power she can find to use against Frav."

No one has asked me what I think. Corri rubbed at the corners of her tired eyes. *But there really is no other choice.*

"What important power can she hope to gain from this Trial?" Gadavar's quiet voice broke Takra's angry stare at Jehennette.

"It is different for each initiate," Imandoff answered with a shake of his head. "No one really understands the full powers of the ancient Mask of Darkness. Yet there is always a change, always an increase of power."

"I feel this is a thing I must do, but I am afraid." Corri's hand folded around Gadavar's.

"You would be a fool not to fear." Imandoff sighed. "I do not know what the Oracle experienced, but I . . . I still dream of it sometimes. For me, the Mask opened new talents and intensified those already existing. There are times I still feel its powers working through me."

"At sunrise of the third day I will be at the lower gates," Jehennette said as she rose. "Your rooms are prepared on the upper floor of this building. That way none will see or question you when you descend into the bowels of Leshy, where the Mask lies. Will you need a guide to the lower gates?"

Imandoff shook his head as he rose to face Jehennette. A sheen of perspiration dampened the sorcerer's face as he answered quietly, "I remember the way well."

Corri sat on the window ledge looking down into the herb garden in the courtyard below, the stone-paved paths bathed in moonlight. The hallway outside her closed door was quiet.

Do not look for fear before it appears, Farblood, she told herself. *That is the way to die a thousand times.*

A faint tapping came at the door, then it opened to reveal a Leshy healer, her blue gown just visible through the folds of her gray cloak.

"Gertha?" Corri held out her hands to the girl who had helped her escape from Leshy when the last High Clua thought to hold her against her will.

Corri and Gertha clasped hands, looking deep into each other's eyes for a moment. The healer's prayer beads, hung at her waist, softly clicked together as she stepped back.

"I knew I would see you again, Corri Farblood," the young woman said in a soft voice. "I dreamed it." Her blue eyes wrinkled at the corners as she smiled.

"Come, sit here beside me." Corri sank onto the narrow bed, the young healer beside her. "Can you tell me anything, my friend, that will help me when I undergo this Trial?"

"No one here in Leshy has undergone the Trial," Gertha answered, her fingers moving over her beads. "But you will never be led astray if you trust in the Lady. Open your heart and mind to Her, Corri. Let Her lead you in the way She wishes you to go."

"It sounds so easy, yet . . ."

"Yet it is so difficult?" Gertha smiled shyly. "We always fight against Her guidance, thinking we can trust better in the things we can see and touch. Even in healing this is so. Yet when I listen with my inner ears to Her voice, the healing works better, even with the worst cases."

"The new High Clua Jehennette, can she be trusted?" Corri's fingers played with the hilt of her belt dagger.

"You need not fear this one," Gertha answered, her face serious. "She walks the True Path, as do her young daughters, Sallin and Merra. Jehennette is a devoted, gentle healer, the best in Leshy, and one who listens always to the Goddess."

"I did not know the High Cluas of Leshy married!" Corri stared at Gertha in surprise.

"Under Jehennette, we may if we wish," the healer answered. "Merra, the oldest of Jehennette's children, is the daughter of a Tuonela warrior from the Black Moon Clan. She was born with much knowledge of how to open the body and heal with the knife, an uncommon practice and much feared by the other healers. Most healers say that if healing cannot take place with only herbs and the hands, then it is the Goddess' will that the sick or injured person should not be healed. Merra is gone from Leshy at this time to study with the feya women of the mountains. She wishes to learn the deeper trances connected with their healing skills." Gertha looked down at her hands.

"I understand. Because Merra is different, she is given little welcome here among the other healers." Corri frowned. "What of the other girl?"

"Sallin is a year younger. Her father was Davin, a merchant. Some whisper that he was from Frav, but how could that be? The girl knows how to draw power from other planes, channeling it through her hands and into the sick."

"So any danger here at Leshy lies not with the High Clua this time, but with the narrow-minded among the healers?"

Gertha nodded, loose strands from the bun at the back of her head falling about her face. "There are always those who fear anyone different. That is why the High Clua has put you and your friends here, away from the others. Have you continued to practice the meditations I taught you?"

"As much as I can," Corri answered, a wry smile curving her mouth. "My journeys have not left much time for meditations."

"Go within as much as you can before you undergo the Trial." Gertha took Corri's sun-browned hands in her pale ones. "I do not know what will be required for the Trial, but I do know that when one goes often to the quiet center within, one can more clearly hear the voice of the Goddess."

"I will," Corri whispered as she leaned forward to touch cheeks with Gertha.

"I must go." The healer stood up, smoothing back wisps of hair from her face. "All healers of Leshy must work in turns, day and night, to prepare medicines. We will be needed, Jehennette tells us, both at the border and here among the Peoples when the war comes. If Frav once more looses a plague, we may be all that stands between life and death for the Peoples." She smiled back at Corri as she opened the door and went into the dark corridor beyond.

The Goddess bless and keep you safe, Gertha, Corri thought as the door closed quietly. *O Lady, tell me how I should prepare for this Trial!* But no answer floated into Corri's mind as she turned back to the window.

The Oracle awoke with a start, the grayness of early dawn faintly lighting her bedchamber. She arose, wrapping a heavy cloak about her slight form as she walked out onto the balcony in the chill, dew-laden morning.

I have done everything I know to do, she thought as she stared down at the garden, all grays and blacks and faint whites in the new dawn. *The Kirisani have been warned to prepare for the coming war with Frav, to store food and hunt out old weapons. All those of warrior ability are here in the Temple, being trained in the arts of the sword and other weapons. Her Own is once more filling with warrior women.* She sighed and pulled the cloak tighter against the morning chill. *The old fortresses are being repaired and stocked as strongholds for the Peoples, if necessary. I have sent word to all the Peoples that the forbidden burial mounds from the last war are true warnings that the Fravashi may once more send plagues upon us. Even the Baba of Tuone has sent word that he instructs his Clans to prepare for war. What more is there, that I should have such fearsome dreams?*

Her mind worried at the edges of the dream that had awakened her in the early dawn until it locked onto a familiar image. She let her mind drift back into a half-dream state and found herself looking once more at the ancient helmet in the cave under the sacred waterfall, the helmet of the ancient warrior woman Varanna.

O Goddess, how could I have forgotten! She turned quickly from the window, one hand searching in the darkness for the rough touch of the bell-rope. *The Dream Warrior must wear Varanna's ancient helmet when she faces the Fravashi armies!*

As the Oracle's fingers encircled the rope, her door opened. Zanitra stood framed in the glow of the corridor lamps. The Oracle moved quickly toward her.

"Pardon, Oracle, but I must speak with you." Zanitra's velvety voice was edged with anxiety.

"What have you seen, Tamia?" the girl answered as her shaking hands lit a lamp. "Have you dreamed also?"

"I could not sleep." Zanitra closed the door and followed the Oracle across the chamber to drop into a chair beside the girl. "I was uneasy, so I sat gazing into the sejda balls. What I saw . . . I do not understand what I saw."

"Tell me!" The Oracle's slender fingers closed around Zanitra's arm.

"I saw the Dream Warrior and my brother Imandoff inside Frav! I have never seen Frav with these eyes, but I know it was Frav. And standing against them was a Tuonela warrior."

"The warrior woman who rode with them?" The Oracle frowned when Zanitra shook her head. "Then who?"

"I do not know. A man I have never seen before. It is so frustrating when the visions are not complete!" Zanitra rose and paced back and forth, her hands clenching and unclenching on her robe.

"Perhaps your vision answers my own questions of the dream that woke me." The Oracle's thin face was edged with golden light over the sharp facial bones. "In my dream I saw Varanna's helmet and knew that the Dream Warrior must wear it in the coming battles."

"Is the war with Frav closer than we thought?" Zanitra turned sharply to face the seated girl.

The Oracle shrugged. "I received no clear answer on that. You?"

Zanitra shook her head. "Nothing," she sighed. "But we dare not ignore your dreams, Oracle. Your dreams have always been true sendings."

"I wish the gift were stronger, that the dreams would show me when as well as what." The Oracle stood, wrapping the cloak tightly around her. "Come, Tamia Zanitra. You and I will go at once to the sacred cave for Varanna's helmet. Then we must send it to the Dream Warrior at Leshy."

"I will take it." Zanitra followed the Oracle out of the chamber, down the maze of halls toward the great underground cavern that led to the sacred cave. "My sword hand is still strong, as is my secret talent."

The Oracle paused, her hand on the great iron gate that separated the corridors from the underground cavern. "Of course. You would never dare let those of Sadko know what powers they forbid lie within you. What power do you hold so close, Zanitra?"

The older woman smiled as she looked deep into the Oracle's dark eyes. "The gift of creating illusions," she answered.

Corri lay a long time on her narrow bed, unable to sleep yet yearning for rest. At last she slipped the owl stone circlet on her head and willed herself to seek the quiet center within, that place of the spirit where the imprisoning body was left behind and her soul and mind sought for spiritual guidance and comfort. As she reached out to touch that otherworld calmness, she felt her spirit-body separate from the physical and found herself hanging near the ceiling of her room.

I will see Tirkul, she told herself. *I must see if Kayth has done the evil he spoke of, or whether Tirkul has evaded the blackness of that control.*

With the quickness of thought, Corri rose above Leshy and turned to face the mountain barrier, far across the wide Tuonela grasslands. Then she passed, unseen, through the dark night sky, speeding over the grasslands rippling gently in the night wind until she hung over the Tuonela warrior's solitary camp near the land bridge over the Kratula Gorge.

Tirkul? Corri's spirit-body stood beside the sleeping warrior, the horse Hellstorm beside him. *Tirkul,* she mind-called again.

Corri? Tirkul's spirit-body sat up, staring at her. *Why have you called me in my dreams? Are you safe?*

He rose, gathered her into his arms, crushing her against his broad chest. She raised her lips and felt a feathery kiss brush her mouth. He pushed her away a little so he could look down into her eyes.

Hush, he said as her mind formed words. *There are things I must say while I have the courage. I was wrong to demand you leave this path ordained by the Lady. You cannot throw aside your duty anymore than can I. My words were shameful. I would not smother you with unwanted love, for that in itself would kill whatever you may feel for me. Such a burden of demanding love may well cause you to open yourself to the enemy, bringing about your death through the ties I thought to bind between us.*

To trust or to love, that is difficult, Tirkul. Corri looked up into his eyes and, with a sudden insight, knew that a part of Tirkul also had moved beyond what he once called love for her. She felt no sadness that this was so, merely a deep feeling of great and loving friendship. *In all my life there was no one I could trust or who truly loved me. I only know that such a blanket of love as you offered made me feel a prisoner. Stand beside me as a friend,*

Tirkul. Help me to do what I must do. I need time and space to learn what love truly is.

Corri felt a strange pulsing begin in her spirit-form, a feeling of energy waiting to rise. *As much as I know of love and friendship, I love you as a close and dear friend.*

I, too, question this feeling of love. Tirkul's eyes were sad. *I never want you out of my life, but I think this is not the meaning of love. Remember, I promised to be at your back whenever you need me. Still, I wish you did not ride into danger.*

I must do what is my destiny. If I turn aside, everything we know of Sar Akka will be drowned in a flood of evil and death. If you come with me, I can offer you nothing, not even life at the end. When this war is done, I may not even live.

I know this, and I am afraid. If I could, I would put my body between you and any danger.

Where the Lady leads me, you cannot go, Tirkul. It is a path I must journey alone.

As a warrior I know this. As a man who loves you as my dearest friend, it makes me angry and sad. I feel helpless, but a part of me knows that such emotions will hinder what you must do. I release you from heart oath, Corri. I would not encumber you in any way.

Corri clutched at him, burying her head in the hollow at the base of his throat. *Do not leave me adrift without any love! Please, Tirkul, do not ask me to break the only line I have, a line that may be as important as the rope you threw to snatch me from the flood waters.*

Ah, my little thief, even though I know there can never be love of man and woman between us, I want you so. Tirkul pulled her down to lie beside him. He moved closer, until their spirit-bodies touched from forehead to hip.

Corri felt the energy whirling within her pelvic area, then rise to burn through her spirit-body to the crown of her head. She felt it jump from her heart to Tirkul's, then match his at the throat, the forehead, and the crown of the head. The energy flashed downward again, shaking her with its intensity as it bridged at the abdomen and finally the pelvic region. She melted into its fire, her body quivering in waves of ecstasy as she and Tirkul blended together in their spirit-bodies in a matching of the age-old physical rhythm of love.

Corri lay in the relaxed aftermath of this strange spiritual lovemaking, watching Tirkul meld back into his physical body. *I do not think this is what loving means, but rather an expression of closeness and caring. What do Imandoff and Takra have together that makes their love different?*

For several moments she watched Tirkul's sleeping face, then turned her thoughts back to Leshy. As she rose to hang over the quiet campsite, preparing to return to her sleeping body, Corri thought of Kayth's threatening words. *I will not let him use Tirkul against the Peoples!* she thought fiercely. *There must be some way I can protect him.*

As she hung there in deep thought, her mind engrossed in recalling the lovemaking and in remembering what she had learned of magic from Imandoff and Halka, she did not see the faint blood-red wave of energy sweep across the Gorge and fasten onto her spirit-body. She only became aware when its relentless force began to draw her into Frav. She fought against the pull, but it was useless.

This has not the feel of Kayth or Minepa. She kept her resistance strong as her mind nibbled at the edges of the entrapping power. *Who else in Frav must I fear?*

She swept over the Gorge, across the sleeping city of Vu-Murt and on over the separate city connected to the Fire Temple. Her spirit-body spiraled gently downward until it passed through the stone wall of a tall building enclosed by a garden-like area.

This time Corri found herself inside a room where she had never been before. Soft draperies hung over the bed; tapestries depicting sexual scenes covered the stone walls. Perfume bottles and pots of face paint littered a small table holding a mirror. The incense burning near the bed gave off a strange arousing, cloying scent.

In the pale candlelight, she saw two forms entwined on the bed, the pale limbs of a woman and the thicker ones of a man. In the air above the physical forms were the spirit-bodies of the two lovers. On the floor by the bed was a pile of rumpled clothing, the dark red robes of a Volikvi priest intermingled with the filmy garments of the woman.

Corri tried to free herself, disgusted at being a captive to the lovemaking of others. But she was held fast as a fly in honey. In a flash she realized that her spirit lovemaking with Tirkul had connected her in some way through the lovemaking of these Fravashi.

Listen! The single word echoed through Corri's mind.

Lady? A sense of protecting warmth swept over her. *Goddess, why am I here?* No answer came. *I may have to listen, but I need not watch,* she thought, turning her attention away from the moaning pair.

Quiet settled in the room as the priest and the woman broke apart. Corri backed up against the wall as far as she could against the pull of the trapping energy.

"Did I not tell you, Zalmoxis, that Kayth was a danger? Not only to Minepa, but to you." The woman's voice was husky, full of post-sexual gratification.

The man grunted and sat up, reaching down for his robes. "Yes, Xephena, you told me." He swung his legs over the side of the bed, bringing his face into the candlelight. "What would you have me do, now that I believe you?"

"Bide your time." The woman sat up, stretched, and pushed back her long black hair, tints of red glowing in the soft light. "Kayth may yet let drop some secret we can use."

"You have snared him with your lovemaking?" The man's broad flat nose and cruel mouth were edged with light, his pale shaven head with its long, deep auburn side-curl over each ear plain to Corri's view. "Be careful, Xephena, that you are not burned by your plotting. This knowledge of lovemaking in the other-body is forbidden to Trow priestesses. Minepa is not one to toy with."

"Do you doubt the strength of my powers, Zalmoxis? I am the one who created the pathway for the shadow-seeker, that ethereal otherworld being that trails the girl. I will make Kayth forget this obsession for heirs through his daughters," she answered. "And when I sit at Kayth's side, then he and his daughters will all die."

"Do you think that Kayth will be taken in by your arts of loving, so that you can scratch him with your poisoned claw blades?" Zalmoxis dropped a bloodstone pendant around his neck. "It will take more than poison to remove Kayth."

Xephena looked straight up at Corri and smiled. "None of you know the extent of my powers," she said softly.

Chapter 13

As soon as the door closed behind Zalmoxis, Xephena rose from the bed. She sensually stretched, cupped her breasts with long-nailed fingers, then smoothed her hands down over her narrow waist and flaring hips. Her painted dark eyes looked straight up at Corri as the priestess smiled.

"Greetings, Dream Warrior." Xephena's voice was sultry, sexually inviting. "I had not set my snare for you, rather for your Tuonela warrior. But I caught a bigger fish—the fabled spirit-warrior who will protect the Peoples from Kayth and his armies." The voice now dripped with contempt. "It seems that you are not as pure as they believe, woman, if you are attracted and entrapped by the powers of my lovemaking spell."

Corri pressed herself back against the wall, the extent she could retreat from the Fravashi priestess. *Nothing in the Prophecies says that I must avoid lovemaking,* Corri said. *Varanna herself had a lover.*

"Varanna!" The priestess shrugged into her filmy clothing, a shadow of contempt twisting her full mouth. "Varanna is nothing. If she lived today, the victory would be mine, not hers. My powers far exceed what Varanna knew!" The gold-decorated girdle about her hips flashed in the candlelight.

Speak carefully, Fravashi. Varanna was led and protected by the Goddess, as am I, Corri warned.

"I go now to sacrifice to a Goddess greater than your Frayma," Xephena said as she picked up tiny curved blades from the table and slipped one over each finger. "The Goddess Croyna is the Eater of Souls, the Giver of dark powers, the One who destroys all in the end. I order you to abide here, Dream Warrior, until I return." The woman's armed fingers wove a web of power in the air between them, a web that settled over Corri's body. "No use to struggle, woman. You cannot break out of my control." The Trow priestess looked back as she opened the door to the corridor. "I will deal with you when I return. I will make you obey my will as neither Kayth nor Minepa has been able to do."

Corri did not answer the Trow, but watched her silently as the door closed. *Goddess, what is there here to learn that You do not help me get free?*

She felt a sensation of both warmth and cold at the back of her neck where her head joined her spinal column. She shivered, fighting the strange power that pressed against her, attempting to enter her spirit-body.

Trust me, daughter. The Lady's voice came soft and clear in Corri's mind. *Let Me join with your spirit. This joining will enable you to be free of the Trow's power.*

Corri pushed aside the fear she felt, and tried to relax as part of the Lady's being slid into her spirit-body. As the energy settled, Corri felt as if she saw through two sets of eyes. The sticky webs of the spell crumbled to ashy specks, which melted away.

Now I will show you the true evil of the Fravashi priests and priestesses, the voice said in Corri's mind. *The Peoples do not* truly know what evil dwells here, an evil that controls the Fravashi people and keeps them from overthrowing their rulers.

Corri's mind withdrew to a state of vague awareness as the possessing power of the Lady moved the girl's spirit-body swiftly through a series of walls, always downward, until she emerged in a great subterranean cavern. At a dark-stained altar near a deep cleft in the rock stood Xephena, thick incense clouds billowing around her. The light of black candles at each end of the altar glittered on the claw blades on the fingertips of the upraised hands.

"Awake, Croyna!" The Trow's husky voice echoed through the high-vaulted cave. "Goddess of Dark Powers, I bring to you the promised sacrifice!"

Corri tried to move away, but found herself forced to watch. On the altar lay a young woman, naked, chained at ankles and wrists to the block itself. Corri found that she could not even avert her eyes as Xephena stepped out of her gauzy robe. The Trow straddled the bound woman, lowering her face to kiss the captive's breasts and abdomen. The claw blades made bloody tracks wherever the priestess caressed the bound woman's body. In the shadows at the edges of the candlelight, Corri saw the veiled forms of other Trow and heard the beginnings of their wild chanting.

As Xephena worked herself into a sexual frenzy, Corri became frantic to leave this scene of degradation. She fought against the controlling power of the Lady until she hung defeated in the smoky air, her eyes still riveted on the twisting form below.

She calls upon Me in another of My forms, the voice said in Corri's mind. *She has twisted my aspect of the Elder One into something evil and degenerate, a warped power to suit her own desires.*

How can that be? Corri felt as if her physical body, left behind at Leshy, was trying to vomit out this filth her spirit-body saw. *You are not evil, Lady. Your power is good and clean.*

Power is power. Its purpose can be twisted by the user of that power. A tinge of sadness colored the voice. *Dark power can be used, although not fully, for goodness, as the power of the light can be partly turned to the ways of darkness.*

Xephena picked up a wickedly curved dagger as she shouted strange words. The blade gleamed in the light as she slowly pushed it upward into the rib cage of the bound woman. The wild chanting drowned out the captive's scream as the knife found her heart. The Trow rubbed the blood over the dead woman's body, licking at it with her pointed tongue. With a great shout, the chanting ended, leaving the subterranean chamber in a heavy silence.

"The sacrifice is accepted." Xephena slid off the dead body and motioned to the priestesses crouching in the shadows. Her body seemed to glow with vitality, appearing now even more voluptuous than it had been. "Give her body to Jevotan, for the God must have His share also."

Two of the priestesses crept forward to free the bound limbs of the victim. They tugged the limp form from the altar block and cast it into the cleft in the floor. An answering cloud of fire-lit vapor rose with the stench of burning flesh.

Now you have seen true evil, the Lady's voice said. *What My children do to each other is evil enough, but what these priestesses do in My name, calling upon one of My forms, is doubly so, for they twist My gift of love into a thing of filth. Love is for creating life, not for taking it in this manner.*

Corri felt herself rise swiftly once more through the stone walls of the Fire Temple until she hung in the star-sprinkled air.

You are My Dream Warrior. You are the only hope of the Peoples for freedom from the terror of these priests and priestesses with their warped minds and misuse of My power. Return to Leshy, My daughter. Put on My Mask of Darkness. I will always be with you.

Corri's spirit-body quivered as the power of the Goddess withdrew. Her thoughts turned to Leshy, but as she began to move through the night toward the Mystery School she felt something snap around her ankle. Looking down, she saw a hair-thin red tentacle running back to the Temple below. She kicked and twisted, finally calling up a bright sword to her hand. She bent, slashed at the tentacle, then fled through the night back to her physical body on the narrow bed at Leshy.

Corri sat up, her heart pounding, her mouth dry. Jerking the owl stone from her forehead, she slid it into the carrying pack and went to splash her face with water from the basin in the corner. She leaned against the stone wall, shivering and shaking, as she fought against the need to vomit from what she had seen. She stripped off her soaked undergarments, replacing them with fresh ones from her travel bags. Still chilled, she dressed in her tunic and trousers.

I cannot let that Fravashi filth pour into the other lands, she thought as she stumbled back to the bed. Her mind continued to see the parody of love Xephena had forced on the bound woman before sacrificing her. *They have twisted every good in life in order to gain power through the dark forces. And I may be the only hope of stopping them.*

She clutched the coarse wool blanket about her, too soul-sick in mind to sleep; yet her physical body shook with exhaustion. Out of the corner of her eye, she saw a shadowy mist in one dark corner of the room. She felt the hair on the nape of her neck rise as the misty form tried to move into the light, but was repelled.

Corri felt an icy coldness reach out to her, then withdraw. When a soft knock came on her door, she leaped from the bed and tore open the door. Gertha stood there in her nightdress, hair loose about her shoulders, her face white. Behind the healer stood the tall form of Imandoff.

"O Goddess, Imandoff, help me!" Corri's voice was only a cracked whisper.

The two pushed into the room, Gertha drawing Corri to one side while Imandoff faced the misty form in the dark corner.

The sorcerer's slender fingers wove a net of light across the corner, trapping the intruding entity, then reached back one hand to the healer.

"The trap, Gertha," he said, his eyes still on the shadowy figure that beat against the net.

From a pocket in her nightdress, Gertha drew out a small, thin, flattened plate, a spiraling line of writing circling from its outer edge to the very center. Imandoff carefully slid the trap into the shadows, then stepped backward. A thin, shrieking cry darted through Corri's mind as the shadowy mist sank into the center of the plate.

"What followed you here, Corri?" Imandoff sat beside the girl and Gertha on the narrow bed.

"I think the spirit-form of a Trow priestess." Corri's hands shook as she clasped them together in her lap. "But how did you know to come?"

"A dream," Imandoff and Gertha answered together.

"If you were followed by a Trow, I will not ask you what you saw her do." Imandoff frowned as he smoothed back Corri's hair. "What I know of the Volikvis is bad enough, but old stories say the Trow are worse."

Corri's raw inner senses screamed a warning just before she saw the trap in the corner crack from side to side.

"Impossible!" Imandoff shouted as he threw himself before the women. "No one can break free of a spirit-trap!"

The shadowy mist shot upward and disappeared through the roof.

"Kayth has the power." Corri's voice was tired. "At least Xephena's spirit-body is gone."

"When strong powers of light come up against strong dark powers, there is always a troubling." Imandoff whirled to Gertha. "Warn the High Clua. The School must be recleansed and resealed." Gertha ran out of the room, her face white with fear.

Corri's inquiry about Imandoff's words died on her lips as balls of light sprang into existence and bounced around the room. The water pitcher and basin in the corner rose to the ceiling, then fell to shatter on the floor. Icy fingers pulled at her hair while evil laughter could be heard in the corridor beyond. Screams and cries of alarm broke out in every room of the Mystery School, shattering the night.

The School was a frenzy of frightened initiates and disturbing phenomena as Corri and Imandoff hurried toward the chapel. Small whirlwinds blew dirt and pieces of herb leaves into their faces as they fought their way with other initiates to the safety of the thrice-blessed building. Corri cried out in pain as her bare toes stubbed against the doorsill.

Inside, Jehennette stood near the white-covered altar, her mouth set with determination. In her hands she held a smoking censer and a bunch of fresh-cut moly. At her side stood a man with a silver bell and a woman clutching a pitcher of blessed water from the School's well.

"Does Frav think us so powerless that they can send their evil creations to trouble this School?" Jehennette asked, her eyes bright with anger.

"It is my fault," Corri said. "A Trow followed me here with her spirit-body when I dream-flew tonight."

Jehennette shook her head. "No, child, the only surprise to me is that they have not tried these tricks sooner." She turned to Imandoff, who now held his sword in one hand. "It is long since I have had to cleanse and seal by ritual."

"Once learned, it is never forgotten." The sorcerer raised his hands for silence. "You must all calm yourselves and chant for power as we clean this intruding evil from Leshy," he said to the initiates crowded before the altar.

Corri heard the splatter of entity-thrown pebbles against the chapel door, the whine of ghost-wind against the glazed windows of the chapel and the gibber of otherworld voices outside as she watched the initiates begin their calming techniques. Soon the chants filled the great room, drowning out the noise of the forces attempting to enter the building.

Imandoff began to circle the room, drawing a line of visible power with his sword. Behind him Jehennette marched with her swinging censer, shaking the bunch of moly at each corner. The woman with the pitcher sprinkled drops of water as she went, the sharp tones of the silver bell rung by the other initiate hard on her heels.

Unwilling to remain behind, Corri followed the sorcerer and the other exorcists out of the chapel and through each building of the School. She felt the oppressing forces of evil entities retreat as the sorcerer and his attendants cleansed and sealed each place they found to be contaminated, until they at last stood once more back at the door to Corri's room.

As Imandoff and Jehennette marched into the tiny room, Corri jumped as a hand grabbed her arm. She whirled to find Takra beside her in the corridor.

"I could no longer stay within the circle Imandoff cast," the Tuonela whispered. "A Tuonela does not leave friends to face danger alone." Takra gave a shudder, then peered through the open door. "All those gibbering faces and things flying about the room set my teeth on edge. Where did they come from?"

"From Frav," Corri answered, her eyes flicking over every shadow in the long corridor. She was aware for the first time of how cold her bare feet were.

"An attack on you." Takra's face was grim as she laid a firm hand on the girl's shoulder. "I thought this place was a safe haven from such attacks, at least by Imandoff's reckoning."

"It is safer than meeting these entities outside with no walls to seal against them." The sorcerer leaned against the door frame, his sword hanging loose in his hand. His face was drawn with exhaustion, drops of perspiration trickling down his cheeks into his beard. He waited until the other exorcists went down the corridor to join the initiates in the chapel. "Corri, what does your heart tell you?"

"I think I should undergo the Trial sooner than three days," she answered with a deep sigh.

"No!" Takra looked from Corri to Imandoff, her sword half-raised.

"Wait longer," Jehennette said, setting her censer and herbs on the floor. "Take time before deciding this, child. Learn more than Imandoff or I can teach you in three days. You will need every scrap of knowledge you can gather for this Trial."

"I agree with Corri." Imandoff slid the long sword into the sheath at his waist. "She must not wait. Postponing the Trial will only give Kayth and his followers time to regain their strength and possibly attack again."

"The child is exhausted," Jehennette persisted, "and it is already near dawn. If she undergoes the Trial sooner than the three days, when will she rest? When will you teach her?"

"I will rest today, then go to the lower gates at nightfall." Corri looked at the sorcerer, who nodded agreement.

"There really is no way to prepare anyone for the Trial, Jehennette." Imandoff's gray eyes held Corri's in a rueful stare. "How can I prepare anyone when each experience is different from all others?"

"Will you be with me?" Corri asked, fear plain on her face. "Or must I go alone to this place of Trial?"

"Only one who has undergone the Trial may enter with the initiate." Imandoff laid his hand on Corri's shoulder. "I will go with you, Dream Warrior."

"No one tells me where I can and cannot go." Takra's jaw was firm, her mouth a tight line of defiance. "I will be with my sister-friend, whatever your laws say."

Imandoff raised his hand to stop Jehennette's flood of protesting words. "You can go as far as the outer door of the chamber," he said. "It is too dangerous for the uninitiated to enter once the Trial is underway. No protests, Takra. This is the way it must be. This is something Corri must undergo alone. Even I cannot aid her, except by my presence."

"I have to do this alone, Takra, for I think this Trial must be a thing of the mind." Corri smiled ruefully. "But I need you and your bravery to guard me against any who might try to stop what I do." Takra nodded.

Jehennette reached up to a peg by the room's entrance and took down a metal disk that she hung on a hook in the center of the door. "While this hangs here, no one in Leshy will disturb you. Sleep all you can, child, then meditate until dusk." She picked up her ritual tools and lightly kissed Corri's cheek before she disappeared down the corridor.

"It is safe," Imandoff said as Corri hesitated on the threshold. "They cannot enter that way again."

Corri stood on tiptoe to kiss the bearded cheek. "My thanks, old man. Now, do you not think you and Takra should rest also? You have fought a hard battle against the forces of Frav this night."

"We will come for you at dusk," Takra promised as she and the sorcerer headed toward the stairs.

Corri cautiously entered the room, her eyes seeking all the shadowed corners. *If you shy at shadows like some timid pleasure woman, how will you react in some creepy underground hole tonight?* she chided herself as she curled up on the bed. She said nothing to the initiate who came to pick up the broken pitcher and basin and replace them with others.

Although she thought she would never sleep, Corri sank into an exhausted slumber just as the chapel bells rang out for morning worship.

Clear, bright sunlight lit the room when Corri aroused at the sound of a tray being slid through the bottom slot in the door. She yawned, then hurried to snatch up the food, hunger strong within her. She savored the fresh bread topped with churned butter, a boiled egg, and dish of stewed fruit, washing it down with hot herbal tea. Once the hunger pangs had eased, she put aside the tray and leaned back against the rough stone wall, letting her mind ease its way into the calm center of meditation.

She saw and heard no one within that calm place. Instead of seeking the Lady, as she would have done at another time,

Corri drifted in that calm, soaking it up, storing it against any future need. She was at peace, all fear of the upcoming Trial only a dim distant memory. When she once more opened her eyes, the sunlight within the room was dimmer as the sun began its fall toward the western mountains.

Corri sat unmoving, her body relaxed as she watched the sunlight slowly move across the floor. The sound of a scratching noise at the door brought her alert and tense. When it continued, she quickly crossed the small room to ease open the door. Gadavar slipped inside, pushing the door shut behind him.

"I had to see you, Corri. You should not be alone at this time," he whispered. "I know the scent of fear, and it hangs over you like a cloud."

"Where were you when we were cleansing the School?" she asked, looking up into his brown eyes.

"Locked in my room by our sorcerer friend. It took me some time to pick the lock." Gadavar smiled down at her. "Imandoff thought it would be safer for me there."

"But did you not see things? Terrible uncanny things?"

"The Green Men have their own magic against the dark forces." Gadavar cupped her cheek with one hand. "Are you unharmed?" His brow wrinkled in concern.

"Only a little shaken by all I have seen."

"Corri." The Green Man breathed her name as he looked down at her, desire plain in his eyes. His hand trembled as he touched her cheek, then caressed her neck, her collarbone, and the hollow of her throat. "Am I too forward in coming here? Perhaps you do not feel the same as I do."

In answer, Corri leaned into his strong arms, her face upturned to meet his lips. He held her tightly as their bodies molded together. She felt the thick muscles of his back bunch and quiver under her hands. His breath came harder as she slid her hands down his ribs to the belt at his waist.

"Make love with me, Gadavar." Corri's voice shook with emotion.

He scooped her up as he turned toward the narrow bed. As he laid her on the bed, his lips slid down the column of her throat and into the opening of her tunic. Corri ran her fingers through his leaf-brown hair as he unlaced the tunic to cup her breasts.

"I can make no promises to you," she whispered as he shrugged out of his clothes, dropping them on the floor beside hers. She caught her lower lip in her teeth as he turned back to her. *He is perfect,* she thought, her heart beating wildly as her eyes trailed over his muscled chest, the long, lean thighs, the strong arms. Gently, he removed her clothing.

"I ask for none." He stroked his hands down her belly, then back up to her breasts.

Corri reached for him, drawing him down, her lips finding his, her body arching to meet him. His gentleness and his love wrapped around her, sweeping through her body and mind like a hot tidal wave. Nothing around her was real except Gadavar's body against hers. Every inch of her skin was alive and aware. The emotions that surged through her lifted her body and mind and soul to a new, sharp perception and joy she never expected to find or experience.

I am drowning, she thought as she released her fears and inhibitions like old worn-out clothing. *I never thought I could feel this way toward any man. Even in my shadow-self with Tirkul I felt nothing like this! If this is love, I never want to let him go.*

The brief physical discomfort gave way to a stronger sense of pleasure. She reached out with her mind to link with his mind, sinking deeper into the ecstasy.

Think with me of strength and safety. Gadavar's firm command drew her even further into the realm of magical loving. *Use the power we raise from our loving to armor yourself for the Trial.*

Corri let go of the last of her inner reserve and felt Gadavar mold the power raised between them into an almost tangible thing, then feed it back into her.

Afterward, as they lay twined together, bodies damp from lovemaking, Corri sensed a difference within herself, a sense of confidence, an eagerness to be done with the Trial and on to the border.

"This may be the beginning of a journey from which I may not return," she said softly, her lips against Gadavar's head where he rested against her breasts.

"I know." Gadavar raised his head until he could kiss her. "I ask no promises from you, Corri. I have done what I can to protect you. Whatever happens, whatever you decide if we both live through the coming battles, remember I love you."

"And if I do not choose you . . . if I live and go another way . . ." The words fought their way through her tight throat.

"My heart will be heavy, but I will understand." Gadavar gathered her in his arms, whispering against her hair. "I have known a pure true love, even if only for a moment. I will carry that love with me into Between Worlds."

Corri felt hot tears trickle down her cheeks. *Why can I not tell him of my choice?* she asked herself. *Why do I speak as if Tirkul still has a hold on my heart?* She swallowed at the lump in her throat. *I am afraid, afraid that if I tell him of my love he will, someday, become someone I can no longer love. And I am terrified that he will not survive the battle, and I will be alone again.*

Gadavar wiped away the tears and gently pulled her head onto his chest, where she heard the steady beating of his heart. Gradually, his whispered words of mountain forests and vivid sunsets in her ears, she drifted off to sleep.

When Corri awoke, she was alone on the narrow bed. Only the faint rays of sunset came through the window, splashing weakly across the floor. She smiled at the few unexpected sore spots, remembering the night with Gadavar and savoring the memory of each word and kiss. Then, like a splash of cold water, she remembered the Trial.

Imandoff will be here soon, she thought. *Goddess, be with me. I am as ready as I will ever be.*

As she reached down to get her clothes, her fingers curled around a silver disk strung on a leather thong. She held it up to better see the scratched design she felt on it.

"Corri," she read aloud, then "Gadavar." Below the words was etched the upturned crescent moon of the Goddess.

She slipped the pendant over her head to lie next to the one given to her by Halka, the Tuonela shakka. Her mind still hazy with sleep, she bathed as best she could from the basin, then quickly dressed. As she tugged on her half-boots, Imandoff opened the door and peered in.

"It is time, Corri," he said. "Takra awaits on the stairs below."

"Gadavar, will he be there?"

Imandoff stepped inside, pulling the door closed behind him. "To a sorcerer, it shows." He smiled gently as he leaned back against the door. "Love carefully, Corri, but take your loving where you can. None of us knows if we will see the morrow. And you who have never known love before, the power of this love may save you when you face alone the evil of Frav. My heart tells me your task would be so much harder without love."

Corri felt a blush rise on her cheeks. "If people do not know you as I do, they might think you and Takra did not love each other. But you do love her, do you not? Even with all the jesting and growling you do at each other."

"That is our personal way of expressing our love." Imandoff cocked his head to one side and smiled. "But for you and Gadavar I think it is different."

"Gadavar . . ." Corri paused and looked away from the sorcerer's intent gray eyes.

Imandoff walked to her side and brushed back her hair from her cheek. "Gadavar did the best he could for you, more than I realized he could do."

"Where is he?" Corri asked, her throat tightening.

"Word came an hour ago, calling him back to the mountains." Imandoff fingered his sword hilt. "Trouble arises at our backs. The Jabed found men to listen to his rebellious words before he disappeared again. Gadavar was needed to help keep the peace in the mountains."

"Letting myself love him is hard, Imandoff. I am so afraid." A tear slid down her cheek.

"I know," the sorcerer answered softly as he wiped it away. "My heart becomes ice and seems to stop beating each time I let myself think of Takra going into battle with you. My love for her has become my life, my very breath, the only reason I now care whether I live or die." He touched Corri's cheek lightly with one hand. "Yet I dare not try to protect her, or it will kill that love. I endure the inner pain of possible loss by simply living for the moment."

I will always love you. I will carry your love with me into Between Worlds. Gadavar's words echoed through Corri's mind.

He knew he could not go with me, she thought. *He knew, yet he gave me what he could, without asking anything in return.*

"I am ready now, Imandoff." Corri straightened her shoulders, one hand pressing against Gadavar's pendant hanging under her tunic. "It is time I faced this Trial and got on about the Lady's business."

Chapter 14

Tirkul's head dropped onto his bent knees as he tried to keep vigil near the bridge into Frav. Hellstorm, his buckskin horse, twitched his ears toward the bridge and snorted. The moon, breaking through the clouds, revealed two figures standing on the stone span. The horse stamped his feet in warning, but Tirkul slept on.

Tirkul, come to me. A parody of Corri's voice rose in the Tuonela's mind. *I am here, on the bridge. Come to me. Together we shall defeat Frav. Come.*

A tendril of power swept across the bridge, pushed into the sleeping warrior's mind, and locked him into Kayth's control. Tirkul rose slowly and began to stagger toward the spell-bound border, his open eyes unseeing, his hands hanging loosely at his sides. On he went, passing through the spells without concern, onto the bridge.

"Take him to my special room, Minepa," Kayth ordered. "I told you he would be the key to victory over the other lands, and so he shall be, when I finish with him."

Hellstorm screamed a challenge, racing straight toward the bridge, then veering aside as Kayth threw a fireball in the mount's face. Minepa hurried the Tuonela warrior along, Kayth keeping the horse at bay, until they passed through the gates at the other end of the bridge.

"I did not think his horse would do battle for him," Kayth mused as he slammed the locking bar into place. "How is it the horse could cross over?" The sound of hooves striking the closed portal echoed through the courtyard in which they stood.

"Animals can pass through the spells," Minepa answered, his hand tight on Tirkul's unresisting arm. "If you had asked, I would have told you."

"What else have you forgotten to tell me, Minepa?"

The Volikvi cringed at the tone in Kayth's voice. He bowed his head, yet his deep-set eyes held sparks of resentment. "Nothing of importance," he said softly.

His mouth twisted with contempt, Kayth turned and led the way into the Temple. Up the back stairs he went, through torch-lit hallways, until he opened a door carved with the leering faces of demons. Tirkul moaned as he crossed over the threshold.

"Quickly, before he fully awakens." Kayth pulled Tirkul toward a waist-high stone block with iron chains and shackles set into the sides. "Down, you enemy of Jinniyah! Now you will serve me whether you will or no."

Minepa and Kayth forced the warrior face-down onto the block and locked the shackles about his wrists and ankles, stretching his body straight and tight against the stone.

"Where am I?" Tirkul turned his head from side to side, his long braids dragging on the dark stone.

"Inside Vu-Zai, Tuonela scum." Minepa grabbed Tirkul's hair with one taloned hand, twisting his head upward. "You will tell us what we wish to know."

"Never!" Tirkul spat at the Volikvi, who dropped his hold. The warrior's face smashed against the stone block, splitting his lip.

"We shall see." Kayth moved into his line of vision, a strange implement in his hand. "How brave are the Tuonela, Minepa? Brave enough to endure this?"

He bent and applied the torture tool to Tirkul's shoulder muscles. The warrior's eyes went wide with shock as burning waves shot through his upper chest and neck. He clenched his teeth, his body shaking uncontrollably.

"That is just the first taste of what I can do." Kayth bent close to the bowed head, his voice low.

"I will never help you." Tirkul's voice was only a bare whisper.

Kayth applied the instrument to the thick muscles of Tirkul's arm. The warrior's hand cramped, his fingers crooking into tendon-stretching positions. The sweat now rose over his entire body, dripped down his face to splatter on the stone block, but he made no sound.

"Let me try." Minepa's eyes were bright with eagerness.

"I want him broken, not dead." Kayth continued to move the torture tool from one place to another on Tirkul's body. "He is no good to us dead."

The burning agony, the deep pain in muscles and joints, went on and on. Before they subsided in one place, they began in another. Tirkul moaned, his head tossing from side to side. At last the taunting voices receded, becoming only a faint echoing within his skull, as he lay half-conscious on Kayth's torture block.

"Now he will move and exist according to my will." Kayth's voice echoed back and forth through Tirkul's skull.

The warrior felt Minepa's bony hands take his head on both sides and hold it in a punishing grip. "Anything forced into the brain will kill him."

"It will not be in the brain." Kayth's fingers probing at the back of Tirkul's neck where it met the skull felt like fire-hot brands to the warrior. "And he will be able to tell no one what I have done."

Tirkul screamed as he felt Kayth push a sharpened point into his neck. The Tuonela warrior tried to fight against the pressure and pain, the fear of what they did, but he was helpless. Minepa's fingers dug into the sides of his head, the long nails drawing blood. Tirkul lost consciousness as Kayth pushed the device deeper into his upper neck muscles.

The key grated sharply, cracking the underground silence, as Jehennette unlocked the great inner gates below the Mystery School. Corri heard her breath, and the breath of those with her, overloud in the heavy stillness of the rock-hewn corridor. The lamps carried by her companions bathed them all in a warm glow, but beyond the gate Corri saw only a thick blackness, a darkness that seemed to reach out, pressing on her chest. Her hands, hidden under her cloak, twisted together in nervousness.

"I will be in the chapel," Jehennette said as she gave the gate key to Imandoff. The High Clua turned to Corri, quickly embracing her. "Perhaps my prayers to the Lady will aid you in this Trial. Surely She would not desert you, Her Dream Warrior, in this time of great crisis, but prayers never hurt."

I feel the fear in her. I, too, am afraid, so very afraid, but this Trial is something I know I must do. Corri looked around at the black wavering shadows, clotted like waiting specters in the stone corridor. *I will center my thoughts on the Goddess and trust Her to guide me through.*

Without another word, the head of Leshy went back up the long rock-lined corridor, the light from her lamp growing ever smaller.

"I cannot enter?" Takra's amber eyes pleaded with Imandoff, who shook his head. "I have hunted the barsark, I have stood guard at the border to Frav, I have danced the sword glee with sharp knives flicking by my skin, I have faced death and injury in many ways." She set her lamp on the floor near her feet. "But never, until now, have I faced such a difficult challenge. To stand by and not interfere, whatever happens to my sister-friend, this is the most difficult of all." Takra fought to keep her deep fear locked inside as she tightened her fists and swallowed back the tears that clogged her throat and dampened her eyes. "You should take the time to give her more training, Imandoff, any training to help her through this."

"Trust me, Takra. There is no training to prepare for the Trial, no matter what Jehennette said. I know," Imandoff answered softly. "And I understand your fears. Even though I will be there with Corri, I also cannot interfere." He pulled open one side of the gate, his lamp lighting his face in sharp planes of light and shadow. "No one must enter, Takra. No one."

"No one shall while I stand guard." Takra's hand fell to her sword hilt. "May you ride with fair wind and sun, sister-friend."

"You owe me an ale when I return." Corri smiled at Takra's quick nod, a half-smile that never reached her eyes. *Goddess, bring me back safely to these friends . . . and Gadavar.* Her thoughts settled for an instant on the tall man before she pushed the image away. "With you guarding my back, what have I to fear?"

Corri raised her fist in the Tuonela salute, turned abruptly, and went through the gate into the darkness beyond. Imandoff led the way down the short corridor to another door. This barrier creaked ominously as it yielded to the sorcerer's hand.

The sorcerer set the lamp on a rock shelf and closed the door, shutting them into a room carved out of the rock itself. The smell of spring water reached Corri's nostrils above the scent of time and age.

In the center of the room was a high-backed chair all of silver, its surface deeply etched with strange symbols and figures. On a rock pedestal near it lay a black helmet with strange faceted eyepieces in the visor. Its dull surface drew in the lamplight, reflecting nothing, while the eyepieces glittered like the eyes of animals or some giant waiting insect.

Such strange things I feel within this room, Corri thought as she looked around. *Old terrors, ancient sorrows, defeats and triumphs, they have left their mark in the stone walls and everything here. What kind of mark will I add to these?*

"Well, old man," Corri said, taking a deep breath. "What do I do now?"

Imandoff laid aside his staff and unbuckled his sword, leaning it against the time-hardened wooden door. "Sit in the chair, Corri, while I bring you what is needed."

Corri moved uneasily in the high-backed seat as she watched Imandoff take a tiny bottle from the pouch at his belt. From the rock shelf that held the lamp he fetched a miniature goblet, which he carried into the darkness behind her. She heard the splash of water as the sorcerer rinsed, then filled the tiny cup. Standing before her again, Imandoff carefully measured two drops of liquid from the bottle, letting each drop sink into the water-filled goblet.

"Why were you chosen to undergo this Trial, Imandoff?" Corri's soft words whispered through the dark corners of the chamber.

The sorcerer paused, the goblet in his hand, as he stared back in time. "A very old priest at the Temple insisted on testing me, although I knew not why at the time. When he was satisfied, he told me that one day I would need the strength that comes from undergoing the Trial of the Mask. I was cocky with my powers and agreed, not understanding the changes it would bring." His words fell to a whisper. "Afterward, I understood why no survivor ever speaks of the experience."

He swirled the goblet three times clockwise while he chanted. "Be thou pure in the service of the Goddess."

Corri felt the hair on her arms rise as Imandoff's powerful voice echoed through the chamber. She felt cold, intensely cold, as if she sat under a deep winter's moon with the sharp breath of the north wind against her naked skin.

"Who seeks to wear the Mask?"

Imandoff's shadowed face seemed to take on the appearance of another, one far out of the past who would brook no unworthy seekers in his realm. She realized that not only Imandoff stood before her, but another of even greater power, one who would judge her by her answers.

"I am Corri Farblood," she answered, her throat dry. "Some call me the Dream Warrior."

"Who are you?" came the question again.

"I am sister-friend to Takra Wind-Rider and companion of Imandoff Silverhair." *Is there some trick answer I must give?* she thought, her thoughts whirling.

"Who are you?"

Corri's hands clenched on the chair arms as she leaned forward. "I am only me," she said, the words breaking as they passed the dryness of her mouth. "I want to save the Peoples from the evil of Frav, the great evil now embodied in my father Kayth." She grew frantic as the face before her showed no emotion or recognition. "I am only me!" she screamed.

"Drink the bitter cup of the Mask and enter the Realm of Terror and Time." Imandoff handed her the tiny goblet, his face once more assuming his own identity. He blinked as she took it from his hand.

"Natira," he whispered. "The Great Judge of Between Worlds! I cannot say whether you are blessed or cursed that Natira should enter this place and put his hand upon what you do, Corri."

"Does it matter?" She looked down at the dark liquid in the goblet. The shaking of her hands moved the water's surface in little waves. "I cannot turn away from this Trial, not if the Peoples would remain free."

"Drink it all at once," Imandoff counseled. "The taste is very bitter." He smiled as she gulped it down, grimacing at the acrid aftertaste.

"What now?" she asked, leaning her head back against the chair.

"In a few moments you will begin to experience a sense of strangeness, a sense of being both within and without your body."

"Like dream-flying." Her vision began to change, making the lamplight, Imandoff, and all she saw around her glow with strange colors.

"I have never been able to dream-fly," Imandoff answered as he leaned closer. "Colors and sounds will intensify, finally fading into visions. This much I can tell you, Corri. What you see or feel or do after that will be for you alone."

She looked up into his shadowed gray eyes and saw the concern there. *He is afraid I will die, or worse. But what can be worse than death before I stop Kayth?*

It would be worse to not die, but some part knows you cannot work to defeat Kayth, her inner mind said. *To live insane with a small part of the mind rational.*

I trust in the Goddess, she firmly told herself. *There is no room for fear in my heart now.* She touched Imandoff's beard with her fingers and smiled. "It has begun then, old man. I see a great light around you, the same as the life-force I see when I leave my body behind and look upon others. Your voice, even my own words, come from far away, as if they echo down a tunnel."

Imandoff straightened, watching the girl's pupils widen and the puzzled look on her face as she stared straight through him. Slowly, he took up the Mask of Darkness and settled it over her head.

"The Goddess bless and keep you, Corri Farblood," he whispered. "Where you now go, I cannot follow. Neither can I aid you in any way." He sat cross-legged beside her on the cold floor, his cloak wrapped around him.

Corri felt the cold metal of the black Mask slip over her head and settle down over her face. The faceted crystal eyes broke her view of Imandoff and the chamber into a thousand tiny pieces. She stared through the eyes, trying to bring the sorcerer into focus. When the pieces of Imandoff sank out of her sight, she settled back in the chair. Reaching out with her inner senses, she felt his presence near her feet and Takra's restless pacing near the outer door.

I am not alone, she told herself. *Imandoff is here with me, and Takra is close at hand.*

Her body grew warmer as the potion worked its way through her veins. Reality slipped away from her grasp. She hung in a swirling place of what at first appeared as deep darkness, then changed to an eye-blinding pulsing of colored light. She fought against the sucking strength of the whirling center as she was pulled in and downward, but her efforts were ineffective against the supernatural force. Nothing she saw or felt could be compared to reality.

No! her mind screamed in fear. *This is not real!* For an instant, her mind steadied. *But it is real. I see it, and I feel the fear it creates.*

Faces swept before her eyes, some out of the past, some unknown to her. *You are dead and gone,* she thought as Grimmel leered at her. The Master Thief's face was replaced by Takra's, twisted in pain. *Do I see her death?* Malya's features melted into those of Xephena, then the Oracle. *I do not understand. This confusion is tearing me apart inside. I must get out!*

Corri fought against the visions until her mind was beaten into exhaustion. She hung in a place of darkness once more, with only a tiny speck of light far in the distance.

What does it matter? The light is too far away, and I am too tired to try to reach it.

In the striving is the victory. Before her stood a robed and cowled figure, its hands tucked inside the sleeves of its robe. *All events and people move within the divine cycles of being. One of great evil has learned how to break the cycles. What will you do, initiate?*

Kayth's face, overlaid with a transparent writhing mask of evil made flesh, appeared before her. *This is no living being, but pure evil out of the depths of the black Abyss!* Corri cried out in fear, thrusting out her hands to shove it away. Kayth's image shattered like a broken glass, and the strange pieces whirled away into the darkness.

She turned to find the mysterious cowled figure still at her side. *Who are you?* she asked. *Why do you allow such evil to torment me?*

I am Natira, Judge of Between Worlds, the Lord of Karma. Goodness can only be judged by knowing what evil is. What will you do to protect the Peoples, initiate?

From the far distant speck of illumination now came strands of light, some straight, others twisted about each other. These threads pulsed with energy, changing colors as they touched each other. The strands swept around her, moving into the darkness as far as she could see. As Corri looked closer, she saw the threads contained pictures: pictures of moving events, forms, and faces of people.

What are these? she asked Natira.

Life-threads. The cowled face turned toward her. *How will you change them to conquer evil and save the Peoples?*

Corri felt a growing panic fill her chest. *Lady, help me!* she cried, her voice echoing through the darkness. *I do not understand what to do!*

A bright form materialized at Natira's side. Corri sobbed in relief as the Goddess took shape, Her gentle smile comforting the girl.

Natira, neutral Judge of all. The Lady's voice soothed Corri's spirit. *Would you hinder my Dream Warrior?*

The way she travels is hard, Lady. The robed figure bowed its head. *She must learn that thinking is not all. She must learn when to act on instinct alone, or she cannot hope to win the coming battle.*

I chose her for her pure heart, for her innocence. The Lady smiled at Corri. *Can you not see, Natira? To that she has now added the armor of love.*

Lady, tell me what I must do, Corri begged. *I am willing to be Your Dream Warrior, but how must I fight?*

The Lady smiled, pointed a finger at the sweeping, twisting life-threads that billowed around them. *Some threads cannot be changed, others can be. Learn which you can change, which you cannot. If you fail to learn, Dream Warrior, the Peoples will lose faith and the evil of Frav will sweep over them like a consuming wave. If you succeed only in part, you can still be a rallying point for the Peoples, but your dream powers will be gone.*

If I succeed? Corri held her breath as she awaited the answer.

Your powers will be strengthened so that you, and you alone, may be the deciding factor in the battle against evil, even as was Varanna.

Even victory has its price. Natira turned his cowled face, and for the first time Corri saw the blazing eyes hidden within the shadowed face. *Some will shun you through fear. Others will seek you for the power you hold. Your life will be changed forever. The choice is yours.*

Then I choose to be the Dream Warrior, Corri answered. *I am what I am, a light-bearer for the Lady. I must save the Peoples and Sar Akka. By walking Her path, my friends, the people I know, will be safe.* She thought of Gadavar deep in the forests of Deep Rising, little Dakhma safe in the Temple, Imandoff and Takra who kept vigil with her, and all the others who had tried to help her in one way or another.

Then be about your work, Dream Warrior.

The voice of Natira faded, as did the two figures before her. Corri hung alone in the vast darkness of space and time, the life-threads dancing and intertwining around her.

Trust my instincts, Natira said. Corri's hands reached out to the nearest tangle of threads, smoothing, unknotting them. To her surprise the strange threads were solid in her fingers, solid but slippery and moving with a life of their own. She looked closer at the flashing pictures within those threads and saw the forms of Gertha and Jehennette moving about a battlefield with their healing bags in hand.

Once she saw Kayth and Minepa creating a firestorm, a storm that flowed over the grasslands, consuming everyone and everything in its path. She fought long and hard to free this thread from others, but did not know when it slipped from her fingers if she succeeded.

Another time, tiny figures of herself, Imandoff, and Takra crossed the stone bridge across the Kratula Gorge into Frav. Corri fought her way along this thread, struggling to see its end, but it slipped away before she saw the outcome.

As she pulled and pried at knots and tangles, her inner senses warned her of Kayth. Clutching at the threads in her hands, she looked up to see the wavering face of her father. His lips moved, his hands raised, as he tried to disrupt her work. Corri saw the waves of energy burst from his fingers, then dissipate into nothingness.

Begone! Corri shouted at him. She dropped the writhing threads to cast balls of power at the frowning face. But her efforts could not reach Kayth any more than his could reach her. Kayth's face began to fade away, even as he struggled to keep his position in this place.

His power is growing in some strange, warped way, Corri thought. *I see it in the muddied colors of the light around him.*

She reached out to catch another tangle, striving to separate the twined threads, to pull them smooth. Some came loose, others knotted tighter against her will. On she worked, desperate to loosen knots, despairing when she could not. She lost all sense of time; it no longer mattered, only her work. Even the face of Takra's child, another smaller baby by its side, did not long hold her attention.

Her breath caught when she looked down upon a life-thread holding the image of Tirkul. Knotted about it was the thread of Gadavar, and knotted still tighter to both was one containing the faces of Kayth and Minepa. Twisting around these were the strands of Imandoff and Takra.

Corri worked feverishly at the threads, tugging, smoothing, praying. One thread broke free to float away in the darkness, then another and another. As her cramped and aching fingers worked on the knots of the remaining strands, they whipped out of her grasp, striking a burning blow across one of her hands and disappearing into the winds of time and space, the loosened knots still writhing. The face and form of a man remained in her sight the longest, his possible destiny filling her with great sorrow.

No! she screamed into the darkness of her vision. *Let me try again!* she begged.

Some threads cannot be freed from their destiny, came the Lady's voice. *I give life and I take it when the life-cycle is finished. None is greater than I.*

Corri felt hot tears run down her cheeks. *This is the way it must be?* she asked.

These are all the possible futures at this moment in time. The more strong wills involved in an event, the harder that event is to change. All choices build a life, moment by moment, thus creating changes in the life-path. But every life must end someday, and that is My law.

A wave of love surrounded her, pushing her out of the darkness of time and space. She felt her fingers cramped around the arms of the silver chair and heard Imandoff's rapid breathing near her feet. Her eyes once more looked at the crystal eyepieces of the Mask.

"Imandoff?" Corri's voice was a harsh croak in the still room.

The sorcerer's hands brushed against her, causing pain to her heightened senses. "Breathe deeply, Corri," he whispered. His quiet voice seemed to scream in her ears.

She cried out as Imandoff lifted the Mask of Darkness from her head and set it on the table. Her chest felt as if it lay under a heavy weight.

"Breathe, Corri, breathe!" Imandoff commanded as he towered over her.

She gasped and sucked in great breaths, felt the crushing weight lift from her chest. She shut her eyes against the glaring lamplight, leaning back into the chair, vividly aware of every line of carving against her back. Hot tears still ran down her cold cheeks.

"I did what I could." Corri felt the tears run faster as in her mind she saw the tangled threads leap from her fingers and disappear into the darkness. "I did what I could."

Imandoff pressed the rim of the tiny goblet against her lips. "This will help," he said, gently smoothing her sweat-dampened hair from her forehead. He took her left hand in his and frowned at the star-shaped burn on the fleshy part where her thumb joined the palm. "We must have Jehennette see to this."

"Imandoff, I could not save . . ." Her tongue seemed blocked. The words she wanted to share were stuck somewhere inside her. She looked up at the sorcerer, pleading in her eyes.

"When I underwent the Trial, certain things I saw I could never share with another." Imandoff knelt beside her, holding her shaking hands. "At times I thought I would go mad, but I endured and did what I was led to do."

"This is why we can never see all of the future, is it not? We never know which events are set beyond change and which are changeable." Corri felt the circulation moving in her legs and feet once more. "If we knew everything that was destined to happen, we could not live with it. Is this what all initiates of the Mask undergo?"

"I think it is, in part," he answered. "What each sees is different, but each must see part of the future. I saw part of the battle with Frav. The Oracle saw that she would become the

Oracle." He sighed and kissed Corri's hands clenched about his. "Any who live through the Trial seem to have a part in this coming battle between good and evil, Corri."

"What really became of those who tried and failed?" Corri loosened his hands and got shakily to her feet.

"Most died. The two who survived are cared for here in Leshy. Their minds are gone. They live in dreams and nightmares."

"And because I survived, I must consider myself fortunate? I wonder." Corri began to carefully walk about the room, each step steadier than the one before. "Knowing what I know, I wonder."

"Come, Takra must be wild with worry." Imandoff took her arm as he opened the door. Reaching out for his staff, he guided her through the portal into the short corridor.

"How long was I wherever I was?" Corri asked as they came to the great inner gates. Imandoff shrugged his shoulders.

"How is she?" Takra peered at Corri as she shut the gate behind them. "Do you know it has been a night and another day, sorcerer?"

"That long?" Imandoff's face was drawn with weariness.

She stepped close to Corri and looked deep into her eyes. "Are you well, Farblood?" Concern crossed Takra's face at what she saw in Corri's face and eyes.

Corri straightened her shoulders and nodded. "I am well," she whispered. "And I still will hold you to that ale." She kept her burned hand turned away from her friend.

"Has anything happened while we were down here?" Imandoff glanced toward the stairs, a puzzled frown on his face.

"Your sister waits above." Takra held the lamp to light their way down the tunnel and back up the stairs. "Zanitra came down to speak with you, but the door was already closed. All she said was 'I should have come sooner.' Do you know what she means?"

The sorcerer shook his head. "If Zanitra came to Leshy, she had a strong purpose." Imandoff leaned heavily on his staff as he climbed the last stairs to the Mystery School above.

Once more within the High Clua's private rooms, Corri sat in a cushioned chair near the window that looked out upon the moon-splashed herb gardens in the courtyard. In her good hand was a mug of hot soup, its healing properties thick upon her tongue when she sipped at it. The burned palm of the other hand was coated with herbal salve and wrapped in a bandage.

My body is rested, she thought as she stared out the window. *But my mind feels as if it has been bruised and beaten. I am not the same as when I walked into that underground chamber. Something deep inside has changed forever. Will Gadavar notice? Will he turn away from what I have become?*

Takra sat, boots up on a small table, while she tore at a leg of roast jakin. Beside her, Imandoff sopped up the last of his soup with a thick piece of bread as he listened to Zanitra.

"The Oracle and I both had similar dreams," the tall woman said, touching the bulky bag at her feet with one hand. "The Dream Warrior must wear Varanna's helmet when she goes into battle against Frav."

"But the helmet was badly damaged and the sword destroyed." Imandoff set aside his bowl to look from Zanitra to Jehennette.

"The sword hilt remained." Zanitra looked at her brother over her steepled fingers. "Even now a blacksmith in the Temple is reforging the blade, according to the ancient methods."

"And the helmet?" Jehennette traced the scrolling pattern on her chair with one finger, her eyes intent on Zanitra. "Our history tells us that part of the eye-visor was destroyed in that ancient battle. Can it also be repaired?"

"I brought it as it is," Zanitra answered. "No one knows what great sea beast's scales went into its making, nor how it can be mended. Perhaps the Goddess will reveal the manner of its repair to the Dream Warrior."

Zanitra rose and carried the bag to Corri, laying it near the girl's chair. "Perhaps meditation with the ancient helmet will give you insight, especially now that you have undergone the Trial. After Imandoff . . ." She paused. "Afterward, there were depths to my brother that did not exist before, depths of knowledge I cannot hope to understand." She turned to look out the window at the darkened courtyard, her hands clasped together.

"The Trial creates changes," Imandoff said, staring down at his empty bowl, his thoughts far in the past. "The initiate who wears the Mask cannot know the extent of those changes until he faces a crisis." His gray eyes rose to catch Corri's in a glance of understanding.

"Imandoff, the city around the Fire Temple is called Vu-Zai, the House of Zai, is it not?" Corri set her mug on the table, then crossed the room to the sorcerer's side. "Who or what is Zai?"

Imandoff looked up at her in surprise. "That is a terrible name out of the far past, long before the Peoples came to these lands. Zaitan was the first name of the Fravashi god." He took her hand as she sat on the chair arm beside him. "When some of the star travelers joined with Frav, they merged the name of their god with that of the Fravashi's, changing the name of the deity to Jevotan."

"What was said of Zaitan, of His powers?" Corri pressed. "I need to know, for I think that Kayth has learned how to tap into those powers as I do the Lady's."

"Lady protect us!" Jehennette's fingers flew to her prayer beads, rolling them one by one through her shaking hands.

Zanitra whirled from her place at the window. "O Goddess, be with us!"

"Zaitan was a powerful, jealous god," Imandoff said, looking up into her eyes. "Until the Volikvis gained control, though, the Fravashi people paid Him homage out of fear, but were not overzealous in forcing His worship onto others. After the Volikvis came to power, Zaitan's strength appeared to grow, as did the Fravashi zeal for religious control. It is said they keep Zaitan, or Jevotan as they now call Him, strong within this plane of existence by sacrificing humans to Him. In magic there is a little-known law that blood gives great power to the magic."

"As in the Valley of Whispers, as the Trow Xephena did to Croyna," Corri said softly.

"Where heard you of this Croyna?" Zanitra demanded. "That one is a blasphemous distortion of the Lady! And what know you of the Trow?"

"I heard and saw . . ." Corri felt the unconscious restriction once more lock up her words.

"She cannot tell us, Zanitra." Imandoff shook his head. "There are happenings of the Trial about which the initiate can never speak." He rose, pulling Corri up beside him and holding out a hand to Takra. "Corri still has not rested enough from her ordeal. I think we all should retire for the night."

The unnatural sound of running footsteps broke the evening stillness. By the time Gertha threw open the door to Jehennette's private room without knocking, all in the room faced the door.

"Pardon, High Clua." The young healer stood with white face, her hands clenched together in an effort to stop their shaking. "The Watcher has seen a terrible thing!"

"Come, tell us." Jehennette beckoned with her hand. "I found one within Leshy," she said to Imandoff, "who can far-see by crystal. He has been watching the border."

"Clan warriors have been taken captive. Taken across the border into Frav!" Gertha bit her lower lip.

"Have Fravashi armies invaded?" Imandoff gripped his sword hilt.

Gertha shook her head. "Only a raid for captives."

"Who and how many were taken?" Takra's cool voice broke the silence.

"The Watcher does not know who, but only a few were made captive," Gertha answered.

"One is too many." Takra's jaw set in a firm line.

Corri found all within the room looking at her. "Then we must go at once to the border. Takra is right. One Tuonela, one Kirisani, even one Asuran, is too many to leave in the bloody hands of the Volikvi and Trow."

Chapter 15

"The last steps toward battle have been taken," Corri said, as the three companions gathered in her room. "I feel as if my very existence has become a catalyst, a spur to war. Perhaps if I had never been born, all this would not be happening." *I saw this in the Trial,* she thought. *Now I must take every opportunity to change the death I saw. It must not happen!*

"You take too much upon yourself, Corri." Imandoff put his hand on her shoulder. "You do not know that your non-existence might have only made things worse."

Corri rubbed a hand across her aching eyes. "If we lose, the Volikvis will kill first all those with talent. Little Dakhma and Athdar, all the initiates, even some among the Green Men. I will do everything I can, even give up my life, to stop them." Her thoughts, her emotions, still felt raw and over-sensitized.

The sorcerer raised her chin to gaze into her eyes. "We each walk the path we are given in this life. You know your path from the Trial, as I do mine."

Takra sat honing her belt knife, a look of deep concentration on her face. "Jehennette will shake this Mystery School in such a way they will never forget. Even now she lays her plans for the healers to journey to the border." She waved the knife at the room about her. "It is time for those of the Mystery Schools to see firsthand how the Peoples struggle through life. Now they must face danger at the border with us, if they want to remain free."

"Zanitra has begun her return to the Temple," the sorcerer answered. "The Temple Watcher will have seen what the Watcher of Leshy read in the crystal, but my sister felt a strong urge to speak face to face with the Oracle. Knowing Zanitra, she will join Her Own on the march to the border. Since both my sword and my powers will be needed at the border, we will ride at first light."

"Whatever danger we may find there, I will remain at Corri's side," Takra said, her strong hands twirling the dagger, then slamming it into its sheath. "I would be no friend if I did otherwise."

Imandoff looked at Takra with a grin and raised one eyebrow. "I would not presume to tell you, a Tuonela warrior woman, where she may or may not go. I might worry, Takra, but I too want you by my side."

"Yes, I must go to the border." Corri felt a great sadness and soul-weariness press down upon her. "I saw all the future possibilities. I changed what I could. Blood or no, I must still face Kayth. And another, even more evil." She shivered. "They want me. Not Tirkul, not the other Tuonela warriors, but me. For without me, you see, Kayth and Minepa cannot hope to control Sar Akka."

"Why do you speak Tirkul's name?" Takra's hands stilled. "The Watcher could not say who was taken."

"Once when I spied upon Kayth, I heard him say that he had plans for Tirkul. If necessary, I will trade my life for his or any of the captured Tuonela."

Imandoff raised his eyebrows in astonishment. Takra's sun-tanned face grew rigid with determination.

"You plan to surrender to the Fravashi?" Takra's hands tightened on her sword hilt. "That I will not let you do, sister-friend!"

"No, I shall not surrender." Corri rubbed at her tired eyes. "But I shall make them think they have eaten fire and drunk darkness before I am finished. How all this will end . . . that I am not certain. I could not follow that life-thread to its con-clusion, nor could I create much change in its direction." She looked at Imandoff, who nodded his understanding of what she could not put into words.

"Never seek the end of any event." Imandoff placed his hand on Corri's arm. "Always deal only with the events of this moment, this day. Then, when the end of the event shows itself, take it by the throat in surprise. Only when you do this will the other possibilities present themselves."

"Truly?" Corri looked up at him.

"But of course." Imandoff smiled. "The Lady never creates a life that leads to a dead end. She always provides a way out of the maze if we are strong enough to see it and take the path that suddenly appears. Even the meshes of time and life can be taken by surprise and forced to yield their secrets, if we are strong in purpose."

"There is so much I do not know. I thought the Trial would make all things clear to me, that no more questions without answers would ever arise. The Trial of the Mask of Darkness is the greatest of initiations, is it not?"

Imandoff cleared his throat. "Tradition tells us there once were other initiations besides the Mask of Darkness. At one time the Mask was only one in a series of ordeals. Ancient records hint at the others and the devices that were used. But the devices and the ways of the ordeals have been lost to us. I think, Dream Warrior, that you are standing on a new path that may yet lead us to recover these ancient ordeals of testing.

If you journey on these new ways, this time I must follow, not lead."

"If you think I let her go alone into any danger, Silverhair, think again!" Takra's amber eyes flashed as she came to stand beside them.

"No, my Tuonela warrior, I did not mean that." Imandoff lightly touched Takra's scarred cheek with his hand. "We shall always stand at her back, you and I. But Corri, I fear, will be forced to journey into areas of the mind and spirit that neither you nor I have ever touched. In that she must lead the way. Will you follow her into that kind of danger?"

"I follow my sister-friend wherever she goes: body, mind, or spirit," answered Takra.

"So say the prophecies." Imandoff nodded, his forehead wrinkled in deep thought. "'And the Dream Warrior shall lead her followers into the ways of Darkness to fight the Footed Serpent at the Gates of Fire.'"

"Fire." Corri's voice was nearly inaudible. "Fire," she repeated, then whirled to grasp Imandoff's arm. "Firestorm! Kayth plans to raise a firestorm against the Tuonela warriors and the Clans! We must ride at once. I need to be closer if I am to defeat his purposes! I do not feel I have the strength to fight him from here."

"Then we ride now." Takra grabbed her saddlebags.

Imandoff went to prepare the horses, while Takra and Corri packed. As the women worked side by side, Corri turned to her friend, a question plain in her eyes.

"Takra, how long can you keep your secret from Imandoff? Soon it will show."

Takra shoved Imandoff's few possessions into his bags before answering. "I got more tesselberry root from Jehen-nette, but the sickness seldom comes now. She says the baby will not show for some time yet." Takra smiled and shrugged her shoulders at Corri's raised brows. "She should know, sis-ter-friend. She has two of her own."

They tarried only long enough to gather fresh provisions and water before leading the horses to the gates of Leshy. Behind Corri's saddle was strapped the bag containing Varanna's ancient helmet.

"Watch for us, Dream Warrior," Jehennette called after them. "My healers and I will follow as swiftly as we can when the war-horn is sounded. Go with the Goddess, my warrior-friends."

Corri, Imandoff, and Takra rode hard throughout the night, crossing the Crystal Sands and heading straight into the Tuonela grasslands. As the first rays of dawn broke over the Takto Range to the east, Imandoff called a halt.

"We must rest the horses and ourselves," he said as Takra guided them to a small waterhole. "We have many days' journey ahead of us before we reach the Mootma Mountains and the border battle with Frav."

"Let us put at least another half-day's ride behind us," Takra urged, staring over the waving grasslands toward the north.

"No, we stop here." Corri slid down from Mouse and clung to the horse's damp sides for support. "My inner senses tell me my dream-powers can reach Kayth from here. Whatever I do, it must be done now." *The Trial and now this hard riding have given me no time to regain my strength. Oh, Goddess, help me to push back the mental fatigue and do what I must.*

Silently, Imandoff untied the blanket from behind her saddle and spread it on the ground. Corri staggered onto it and collapsed into a cross-legged position. She felt the headband with the owl stone slide onto her forehead and the brief touch of Takra's hand. As Corri went inward to begin her dream-flying, she heard the faint, receding voices of her friends.

"She is exhausted." The worry in Takra's voice appeared as pink and violet circles in Corri's mind, colored smoke rings that floated around her body.

"She knows best what she must do and when." The conviction in Imandoff's voice created silver shafts that speared through the colored rings, shattering their clinging threads.

Corri floated above her body, rising swiftly into the dawn-tinged sky of the grasslands. She felt an icy wind of the spirit sweep from the mountains in the north straight toward her. She shivered as its soul-chilling breath tried to wrap itself around her floating body.

No, you cannot trap me. Corri cast the wind aside with a wave of her hands. *I come, Kayth. I come for you and your evil one, the one who smells of old blood and older blackness of the soul. There is no place you can hide that I cannot find you this time.*

Quickly, she willed herself to the border between Frav and Tuone. Below her she could see the thin Tuonela forces gathered near three widely separated places. Swords flashed and the voices of men and women screamed their battle cries.

I saw all this before, Corri thought. *I saw this but could not affect the battles. That means there must be another area of danger, the place where Kayth will brew his firestorm.*

She looked closer and saw the spells that sealed the border between Frav and Tuone. They glowed in a silver-blue line stretching from the far east in the Mootma Mountains to the western coastline of the Zuartoc Sea. Before each of the battle-places, the glow was gone, a hole broken through the ancient spells.

There must *be another break. Kayth and his evil Soothsayer cannot create the firestorm on Fravashi soil. I feel it! They must cross into Tuone, but where?*

She sped west along the border, the deep blue of the Zuartoc Sea in the distance. As she neared the smoking mountain that marked the site of Vu-Murt and Vu-Zai, the Volikvi center, she saw the deep chasm of the Kratula Gorge. Across the Gorge, reaching directly from the heart of Vu-Zai, stretched an ancient natural land bridge of stone. And on that bridge she saw and felt the tainted life-forces of Kayth and the evil Minepa.

But the spells hold there, she thought. She saw no break in the silver-blue line. *Illusion? And where is Tirkul?*

She looked closer at the scene below and detected a faint, almost imperceptible wavering in the force of the spells. Kayth and the Volikvi priest crossed the end of the bridge into Tuone as she watched. The Volikvi held a black stone before him, its shimmering rays beating against the spells at the end of the bridge.

No! Corri clamped down on the anger and fear that threatened her control. Stumbling behind Kayth, with only a thin cord around his neck as a lead rope, was Tirkul. Tirkul's hands were free, but he walked stiff-legged as though he willed his body to stop but could not make it obey. *Lady, help me!*

Before Corri the golden glow of the Goddess emerged. *I cannot interfere,* said the beautiful voice. *You must choose what you will do and how you will do it.*

Why Tirkul?

His life-force is strong, and he is Tuonela, came the reply.

They would tie his life-force and his knowledge of the grasslands to their magic?

Just so. The glow was beginning to fade. *Wait until the power builds. Blood is used to bind it.* The glow was gone.

Control yourself, Farblood, she thought. *Do not explode your power this time, like some inexperienced Temple novice.*

Carefully, Corri gathered to herself the anger, fear, and mental pain she felt within. She gathered it as a potter would gather clay, molding it into a compact form between her shadowy hands.

Corri, let me see through your eyes! Imandoff's voice sounded in her head.

She sent a tendril of thought back to the sorcerer, then opened her mind to what was happening below.

They are over the spell-bound border now, she said, as if Imandoff stood beside her. *I cannot see how they crossed, unless it is through the black stone the evil one carries.*

That does not matter now. The calm voice of the sorcerer gave her strength. *Remember the Valley of Whispers, Corri. The Volikvi had to build his spells first before he could call upon the stolen blood of Takra's friend. Wait.*

This Volikvi is different, I know. If I just touch the outer edges of his life-force, perhaps I can break his spell-casting.

No! Imandoff's shout sent her dream-body spinning. *Do not touch his life-force at all! Let me see them again.*

Corri hovered lower over the scene. Kayth stood back, holding the rope that guided Tirkul, while the Fravashi priest slowly paced among the fumes of his stinking incense. The Tuonela warrior stood as stiff and still as a statue; only his eyes were alive, flashing with rage.

It is only Minepa, who calls himself the Soothsayer of Jevotan. He never felt my presence when I spied on him before.

Minepa! Corri heard and felt the fear in Imandoff's voice. *Beware, Corri, for he uses a power-sink stone, one that has been fed evil power for long and long. Wait until he is about to draw Tirkul's blood, then strike!*

Corri felt the first blow of power rise up from Minepa's spellcasting. It shook her form like a blast from a grassland storm. She fought to keep her place above the Gorge, pushing back against the dirty flow of twisted magic, finally causing it to divide and pass her on both sides without touching her life-force. She felt as if her mind and all her senses had been scraped raw from its first contact. The shimmering black stone lay at Minepa's feet. From it came the tiny beginnings of a whirling fire.

Now, Minepa's magic appeared to her as a swirling cloud of black laced with flashes of dark red, the color of old blood. The Volikvi was chanting, one hand gesturing toward Tirkul, the other directed downward to the stone of power. Corri strained to hear, and the voice came clearly through the air.

"Jevotan, hear me! I give You the blood of this Tuonela warrior that Your power may grow and break apart the spells holding us from bringing all the Peoples under Your rule." The voice droned on in some unintelligible language so filthy in its touch on Corri's mind that she drew back slightly.

Below, she saw Minepa's black robes move from the winds of the miniature firestorm within the black stone. A tiny whirlwind of fire steadily grew larger as it slowly began to rise upward. With her mind, she reached out and tried to smother it.

Kayth's head snapped up, and he stared upward straight at Corri's invisible form above them.

Daughter, you have once more come to me. The mental voice broke through Corri's barriers. *Join your powers with mine and we can break the last strand of Minepa's power. With you at my side, I will no longer need him. Do it now while he is obsessed with his magic.*

No. Corri held her mind still as she furtively continued to mold her gathered power between her hands. *There is a taint to your life-force that sickens me.*

Then I, with Minepa's aid, will bring you to me whether you will it or not. There was an assured smugness to Kayth's words.

Tirkul's bent head raised to look where Kayth did, a puzzled frown on his bruised face. His free hands slowly began to fumble at the loop of cord around his neck. As his hands touched the cord, he cried out as if he touched hot coals.

Minepa jerked his head upward, following Kayth's gaze, at last aware that an opposing power hung over him. He flung up a hand, pointing the long fingers directly at Corri.

Instinctively, she deflected the blaze of power with one hand, shouting *Frayma!* At the same time, she threw her gathered power in a brilliant stream of energy straight onto the cord linking Tirkul and Kayth.

With a curse, Kayth leaped back as the power burned the cord in two. He turned and ran for the bridge over Kratula Gorge.

The firestorm, now shoulder-high above the black stone at Minepa's feet, wavered and spun out of control. It darted upward from its growth-point, a small whirlwind of death and destruction, to swirl across the Gorge and strike against the smoking mountain on the other side in a roar of sound and blast of flames. It pounded itself into oblivion against the bare stones of the great mountain.

Frayma! Corri shouted again.

Tirkul staggered back against a jutting of rock, frantically pulling the burning cord from around his neck. He snarled at Minepa, but seemed unable to move toward the Volikvi. Minepa sprang at the Tuonela warrior, quick as a striking snake, his dagger upraised in one hand.

"Die you shall, Tuonela unbeliever!" the priest cried. "No one can save you now. For I am the Soothsayer of Jevotan, and my words and will shall be done!"

Frayma! Goddess! Corri shouted a third time.

Out of the landscape of great rocks' cracked and broken teeth, in answer to her silent cry for help, Corri saw the flying form of Hellstorm, Tirkul's mount, as he raced forward. The horse screamed its rage, its eyes wild, teeth bared, a rope of foam streaming back from its jaws. Minepa hesitated for an instant, forgetting about Corri, as the great horse paused once to rear, striking at the air with its sharp hooves.

She watched as Minepa, his concentration shattered, ran for the bridge across the Kratula Gorge. He ducked behind the scattered monolithic rocks, working his way ever nearer to the bridge, staying out of sight of the enraged horse. When Hellstorm broke off the hunt to return to Tirkul's side, Minepa dashed for the bridge.

Ride, Tirkul! Corri poured her words directly into the warrior's mind. *You are free!*

"I ride, Dream Warrior." Tirkul stumbled to the lathered and prancing Hellstorm. He pulled his beaten body up onto the saddle.

Go to the Tuonela defenders of the border, Corri ordered. *I . . .we shall meet you there.* She felt her strength waver. *Ride, Tirkul, for I may yet have need of your strength at my back.*

Hellstorm turned and picked his way back along the Gorge, Tirkul bent low over the horse's neck. Corri felt her throat tighten in grief as she watched him ride away toward the Tuonela forces. As she tried to follow him, she felt herself pulled back toward her body on the Tuonela grasslands.

Farewell, Tirkul, she whispered. *I have brought you nothing but sorrow and pain. May your future-days be better, though I think they will not be for me.*

She looked back over the grasslands, golden brown in the sun. The faint blue smudge of Deep Rising marked the far distant southern horizon. She willed herself back to her physical body. This time, instead of the swift forward movement of return, Corri saw before her a black opening in the air and felt herself being sucked into it. She tried to struggle against the pull, to cry out, but her dream-body and voice were paralyzed.

Her whirling movement stopped, and she found herself in a place of darkness over-warm from concealed fires. She put out a hand and felt the slickness of rock under her fingers.

A tunnel, Corri thought as she looked around at the glassy-black surface. *But this is not rock. Not the kind of rock I know.* She reached out again and stroked the walls with her hand. *This is like polished gem. Slick and black as night!*

A rising chant of voices reached her, echoing strangely through the half-lit tunnel. A flickering glow pulsed sporadically against the black walls, as if from the reflections of a thousand distant lamps. She willed herself to move forward. Gradually upward the tunnel led, then turned in a bend, coming out on a rough platform high above the floor of a huge cave.

Corri looked around her in wonder. The cave walls were as slick and glossy as those of the tunnel behind her, bringing to her mind the Cave of the Maidens high in the Barren Mountains and the evil place of the Trow priestess.

This is the place where Xephena performed her filthy sacrifice. She turned her mind away from the bloody memory.

Below, the floor was cut into two sections by a huge crack, the ends close together and the middle portion very wide.

Across the narrow ends of this crack were two wooden bridges. There was an unnatural heat to this place, as if an infernal fire burned far below in the deep gouge in the earth. Dark holes marked several more tunnels that exited directly onto the cavern floor. She could see three on the opposite side, across the bridges, and guessed that there were more below her platform.

I should not be here! Corri stared at the cavern floor where thousands of candles burned, their flickering reflections mirrored again and again on the glassy walls. *This place has the smell and taste of old and deep evils.*

She started to use her senses, seeking a way out, and gagged at what she found. The lingering scent of old blood given in terror tainted the very air and rock. The cries of men and women long ago raped and tortured here clung to everything.

Out! I want out! she thought. She tried to retrace her path but found the way barred to her.

Lady, help me! There was no response to her cry.

To her right Corri saw a narrow stairway cut into the rock. She followed it down, her dream-body floating along the steps as if she were half in her physical body. At the bottom, she edged along the walls until she came to the crack itself. Peering over, she saw the glow of fire far below. A sulfur stench puffed from the crack, reminding her of incense used by Minepa and the Volikvi in the Valley of Whispers.

The approaching tread of footsteps echoed from one of the tunnels. The rise and fall of chanting voices cut through the still air. She felt her life-force quiver before the strangely worded sounds. Fear rising within her mind threatened to engulf her thinking. In terror, Corri ran-floated across the nearest bridge and forced herself to enter the pitch-black entrance of the nearest tunnel.

She pressed herself against the wall while her heart thumped wildly. Into the cavern behind her marched a long line of Volikvi priests, their dark red robes swinging to their measured steps, their long hair hanging in tangled mats about their heads. In their midst was a Tuonela warrior, his eyes wide, the whites showing in fear, his booted feet dragging in reluctance. Only a single cord around his neck guided him, but the warrior seemed as unable to break free as Tirkul had been when Kayth lead him.

"Jevotan, we bring You meat and drink!" called the Volikvi leader. Corri recognized the man with whom Xephena had coupled, the Volikvi priest named Zalmoxis. The other priests dragged the warrior to the very edge of the great crack. "Give us victory, and through us You will be given the highest of praise. For our victory will bring You all the souls of Sar Akka!"

The Tuonela bared his teeth and groaned as the Volikvi leader drew his dagger, its wavy blade glinting in the candle-light. He grabbed one of the warrior's arms and pressed the sharp knife edge to a vein. As the blood spurted forth, a lesser priest stepped forward with a bowl to catch the liquid.

Corri tried to gather energy between her hands but managed to create only a small ball of light. With great effort, as if she moved through clinging mud, she threw the energy ball across the cavern to splash against the life-force glow of the Tuonela.

The Tuonela warrior struggled against his captors and suddenly spat straight into the face of the sacrificing Volikvi. A wild Tuonela yell broke the silence as the warrior struck out around him. The bowl of blood crashed, shattering on the stone floor. The warrior was the center of a snarling, struggling mass of Fravashi priests. Suddenly, the mass of fighters slipped over the edge of the crevasse and fell into the glowing darkness below. A cry of "Tuone!" broke through the screaming of the doomed Volikvis as warrior and priests fell to their deaths.

The Volikvi leader watched without sign of emotion, then turned to the remaining priests who stared in horror at the crack.

"Search the Fire Temple," he ordered. "Some sorcerer is here." He pointed across the bridge to Corri's hiding place. "Either we have been infiltrated by one from across the border, or there is a traitor among us."

"But how can that be, Zalmoxis?" The priest who had held the bowl quickly backed up in terror as the leader glared at him.

"Have you thought, hell-spawn, that someone among us may make common cause with the Peoples? Search!"

Corri fled down the dark tunnel as the Volikvis began their cautious crossing of the wooden bridge. The farther she went, the more she felt as if she struggled through deep mud. Only an occasional torch stuck in a wall socket lit her path. In this strange state, Corri could not see in the darkness, but had to depend on the torches. She fought on, her heart thumping in her ears, her breath rasping in her throat.

What is happening? she asked herself. *Never before have I felt like this when dream-flying. I cannot fly, I must gasp for breath.*

Corri leaned against the tunnel wall, fighting to calm her heartbeat and breathing. She found she could still use her inner senses to a degree. She strained to catch any sound of the pursuing Volikvis.

"Whoever came this way is either crazy or very unafraid." The voice of one of the priests was faint. "This way leads only to the den of the Footed Serpent."

"Quiet!" another replied. "The beast will hear you."

"Have you ever seen it?" a third man scoffed. "I do not believe it exists."

"It exists," the first answered, a quaver in his voice. "I watched it once as it fed on the sacrifices Minepa chained in its cavern. It seemed to do more than come up out of the black waters of the lake. It seemed to come from another dimension into this one. It is huge, a nightmare thing of great strength and strange power." There was a pause. "If you wish to see it at close hand, as the next sacrifice, state your disbelief loudly. Zalmoxis has ears everywhere."

Corri moved forward again, coming at last to another platform set high above a black lake with a narrow strip of shoreline. The lake cavern was so huge that the opposite shore was hidden in thick shadows. Few torches lit this enormous space, except on either side of the tunnel mouth in which she stood and at the mouth of a tunnel far below to her left. Four sets of manacles and chains hung from the wall below where she stood. She checked behind her with super-sensitive hearing.

"I go no farther than the door to the den," declared one of the priests. "Sacrifice pit or den of the Footed Serpent, it is all the same."

"Agreed," said another. "We can clearly see the floor without going in."

Corri frantically looked for a staircase, found it, and made her way down. She edged along the narrow shoreline, the steep wall at her back, her eyes constantly on the black water before her. The lake's surface was glassy-smooth like the walls around it, except for an occasional strange ripple and bubble. She was arm's length from the tunnel mouth when the Volikvi priests peered cautiously out over the rock platform far above.

"I see no one," one of them whispered, then clamped his hand over his mouth. "Can it hear us?" The man's voice was barely audible, even to Corri's sensitive ears.

I must be enough in my dream-body that they cannot see me, Corri thought.

She dived into the tunnel and moved as swiftly as she could along the semi-darkened place. Here again, torches occasionally lit the path. After what seemed like hours of struggling against an invisible force, Corri saw more light and heard voices. She flattened herself against the tunnel wall and inched forward. The tunnel opened into a guard-room surrounded by the barred doors of cells cut into the rock itself.

"You cannot win, Fravashi scum!" shouted a man from one of the cells. "Nathsa would not have gone to his death alone, regardless of what spells your stinking priests put on him!"

"Quiet, Tuonela garbage!" The huge jailer snapped his whip at one of the cell doors. "Your turn will come soon enough. Jevotan is ever hungry. At the end you will beg and whine like all the rest." He laughed, scratched his huge belly, and went back to his stool near a steep exit tunnel in the far wall.

Corri tried to call up another energy ball, but only a faint spark glowed between her hands. *Hell-fire!* she thought. *This place must be sealed against what I can do.*

A guard pounded down the far tunnel and into the prison.

"Orders from Zalmoxis to check the tunnel as far as the den," he said. "The High One thinks someone may have penetrated the Fire Temple."

"Impossible!" The huge jailer slapped the whip against his thick leg.

"Then you tell that to Zalmoxis." The new guard stared at him.

"I will check." The jailer grumbled to himself as he stamped across the prison toward Corri's tunnel.

What now? I cannot take the chance that perhaps he can see me.

Corri frantically looked around and spotted a crack high up near the ceiling of the tunnel. The walls of this tunnel had tiny irregularities in its surface. *Since I cannot float, I must climb.*

Quickly, Corri scrambled upward, her shadowy fingers catching in the minute crevices until she could pull herself into the black fissure near the ceiling.

The guard grumbled his way past her without looking up.

Lady, smile on me. She sent a silent prayer to Frayma. *I really do not want to have my dream-body stuck in a hole in Frav.*

Corri wiggled her way through the crevice, its rocky sides scraping against her dream-body. The farther she went, the easier it was to move.

I wonder if I will be scratched and bruised when I get back. If I get back.

With a jerk Corri felt as if she had broken through some invisible barrier. She flew up the remainder of the crack as if she were a breeze chasing its way across the grasslands. When she emerged, she floated along the side of the smoking mountain near the bridge across the Kratula Gorge, her dream-powers once more hers.

Lady! Corri's silent call went out and this time was answered.

Well done, my Dream Warrior. The Lady emerged before her, her scintillating golden glow warming and healing Corri's spirit. *I could not come to you within that place. Evil has grown stronger there, and prevents my entering. Remember what you have seen, Dream Warrior.* She faded away.

Mother of Mares, when will this end? Corri was bone-tired. No answer came to her question. She felt a tugging at her dream-body, a calling of her spirit from far out in the grasslands of Tuone before her. Unresisting, she let her form streak swiftly back over the rolling grasslands and dive into her immobile body.

Chapter 16

"Corri?" Imandoff's voice finally broke through the cloud of weariness that enveloped her. "What happened?"

She opened her eyes into brilliant sunlight, then quickly closed them. She felt Imandoff's strong fingers dig into the rigid muscles of her shoulders and neck, massaging until they loosened and relaxed.

"Drink this." Takra put a flask to her mouth as Imandoff propped Corri up against his kneeling body.

Corri took a deep drink, sputtering and gasping as the mountain water burned in her throat.

"I have been in the Fire Temple of Frav." Corri's voice was hoarse. "And Tirkul . . . he is hurt but free and riding back to the Tuonela defenders. Kayth did capture him, as I feared."

"By the hell-fires of Frav! You frightened us, Dream Warrior." Corri looked up into Takra's tired face. "The way you screamed, even Lightfoot and Mouse nearly bolted. Keeping guard over you while you are wherever you are, fighting

301

against only the Goddess knows what, is worse than taking a sword slash across the face in battle." Takra grinned at her.

"Minepa and Kayth?" Imandoff spoke quietly next to her ear.

"Still alive." Corri slumped back against the sorcerer. "Minepa, the Soothsayer of Jevotan, is evil enough, but Kayth is far worse. He has made a bargain with evil straight from the Abyss, and his power grows." Her voice cracked with hoarseness.

"If Minepa should die, Silverhair, what would happen to his powers?" Takra squatted back on her heels and stared at the sorcerer. "Would it go into nothingness? Or could it be taken in and used by another?"

"I do not know, Wind-Rider," the sorcerer answered. "There are two ways of thinking about that. One way says that the power simply disappears back into Between Worlds. But another states that the power can be captured and used by any sorcerer if he or she is powerful enough."

"That can give a grown warrior nightmares," Takra growled as she started to take a swallow of mountain water, then stopped with the flask halfway to her mouth. Without drinking or saying a word, she passed the flask to Imandoff.

Imandoff gave her a quick look of curiosity but said nothing.

"We must ride on to the border." Corri struggled to get up.

"You must rest, at least until morning." Imandoff pushed her back on the blanket.

"I cannot waste a day!"

"A day?" Takra looked at her in astonishment. "Sisterfriend, the sun now hangs near the western horizon."

"Corri, you have been gone from your body for nearly all the daylight hours." Imandoff moved up beside her so he could look into her face. "The last we heard was when you shouted to Frayma three times. Then you lay in a sleep that we could not break. We had begun to fear that you would die in that sleep until Takra saw you open your eyes. And you have had no rest after the Trial in Leshy."

Corri lowered her head to her hands. "Oh, Imandoff, I thought this might be the final battle, this dream-flying battle with Minepa and Kayth, but it is not. I must enter the Fire Temple at Vu-Zai. The path leads there."

Imandoff's face was grave, and Takra shuddered. Corri lifted off the headband with the owl stone and set it carefully aside.

"I cannot leave this half-done. That would be worse than never having done anything at all."

"You will not go alone, sister-friend." Takra's hand rested on her dagger hilt. "I will be there with you."

"And I," echoed Imandoff, reaching out to take her cold hand. "And Tirkul, when we find him."

"I know that you and Takra will be with me," Corri whispered. "But I do not know about Tirkul."

"Do not give in to despair." Imandoff squeezed her hand. "It will take more than a Fravashi to put an end to this sorcerer." He tipped Corri's chin up and waggled his eyebrows.

"Or to the rest of your friends, Dream Warrior." Takra rose and took up her bow. "We eat grassland hens tonight, Silverhair. I am weary of dried meat and hard bread." She stalked quietly off through the tall grass.

Imandoff watched Takra with a thoughtful stare as she disappeared into the dusk. "Have you noticed anything different about the Wind-Rider?" he asked.

"You mean more different than usual when she is preoccupied?" Corri shrugged off the question with a shake of her head.

"Imandoff, will there ever be an end to this constant journeying and fighting?" Corri propped her elbows on her knees, then leaned onto her hands. "Will there ever be a time of peace when we do not have to watch our backs?"

"Perhaps." The sorcerer stacked small pieces of dead brush to make a fire. "But think how dull life would be if there was not occasional excitement." He grinned at Corri. "You would be as bored as I in a few days."

"Probably. But I would like to give it a try sometime."

Corri rubbed her aching forehead and stared to the north. In her mind she could clearly see the stone land bridge that led from Tuone into the Fravashi sacred city of Vu-Zai, with the great mountain guarding it.

"Have you ever managed to cross the border and get into Frav?" she asked.

"No, but I wonder now why I never tried. The Volikvi priest we trailed into the Valley of Whispers had no difficulty. With what we learned later, I assumed that Kayth helped him." Imandoff sat back on his heels and stared at the darkening northern skies. "The Fravashi traders I found in Nevn have crossed for generations, long before Kayth's influence and power. Like everyone else, I once thought the stories of Fravashi crossing into our lands were born of too much mountain water on a dark night. After all, the border was supposedly secured with unbreakable spells."

"If Kayth and the trading families can come this way, then we can go into Frav." Corri pulled out her booter-knife and idly drew it back and forth through her fingers. "You know, Imandoff, I am not afraid of taking that journey now. Does that mean I am crazy?"

"No crazier than he is." Takra appeared suddenly out of the surrounding dark into the light of the campfire. "Or you, with your dream-flying. Or me. It means you are doing what is necessary and the hand of Frayma is over you."

"The Tuonela have always been crazy, Wind-Rider." Imandoff grinned up at Takra, then raked back the fire with a stick, exposing a bed of thick coals. "Sane people do not stand up in the saddle of a galloping horse."

The birds the Tuonela warrior held were coated in mud from the spring. She thrust them into the outer coals and squatted down beside Corri.

"Then sane people must miss all the joy in life, Silverhair. Begin to worry, sister-friend, when you are paralyzed with fear and cannot take the next step. Fear dulls the senses and weakens the sword arm. It often makes you face the wrong enemy."

"I am a thief, not a warrior, Takra." Corri tossed the booter into the air and caught the hilt cleanly as it fell, twirling, back down. "I think this journey into Frav may take the skills of a thief. I know Imandoff can sneak around on inn roofs and into dark tunnels, but how good are you at such things?"

"You mean we might have to go back underground?" Takra shuddered. "I hate crawling around inside a mountain."

"I hate heights," Corri answered. "But if it means putting an end to Kayth's evil power, I will walk a sword's edge on the top of the Fire Mountain."

"You need not go, Wind-Rider." Imandoff took out his pipe and tamped it full of smoke-leaf. "We will need protection at our backs. You and Tirkul can stand guard at the point where we cross the border." He called up fire with a snap of his fingers and puffed at the pipe.

"Never!" Takra's eyes flashed with anger. "You are not leaving me behind, Silverhair!"

"At least we now have a little more time to make our plans." Corri sliced a blade of grass into tiny strips with her knife. A sense of calmness began to flow through her mind and spirit. "The frantic urgency is leaving now. Kayth will be licking his wounds and planning his next move."

"Do you wish to go back to the Clans for a time?" Imandoff sent a smoke ring spiraling up beyond the firelight, into the darkening sky.

Corri shook her head. "With distrust of strangers burning over the grasslands, you and I would not be welcome at this time. Besides, there is no time for that, that much I know. No, my way lies to the north. Have you ever wondered, sorcerer, what the Footed Serpent is? I think we shall find out."

"The future will care for itself, Dream Warrior." Imandoff pulled the birds out of the coals and knocked off the mud. "But, like you, I am always curious about things I have never seen." He tossed a bird to Takra.

"Curiosity has a way of stepping on your fingers when you least expect it." Takra yelped, then tossed the bird carcass from hand to hand to help it cool. "But, knowing you, Silverhair, you will probably stamp back."

Imandoff grinned as he tore off a strip of meat. "I told you when we destroyed the Volikvi priest in the Valley of Whispers that life with us would never be dull."

"I remember," the warrior woman answered. "And I have had many a day to regret your company."

Corri looked away from the emotional glance exchanged between the sorcerer and Takra. *Some day,* she thought, *I want to know that close feeling with someone. I have made the choice of Gadavar in my heart, but how can I tell him? I know this feeling I have for Tirkul is only deep friendship, but have I jumped into quicksand, doing what I did with him?* She remembered her last glimpse of the Tuonela as he rode away, bent over Hellstorm's saddle. Then Gadavar's promise echoed through her mind. *Will I even live to know the joy of Gadavar's love?*

Be at peace, daughter. The Lady's soft voice came clear to Corri's mind. *Trust Me to lead you into the right paths.*

Corri relaxed as a feeling of warmth and love flooded over her. *I can do nothing else,* she thought. *I put myself and my battle companions into Your keeping, Lady.*

"Look!" Takra's excited voice broke into Corri's thoughts. Three falling stars traced their glowing paths across the black sky to the north.

"A strong sign of the greatest luck," Takra said.

"Of course," Corri answered. "The Lady shows us Her will and Her way." She smiled at Imandoff and Takra. "You two have been idle long enough. When you get bored, you begin bickering with each other. Perhaps one of you should stay behind just so the Fravashi will not hear you and know of our coming." She smiled.

"Never!" Imandoff and Takra said, then looked at each other and laughed.

"I want to discover the reality behind this prophesied Footed Serpent," the sorcerer said.

"And I want to spit on the altar of Jevotan." Takra waved her hand toward the north.

Corri shook her head. "I still think I am companying with crazies." She grinned and ducked Takra's swing.

"What do you think of children, Silverhair?" Takra suddenly asked.

"They are the hope of the future," Imandoff answered, looking at her in surprise. "Difficult to endure at times, but wonderful in their curiosity for all things."

Corri held her breath while Takra nervously picked at the roasted bird in her hand.

"I carry your child," the warrior woman finally said softly. "But that will not keep me from journeying with Farblood!" Her eyes flashed as she raised her head, her chin firm.

"My child?" An expression of surprise, followed by joy, filled Imandoff's face. "My son or daughter?"

Takra nodded, her cheekbones flushed. "But do not think you can tell me what I can and cannot do, simply because this is your child inside me."

"Most men seem to want sons," Corri said, slicing off a strip of meat with her dagger. "What do you want, old man?"

"I only care that Takra and the child come safely through the birth. But perhaps it will be twins." Imandoff's dark eyes flashed with amusement at Takra's open mouth.

"One child at a time is enough, Silverhair," the warrior woman grumbled. "And you will take your turn caring for it, as do all Tuonela men."

"I cannot refuse anything you ask of me, Takra Wind-Rider," he answered, reaching out to catch her hand. "So this was the cause of your sickness. And you knew?" He glanced at Corri.

The girl nodded as she continued to pluck meat from the bird carcass. "Being with child is a woman-thing. It was not my place to tell you, old man."

"Ah, women." Imandoff shook his head. "One of the great mysteries of life. A source of unending curiosity to me."

The three grinned at each other, unspoken waves of friendship sweeping over them. The teasing continued as they ate. The low fire was a shining spot of light in the darkness, a spark of freedom against the storm cloud of war hanging over Sar Akka.

The three rode on toward the northern mountains, only once seeing the herds and wagons of a Tuonela Clan in the distance. But they were not approached by any Clan out-riders. Day by day, the Mootma Mountains grew closer, more distinct on the horizon.

Corri had been restless all that day. Something pricked and pulled at her inner senses, causing her to push the horses to their limit.

"Corri, we must stop and rest the horses." Imandoff's words cut through her concentration, an irritation that rubbed raw against her nerves. "Besides, we are within a short day's journey to the border, and it is getting near dark. We cannot safely ride farther today. What drives you, girl?"

Corri bit back harsh words. "Something is not right." She groped for words to explain what she could not explain to herself. "I cannot put my finger on it, but something is very wrong."

She dismounted and let Mouse's reins trail in the long grass. Out of habit, Corri dug out the piece of cloth she kept for the horse and began to rub down her mount.

Imandoff wiped down Sun Dancer and Lightfoot while Takra slipped off through the gathering dusk to hunt prairie birds for their evening meal.

After making certain Mouse was loosely tethered near the other horses at the small waterhole, Corri tramped down a section of grass and spread her cloak over the sweet-smelling mat. As she idly watched Imandoff start a cooking fire and lay out the hard journey bread they carried, Corri became aware that she was clenching and unclenching her fists in frustration and nervousness.

What is happening? she thought. *This nervousness does not come from the journey or what lies around us.* She began to think about the people she knew and cared about, reaching out with her inner senses to feel for danger around them. *Halka? No, there is no feeling of danger about the shakka and her Clan. The Temple in Kystan is calm and secure. Leshy and Sadko are also quiet.* She reached out to Gadavar in the dark forests and felt only a prickle of anticipation as he mentally drove away a sharrock that had wandered too close to humans.

"Have you found what you seek?" Imandoff's soft voice aroused her once more to the present.

"No. Is the danger coming to us, Imandoff? Sometimes I miss what is right around me."

"I think not," he answered. "I feel no warnings. The horses are calm." He pointed one long-fingered hand at the mounts that quietly grazed not far away. Their only movement, besides the bite and pull at food, was a slight twitch of an ear when some grasslands bird called or the wind rustled over the long grass.

"Perhaps it is at the border." Takra stepped silently into the small circle of firelight, a brace of prairie hens dangling from one hand, her bow clutched in the other. The birds were gutted and plastered with mud, ready to roast in the bed of coals. "Have you received any news about Tirkul in your dreams?"

"When I last reached out to him, he was sleeping." Corri looked away into the dark. *I am not ready to share my decision about Tirkul, even though Takra guesses and Imandoff would understand.*

Imandoff raised his eyebrows in disbelief, but said nothing. He stirred the coals over the mud-plastered birds. Takra sat down beside Corri on the cloak and touched her shoulder with one hand. The faint whistle-clack of the drylands hachino sounded loud as the flock of birds rose suddenly into the dusk. This was followed by the high-pitched grunt of a herd of gribbels not far away.

"Perhaps I should shoot a gribbel so we will have meat to take with us." Takra reached for her bow, but Corri stopped her with a hand on the warrior woman's knee. She liked to watch the waist-high deer, their long ears constantly cocked to hear the smallest sound as they grazed.

"Let them go," she said quietly. "There is enough danger and death in the land." *Danger and death, yes, that feels right. But who is in danger?*

Corri said little as they ate. Her thoughts kept straying back to Tirkul, but she jerked them away each time. *He is safe with the Tuonela,* she told herself. *His wounds did not look that bad.*

She lay awake for some time, wrapped in her cloak against the chill of the night. Imandoff snored softly and Takra moved restlessly, her leather tunic squeaking as she turned. Corri's last thought, as she felt herself sliding into sleep, was of the Tuonela warrior and the rift between them.

Corri found herself hovering above their tiny camp. She turned in a circle, sending out her inner senses, seeking any approaching danger. There was none behind them or to either side. But when she faced the north, she felt an urgency to go there.

The Fravashi border? Corri shivered and sent a mind-seeking thought for Volikvis. There was no response to that danger, just the continued pulling sensation as if she needed to meet someone. *Kayth!* As soon as the word surfaced in Corri's mind she was aware of a slight tendril of thought coming her way. She immediately shut down any feelings toward Kayth, and the sensation went away. *If not Kayth, if not the Volikvis, then who?*

Her curiosity won. Swiftly, Corri flew over the grasslands to the rugged mountains to the north. Below her lay the star-bright sparks of the Tuonela campfires, spaced along the border at long intervals. No feeling of outside danger rose to meet her questing thoughts.

I will look at Tirkul, just for a moment, she told herself. *Then perhaps this feeling will go away.*

As soon as she thought of the Tuonela warrior, she found herself streaking to his side. He lay on his back near the low fire of a Clan camp, covered with several blankets. His pale blonde braids shown silver in the reflected light. Bruises and a multitude of small abrasions marked his face and arms, signs of the Volikvi capture and abuse.

Corri hung there in the chill air, watching the almost imperceptible rise and fall of Tirkul's chest. *Something is wrong here, here in this place. But what?* She looked around at the sleeping camp, the watchful guards stationed in the dark at the perimeter of the camp. She glanced back at the injured warrior and saw a gray mist rising from his brow. Her heart pounded in her throat as she watched. *He must not dream-fly while his body is so weak!*

The dream-body of Tirkul rose up to meet Corri. It swayed in the breeze that crept around the sheltering rocks of the Tuonela camp. Bewildered, Tirkul jerked his head first one way, then another.

Tirkul. The single word shot from Corri's mind into that of the Tuonela warrior. Instantly they hung facing each other.

I am dying, Dream Warrior. Tirkul's outstretched shadowy hands brushed against her life-force.

No! Do not accept death or seek it. I need you for the final battle, warrior.

Honor demands my death. Tirkul moved very close, looking down into her eyes with longing. *I have no choice, Corri. I was captured by the Volikvis but did not die under their hands. I would rather make the long journey to Vayhall than to bring dishonor to my Clan or danger into Tuone.*

It is not your time. I know it!

I would rather die than become a slave to Kayth and his evil,
came the enigmatic reply.

You are safe now, Tirkul. See, all around you are Tuonela war-
riors. Kayth cannot make you his slave.

The deed is done. Tirkul's pale form quivered, and he raised
one hand to his head. *The pain! I cannot think of what happened.*
Let me go. The misty form turned away from her.

No! Your part in this life is not finished, Tirkul of the Clan of the
Asperel. Corri felt herself heat with anger. *We have unfinished*
business, Tuonela warrior. If you would be rid of me and your life,
you tell me face to face. Imandoff, Takra, and I ride even now to
join you.

Tirkul turned to look at her then, and smiled sadly. *Stub-*
born little thief. Sometimes you are like a desert burr in the
trousers. But it is better if you let me go into Between Worlds, Corri.
It is best that I die after falling into the hands of the Volikvis.

Male pride, that is all it is. You would desert me because of your
hurt pride. Corri moved closer. *You would take the easy way and*
desert me when I need you most.

Tirkul's misty form took on a faint red glow as his anger
rose. *A blow to the back, Dream Warrior. Your tongue has sharp-*
ened since we last spoke. He frowned at her.

Calling upon deep instincts, Corri gathered her power into
her cupped hands, then sprang suddenly at Tirkul, forcing his
misty form back down into his sleeping body. She then
smoothed the brilliant light in her hands completely over him,
whispering softly, *Sleep and heal. Sleep and heal.*

For long moments she watched to see if his dream-body
would try to escape once more, but at least for a time it was
secured within the fleshly form. With one last touch against
his cheek, Corri turned and sped back across the grasslands to
their camp.

akra and Imandoff were grim when Corri tried to tell them about Tirkul the next morning.

"We must reach him soon," Corri said, "or I fear he will die. Perhaps if we, his friends, are near him, he will fight to live." Imandoff nodded, then began to break camp.

They rode on toward the northern mountains with the dawn, finally coming into a Tuonela border camp just as it was becoming too dark to clearly see the trail. The fresh scent of pine and fir around them lifted Corri's spirits after days of smelling sun-baked grass on the Tuonela prairies.

"Is Tirkul of the Clan of the Asperel here?" Takra asked as she came to the fire with Imandoff and Corri. Their tired horses, rubbed down and unburdened of saddles and bags, now grazed with the other mounts in a nearby forest clearing.

A Tuonela warrior sharpening his long dagger near Imandoff's feet paused, then pointed the knife into the semidarkness at the far side of the encampment. "He is there. Kulkar is with him."

Without a word, Takra shouldered her saddlebags and rounded the fire, Corri and Imandoff at her heels. Under the low-sweeping branches of an ancient fir tree they found the leader of the war band squatted near a blanket-wrapped form.

"I greet you, Takra Wind-Rider." Kulkar rose to look closely at Imandoff. "And you, Silverhair. Frayma has heard my prayers for help. We have done what we can for Tirkul, but still he wanders in his mind." His dark eyes were suspicious as Corri dropped her saddlebag and knelt beside Tirkul.

"She is the Dream Warrior," Imandoff said in answer to Kulkar's unspoken question.

Tirkul lay quiet, the only sign of life the rise and fall of his chest. Flickering light from the campfire sharpened his cheekbones and edged his jaw, forehead, and the bridge of his nose. Corri bent close, then drew a shocked breath. On both sides of Tirkul's head were a series of deep gouges, as if talons had scored his flesh, even through his braided hair. Dark shadows of fatigue and pain outlined his mouth and smudged his eyelids.

I did not think he was so wounded! Her heart ached for the pain and shame Tirkul must feel. *This was done to him only because of what he feels for me. To Kayth and Minepa, friendship, like love, is only a weakness to be exploited.*

"Are his wounds serious?" Imandoff asked the warrior leader, but Kulkar shook his head. "Do you know the cause of his sickness?" Imandoff watched Corri smooth back Tirkul's sweat-dampened hair from his face.

"We know only that he was taken into Frav, although not with the others who were captured. He acts as if he were tortured, but the marks are few," Kulkar answered. "We do not know how he escaped. He came alone to our camp two nights ago."

"The other Tuonela who were captured, what of them?" Kulkar shrugged at Imandoff's question.

"One died bravely, taking several priests with him." Corri winced at the memory. "Others were still alive the last I knew."

The sorcerer knelt at Tirkul's side, across from Corri, and slowly ran his long-fingered hands above the warrior's still body. "I find small pains in the body," he said at last. "But there is something else, something I cannot name. Does he have any serious wounds?"

"Except for scrapes and bruises, only a small cut on the back of his neck." Kulkar's voice dropped to a low murmur. "At times he moans with pain, holding his head, speaking with people we do not know and cannot see. Nothing we do gives him any relief. Every night he screams out in terror with strange dreams. The others speak of tormenting night demons sent by the Volikvis."

Corri dug into her saddlebag, finding the owl stone circlet by feel in the shadowed firelight. Sitting cross-legged, she slipped the band over her head, centering the stone above her eyes.

If there are no great wounds, what causes the strange play of energy about his head? she thought as she looked at Tirkul's body through the owl stone. *There is a disturbance in his life-energy there.* She centered her inner vision on the warrior's neck to discover a tiny dark spot near the base of his skull. *Such a small wound should not cause Tirkul these problems.* The warrior began to moan softly and tried to move away as Corri gently touched his face.

Corri pushed up the circlet and looked at Imandoff, who watched her silently. "As Kulkar said, there are no wounds great enough to keep Tirkul like this."

"Perhaps his mind is bruised from the Fravashi treatment. As soon as you released your inner sight, he calmed. I will reach into his mind and attempt to keep him quiet while you draw upon the healing energies of the stone."

Imandoff closed his eyes and laid his hands on each side of the warrior's head. Tirkul at once began to moan and twist, attempting to get away from the sorcerer's touch. Imandoff's hands tightened, his brows pulled together as he concentrated.

With the owl stone once more in place, Corri slid one hand under Tirkul's neck until her fingers cupped over the tiny wound at the base of his neck. Tirkul screamed as the stone's energies poured from her hand into his head. He tore his arms free of the blankets, knocking Corri away.

What did I do? This is some barrier that keeps the healing energy from entering, but what? Oh Goddess, I meant only to help, not hurt.

"There is a barrier in his mind," she said as she removed the circlet. "I cannot reach him, nor will he allow me to attempt any healing. What can we do, Imandoff?"

Tirkul once more lay quiet. Imandoff knelt with his hands on his knees, looking intently at the pain-washed face of the semiconscious warrior. Takra's fists were clenched at her sides.

"In the morning we must take him down to the Clans," she said, chewing on her lower lip. "He will be safe with the shakkas until a way can be found to cure him."

"That is the only hope," Kulkar said. "We can spare no one to take him to the shakkas, nor to care for anyone seriously wounded. We must be constantly alert for attacks from Frav now. If he remains here long, I cannot even promise protection should the Fravashi stream across the border here."

Imandoff nodded as he stood up. "Tonight, though, I want to look at the border for myself. There must be some way to strengthen the old spells, to prevent these attacks."

"Tirkul will be safe here while you are gone." Kulkar turned and motioned to a warrior to watch the now-quiet Tuonela. "Take care, Silverhair. We never know when the Fravashi will attack next, or where."

Imandoff led his companions through the dark trees, away from the camp. The sliver of moon gave little light as they entered a rock-strewn area with a faint blue glow running from east to west. Takra cursed softly several times as she stubbed her toes on shadowed rocks, her soft voice unnaturally loud in the silence.

"This is the place." Imandoff stopped so suddenly that Corri ran into him.

"What place?" she whispered.

"The Fravashi traders, the ones I met in Nevn, cross the border here." The sorcerer pointed out two cairns of rocks set far enough apart that a loaded horse could pass easily between them. He dug into his belt pouch, pulling out a circular piece of wood on a thong. Carefully hanging it in plain sight on a tree limb near one of the cairns, Imandoff cupped the medallion in his hands and whispered silent words over it. "If I have counted right, and I am certain I have, they will return this way either tonight or tomorrow."

"What is that to us?" Takra said, her eyes nervously scanning up and down the spelled border.

"I wish to talk to them," Imandoff answered. "As allies, they could pass on news and rumors of Fravashi plans. And perhaps they know what the Volikvi have done to Tirkul."

"Do we wait here?" Corri looked about her at the black shadows of the forest and shivered.

"We will return to camp. The medallion will alert me to their presence, and the traders will wait for us. If fighting breaks out here tonight, then they must hide until it is safe to cross the border. Either way, I shall know the traders are nearby." Imandoff turned back toward the Tuonela camp, Corri and Takra at his heels.

Chapter 17

Once more Tirkul heard the strange evil voices within his mind, whispering to him, enticing him, then ordering him. Calling upon all the mental discipline he knew, he resisted the demands. He felt his nerves and muscles quiver in response to the mental orders, but he fought back, willing his body to stay where it was. The voices stilled, and he lay bathed in perspiration, his body twitching from the assault, his mind cringing from the memory.

The headaches returned, a sudden pounding, crushing pain that set him writhing and moaning. He bit his lower lip to hold back his cries and felt the blood trickle down his chin. His body arched on head and heels as his fingers dug into the soft padding of dead fir needles and dirt beneath him. Just as he began to spiral downwards into the darkness of unconsciousness, Tirkul felt something within him give way, as if a portion of him stepped outside the gnawing agony. The pain receded, leaving him aware that it lurked at the edges of his consciousness, ready to leap up again.

You will return to Frav! Minepa's compelling eyes hung in Tirkul's inner vision. He could not turn aside from the sight of those eyes. *You must return to me, or you will die of the pain.* The Volikvi's taloned fingers lifted into his line of vision. The pain crushed down, tearing at the inside of his head like great hooks in his brain; every nerve in his body screamed from the torture as if his skin and flesh were slowly being ripped away. The agony lasted just for an instant before withdrawing again, but it was violent enough to leave Tirkul shaking and sick. *I have the power to remove the pain, Tuonela. Only I can take away this agony.*

"I will not!" Tirkul's mumbled words reached the guard, who shook his head in sympathy.

Then return for this! Tirkul saw Corri chained to the stone block, Minepa's hands rubbing up and down the girl's nude body. *Return, and I will free her.*

Tirkul's eyes snapped open. He listened to the quiet voices of the warriors about the campfire, the faint rustle of dead needles as his guard moved away to join them. He struggled up, sliding out of the blankets, his eyes alert to every movement in the circle of men. Stealthily, Tirkul crawled back in among the trees, then rose and stumbled toward the spell-bound border, using all the scout-craft he knew. Once he froze motionless as three figures passed near him in the dark, but his numbed mind recognized none of the night walkers.

Suddenly, behind him, Tirkul heard shouts from the warriors in camp, and he dashed blindly toward the border. Ahead lay the Kratula River, shallow here before it began its way through the ever-deepening Gorge. His controlled mind registered no barrier as he waded through the faint silvery blue haze of the spells hanging over the river. He stumbled up the bank and into the trees on the other side.

Gasping for breath, Tirkul leaned against the moss-covered trunk of a tree, deep in the shadows, and watched the Tuonela torches marking the clansmen's search. The firefly wink of the torches drew ever closer until the warriors milled about the Tuonela side of the border. Their voices reached him clearly, but the words had no meaning.

Tirkul turned away and crept on through the trees, following the directions planted in his mind. Soon he found himself at the edge of a road where robed figures waited.

His sudden silent appearance out of the black forest startled the watchers. There was the clink of weapon against sheath as Tirkul stepped onto the dusty track.

"Take me to Minepa," the Tuonela ordered, his hoarse words shattering the stillness.

"Come, we have a mount for you." A robed figure led out a horse, laying the reins in Tirkul's outstretched hand.

"Should we not bind him?" Tirkul caught a gleam of armor as another man stepped close beside him, sword in hand.

"No need," the first figure answered. "He will go willingly."

The cloak slipped back slightly, and Tirkul saw the robe and pendant of a Volikvi priest. The Tuonela warrior hesitated for an instant as his mind fought against the implanted messages, trying to send out signals of danger. Then he mounted and turned the horse's head toward Vu-Zai, the Fravashi soldiers around him.

"You must wear this." The Volikvi rode close, slipping a black medallion over Tirkul's head. The warrior looked down at the pendant lying on his chest, then up into the shadowed eyes of the priest. "Only if you wear this can you enter Vu-Zai."

The last of Tirkul's misgivings were smothered by the power of the pendant. *There is nothing to fear,* he told himself. *I will go to Minepa, take Corri, and leave again. No one can hold me against my will.*

Yes, that is the way of it, the subtle voice whispered in his mind. *There is no need to resist. Do what you are told, and everything shall be as you wish.*

Without a backward glance at the border, Tirkul rode off into the night with the Volikvi and the Fravashi soldiers.

*W*e saw him cross the border!" Kulkar stood, hands on hips, looking straight into Imandoff's eyes. "Tirkul is no traitor, yet he ran from his own people."

"You said there was nothing on him that was unnatural, not of Tuonela making. Yet he deliberately crossed over into Frav." The sorcerer frowned as he thought. "There had to be something used as a caller."

"There was nothing. The Volikvis must have marked his spirit," answered Kulkar. "Nothing else makes sense."

Imandoff shook his head. "To be possessed by the will of another, there must be an object, something to link the two."

"There is another way." Corri's quiet words stilled the warriors gathered around them. "Kayth and the Volikvis use strange boxes to help them get through the spells at the border, is this not so? And these boxes have never been seen before among the Fravashi before Kayth's coming?"

"This is so." Takra stood staring at the black tree shadows across the spell-marked river. "Our history says nothing of such things."

Corri took a deep breath and plunged on. "I should have guessed. The object used to control Tirkul was not on the outside, but on the inside, where no one would see it."

"The wound in his neck!" Imandoff half-drew his sword, then slammed it back in the sheath. "We cannot leave Tirkul in the hands of the Volikvis. What did Kayth and Minepa see in him, what hidden power do they suspect? I must go into Frav and bring him back. We cannot take the chance that Tirkul's presence among the Volikvis will not tip the scales of war in their favor."

"I think you are following the wrong trail, Imandoff." Corri took hold of the sorcerer's sleeve to get his attention. "Kayth was able to get at Tirkul because of his thoughts of me. It is me Kayth wants, not Tirkul."

"If Kayth's power grows as you say, he would have launched his attack straight at you, Corri. You have not come into your power enough to hide your presence from him. All he need do is send Volikvis and warriors over the border and take you." Imandoff paced two steps, then back again. "No, I am not seeing something, but what?"

"Perhaps it is because Tirkul believes he is Varanna's lover, the Tirkul of the ancient legends, come back," Takra said.

"Perhaps," Imandoff answered. "Whatever the reason, Corri and I will go into Frav this night." He turned to go back to camp.

"Not alone, you will not." Takra's muscled hand tightened on his arm, stopping the sorcerer. Her pale brows drew together in determination.

"Corri and I can move through Frav with no one wiser, but you, Takra, your fair hair would shout Tuonela to the first guard, the first Fravashi we passed."

"Then I will darken my hair. You do not leave me behind, Silverhair. Tirkul is my clan-brother. It is my right to go with you."

The two stood glaring at each other until the murmurs of agreement from the warriors broke Imandoff's gaze.

"It is her right," Corri said, "and mine. We are wasting time, Silverhair. There is also the matter of those who wait for you in response to your medallion. Do what you must with them, then let us ride into Frav. Every minute we delay means they take Tirkul farther into dangerous territory."

"Yes, we must catch up with them before they take him into Vu-Zai." Imandoff turned to Takra. "If you must come, Wind-Rider, bind up your hair and wear Corri's hood. And say as little as possible when we are in Frav. Your speech will quickly mark you as Tuonela."

They hurried back to the rough camp. As Imandoff and Takra saddled the horses, Corri took the bag containing Varanna's helmet to Kulkar. Into the bag she placed the precious owl stone set in the ancient silver circlet.

"I dare not take these into Frav," she told him. "Can you spare a rider to take this east to Frayma's Mare?"

"For you, Dream Warrior, any rider would go." Kulkar held up his clenched fist in a warrior's salute.

They led the horses back to the border-point where Imandoff's wooden medallion hung to find a small band of dark cloaked traders waiting for them. Takra's long pale braids were bound tightly around her head, her brows and lashes darkened with ashes. She wore Corri's hood pulled far forward to hide the Clan tattoo on her cheek.

"We would go into Frav with you," Imandoff told the leader of the Fravashi band after explaining what happened. "Which road will the Volikvis take?" The sorcerer stared at the pale foxfire of spell-light hanging over the Kratula River.

"It is several days' journey through Frav to Vu-Zai," answered the man, scratching his bare chin. "They will head first for Vum. But why do they want this Tuonela warrior?"

"We are not certain. Perhaps Minepa thinks to use him to gain full entrance for Fravashi warriors into Tuone." Corri mounted her horse and turned Mouse's head toward the river. "The why does not matter. Tirkul is captive. We are wasting time."

She kicked Mouse with her heels and rode down into the water. She felt only a rough tingling against her skin as she broke through the spells. As the horse climbed the far bank, Corri turned and motioned to the others.

"I know I can suspend my belief and pass through the spells," Imandoff said as he moved close to the Wind-Rider. "But I do not think you can. Ride back to the others, Takra."

"No! Do what you must, Silverhair, but get me across the border." Takra mounted Lightfoot and sat, her hands clenched on the reins. "And no tricks, sorcerer."

With a sigh, Imandoff pulled himself onto Sun Dancer, then rode up beside her. Leaning close, he touched the center of her forehead with one long finger. The words he whispered were only a murmur to the traders, but Takra's eyes lost their focus and stared straight ahead.

"We must hurry. The border guards must not see us cross." The Fravashi trader signaled his people.

The traders guided their mounts and pack mules down to the water with Imandoff and Takra following. Once across, Imandoff again touched Takra's forehead, and her eyes focused on her surroundings.

They rode on without words, the only sounds being the jingle of horse brass and the creak of leather, as they followed a narrow rocky trail into Frav. Before daybreak they were riding through the outskirts of Vum.

"Here." The lead trader pointed to the open gates of a house surrounded by a walled courtyard. "This is the house of my family. No one here will dare speak of your presence. I will inquire discretely about this Tuonela." He handed the reins of his mount to a servant, then quickly guided the three into the large house, where they were given rooms.

"We will get nowhere if we wait for this cowardly Fravashi to seek news of Tirkul." Takra paced up and down the upstairs room, her hand clutching her dagger hilt. "How do you know he will not betray us?"

"He dares not," Imandoff answered. He sat calmly smoking his pipe, his booted feet propped up on a second chair. "The very fact that we shelter in his house would bring a death penalty down upon him and his family."

Corri finished sharpening the last of her daggers and slipped each back in its place—one openly in her belt, one in her boot, and the tiny lady's knife she had begged from Imandoff into her shirt. She tugged on her hood that Takra had cast aside as soon as they were safe within the trader's house. Her leather trousers and tunic were thrown on the bed, and she now stood clothed in Fravashi cloth trousers and shirt. She fingered Gadavar's silver amulet that lay hidden under the shirt.

"One thing I noticed as we rode into Vum, red hair, at least among men, is not unusual here in Frav," Corri said. "Even one of the trader's daughters has red hair, although she takes great pains to keep it concealed."

"I will not let you go into the city alone." Imandoff's feet hit the floor with a thud.

"It is not for you to tell me what I can and cannot do." Corri glared at him. "In Hadliden I was often sent among strangers and never once did anyone guess that I was a woman. The Fravashi tongue is basically the same as the other Peoples, and I have a quick ear for picking up accents."

My instincts tell me that I am the only one who can discover where Tirkul is kept. And the Judge Natira said to follow my instincts. She stared back at Imandoff. *I am so afraid, old man, but this I must do. Try to understand.*

"Think, Silverhair." Takra's firm words, her upheld hand, stopped the sorcerer's protests. "Although I like it no better than you, Corri was a skilled thief in Hadliden. She has the talents to get her out of most trouble she may encounter, even in a strange city. I, too, do not want her to go alone, but I can see no other way. We cannot wait for the trader to find Tirkul. Time is against us."

"But Corri has no contacts here," Imandoff protested.

"True, but neither do you. I know how to skulk about markets, listening and watching. The arrival of the Volikvis with a Tuonela warrior will not have gone unnoticed." Corri went to the open window and looked down into the busy courtyard. "The servants are preparing to go to the markets for food. I will join them, then slip off by myself."

Imandoff sighed and nodded. "What you say makes sense. But take no chances, Corri. You are a dear friend, and I do not want to lose you."

Corri eased open the door and looked down the hall before slipping out of the room. She walked with her head slightly down, her ears alert to everything around her, as she passed through the lower hall and out into the courtyard. She loitered near the kitchen door until the cook's helper and several servants came out on their daily trip to the markets. Grabbing a woven basket near the door, Corri fell into line and walked unnoticed out of the trader's compound into the streets of Vum.

The alertness and the heightened senses she had used as a thief swiftly came back as Corri followed the servants through the crowded markets from shop to stall. She eyed all the alleys as possible escape routes, checked the positions of the few Fravashi soldiers, and memorized the bargaining manners of the people milling about the great square just inside the city wall. Her sharp ears assessed the Fravashi accent, filing it away for possible future use. When the cook's helper had led the servants far enough into the market crowds, Corri quickly slipped behind a booth of vegetables and lost herself in the mass of people.

Where would Volikvis go with a prisoner? she asked herself as she wandered about the square, trying to look as if she were on an errand. *Is there a temple here or would they go to an inn?*

"Have you heard?" The loud voice of a man behind her drew Corri's attention. "Zalmoxis came to Vum early this morning with a Tuonela warrior."

"What do they want with just one?" asked the man walking beside him. "The Volikvis rarely consider one prisoner for sacrifice in the Temple as fitting."

"Perhaps this is the fabled Dream Warrior," the first man said. "If the Volikvis hold the Dream Warrior, there will be little fighting spirit in the other Peoples when our warriors attack at the Harvest Moon. Do you suppose Zalmoxis took the Tuonela to the Temple of Pleasure where he stays so often, or is he softening him up in the Temple of Jevotan?"

"Do not talk so loud! The Volikvis are nervous, sending their spies everywhere. They arrest anyone who disagrees even a little with them or asks questions. Yesterday they took away Yulak for words spoken in the privacy of his own courtyard." The second man made a warding sign with his fingers.

"Yulak speaks traitorous words." The first man bumped into Corri as he turned to face his friend. "Yulak, like others, believes that we should not force our religious beliefs on the other Peoples, that we should not attack them, that the Volikvis should not make blood sacrifices of humans."

"Perhaps Yulak is right." The second man's voice was barely audible above the noise of the crowd. "Long ago, our God demanded no such sacrifices. The Fravashi held to their own customs and went their own way in peace. This our ancient history tells us."

"If you feel this way, why do you not go straight to the Temple of Pleasure and tell Zalmoxis yourself? As long as you speak such blasphemous ideas, keep your distance from me!" The first man drew back from the other and pushed angrily through the crowd.

Corri eyed the remaining man from under the edge of her hood. He stood looking across the market square, his eyes raised to a tall red tower seen over the roofs of the surrounding buildings.

"I send my blackest curse on that Trow temple. May all the Volikvis and Trow burn in the fires of hell!" the man swore softly, before turning on his heel and walking away.

So that is the Temple of Pleasure, Corri thought. *If Kayth plans to attack the Peoples before the Harvest Moon, the time is short, for the Harvest Moon is only five months away. Even though the Fravashi plague us with raids, these are just a smoke screen to hide their actual plans. I must find Tirkul. If he is in that Trow temple, somehow I must bring him out.*

She began to pick a cautious way through the streets in the direction of the red tower. Within a short time she reached a low-walled enclosure, the red tower within it like a giant finger pointing to the skies. Lining the streets around the Temple of Pleasure were shops selling perfume, religious jewelry, exotic fruits and flowers. Across from the open gates stood a tavern, the Sea Kern.

As Corri stood looking up at the white bird with red wing-bars on the tavern sign, she felt a prickle of danger crawl between her shoulder blades. Instinctively, she hunched her shoulders and stepped close to the building, trying to look like the other servants who passed up and down the street.

Corri bowed her head as a Volikvi priest and a woman well wrapped in gauzy veils walked past and into the Sea Kern. The woman's thick, sweet perfume stung her nose, bringing back vivid memories. Looking up from the shelter of her hood, Corri saw the dark red side-curls against the man's shaven scalp, the long-nailed fingers where the woman held her veil across her face.

O Goddess! It is Zalmoxis and Xephena. Corri took a deep breath and pushed down the mental scenes that flooded her mind. *If they are here instead of at Vu-Zai, it must be because of Tirkul. But why do they come to a tavern instead of going to the Temple? Anything those two do or anyone they meet could be of great importance.*

Corri set the basket down against the tavern wall and slipped in behind the priest and Trow. Once inside, she shook off her servant guise, straightening her shoulders and looking about her with sharp eyes. Zalmoxis and the Trow went directly to the back of the great room, the patrons pulling aside as they passed. Corri caught a glimpse of a man as the two pushed through a curtain into a sheltered alcove.

Quickly, she moved into the booth next to the alcove, taking the mug from the hands of a sailor snoring with his head on the dirty table. She leaned back against the wall, as if she too were drunk and half-asleep.

I must know what they say, she thought. Gently, with great control, Corri allowed her spirit-form to slip a little from her body. The murmur of voices in the alcove behind her became clearer as her inner senses sharpened.

"How much time will we have before this Tuonela is taken on to Vu-Zai?" Zalmoxis asked.

"Kayth is even now on his way to Vum." The deep voice of the second man was cautious. "If you think to use this Tuonela against Kayth, you must work quickly. Why is he so important to Kayth?"

"We do not know, only that Kayth wishes greatly to have him within his hands." Xephena's voice sounded edgy, tired.

"For that reason alone we wish to have time with this Tuonela. He must have some power we have not seen." Zalmoxis thumped the table with his hand.

"Power, now that reminds me. Word is that Kayth is growing stronger. No one nay-says him on anything, not even Minepa." The second man's voice dropped to a whisper. "All must now call him Jinniyah."

"Jinniyah!" Xephena's voice rose, then dropped again. "Are there signs that he is gaining the ancient powers?"

"There are signs," the man answered. There was a scrape of bench as the man rose to leave. "I must return to the Temple of Jevotan or there will be questions."

Corri continued her pose as a drunk as the man left the booth. He paused briefly beside her table, then left the tavern.

"If Kayth is coming into the powers of Jinniyah, we must move quickly to stop him." Zalmoxis leaned back against the wall near where Corri sat. "What of your forbidden powers, Trow?"

"I cannot use them to the fullest," Xephena answered. "That cursed sorcerer and his trap left me drained. As yet I cannot even dispel the shadow-seeker. It still haunts my dreams." The Trow's voice was tight with nervousness.

"We must find some way to influence the Tuonela warrior before Kayth arrives and takes him from the Temple of Pleasure." Zalmoxis slapped the table again with his hand. "We dare not remove the Stone of Darkness he wears, yet the Stone sharpens Kayth's control over him. There must be another way!"

"There are drugs," answered the Trow. "Fill him with those, then give him to the Trow at the Temple. Sexual magic is something Kayth has not yet discovered. It may well be enough to break the link."

Corri carefully recalled her spirit-form and felt it settle once more in its proper place. Setting the mug on the table, she pushed out of the booth and started across the tavern room. Before she had gone five steps, a harsh voice broke through the tavern noise.

"You! The boy in the hood, come here!" Corri turned to find Zalmoxis pointing at her.

What do I do? If I run, he will surely know something is wrong. If I go to him, will he and the Trow recognize me?

Corri hunched her shoulders and shuffled back toward the Volikvi, her heart pounding.

"Go to the Temple jeweler on the corner and tell him that Zalmoxis wishes you to get the medallion he ordered." The Volikvi barely looked at Corri as he took a gold piece from his belt pouch. "Bring it to me at the Temple of Pleasure." He grasped Corri's shoulder as she turned to go. "If you delay, I will take you to the altar of Jevotan myself."

Corri hurried out, paused until she spotted the jeweler's sign at the corner, then ran down the crowded street.

If I fail in this errand, Zalmoxis will turn out the soldiers to search for me. There is nothing for it but to take this medallion into the Temple of Pleasure. She paused outside the door as a sudden thought flashed across her mind. *Tirkul is there!*

Corri pushed open the door, hesitated before she entered the crowded workroom. *I can play an imbecile. That should cover my accent.*

She allowed her mouth to hang slack and one foot to drag as she shuffled into the shop. "Zalmoxis," she lisped, holding out the gold piece to the first workman she saw. "Zalmoxis." She pushed the coin at the man.

"Master, a slave here for the medallion," the man called out, pushing away her hand.

A short man, his back bent from long hours over his work, came forward with a small bag in his hand. "Take to Zalmoxis," he said as he took the coin from Corri's hand. "Go to Temple." He pointed in the direction of the red tower. "Go Zalmoxis."

Obediently, she took the bag and started for the door.

"Why do they use idiots?" the master jeweler said. "Seems like that kind would be losing things all the time."

"They do not ask questions," answered one of the workmen.

"True enough," Corri heard as she shut the door behind her.

Corri's hands shook as she walked through the open Temple gates and up the paved garden path to the great doors. *Now what? Am I supposed to know where to go or do I just blunder in and ask for Zalmoxis?*

"Here, you. What do you want?" A guard near the doors stopped her with a rough hand.

"Zalmoxis. Go Zalmoxis." Corri tried to push the bag into the guard's hand but he pushed her away, opened the door and pointed toward an ornate stairway.

"Zalmoxis up there." The guard pointed up the stairs. "By the dry tits of Croyna, where does he find these imbeciles?" the man muttered as she shuffled across the tiled floor and began her climb.

The stairs opened onto a long hallway lined with doors. Corri paused, uncertain where to go. As she stood there, the bag hanging in one hand, one of the doors opened and a Trow came out. She was scantily clad in a gauzy robe, her nipples gold-painted, a girdle dropping its swaying fringes between her legs. The Trow frowned at her, then stood aside as a man came out of the room. The Fravashi ignored her as he pushed past to go down the stairs.

Here goes nothing, Corri told herself as she shuffled to the Trow. "Zalmoxis," she lisped, holding out the bag.

"I am not Zalmoxis," the Trow said, taking Corri roughly by the arm. "I suppose you are another imbecile that old man uses in his attempts at sex magic," she muttered as she dragged Corri down the hall.

"Stay here," the Trow ordered, pushing Corri down onto a bench behind a heavy curtain at the end of the hall. Behind the bench was a window, open to the garden below. "Stay. I take to Zalmoxis. Good boy, stay." She took the bag from Corri's limp fingers and disappeared into the room nearby.

There must be a way to find Tirkul, Corri thought as she edged farther behind the curtain. She knelt on the bench to peer out the open window. A narrow balcony stretched the length of the building. Cautiously, she looked down but could see no one in the gardens through the thick pierced railing.

Zalmoxis and Xephena may let slip where they have him hidden away. The only way to find out is to eavesdrop.

She stepped over the low sill and onto the narrow balcony. An ornate strip of carving jutted out onto the balcony, shielding the view of what must be a window. As she quietly moved to the carving, she saw that the window of the room the Trow had entered was open, but the curtains drawn. Behind her she heard a door shut and the Trow's voice calling. She flattened against the building, hiding behind the jut of carving.

When the Trow did not come onto the balcony, Corri silently made her way to the open window. Crouching below the low wall of the balcony, she knelt at the window, intently listening to the low voices within the room. A tiny gap in the curtains allowed her to see inside. Zalmoxis sat in a cushioned chair while Xephena lounged on the wide bed.

"Well, where is the boy?" Zalmoxis asked.

"I put him on the bench near the window but he is gone." The Trow nervously plucked at her gauzy robe.

"No matter." Zalmoxis dismissed her with a wave of his hand. "Go back to your duties."

"We must begin the conditioning of the Tuonela at once," Xephena said as she leaned back on the red and black pillows.

"Which Trow will you use?" Zalmoxis took the gold medallion from the bag and attached it to his belt. "Surely you will use others to begin." His glittering dark eyes raked across her almost-nude body.

"I will give him drugs to break down his resistance and heighten his sexual needs and prowess." Xephena moved her hips sensuously, cupping her breasts with her hands. "Then when the others have coupled with him and he reaches the pinnacle of his sexual height, I will go to him. At the peak of lovemaking, I will bind him to me and give him orders that even Kayth cannot break. The Tuonela has a wonderfully strong body, one that will last for hours."

Zalmoxis licked his lips as he stared at her. "Where is this Tuonela now?"

"He is safe within the outer Temple room, the place where the Trow initiate the Volikvi novices into our part of Jevotan's religion." Xephena wiggled her hips again. "Since Kayth does not believe in the power of sexual magic, he will not expect him there."

Zalmoxis stood, his hands quivering as he plucked at the fastenings of his robe. Just as his fingers pulled loose the top clasps, someone banged loudly on the closed door. Then the door flew open to reveal a Fravashi guard, his eyes looking straight ahead, his body snapped to attention.

"I beg your forgiveness for intruding, sir, but a party of priests from the Temple at Vu-Zai are at the gates of the Temple of Pleasure. And the man Kayth is with them!"

Chapter 18

"So soon!" Xephena hissed, sitting up on the bed, her mouth pursed in disapproval. "Can we delay his seeing the Tuonela?"

"Mistress, the man Kayth is even now on his way to the initiation room." The guard continued to stare straight ahead, no expression on his face.

"We must go up at once!" Xephena slid from the bed, rearranging her diaphanous robe to reveal her scarlet and gold-painted nipples. "Talk to his men," she ordered the guard. "If they are willing, get them to the most persuasive of the Trow. And listen well, Thidrick, to all their talk."

The guard stood aside as Zalmoxis and Xephena hurried out of the room. "May you fight among yourselves and bring down this reign of madness," the guard muttered as soon as the two were beyond hearing.

"Are you certain you saw someone on that balcony?" A guard's voice from the garden below brought Corri instantly alert. "No one can get to that balcony except through the Temple."

"Nevertheless, you will go see," answered the cold voice of a priest.

Corri frantically looked up and down the balcony. She saw other juts of carving, which seemed to frame each window, marking other possible avenues of escape. *If the rooms are not occupied,* she thought wryly. *And even if I get in, where will I hide if they search the Temple?*

She crawled back to the open corridor window, listening all the time for any sign that the priest still remained in the garden below. Quickly she pulled herself over the sill and slipped behind the heavy curtain, expecting at any moment to hear an alarm raised, but none came.

Safe so far. But I cannot stay here. This is the first place they will come. And I doubt that playing the imbecile will work with Kayth's companions.

As Corri stood, undecided as to her next plan of action, a thick hand whipped around the curtain. Before she could reach one of her knives, she was jerked from her hiding place, her arm locked behind her back in a punishing hold.

"Whose spy are you?" asked a deep voice by her ear. The guard reached with his free hand to jerk down her hood. "By the God, a fiery-haired one! Are you a novice here, girl?" The guard loosened her arm and turned her to face him.

"I am no Trow, novice or otherwise." Corri frowned as she rubbed at her arm.

"Then, girl, this is no place for you. Come quickly!" The guard grabbed her again by the arm, pulling her toward a narrow opening halfway up the corridor. "Cover your head," he whispered as he led her down the dark stairway past the ground floor and on down into a basement.

The room at the foot of the stairs was awash with lamp-light. Corri bent her head after a glance showed several guards dicing in one corner, while others sat eating at a long table.

"Taken to boys, Thidrick?" called one of the men. "Did the Trow refuse you?" Coarse jests and laughter filled the room.

"Watch your tongue," Thidrick growled as he dragged Corri the length of the room and through a curtained entrance.

"Stay quiet!" he whispered, pointing to a stool in one corner. "Most of them will leave for duty soon. The guards who come down will not have seen me bring you here, so they will have nothing unusual to report to Zalmoxis or Xephena."

Corri sat on the stool, clasping her shaking hands on her knees. Thidrick poured a mug of warm ale and handed it to her. He continued to stand near the curtain, one hand on his belt knife, his head bent as he listened to the men in the room beyond.

A great gong rang through the Temple, its vibrations carrying down the narrow stairway. There was a scrape of benches, the clink of metal as the men left to relieve the guards on duty above.

"Now tell me, girl, why are you here and where are you from?" Thidrick stood before Corri, a mug in one hand, the other resting on his knife hilt. "If you do not know that all red-haired women are taken to become Trow, then you are not from Frav."

Corri looked up into the very dark brown eyes, deep set under heavy black brows. *What he said about Zalmoxis, perhaps he will help me,* she thought. *I must get to Tirkul somehow, and I cannot without help.*

"Why do you help me?" she asked.

"My younger sister had red hair. The Trow took her." Black anger crossed Thidrick's face for an instant. "She killed herself rather than become one of them."

"I am not from Frav, I am from Asur," Corri finally said, watching the surprised lift of Thidrick's brows.

Thidrick smiled, one corner of his mouth lifted in a pseudo-sneer from an old scar there, a scar that showed white against his golden-brown skin. "No Asuran has red hair, girl. Try again."

"I swear by the Goddess, I am from Asur."

"You swear by the Goddess? Do that to the wrong ears and Xephena herself will take you to the altar and tear out your heart with her own hands!" Thidrick pulled off his rimless metal helmet and scrubbed one hand through his curly black hair. He sat down suddenly on the bed beside her, staring into her eyes. "I hear whispered talk of the ancient Prophecies that the Dream Warrior has come. Is this what the other Peoples also say?"

Corri nodded. "I have seen the Dream Warrior." Her eyes dropped to the star-shaped mark on the mound of her thumb, a permanent visible reminder of the Trial she had endured. *How strange,* she thought. *Except for the first few days of pain, I completely forgot it. And no one comments. Can they not see it?* She looked up at Thidrick. *No, I do not think others can see it.*

"Then there is hope." Thidrick ran his hand down his leather knee-breeches. "There must be an end to this madness of religious conquest, this sacrificing of people on Jevotan's altars."

I have to trust him, Corri thought. "I must know what this Kayth says, what he plans. And I must speak with the Tuonela warrior held here."

"You ask me to give you the moon, girl." The guard rose to pace about the room. "To take you to a place where you can listen to this Kayth, that I can do. But the Tuonela, not while he is in the Temple."

"Thidrick, are there many Fravashi who do not want this war?"

"Many," Thidrick answered, "but they dare not say so where any who spy for the Volikvis and Trow can hear them. If there were only some sign we could wear when the war comes, some symbol that would tell the other Peoples that we are not with Kayth and Minepa."

"Perhaps there is a way." Corri set the mug on the floor by her feet. "You said it yourself—the moon." The guard looked at her, puzzled. "If those of the Fravashi who desire peace wear a moon crescent, horns upturned, will it arouse suspicion?"

"I cannot see how it would," the man answered. Then he smiled as he followed Corri's line of thought. "I see. Any wearing that symbol could be identified by the other Peoples and spared. But how will the other Peoples know the meaning of that symbol?"

"I will tell them," Corri answered. "But you must help me in what I need to do so I can return across the border."

Thidrick set aside his mug and settled his helmet over his black curls. "Come," he said. "And upon your life, girl, do exactly what I say."

Thidrick peered around the edge of the curtain, then signaled her to follow him. Once more they crossed the room, this time to the cat calls of different guards just off duty. Thidrick used the narrow stairway as far as the ground floor, then quickly led the way behind a carved panel that cut off the back of the room from the great doors. He pressed his thumbs against two indentations in the wall, opening a secret stairway. Without a word, he pulled her through, easing the section back into place.

"We must take great care," he whispered. "This way is not used by many, but one never knows if one of the Trow will be here. If I must leave, for whatever reason, do not move from where I take you."

They climbed the long flights of stairs, up two floors as much as Corri could calculate. At last they came out behind another carved panel. Cushioned benches ran along the foot of the panel.

Thidrick leaned close to her ear, his voice barely loud enough to be heard. "If anyone comes, go through that door."

He pointed to a gilded door to the left. "This is where they bring the Trow novices to watch when the older priestesses initiate the new Volikvi priests. That room is only for Temple supplies."

Corri nodded, her eyes intent on the people she could see through the carving of the panel. *Kayth! Zalmoxis and Xephena.* She caught her breath. *And Tirkul!* She eased closer to the paneling. *Kayth must never know I spy on him.* She dampened her inner senses, praying that Kayth's power would not seek her out.

Through the carving she saw a scarlet-covered bed filling a narrow section of the room. Tapestries of explicit sexual acts covered the walls as far as she could see.

"I see he is well controlled." Kayth's cool voice easily reached through the paneling. "But we must make certain that he does not fight the caller placed within his body. He must want to stay in Frav."

"Then let the Trow condition him," Xephena purred. "When he learns the joys we can give him, he will not want to return to Tuone." She moved close to Tirkul, rubbing her body against his.

"Perhaps," Kayth answered, "but I have no trust in you, Xephena. The device in his neck remains. When I finish with him, it is a means to trap his shadow-self after death."

"What use is this Tuonela warrior to you, my lord?" Zalmoxis moved into Corri's view. "He has no great powers."

Kayth's glance at Zalmoxis was cold, detached. "I am Jinniyah. Do you question me?" Zalmoxis cringed. "Do you not know, Volikvi? This is the reincarnation of Varanna's Tirkul." He smiled coldly at Tirkul. "This time Tirkul must die before the battle with the Peoples, and the Dream Warrior will live as my prisoner, live to bear my child. A great child!"

Kayth moved to the low altar-bed and smoothed the deep red coverings that hung over it. "I, and only I, have been able to read and understand the Books of Jinniyah, the great Books of Darkness, whose secrets have lain for hundreds of years in the Fire Temple at Vu-Zai. I have bridged the space between this world and the darkness of the Pits. I, Jinniyah, speak with Jevotan's demons. I can call up their power!"

Kayth turned suddenly and laughed, a wild echoing sound. Zalmoxis and Xephena drew away from him, but Tirkul stood unmoving, as if he heard nothing.

"Yes, let the Trow work their spells on him while they may," Kayth said. "Take him about the city as if he were a favored lord. Ply him with drink and women, anything you think will help to break his will. For at the Harvest Moon, on the eve of the invasion, I myself will cut out his beating heart for Jevotan. The demons have told me that if Tirkul dies on Jevotan's altar, the Prophecies will not come true. Frav will win the war, and I, Jinniyah, shall rule all Sar Akka!"

That is not what I feel! Corri thought. *Never have I found a connection between Tirkul and Varanna's lover. Is it possible that the demons with whom Kayth works feed him lies among the bits of truth?*

Still laughing to himself, Kayth strode out of the drapery-hung room, slamming the door behind him.

"He is mad!" Zalmoxis stepped close to Xephena. The Trow stared at the closed door, a thoughtful look on her painted face.

"Perhaps, but he holds the power he claims." The skeleton-thin figure of Minepa moved into the line of Corri's vision. "I have seen the demons he calls up and heard him talk with them." The Volikvi thrust his sharp-boned face close to Tirkul. "Break this one," he ordered. "I want to see him whine and beg on the altar of Jevotan. I want to hear him curse his Goddess as he dies under Kayth's knife." Minepa turned on his heel and followed Kayth.

"I will begin the work," Xephena said as she ran her hands over Tirkul's chest. "Then Thidrick can take him about the city, to every tavern, until he learns to lose himself in drink

when he is not in my arms." She led Tirkul to the altar-bed
and pushed him, unresisting, down upon it.

Zalmoxis watched the Trow run her long-nailed fingers
over Tirkul's body for a few moments before he silently left.

Fight her, Tirkul! Fight! Corri clenched her fists. *This is rape
of the mind as well as the body,* she thought. *This is why he
wanted to die. No Trow, no Volikvi, deserves to live! Their filth and
evil have beaten the Fravashi people to their knees for centuries
through such as this! But I dare not interfere now or I will never get
Tirkul out of here.*

She jumped as Thidrick touched her arm. "We must leave,"
the guard whispered. "This is no thing for a girl to see." He
pulled her after him down the stairs, leading her this time out
a back way to a small rear gate.

"Thidrick, can you arrange to bring Tirkul alone to a tavern
where I can meet with him?" Corri said quietly as they
approached the guarded gate.

"I will try. Tomorrow night be at the Prancing Mare."
Thidrick nodded to the guard as he passed through the gate
by Corri's side. "If Zalmoxis and Xephena plan to use the
Tuonela against Kayth, they must quickly drown his will. Yes,
I think by tomorrow night we can be at the Prancing Mare."

orri crept back through the darkening streets of Vum,
slipping silently and unnoticed into the house of the trader.
She found Imandoff and Takra preparing to search the city
for her.

"By the hell-fires of Frav," Takra said through clenched
teeth. "We thought for certain you were Kayth's captive. The
trader brought word that he is now in Vum."

"I saw Kayth." Corri sank down on the bed, resting her
head in her hands. "And I saw Tirkul."

"But they did not see you?" Imandoff sat beside her and
lifted her chin to look into her eyes. "Where is Tirkul?"

"In the Temple of Pleasure. We were right when we guessed that the wound in Tirkul's neck might hold a caller. Imandoff, Kayth captured Tirkul so he can offer him on Jevotan's altar just before the invasion at Harvest Moon! By such a deed, he thinks to change the Prophecies and trap Tirkul's shadow-self after death."

"Harvest Moon? So little time for the Peoples to prepare." The sorcerer scratched his beard as he thought.

"Can he change the Prophecies in this manner, by killing Tirkul before the battle begins?" Takra set one foot on a chair and leaned on her knee.

"I do not see how," Imandoff answered.

"He can if Tirkul is truly the reincarnation of Varanna's Tirkul." Corri looked at the surprise plain on Takra's face, the frown of deep thought from Imandoff. "I heard Kayth say this when I spied on him. But I do not think Tirkul has any connection with the ancient warrior-lover."

"You were close enough to Kayth to hear his words?" Imandoff rose and paced to the window. "That was a dangerous thing to do, Corri."

"Thidrick, one of the Temple guards, was with me."

"You went into that place and trusted someone there!" Takra threw up her hands as she turned away.

"This Thidrick, why did he help you?" Imandoff turned his head to look at her.

"Thidrick does not believe in this religious war. He told me that many other Fravashi feel the same." Corri stood and stretched. "Those who do not wish to fight the other Peoples will wear a crescent moon, horns upturned, when the war begins. In this way, we will know friend from enemy."

"You arranged this?" Imandoff smiled and shook his head when she nodded. "Out of the mouths of the uninitiated often comes wisdom. That all Fravashi will not fight, this will be welcome news across the border. But we are no closer to rescuing Tirkul."

"Thidrick will bring him to the Prancing Mare tomorrow night. I will meet him there."

"You will not go alone!" Takra moved to Corri's side, her brows drawn down.

"I must see Tirkul alone," Corri said stubbornly. "I do not know what Thidrick would think if you were with me. And alone with Tirkul, I may be able to reach through the defenses Kayth has set."

"Every tavern I know has a back alley." Imandoff reached for his pipe, tamping it full of smoke-leaf. "Takra and I will wait in the alley, close enough if there should be trouble."

"But I go in alone." Corri's jaw set.

"Agreed." The sorcerer snapped his fingers to light the pipe, then sent a puff of smoke toward the ceiling.

"This Fravashi trader, he will not let us go wandering about the city." Takra pointed at the closed door.

Imandoff smiled. "I have ways to get us out without being seen, Wind-Rider."

"Probably over the roofs and along narrow ledges," Takra muttered.

Corri awoke, gasping for breath, her heart pounding. She sat up, the blankets clutched around her, and looked carefully into all the shadowed corners of the room.

I did not dream-fly, she thought. *Yet Kayth was at the edges of my dreams. How did he discover that I am in Vum?*

"What is it, Corri?" Imandoff's soft whisper came from the bed he and Takra shared at the far side of the room.

Corri bent her head to her drawn-up knees as she willed herself to be calm. She heard the soft pad of feet as Imandoff came to her side. The sorcerer sat on the narrow bed beside her, gently stroking her hair.

"Kayth knows I am in Vum," she whispered.

"Does he know where?"

Corri tested her inner senses before answering. "No. He only knows I am within the city."

"Sister-friend, will you still meet with this Thidrick and Tirkul?" Takra's bare body glowed in the moonlight coming in through the open window as she crossed the room to Corri's side.

"I must. This may be the only chance we have of rescuing Tirkul. I cannot leave him here."

"I wonder . . ." Imandoff drifted off into thought. "It would seem, Dream Warrior, that your powers have grown since you underwent the ordeal of the Mask. Before, Kayth would have known at once exactly where you were. Yet you spied on him without attracting his notice. And now he only vaguely knows you are within the city."

"I think we should be ready to move out as soon as we get Tirkul away from the Temple." Takra moved restlessly about the room. "What of the trader? Can he be trusted if his family is in danger?"

"He has already made plans for the time of war," Imandoff answered. "Those of his family who cannot cross the spells at the border will be taken in by friends and distant family in other cities. I think it is time for him to flee." The sorcerer rose and crossed the room to pull on his trousers and tunic. "I will speak with him at once." He silently went into the hall, closing the door behind him.

Before dawn, there was a quiet bustle about the trader's compound as most of his family and servants packed and began to move out to safe havens about the countryside. The trader himself and the few family members and servants able to cross the spellbound border waited anxiously, afraid that if all left at the same time it would attract unwanted attention.

"My father will send out small groups throughout the day," the trader's red-haired daughter confided to Corri when she brought up the morning meal. "Although my father is angry with me, I will not go until the last."

"But if they catch you, you will be taken to the Trow." Corri looked at the girl in surprise. "Why do you stay?"

The girl looked over her shoulder, then, certain that no one listened, she leaned close. "I am a healer," she whispered. "Even my father does not know of this forbidden talent. I know that you came to rescue one of your people from the Volikvis. I think you will need my talent before you reach the border." The girl smiled. "My name is Balqama. My father named me after our far distant ancestress who discovered the secret to crossing through the spells."

"We may have to ride fast and hard," Corri said, watching the girl's dark eyes. "And there is certain to be fighting before we reach the border."

"I can ride," Balqama answered, straightening her shoulders. "And I can use a knife if necessary. My father has often teased me that I am a Tuonela in disguise." She lifted her skirts to reveal a sheathed knife strapped to her thigh. "I will dress in some of my brother's clothing. Do what you must. When you are ready to flee Frav, I shall be waiting here with the horses."

The day dragged as Corri, with the help of Balqama, packed the saddlebags. Imandoff explained to the trader girl their plans for rescuing Tirkul. Balqama drew a map of the streets leading to the Prancing Mare, then marked out the way they could take using alleys and little-used side streets.

Throughout the day, small parties left from the compound. As the last prepared to leave, the trader argued with his daughter, but she steadfastly refused to go with him. Finally, the girl simply hid until her father could wait no longer and rode out.

When the sun was well down, Balqama brought a tiny vial to Corri, pressing it into the girl's hand. "Use three drops of this in your friend's drink if you can," she instructed. "At first it will only make him drowsy, open to your suggestions. After a time, he will fall into a light sleep. In this way we may get him out of Vum without a struggle."

Corri tucked the vial into her belt pouch. "May the Goddess bless you, Balqama. It may well be your wisdom that gets us out of this alive."

"I have no love for the Volikvis and Trow." The girl's dark eyes hardened. "I have lived my whole life in fear because of them. For this, and the freedom to walk with my head uncovered, to be what I am—a healer—I wish you well."

The streets were dark when Corri and her companions made their way toward the alley behind the Prancing Mare tavern. No one stopped or questioned them as they slipped from side street to odorous alley across the city. Takra, her pale hair covered with a hood borrowed from Balqama, strode with one hand constantly near the sword at her side.

When they finally reached the garbage-filled alley behind the tavern, Corri nervously checked the slide of her knives, the set of her hood.

"What if this Thidrick does not come?" Takra whispered.

"He will." Corri eased open the grimy door and peered down a short darkened hallway. Loud voices and laughter came from the tavern's common room beyond the curtain at the end of the hall.

"Walk with the Lady." Imandoff clasped Corri's shoulder. "And take care, Dream Warrior."

Corri slipped inside, slowly making her way down the hall. When she reached the curtain, she eased it aside, her blue-green eyes flicking across what she could see of the room.

Where is Thidrick? The curtained booths were beyond her line of vision. *Well, there is nothing for it but to go in.*

Corri fell easily into the role she had used before, that of an imbecile. Her back hunched, mouth open, her lips slack, she shuffled out into the room. She wandered from table to table, lisping and begging for drinks. She was either ignored or roughly pushed away.

Now for the booths, she thought, working her way toward the curtained alcoves at the rear of the tavern. *Thidrick is here somewhere, I know it.*

The first curtain she pulled back revealed a sailor with his hands up the skirt of one of the barmaids. The girl swore and threw her drink at Corri, splashing the sour ale down the girl's front.

As Corri paused before the second curtained booth, a heavy hand reached through and jerked her inside. Corri found herself on the bench beside Thidrick with Tirkul sitting unresponsive across the table.

"Whatever you must do, do it quickly!" Thidrick whispered gruffly. "This Kayth has stirred up the whole Temple, ranting and raving. He is looking for someone he calls the Dream Warrior. Within the hour the guards will all be out in the streets of Vum with Kayth and the Volikvis."

"Tirkul," Corri said softly, reaching across the table and taking the warrior's hand in hers. "I am Corri, remember?"

Tirkul's eyes moved to look at her, but the expression on his face was slack. His hand twitched in hers.

I must do something to make him listen to me, she thought. "Look at me, Tirkul," she ordered. "I am the Dream Warrior. I call you to ride with me to battle."

The warrior's eyes focused on her, widened as he fought against Kayth's control. "I am ready, Dream Warrior," he said hoarsely. He fumbled at his belt for his missing dagger.

"The Dream Warrior!" Thidrick looked at her in awe. "Is this true?"

"It is true." Corri still clutched at Tirkul's hand, keeping him from rising to his feet.

"Let me ride with you," Thidrick said, the look in his eyes a plea. "I have passed the word about the moon sign. If I stay, I am a dead man. Kayth will lose no time killing me for the loss of this prisoner."

Corri froze, her eyes wide as her inner senses ruffled with a warning. "He knows!" she whispered. "Kayth knows where I now am!" She fumbled at her belt pouch for the vial. "Give me his drink," she ordered. "Somehow Kayth knows what happens through Tirkul. If he drinks this," she tipped three drops into the ale Thidrick handed her, "it will make him sleep."

Thidrick leaned over the table and pressed the mug to Tirkul's lips. "Drink it all," the guard ordered, and Tirkul obeyed.

"Now we must get him to the alley, where friends await." Corri slid the vial back into her pouch. "This stays behind." She leaned over the table, jerked the black pendant from Tirkul's neck, and tossed it aside.

"Easy enough." Thidrick motioned her out of the booth. He pulled Tirkul to his feet, slung one of the Tuonela's arms across his shoulder, and propelled him toward the curtained hallway with Corri on their heels.

"By the hell-fires of Frav, who is this?" Takra's voice, followed by the hiss-ching of her drawn sword, reached Corri's ears as the girl eased shut the tavern door.

"This is Thidrick, the one who helped me," Corri answered. She turned swiftly toward the alley entrance, where several horses and a rider were silhouetted against a faint light. "Balqama here?" The trader girl was dressed in men's trousers and tunic, a hooded cloak fastened over her shoulders, her hair covered by an inner hood.

"Hurry!" Balqama motioned with one hand, then turned in the saddle to look back at the street beyond.

Thidrick helped Tirkul down the slimy passage and boosted him onto one of the horses. Takra, sheathing her sword as she went, was the last to leave the alley darkness.

"Thidrick goes with us," Corri said as she mounted Mouse. "His life is forfeit if he stays." Balqama pointed to the pack horse.

The trader girl turned her mare and rode out onto the empty street. But instead of riding back toward the compound, she headed to the south.

"Word came from friends that the Volikvis are guarding all
the city gates," Balqama whispered as Corri pushed up alongside. "We must go another way, and hope that they have not
yet reached that road."

"Bind his eyes," Corri softly called back to Takra, who rode
beside the Tuonela warrior. "Kayth can see through his eyes,
or read through his mind, I do not know which."

Imandoff reached down to tear off a piece of the hem of his
gray robe and handed it to Takra, who then bound it about
the warrior's eyes. Tirkul clung grimly to the saddle, silent and
swaying.

They rode on through the streets of Vum, hands on
weapons, waiting for a challenge to be flung out of the dark,
but none came.

"The gate is open but I see no guards," Balqama whispered,
pointing toward a narrow opening in the wall ahead. "Shall I
ride on alone until we know if it is safe?"

"No," Corri answered. "The hunt is up behind us. We will
chance it."

She kicked Mouse into a trot toward the narrow gate. There
was no challenge, no guard in sight, as they passed through
the wall and out into the Fravashi countryside.

*L*et them go." Minepa's hoarse whisper froze the three
armed men at his back. "When they are well away from Vum,
then we will take them, but not until."

Then this Dream Warrior will be in my hands, not yours, Kayth,
the priest thought to himself. *I will force her to use her powers
against you. We shall see who rules Frav, who gains the final power
from the Books of Darkness, and who controls all Sar Akka! I am
the Soothsayer of Jevotan, and I say this shall be so!*

The skull-thin face turned in the faint moonlight to follow
the line of riders as they hurried down the road toward the
border with Tuone. The cruel lips lifted in a smile, a grimace
that caused the guards with him to shiver in fear.

Chapter 19

$\mathcal{B}$alqama set the pace as they rode away from the city of Vum. Throughout the darkest part of the night they pushed steadily on, resting the horses often. Corri was jittery, the warning prickle between her shoulder blades a constant irritation. She frequently stopped to look at their back-trail, seeking signs that they were followed.

"I know someone is behind us," she confided to Imandoff as they rested on the upper slopes of the Mootma Mountains, within an hour's ride of the spell-bound border with Tuone. "I see and hear no one, but I know we are followed."

"Tirkul is coming awake." Takra dropped down beside the sorcerer. "I do not know if this is a good thing, for he is in more pain the farther we get from Vum."

"Kayth wills him to return," Corri answered. "He fights against the compulsion."

Thidrick nervously fingered his dagger. "When he stops fighting the call to return, then beware, for he may well turn against us."

"I think not." Imandoff watched Balqama bathe Tirkul's face with water. "A part of him must still be aware of what Kayth plans. Did you not say that Kayth spoke freely in front of Tirkul?"

Both Corri and Thidrick nodded.

"If he knows, then he will kill himself rather than return to the clutches of Kayth and the Volikvis." Takra shrugged off the confining hood and pulled loose the pins that held her pale braids tight to her head. "From now I ride as a Tuonela warrior. Any Fravashi who stands between us and the border dies under my sword."

Thidrick looked at her, his dark eyes widening. "Another Tuonela!" He smiled broadly. "And a warrior woman, a thing I never believed until now." The guard turned to Corri. "Can you remove the caller? With the caller destroyed, it will be difficult for the Volikvis to find us."

"Imandoff, we must try." Corri pulled out her booter knife.

"I have deadened the pain for now. He is asleep." Balqama squatted beside her companions. "If you would remove this caller, we must do it now. He should remain in a light sleep until we reach the border. Do you have any sea fire?" the girl asked.

"Sea fire?" Imandoff rose and fumbled in the saddlebags for the flask of mountain water. "Is this what you mean?"

Balqama pulled loose the cork, sniffed the contents, then tipped up the container. She choked, coughing several times. "Yes. I will use this to cleanse the knife and the wound."

"Have you cut into the body before?" Imandoff pulled Takra to her feet. At Balqama's nod, he motioned to Corri. "We will hold him down while Balqama removes this caller. Dream Warrior, you must use all your power to keep Kayth from knowing what we do."

Takra rolled the Tuonela warrior onto his stomach, straddling Tirkul's hips to keep his body still. Thidrick knelt with his knees on the warrior's outstretched arms, the blonde head tightly grasped between his strong hands. Imandoff knelt to hold fast Tirkul's ankles. As Balqama poured a little of the mountain water, first over Corri's booter knife, then over the neck wound, Tirkul moaned and twisted to get free. Shutting her ears to Tirkul's moans, Corri sat cross-legged nearby and allowed herself to slip into a light trance.

As her spirit-form slipped free to hang over the scene, Corri stretched out with her inner senses, feeling gently for any sign that Kayth was aware of them. She found no telltale marks of Kayth, but a fleeting tendril of thought brushed against her in warning.

If Kayth does not know where we are, then who follows? She stared down at Tirkul's limp form, reassuring herself that his spirit-body was still locked within the physical body. *I must know who trails us.*

Corri let her dream-form float higher, then turned to retrace the route they had fled into the mountains. A short distance behind them, she saw the shadowy forms of four riders, pushing hard on their trail. She swooped lower until she could distinguish faces.

Minepa! Corri threw herself away too late. *O Goddess, he knows!* She saw Minepa raise his face to stare upward at her, a cruel twist on his lips. The guards around him rode on without any sign that she was there.

Swiftly, Corri willed herself back to the others. She dove at her physical body, entering it with a slamming thud. She felt sickened as she opened her eyes. For several minutes, the shadowed scenery around her twisted and rolled in a dizzying fashion. Corri swallowed hard, then turned her aching eyes to Balqama, who sat back on her heels, the caller device in one hand.

"Give it to me," Imandoff ordered.

The sorcerer gingerly took the device and walked several paces away where he placed it on a flat rock. Taking another stone in both hands, the sorcerer threw it on the caller. There was a blinding flash of light, a burst of red-tinged flame, and a stench that set them all choking and coughing.

Takra leaped up and began slapping at the smoldering sparks on Imandoff's robe. "You are on fire, Silverhair. Would you light a beacon for whoever trails us?"

"I am on fire for you alone, Wind-Rider." The sorcerer gave her a quick kiss on the cheek.

"We must ride at once." Corri managed to get to her feet, but found the ground still rose and fell around her. "It is not Kayth who follows, but Minepa himself."

Balqama tied the bandage they had used on Tirkul's eyes around his neck, covering the seeping wound. "We dare not ride hard until he wakens."

"You ride on one side of him, I on the other," Thidrick said. "This way, if he starts to fall, we can at least keep him from being trampled by the horses." Balqama nodded agreement.

"I will play rear-guard." Corri staggered to Mouse, pulled herself into the saddle.

"You are no warrior, Farblood." Takra stood beside her, with one hand on Corri's leg.

"I am a warrior who fights in ways you cannot know, sister-friend," Corri answered. "This battle, which will surely come before we reach the border, will not be fought with sword and dagger alone."

"I understand." Imandoff mounted Sun Dancer and gestured to Takra to take Lightfoot. "Nevertheless, Takra and I will do what we can."

They pushed on into the mountains, reaching the slope down to the border just as the sun rose. Although Corri stretched out her inner senses searching for Minepa and his men, she found only a confusing blankness behind them. Tirkul was almost fully awake when they sighted the spell-bound border into Tuone.

"They wait!" Takra's cry broke the still morning air as she pointed toward the border, just beyond the Kratula River.

Shading her eyes, Corri saw a cluster of Tuonela warriors pacing the far banks. She jerked around as a sudden pounding of hooves came from behind.

"Ride!" she screamed, and Thidrick slapped Tirkul's horse.

Takra and Imandoff drew swords, Thidrick beside them, as they turned to meet the Fravashi guards. Corri pulled Mouse to one side, yelling "Frayma!" to draw Minepa's attention. The Volikvi showed his teeth as he turned his horse to meet her.

From the corner of her eye, Corri saw Tirkul slip from his mount, fall to the rocky ground and lie still. Balqama leaped down beside him, her knife in her hand as she crouched over the fallen warrior.

The battle with the guards soon turned from horseback to ground as Minepa's guards leaped down in an attempt to attack the horses. Thidrick jumped onto his opponent, bearing the man to the dusty ground where they rolled back and forth, neither able to use their swords. In a quick twist, Thidrick kicked off the man, then rolled and came up with his dagger in one hand. Before the guard could regain his footing, Thidrick was upon him, delivering a sudden thrust through the ribs.

Takra and Imandoff battled the remaining guards in a flurry of sword-play, while Thidrick retrieved his sword and ran to Balqama and Tirkul. There he stood guard over the fallen Tuonela and the trader girl.

Minepa drew closer to Corri, his bone-thin face bright with eagerness. In his hand was a skull-topped rod, now glowing with a sickening purplish red fire. As he pointed it at her, Corri clutched at the saddle and willed herself out of her body. With a snap that echoed through her head, she shot upward to hang over the scene.

You are mine! Even though you retreat into spirit, your body is mine! Minepa drew rein beside Mouse and reached toward her physical form with taloned fingers.

Never! I am Soothslayer for the Goddess! Corri screamed the words into the priest's mind as she threw down a bolt of power. *I would kill my body rather than let it fall into your hands!*

The power bolt splashed on the ground before Minepa's horse. It reared, spilling the Volikvi onto the rocks and dead pine needles. The priest sprang up, the skull-topped rod again pointing at her physical body.

I will kill the body for you, girl. And your spirit will be bound to me forever! He chanted strange words as he aimed the rod.

Corri gathered more power from the air about her and threw it onto the rod. There was a deep purple, almost black flash as the rod disintegrated into flying shards.

Minepa showed his teeth in a snarl. From his belt he drew a wickedly curved dagger. He turned to strike at Takra's exposed back as she fought with one of the Fravashi guards. Corri blasted the ground between them, startling the guard, who fell with the Wind-Rider's sword in his throat.

Minepa darted aside, then sprinted toward Balqama where she still knelt over Tirkul.

A wild scream from an angry horse rose above the clamor of battle. Hellstorm tore loose from the Tuonela who held him and raced through the river. His ears laid back, his teeth bared, the horse pounded up the bank toward his fallen master.

Thidrick stood ready, but Minepa ducked under the sword-swing. The priest's dagger grated across Thidrick's armor, raking across the metal until it pierced his upper sword-arm. Minepa's fist, backed by a sudden strength borne of fanaticism, took the man in the side of the jaw and Thidrick crumpled to the ground.

"Beware!" Takra's shout followed by a Tuonela war cry sent a chill through Corri as she saw Minepa's path of attack.

No! Tirkul and Balqama are defenseless. The girl is no match for the priest!

Corri threw the concentrated remainder of her amassed power onto the top of Minepa's head as he raised the knife to strike at Balqama. She saw it burn its way through the top of Minepa's skull, brains splattering as it bored on through the head and into the body to the heart. The Volikvi crumpled into a bloody heap at Tirkul's feet, the dagger shattering against the rocks. The war-mount danced over the priest's body until nothing remained except pounded flesh and splintered bone.

Balqama still protected Tirkul's limp form with her own body. Thidrick sat dazed beside her, one hand tightly gripping the bleeding wound in his arm. Imandoff walked to the horses, one arm around Takra, his cloak splattered with blood.

Corri, return! Imandoff's thought sounded in the girl's head.

As she began the descent to her physical form, still frozen in position on Mouse, Corri sensed a new danger coming fast behind them. Her instincts warned her not to seek this danger or investigate the ominous scent of power that flowed before it.

Kayth comes! Corri dived for her body, still sending a warning to her friends. *Ride!*

She opened her eyes to the same sick disoriented feeling she had experienced before. Both hands were tightly clasped on the saddle. Takra was boosting Tirkul onto Hellstorm, while Imandoff helped Thidrick into the saddle. Once mounted, they turned the horses toward the river and freedom.

$\mathcal{T}$here he is." Imandoff's quiet voice broke the strange silence that hung over the Tuonela warriors who faced the spellbound border.

A figure with bright red hair pushed to the front of the band of Fravashi warriors. "Corri Farblood! You who call yourself the Dream Warrior. You shall pay and pay dearly for invading Frav. When the time is right, girl, you will watch your friends die on the altar of Jevotan! I, Jinniyah, have spoken!" Kayth turned back toward Vum, his men following in his wake.

Corri wearily turned her head to stare across the river at the Fravashi soldiers massed there. "We were lucky, old man. We got out before Kayth could catch us. If I had been forced to face him on his ground at this time, I do not know if I could resist his power."

"So you are truly the Prophesied Dream Warrior." Thidrick stood beside them, a bandage over his wound. He smiled, one corner of his mouth pulled upward by the old scar. "I never thought to see the Prophecies alive and breathing. And in a girl at that. All in Frav thought the Dream Warrior would be a man, if the Prophecies did come true."

"What think you of the Fravashi plans for conquest?" Takra stood, her hand resting on her sword hilt. Her amber eyes challenged the guard.

"You have no reason to trust me, warrior woman, that I know and understand." Thidrick rubbed at the black curls that hung from under his round helmet. "But I have no reason to love the Volikvis." His voice hardened. "Understand this, I do not fight against Frav. I fight against the Volikvis, the Trow, and that man Kayth!" He pointed a finger at the distant backs of the retreating Fravashi force.

"That is enough to receive you as a friend," Imandoff said. "What can you tell us to help prepare for the coming battle?" The sorcerer put his arm around Thidrick's shoulders, walking off with him toward the Tuonela who clustered to one side.

"What of Tirkul?" Corri asked, watching Balqama sitting beside the Tuonela warrior. The trader girl had removed her concealing hood, her long red hair a brilliant glowing banner in the sunlight.

"He is weak." Takra eyed Corri closely. "He clings to the trader girl, and she, I think, has some liking for him. Does this bother you, sister-friend?"

"No," Corri answered firmly, and knew she meant it. "My heart has gone a different way. I think, deep inside, Tirkul knows this, too."

I hope Tirkul will always be my friend, she thought, *but I cannot love him as I do Gadavar. Even Gadavar's love I must set aside. If I am to change that one life-thread I fought to untangle, I must create every change possible. That life-thread must not end in untimely death.*

"What if Tirkul is to repeat the life of Varanna's Tirkul in this battle? If he is that Tirkul, are you Varanna?" Takra watched Balqama smile at Tirkul as she gently touched his cheek.

"I know within my heart that Tirkul is not Varanna's Tirkul born again. Neither do I believe myself to be Varanna reborn. If I were, I would know it somewhere inside. In this much, the story is not repeating itself."

A look of relief crossed Takra's face. "How can we know if we choose the right actions to win this battle? What if we choose wrong?"

"We can only do what we feel is right, Wind-Rider." Corri sighed and shook her head. "I may be the Dream Warrior, I may have seen part of the future, but I am not the only one who will decide future outcomes. Each decision made by every person involved will tip the outcome one way or the other. And in the end, when we have done all we can, the Goddess and Natira the Judge have the final say."

"And perhaps the powers of Darkness," Takra answered. "If in this battle against the Fravashi you are not Varanna reborn, but Kayth is possibly Jinniyah, what hope have we?"

"There is always hope as long as there is breath." Corri walked with Takra to the horses. "True, Tirkul is wounded, but he will be able to carry a sword before the battle begins at the Harvest Moon. Minepa is dead, so I will not have to face him again."

"And two Fravashi now ride with us," Takra murmured. "Small changes, yes. But I do not like the thought that you must face Kayth."

"I must because I chose to," Corri answered.

"We will send Tirkul back to the Clan of the Asperel." Imandoff came to their side, his gray eyes serious as he looked at Takra. "It would please me if you would take him."

"And stay out of battle?" Takra bristled. "No, Silverhair. I will fight for our child," she touched her stomach, "among the warriors, not skulking behind like some pampered Asuran. If we do not hold the line at the border, the Fravashi will sweep through Tuone, killing all in their path who resist. I would fight beside you, for fight I must, wherever I am, if they break through."

Imandoff bowed his head and sighed. "I had to try. I love you, Takra, and I fear for your safety and the safety of our child. Yet I know you are right to feel this way."

"I know," she whispered, cupping his face with her hand. "I too am afraid, afraid I may die and the child with me. Afraid that if I live and you are killed in battle, this child will never know her father."

"*Her* father?" Imandoff grinned and pulled her close to kiss her. "Are you so sure it is not a son?"

Unnoticed, Corri walked away. She wandered through the rough camp to retrieve her Tuonela clothing, then found a spring where she could wash before dressing. As she tucked the last of her hidden knives into place, she sat on a moss-covered boulder by the spring and let the warm sunlight wash over her. Her hand automatically pulled forth the silver medallion from Gadavar, caressing it and in a strange way drawing from it strength and comfort.

There is no choice. I must face Kayth, I must destroy his dark powers. What he and the Volikvis do is the greatest of evils. She broke off a blade of grass, twisting it between her slender fingers. *But what I have set in motion will also create great unrest and warring among the Fravashi themselves. Did I do the Lady's will or my own, because I have such a hatred for the plans of the Volikvis and Trow?*

"Dream Warrior, I would speak with you." Balqama's soft voice startled Corri.

"Sit." Corri gestured to the rock on which she sat.

"I have heard words from the Tuonela." The Fravashi girl paused, then hurried on. "They say that you and Tirkul took heart oath, their spoken agreement for marriage. Is this so? I will not interfere if you ask it."

"The heart oath was broken before Tirkul rode to the border," Corri answered. "He demanded of me what I could not do, give up my role as Dream Warrior for the Goddess. We are strong friends now, but not lovers. Let his heart go where it will, Balqama. If it goes to you, love him."

Balqama sighed, reaching out to gently touch Corri's knee. "It must be difficult to carry such a burden alone. I did not know until the Tuonela warrior woman told me that Kayth is your father. You face a terrible task, Dream Warrior. You must slay your father in order to free all the Peoples, even the Fravashi, from the evil that descends upon them."

"Your father, do you know where he has gone?" Corri looked at Balqama's freckled face.

"He went to the city of Nevn, but I shall not join him." The girl bent her head, a tear trickling down one cheek. "Although he has no love for the Volikvis and the religion they have twisted to suit their purpose, he cannot accept my healing talent. In Frav, healing is permitted by the knife or drugs but never by calling power through the hands. The penalty is death. My father cast me out when I told him that I can do this healing."

"But he waited for you till the last."

"He waited only because he thought I would give in." Balqama sighed and looked down at the ground.

"You told him to leave without you. You chose to stay to help us." Corri looked at the girl in a new light. "You placed yourself in danger for Tirkul, and for us."

"I cannot pretend to be what I am not," Balqama answered, the tears flowing down her face. "I must use the talent within me. I cannot cast it aside."

"Thank you," Corri said softly, taking the girl's hands in hers. "You have reminded me of my duty. And you have lightened my heart."

"I do not understand." Balqama raised tear-bright eyes.

"Be happy with Tirkul, Balqama. A healer he can understand and accept."

"Balqama! Come quickly!" Takra charged through the trees and underbrush, her face white.

"What happens?" Corri leaped to her feet, one hand falling automatically to her knife.

"It is Tirkul." Takra motioned frantically with one hand. "He tried to get a knife to kill himself."

"Why?" Balqama asked as she ran toward the camp, Takra and Corri at her heels.

"He feels he has brought shame to his Clan. Because he was captured and taken to Frav." Takra pounded close behind the girl.

"The Trow!" Corri said breathlessly. "Xephena plied her filth on him."

Balqama threw herself on the ground beside the Tuonela who held the struggling Tirkul. "What is this?" she shouted and landed a ringing slap against Tirkul's cheek.

"What?" Tirkul's voice was full of surprise. "Why?"

"I never thought to see a Tuonela coward!" Balqama's cheeks were flushed, her mouth quivered. "To kill yourself because you fell under the power of Volikvi evil, that is a coward's way out!"

Tirkul sat up suddenly, his fists clenched, his eyes flashing. "I should have fought harder!" he shouted at her.

"You fought long and hard against the caller." Kulkar stood, glaring down at Tirkul, his hands on his hips. "No man could have fought a greater fight. Now you would kill yourself when we need you most?"

"Male pride." Takra curled her lip in disgust. "I thought better of you than that, Clan-brother."

Tirkul's dark eyes locked with Corri's. "Dream Warrior . . ."

"There is no pity in me for this thing you tried to do, Tirkul." Corri drew herself tall, settled her mouth in a hard line. "Frayma Herself brought you safe out of Frav, giving you this Fravashi healer to aid and comfort you. If you would take the coward's way out, then do it. Kill yourself and be done with it!" She turned on her heel and stalked away.

Once back at the spring, Corri curled up on the boulder, her head on her knees. *Lady, did I say the right words?* Her mind played back the heart-wrenching scene, Tirkul on the needle-covered ground with Balqama beside him. *It is the hardest thing I have ever had to do. Was I wrong?*

No, My Dream Warrior. Your words saved his life and his sanity. A blanket of comforting warmth settled over her spirit at the Lady's voice in her mind. *You took the knowledge you have learned, added that knowledge to your instincts, and made the right choice.*

Corri felt the presence of the Lady gently enfold her. The depression that had threatened to drown her spirit lifted. She relaxed in the sun's rays.

Will Gadavar and I survive to explore this love I feel between us? Will we ever know the depth of feeling I saw between Tirkul and Balqama, between Imandoff and Takra? she asked herself. *The child conceived in love between Imandoff and Takra must be born into freedom. I will hold to the thought that we will survive, that the Peoples will remain free, that Takra's child will be born in peace and love.*

Corri sat alone for a long time, the sun warm upon her body, the Lady's love wrapped around her. As she drifted down toward sleep, she heard from far off, at the edges of her hearing, the sound of a baby's cries, and she felt a soundless answer from within her own spirit. As she reached out, she could almost see the tiny child, and her tired body fell into a deep, dreamless sleep.

The next morning at daybreak Corri rode out with Imandoff and Takra to escort Tirkul and Balqama as far as the Tuone grasslands. As they prepared to part company, Tirkul rode up to Corri. He sat for several minutes, silent and head down, before he spoke.

"You were right, Dream Warrior. Sometimes it is harder to live than it is to die."

"I know," Corri answered softly. "Neither you nor I have an easy road to travel, Tirkul. But you have Balqama to travel it with you."

"You are not angry that you and I no longer have heart oath?" Tirkul raised his head to look into her eyes.

"It was not meant to be. My road to the coming battle must be walked alone." Corri smiled, then glanced at Balqama, who waited out of hearing. "Be kind to Balqama, Tirkul. She is a healer with the hands, which has made her an outcast from her family and her country. She told her father of this gift, knowing it could mean her death, but she felt drawn to aid us. She has no one but you now."

"I will cherish her. I learned from the mistakes I made with you in demands. I will try hard not to cage Balqama." Tirkul's words were soft. "Ride with the Goddess, Dream Warrior. And when you need me in battle, I will be at your side."

He rode back to the Fravashi girl and leaned over to kiss her cheek. Together they rode out into the wind-swept grasslands.

May the Lady bless you both, she thought as she watched them ride away. *My heart dreaded this parting from the first time I made the decision not to be with you, Tirkul. But I do not feel sad, as I feared I might, just happy for your true happiness.*

"You were very brave, Corri." Imandoff pulled Sun Dancer up beside her.

"No, old man. It was meant to be this way. I just did not see it for a time. Now, let us go to Frayma's Mare. I will need Varanna's helmet and the owl stone for the coming battle."

They rode throughout the day, taking their time, talking together of what they would do after the war with Frav was over. By sundown they rode into the camp of Frayma's Mare to be wildly greeted by the women warriors and Norya, the shakka.

Imandoff and Takra talked and laughed while the sorcerer drank mountain water with the women warriors far into the night, but Corri silently crept away. She spread her blankets near Norya's wagon, the bag containing the ancient helmet and stone beside her, and crawled into the warmth of the covers, bone-tired in body and spirit.

"Dream Warrior, may I speak with you?" The old shakka Norya came out of the shadows and sat down, leaning back against the wagon wheel. "There is a peacefulness within you that you did not have before you rode out with Dakhma. You have grown stronger, firmer of purpose."

Corri propped her head on one elbow and looked at the shakka's eyes reflecting the light of the campfire. "Yes, I have grown," she answered softly. "The anger I carried with me for so many years, the distrust, the fear of not being good enough, it seems to have disappeared, Norya. Is this not a strange thing?"

The shakka gave a soft chuckle. "It happens to all who take responsibility for their lives. Yet, when it happens to us, we all think it is strange. Every living person has challenges, Corri. Life gives them to us whether we want them or not. How we come through the challenges determines whether we are fit to be leaders, shakkas, feya women, the Baba, or the Oracle. Or just a child of the Goddess." She leaned over to brush the hair back from Corri's forehead. "I am pleased that you carry no pain from parting with Tirkul. Tirkul found the woman he needed. You needed more than he could ever give, Dream Warrior, and I think you have found it in another."

"Perhaps." Corri smiled at her. "My heart sings when he is near. But perhaps that is only lust and not love."

"Oh, there is always lust, even in love," the shakka said and chuckled. "Else there would be no children." She rose and dusted off her leather trousers. "When this war is over, you will see I am right. Enjoy him, Corri, for I feel he is a rare treasure. Sleep well." She disappeared back into the wagon.

Eyes on the stars visible through the swaying trees above her, Corri thought back on what she had seen during the ordeal of the Mask. *Did I do enough? Did I change the right things?* Questions whirled around in her mind. *The one life-thread, the one where . . .* her mind shied away from giving a name, *he died, can that still be changed? I did not see Tirkul and Balqama together in the threads. Perhaps others can also change the way the life-threads go.*

Her eyelids began to droop with weariness. She fell asleep with the sounds of Tuonela laughter in her ears.

Dream Warrior, hear me. The Lady's voice brought Corri's mind awake.

I hear, Goddess. What would You have of me?

You have done well, daughter. In the coming battle against evil, I will lead you. I will always be at your side. The war-clouds draw closer, but fear must find no place in your heart, daughter. The power you need will come when the time is right.

Corri saw the ancient helmet in a pool of bright light. As she reached out for it, she felt a stream of power flow up her arm and into her body. Her other hand reached out, drawing to her a strange sword, its hilt of an unusual gleaming substance.

Lady? Whose are these?

Yours, came the answer.

Corri woke with a start to find Varanna's helmet clutched in one hand. *It was a dream,* she told herself as she sat up, the morning air chill on her bare arms. *Or was it? Yes, the sword is not here, but still being reforged at the Temple.*

The power you need will come when the time is right. The Lady's words echoed in Corri's mind.

Imandoff came from the fire, a cup of hot stickle leaf tea in his hand. "Here, drink this. Good for the blood," he said as he sat down beside her. "Have you decided to wear Varanna's helmet in battle after all?"

"Yes, I will wear it as it is, although I do not understand why it is necessary." Corri looked down at the strange, damaged helmet in her hand, light in weight, yet tough enough to turn aside a sword. "I think I will also carry Varanna's sword, though I do not know how to use it." She laid aside the helmet, taking the cup of hot tea.

"There is an old legend about the taking up of a warrior's weapons and war-gear." Imandoff pulled out his pipe and tamped it with smoke-leaf. Corri leaned over to light it with fire snapped from her fingers. The sorcerer grinned at her, then continued. "The old stories say that if you take up the armor or weapons of a fallen warrior, one who died with an unfinished task, you will be filled with the will and the power of that warrior, for good or ill. I have never tried it myself, but I have found many of the old tales to be true." He stared at Corri through his pipe smoke with half-closed eyes.

"Pray it is so, old man. I will greatly need Varanna's power before this war is finished." Corri set aside the cup of tea and hugged her knees. Her thoughts turned to Gadavar; a part of her mind could sense him as he walked the forests of Deep

Rising. "Imandoff, how do you know when you have found the right love to share your life?"

"It generally finds you when you least expect it." The sorcerer blew a smoke ring, watching it rise until it broke apart on the needled limbs above. "Love is caring for another more than you care for yourself, a desire to share that person's company, but still keeping your own identity and goals, and letting them keep theirs." He waggled his eyebrows and grinned. "And of course there are the physical pleasures of love."

"What will you do with this coming child?" Corri asked, smiling up at the sorcerer. "If the war is at the Harvest Moon, and my instincts say it will be, she will be born in the deep winter after, you know."

"I know." Imandoff stared across the camp at Takra, who stretched and yawned from the cocoon of her blankets. "I will trust in the Lady that Takra and the child come through unharmed. And I will love the child because it is part of Takra, part of our love." His gray eyes slid back to Corri, looking deep into her thoughts. "As you will love your own child one day."

"My child?" Corri threw aside the blankets and tucked the helmet back into its carrying bag. "What have I to teach a child, old man?"

"All the ways to climb over roofs and walk on high narrow ledges, no doubt." Takra yawned as she came to stand beside them. She turned to Imandoff with a mock frown. "And you, Silverhair, you will not teach our daughter to crawl about in dark places under the ground."

The sorcerer took her hand and pulled her down beside him. "Would you deny her the excitement of discovering long-forgotten treasures?" he asked as he kissed her cheek.

"I know," Takra said with a wink at Corri. "You are companying with crazies."

"I think you have infected me with your disease of craziness." Corri grinned. "We have gotten so used to excitement, what will we do when things grow quiet?"

"Probably find dark holes filled with black jumpers and other such things to explore." Takra shivered, then punched her elbow into Imandoff's side.

"But of course. Life must not be dull," Imandoff answered, pulling the warrior woman into the circle of his arm.

"That it will never be with you around, old man." Corri smiled as she strode off toward the cookfire and breakfast.

About the Author

I was born on a Beltane Full Moon with a total lunar eclipse, one of the hottest days of that year. Although I came into an Irish-North Germanic-Native American family with natural psychics on both sides, I had to learn discrimination in a family of closet psychics. I seriously began my quest for knowledge in the occult fields more than thirty-five years ago.

I have always been close to Nature. As a child, I spent a great amount of time outdoors by myself. Plants and animals become part of my life wherever I live. I love cats, music, mountains, singing streams, stones, ritual, and nights when the Moon is full. My reading covers vast areas of history, the magickal arts, philosophy, customs, mythology, and fantasy. I have studied every aspect of the New Age religions, from Eastern philosophy to Wicca. I hope I never stop learning and expanding.

Although I have lived in areas of this country from one coast to the other, Oregon (my birthplace) is my home. I am not fond of large crowds or speaking in public.

I live a rather quiet life with my husband and our cats, with occasional visits with my children and grandchildren. I collect statues of dragons and wizards, crystals and other stones, and of course books. Most of my time is spent researching and writing. All in all, I am just an ordinary Pagan person.

To Write to the Author

If you wish to contact the author or would like more information about this book, please write to the author in care of Llewellyn Worldwide and we will forward your request. Both the author and publisher appreciate hearing from you and learning of your enjoyment of this book. Llewellyn Worldwide cannot guarantee that every letter written to the author can be answered, but all will be forwarded. Please write to:

D. J. Conway
℅ Llewellyn Worldwide
P.O. Box 64383, Dept. K162-7
St. Paul, MN 55164-0383, U.S.A.

Please enclose a self-addressed stamped envelope for reply, or $1.00 to cover costs. If outside U.S.A., enclose international postal reply coupon.

Stay in Touch . . .

Llewellyn publishes hundreds of books on your favorite subjects. On the following pages you will find listed some books now available on related subjects. Your local bookstore stocks most of these and will stock new Llewellyn titles as they become available. We urge your patronage.

Order by Phone

Call toll-free within the U.S. and Canada, 1–800–THE MOON.
In Minnesota, call (612) 291–1970.
We accept Visa, MasterCard, and American Express.

Order by Mail

Send the full price of your order (MN residents add 7% sales tax) in U.S. funds to:

Llewellyn Worldwide
P.O. Box 64383, Dept. K162-7
St. Paul, MN 55164-0383, U.S.A.

Postage and Handling

- ◆ $4.00 for orders $15 and under
- ◆ $5.00 for orders over $15
- ◆ No charge for orders over $100

We ship UPS in the continental United States. We cannot ship to P.O. boxes. Orders shipped to Alaska, Hawaii, Canada, Mexico, and Puerto Rico will be sent first-class mail.

International orders: Airmail—Add freight equal to price of each book to the total price of order, plus $5.00 for each non-book item (audiotapes, etc.). Surface mail—Add $1.00 per item.

Allow 4–6 weeks delivery on all orders. Postage and handling rates subject to change.

Group Discounts

We offer a 20% quantity discount to group leaders or agents. You must order a minimum of 5 copies of the same book to get our special quantity price.

Dream Warrior

D. J. Conway

Danger, intrigue, and adventure seem to follow dauntless Corri Farblood wherever she goes. Sold as a child to the grotesque and sinister master thief Grimmel, Corri was forced into thievery at a young age. In fact, at eighteen, she's the best thief in the city of Hadliden—but she also possesses an ability to travel the astral plane, called dream-flying, that makes her even more unique. Her talents make her a valuable commodity to Grimmel, who forces her into marriage so she will bear a child carrying both her special powers and his. But before the marriage can be consummated, Corri escapes with the aid of a traveling sorcerer, who has a quest of his own to pursue. . . .

Journey across the wide land of Sar Akka with Corri, the sorcerer Imandoff Silverhair, and the warrior Takra Wind-Rider as they search for an ancient place of power. As Grimmel's assassins relentlessly pursue her, Corri battles against time and her enemies to solve the mystery of her heritage and to gain control over her potent clairvoyant gifts . . . to learn the meaning of companionship and love . . . and to finally confront a fate that will test her powers and courage to the limit.

1-56718-169-4, 320 pp., 5¼ x 8, softcover $14.95

Beneath a Mountain Moon

Silver RavenWolf

Welcome to Whiskey Springs, Pennsylvania, birthplace of magick, mayhem, and murder! The generations-old battle between two powerful occult families rages anew when young Elizabeyta Belladonna journeys from Oklahoma to the small town of Whiskey Springs—a place her family had left years before to escape the predatory Blackthorn family—to solve the mystery of her grandmother's death.

Endowed with her own magickal heritage of Scotch-Irish Witchcraft, Elizabeyta stands alone against the dark powers and twisted desires of Jason Blackthorn and his gang of Dark Men. But Elizabeyta isn't the only one pursued by unseen forces and the fallout from a past life. As Blackthorn manipulates the town's inhabitants through occult means, a great battle for mastery ensues between the forces of darkness and light—a battle that involves a crackpot preacher, a blue ghost, the town gossip, and an old country healer—and the local funeral parlor begins to overflow with victims. Is there anyone who can end the Blackthorns' reign of terror and right the cosmic balance?

1-56718-722-6, 360 pp., 6 x 9, softcover $15.95

Lilith

D. A. Heeley

D. A. Heeley

The first book of the occult Darkness and Light trilogy weaves together authentic magical techniques and teachings of the Hebrew Qabalah with the suspenseful story of the spiritual evolution of Malak, an Adept of the White School of Magick.

Malak and his fellow magicians from the White, Yellow, and Black Schools of Magick live on Enya, the lower astral plane of the Qabalistic Tree of Life. Malak's brother and arch-rival, Dethen, is an Adept of the Black School. Dethen plots a coup to destroy the White School completely and begin a reign of terror on Enya—with the hope of destroying the Tree of Life and the world—and a colossal battle between Good and Evil ensues. As the Black Adepts summon the Arch-demon Lilith into Enya, Malak is faced with a terrible choice: should he barter with the ultimate evil to free his wife's soul—even if freeing her condemns other innocent souls forever?

The second half of *Lilith* takes place 1,000 years later, in feudal Japan. Malak has been reincarnated as Shadrack, who struggles with an inner demon who will not be denied. He must conquer Lilith's evil or there will be a bloody rampage amid the Shogun's Royal Guard. . . .

1-56718-355-7, 256 pp., 6 x 9, softcover $10.00

Cardinal's Sin

Raymond Buckland

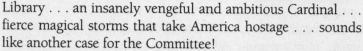

Magical secrets found in an ancient gri-
moire hidden away in the Vatican
Library . . . an insanely vengeful and ambitious Cardinal . . .
fierce magical storms that take America hostage . . . sounds
like another case for the Committee!

The story begins in the United States, where coastal hurri-
canes, flooding rains, and tornados have cost the country bil-
lions of dollars and thousands of lives. As it becomes clear
that these storms are not natural, the Committee—a covert
group of psychically talented people formed by the U.S. gov-
ernment to neutralize malignant paranormal forces—joins
minds to determine how and why these devastating, magical
storms are being caused—and by whom.

Enter Patrizio Ganganelli, a crazed Roman Cardinal obsessed
with avenging his mother's rape during WWII by American
soldiers. As the Cardinal plunders the Vatican's secret magic
library to evoke demonic forces against the United States, the
Committee joins forces with a Wiccan Priestess to counter the
Cardinal's attack. But the Goddess alone may not be able to
defeat this evil entity—someone needs to die. . . .

1-56178-102-3, 336 pp., mass market, softcover $5.99

Flying Without a Broom

D. J. Conway

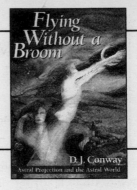

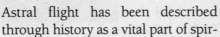

Astral flight has been described through history as a vital part of spiritual development and a powerful aid to magickal workings. In this remarkable volume, respected author D. J. Conway shows how anyone can have the keys to a profound astral experience. Not only is astral travel safe and simple, she shows in clear and accessible terms how this natural part of our psychic make-up can be cultivated to enhance both spiritual and daily life.

This complete how-to includes historical lore, a groundwork of astral plane basics, and a simplified learning process to get you "off the ground." You'll learn simple exercises to strengthen your astral abilities as well as a variety of astral techniques—including bilocation and time travel. After the basics, use the astral planes to work magick and healings; contact teachers, guides, or lovers; and visit past lives. You'll also learn how to protect yourself and others from the low-level entities inevitably encountered in the astral.

Through astral travel you will expand your spiritual growth, strengthen your spiritual efforts, and bring your daily life to a new level of integration and satisfaction.

1-56718-164-3, 224 pp., 6 x 9, softcover $13.00

Magical, Mythical, Mystical Beasts

D. J. Conway

Unicorns . . . centaurs . . . bogies and brownies. Here is a "Who's Who" of mystical creatures, an introduction to them, their history, and how they can be co-magicians in magickal workings. Ride Pegasus on a soul journey to the Moon. Call upon the Phoenix for strength and renewing energy when facing trials in life. In ancient times, magicians knew the esoteric meanings of these beings and called upon them for aid. This ability remains within us today, latent in our superconscious minds, waiting for us to re-establish communication with our astral helpers. Short chapters on candle burning, ritual, and amulets and talismans help you more easily and safely work with these creatures.

1-56718-176-7, 272 pp., 6 x 9, 80 illus., softcover $14.95

Maiden, Mother, Crone

D. J. Conway

The Triple Goddess is with every one of us each day of our lives. In our inner journeys toward spiritual evolution, each woman and man goes through the stages of Maiden (infant to puberty), Mother (adult and parent) and Crone (aging elder). *Maiden, Mother, Crone* is a guide to the myths and interpretations of the Great Goddess archetype and her three faces, so that we may better understand and more peacefully accept the cycle of birth and death.

Learning to interpret the symbolic language of the myths is important to spiritual growth, for the symbols are part of the map that guides each of us to the Divine Center. Through learning the true meaning of the ancient symbols, through facing the cycles of life, and by following the meditations and simple rituals provided in this book, women and men alike can translate these ancient teachings into personal revelations.

Not all goddesses can be conveniently divided into the clear aspects of Maiden, Mother, and Crone. This book covers these as well, including the Fates, the Muses, Valkyries, and others.

0-87542-171-7, 240 pp., 6 x 9, softcover $12.95

Dancing with Dragons

D. J. Conway

You can access one of the most potent life forces in the astral universe: the wise and magickal dragon. Dragons do exist! They inhabit the astral plane that interpenetrates our physical world. Now, *Dancing with Dragons* makes a vast and wonderful hoard of dragon magick and power available to you.

Dancing with Dragons is a ritual textbook that will teach you to call, befriend, and utilize the wisdom of these powerful mythical creatures for increased spiritual fulfillment, knowledge, health, and happiness. Here you will find complete, practical information for working with dragons: spells and rituals ranging from simple to advanced workings; designing ritual tools to aid you in using dragon energy; channeling power using the lines of dragon's breath (energy lines that run through the Earth); and using the true language of dragons in ritual and spell-casting with herbs, oils, stones, and candles.

Dancing with Dragons is a joyful experience. Whether you are a practicing magician, a devotee of role-playing games, or a seeker who wishes to tap the dragon's vast astral power, this book will help you forge a friendship and magickal partnership with these astral creatures.

1-56718-165-1, 320 pp., 7 x 10, illus., softcover $14.95